INVASION

DC Alden

First edition published 2006.
This revised edition reprinted in 2015

A CIP catalogue record for this title is available from the British Library.

ISBN 978 0 956 90800 1

Also by DC Alden

The Horse at the Gates
The Angola Deception

"So, fight them till all opposition ends and the only religion is Islam."

Qur'an 8:39

Prologue

The streets were deserted. Not a breath of wind stirred the warm air that cloaked the city as it slept. From the inky blackness of a derelict building, two boys waited in silence, biding their time until long after midnight, when the roads and pavements would finally be emptied. They waited a while longer, then picked their way carefully through the empty house and moved silently out on to the street. They kept out of the glare of the street lights, seeking every shadow, every patch of gloom, every unlit side street. As they moved, their eyes scanned ahead, their ears alert to the sounds of the night. For these boys the hours of darkness held many dangers. Normally, their presence here would be tolerated, their movements checked, their actions monitored. Now, after the setting of the sun, their very presence within the city limits would result in immediate arrest. Or worse.

They were brothers by birth, in their late teens. They sported close-cropped haircuts and were dressed in the black, loose-fitting clothing and rough sandals of common Workers. As unbelievers, they were forbidden to enter the city between sunset and sunrise; instead, they were banished throughout the hours of darkness to the crumbling London suburbs along the southern banks of the Thames. Their day had started like any other, boarding the transport trains at Clapham Junction where thousands thronged on the dilapidated platforms to ride the open railcars into the city. The sun was already up as they clattered past the wild sprawl of Battersea Park and across the rusting railway span that straddled the slow-moving river, crammed with hundreds of others inside the hot and noisy cars. The train rattled on towards the end of the line, rusted carriage wheels squealing in protest as the train shunted to a halt inside the huge terminus at Victoria station. Soon the platforms were filled with thousands of black-clad Workers and the boys moved with the throng, funnelling through the security turnstiles, their identity wrist bracelets scanned by scowling guards. They crossed the concourse, where ancient shops and storefronts lay abandoned, and moved down into the Underground station, where they boarded the filthy subway trains that ferried them to their places of employment across the city. Only Workers used the subway, the air below ground stale and polluted, the infrastructure decayed, the accidents frequent and deadly. But not today.

The boys alighted from the subway at Justice, climbing the lifeless and poorly lit escalators, passing the faded signs that read Westminster, Jubilee Line, District and Circle. An underground tunnel brought them up inside the basement of the Chambers of Justice itself, a beautiful glass and marble complex where the highest court in the land was situated, where constitutional points of law were argued and debated, where the most important cases were heard and ruled upon. It was a place of clerics, of lawmakers and justice ministers; a place where the prosecutor general himself and his high council ruled over this most westerly of Arabian territories. And it also housed the Inner Chamber.

Down in the basement, the boys gathered their cleaning materials and loaded the cart, pushing it towards the service lift. They trundled past the supervisor in his office who cursed them loudly. Up on the ground floor, their security bracelets were scanned again and they went about their duties, navigating the lofty hallways in silence, polishing floors and buffing marble heads until they finally arrived at their most important assignment of the day: the Inner Chamber itself. Inhabited by one hundred and thirty area clerics and presided over by the prosecutor general and his high council, the Inner Chamber was the nerve centre, the inner sanctum of the Arabian legal system. Situated directly beneath the building's huge central dome, the Inner Chamber was made up of circular terraced marble seating that surrounded a raised podium, the smooth walls ringed by the statues of previous prosecutor generals. Overhead, the giant rotunda was inlaid with display screens that depicted a moving montage of Arabian jihadist victories throughout the ages, from the capture of Jerusalem in ad 638 through to the routing of the Chinese armies on the Mongolian plain some thirty years ago. New arrivals were often distracted, staring in wonder at the digitally rendered battle scenes that raged in silence above their heads. It was a truly imposing room, a sacred inner temple, and access to it was strictly regulated to members of the high council – and the maintenance staff, of course.

The boys wheeled their cart to a stop outside the Inner Chamber's huge oak doors. They were three metres high and adorned with the most intricate and beautiful carvings either of them had ever seen. Guarded by two ceremonial soldiers wearing traditional Arabic dress, the boys were ushered into an anteroom, where they removed their sandals and washed their feet in accordance with the law. The boys did so thoroughly, for they had been trained to be meticulous, to adhere to every rule, observe every detail. They could not, dare not, arouse any suspicion. Their mission depended on it.

They were ushered into the stillness of the chamber. They were expected to work in complete silence and the single guard who joined them inside ensured they did just that. He took up his usual position against the wall and began inspecting his fingernails, while the boys rummaged around the cart for the correct cleaning materials. There was much to do. The glass dome was always cleaned first, before the sun rose too high and the heat became unbearable. Using special tools and working on a well-hidden platform, the boys circumnavigated the glass structure, ensuring that the surface was spotless and the inlaid screens were functioning correctly. When that laborious task was complete, they made their way down the curved banks of steep marble terracing, plumping the rows of silk cushions and polishing every surface to a high sheen. Down on the main floor, one boy concentrated on buffing the marble while the other one, the red-haired one, went to the podium.

The ornate lectern was the centrepiece of the hall. It stood on a platform that offered the speaker an acoustically commanding aspect of the Inner Chamber. The boy dusted every crevice of the podium, ensuring that the glass autocue was gleaming like a mirror and the microphone cleansed with antibacterial wipes. He worked slowly, methodically, his eyes often flicking undetected toward the lazy guard against the wall. An hour passed. Both boys stood by the doors, awaiting inspection by the supervisor. When he finally arrived, he examined their work carefully, grunted his satisfaction and dismissed them both with a curt wave. For the rest of the day, the boys joined the maintenance resource pool, performing a variety of menial tasks around the building and the manicured gardens outside. At dusk, they returned to the station for the journey back across the river. Bracelets scanned, they ambled along the platform, lost amongst the thousands of other Workers who pushed and shoved aboard the waiting trains. Biding their time, the boys lingered until the last transport of the day was ready to depart; they then cut through the throng, finding space on the last car as instructed. The platform soon emptied and, with a loud hiss and violent clanking of metal, the train shunted slowly out of the terminus. Now it was time.

In the crush of the carriage, their security tags were swiftly and expertly removed by unseen hands. Rubbing their wrists, the two boys forced their way to the side of the car as it rattled out of the city and across the river. To the west, the sun had dipped below the horizon and the clear blue sky had begun to darken, the first stars of the evening twinkling faintly overhead. As the train cleared the bridge and slowed to negotiate an ancient set of points, angry shouts suddenly erupted on the other side of the carriage. Fists flew and people surged forward, craning their necks to see what was happening. In the diversion, the two boys slipped silently over the side and dropped to the ground, rolling away from the rusted steel wheels. They scuttled across the tracks, disappearing into a large clump of overgrown bushes as the shouting faded and the train picked up speed once again, accelerating into the distance. The boys squatted in the undergrowth, breathing hard, neither daring to move a muscle. There they waited until night had fallen completely. Under cover of darkness, they slipped back across the rail bridge, crouching low against the parapet, freezing like statues as an Arabian patrol boat cruised along the black waters of the Thames below, its bow cutting quietly through the river, its searchlight playing across the southern shoreline. Once across the bridge they skirted the marshalling yards, avoiding the station that was bathed in the harsh glare of security lights. They kept to the shadows, black veils covering their faces, pale hands thrust deep into their sleeves. They picked their way carefully across the tracks and sidings, making their way without incident to a row of deserted houses that backed on to the perimeter fence, ducking quietly beneath the rusted mesh fencing, forcing their way through deep foliage into one of the empty buildings. Inside, a cautious route was picked around the rotting timbers and piles of rubble to the front of the house. Crouching motionless in the darkness, they watched the street outside. If they were captured here, across the river after curfew, the very least they could expect was a long, painful spell in the damp cells of the Khali Detention Centre. Or they could simply be shot dead in the street. The boys understood these risks and accepted them willingly.

Away from the patrols and the railway yards, the streets of London were quiet and peaceful. There seemed to be few people around and the boys saw only one vehicle, an electric tram that hummed quietly across a distant intersection. The streets were sparingly lit, and they kept to the shadows until they finally reached Warwick Square. The houses here were large detached affairs, occupied by rich merchants and financiers, the wide frontages decorated with palms and giant ferns that spilled across the smooth pavements. They searched for one house in particular and spotted it almost immediately. One hundred metres ahead, on the north side of the square, was a magnificent six-storey dwelling, nestled between two others of similar opulence. In a top-floor window, a single light shone through the slats of a wooden blind. It was the all-clear signal. Adjacent to the house was an alleyway and the boys slipped into the dark passage undetected. They felt their way along the wall until they passed through a wooden door, leaving the gloom of the alley for the exquisitely landscaped rear garden of the property. Huge palm trees ringed the high walls and a rearing horse-shaped fountain dominated the manicured lawns, the water gurgling softly in the night air. The boys made their way across the patio where a glass wall slid silently open to receive them. The summer room was decorated with tall plants and cane furniture, the cool air climate controlled. As their eyes grew accustomed to the darkness, they noticed the portly silhouette of a man standing in a doorway across the room, beckoning them silently. They followed him along a tiled corridor to a large entrance hall that was lit by several huge, sweet-smelling candles and dominated by a magnificent staircase that curved upwards to the floors above. The portly man waited until they had passed into the hallway, then closed and bolted the door behind them. They faced each other silently in the flickering light; then, as if on cue, the young boys bowed their heads.

'Thank you, Your Eminence, for your hospitality and your courage,' they whispered together.

The man laid a chubby hand on each of their closely cropped skulls. 'Rise, my young friends. You have displayed much courage yourselves this night. Wait for me in the library. Ali will bring you food. I will join you later.'

He gestured to a set of double doors across the hall. The boys stepped timidly into a large, high-ceilinged room, lit by more candles and ringed with bookshelves, all of which were stacked with thousands of gilt-edged volumes. The boys stared in wonder. Books were a rare sight across the river, both a commodity and a luxury enjoyed by those that possessed them. The boys were drawn towards the shelves, running curious fingers across the embossed titles and thick spines of the neatly arranged volumes. These were the works of their literary fathers – Shakespeare, Dickens, Betjeman and others. Forbidden, illegal words. On the opposite wall hung rich tapestries and an impressive oil painting that depicted several Bedouin warriors traversing a stunning desert vista.

The boys spun around as the door opened and the emir's manservant, Ali, entered, wheeling a serving trolley before him, laden with silverware and glasses. With a flourish, he removed plate covers in a cloud of steam.

'With the master's compliments. Please enjoy.' He backed out of the room, closing the door behind him.

The boys moved quickly, attacking the roasted chicken legs, the plates of steaming rice and fresh peppers, the bread rolls and butter, lest the opportunity was somehow snatched from them. On the lower shelf, frosted decanters of chilled, clean water stood by, waiting to quench their thirsts. By the time they'd eaten their fill, the trolley had been reduced to a collection of empty plates and greasy bowls.

The boys flopped on to the sofas, reclining amongst the mounds of soft cushions. One of them belched and the other followed suit, producing a satisfied blast of air, they laughed long and loud, the tears streaming down their cheeks. After a while their amusement subsided and they sat quietly, watching the shadows of the candle flames dance lazily across the walls. Their journey tonight had been nerve-wracking, each moment a potential heartbeat away from discovery and arrest, torture and death. But they had made it this far.

They had been called, as had many before them, to undertake a mission of great importance. They'd spent the last week being briefed by faceless men in darkened rooms across the slums of Vauxhall, listening intently, devouring the details. They were young, eager to strike back. For them, the chance to fight was a privilege, an opportunity for their people to rejoice in the camps, to cross the river with a tight-lipped smile of satisfaction, to see the looks of hate in the eyes of the city dwellers. And yes, maybe fear. Fear was the key. For this mission, however, the price would be high. Arrests would be made; husbands separated from wives, sons from mothers. People would disappear, mostly men and always the strong ones, shipped to the east to be sold in slave markets across Arabia or used as penal troops in the border wars with the Chinese. The rumours were wild and numerous, but ultimately of no concern. The boys wouldn't be caught. Well, not alive anyway.

They had learned the history of their nation, a once-proud people now reduced to an existence of hard labour and servitude, but still united in adversity, the gene of rebellion passing from generation to generation. From a young age they'd learned of the suffering, the humiliation, the deaths of countless others, until they craved for vengeance. Separated from their parents by sickness and death, the boys had been given new identities. They'd also been given notice; they were soldiers now, cloaked by their anonymity, their backs seemingly bowed by menial servitude behind the walls of the city, but soldiers nonetheless. And, one day, they would be called.

The door to the library opened and the boys snapped awake, struggling to their feet. The emir motioned them to sit. He plumped up the cushions on a deep sofa and sat down, smiling broadly.

'You are fed, yes? It was to your liking?'

The boys nodded gratefully. 'Yes, Your Eminence. Thank you.'

'Good. Soon the sun will rise and the day will be upon us, a day that will be remembered for many years to come. And you, my young brothers, will be the cause of great rejoicing amongst our people. But there is much to do and much you will need to learn in the few short hours we have. Are you ready to learn, young brothers?'

The boys sat a little straighter. When they spoke it was with determined, even voices. 'We are ready, Your Eminence.'

Western Arabian Desert
4th June 2029

The moon shone brightly as the unmarked Black Hawk helicopter skimmed low over the desert dunes, rising and falling with the contours of the sandy slopes below. Inside the helicopter's large troop transport bay, four men were strapped tightly into their seats. They sat in silence; even with their headsets on, the noise and vibrations of the aircraft were enough to give a man a headache. And one of the men already had such a headache.

General Faris Mousa shifted uncomfortably as the helicopter thundered over another towering dune and dropped, like a stone, towards the desert floor on the other side. Allah spare us, he grimaced. Another ten minutes of this and the pounding inside his skull might well develop into a migraine. Stress, that was the problem, he concluded. Too much stress, too many plates to juggle. But was it any wonder when one considered what lay ahead? He rested his forehead against the cool Perspex of the window as the empty desert flashed beneath them in the darkness. He smiled ruefully; his God-given name, Faris, meant 'horseman' in Arabic. What he wouldn't give to be in the saddle of a beautiful Arab mare right now, cresting a sand dune under the silver moon, travelling the silent desert guided only by the stars. Maybe in the future, when all this was over and God's work was completed. Maybe.

Mousa watched as the pale desert sands rose and fell beneath the Black Hawk. Up, down, left, right; quite disorientating, if one was not used to it. Of course, Mousa was used to it. As a general in the Arabian Special Forces, he had endured many things on his rise to the near pinnacle of his profession. The two rows of decorations above the breast pocket of his camouflage jacket, in addition to the paratrooper's jump wings on his shoulder, were testament to his courage.

As well as his physical abilities as a soldier, Mousa also prided himself on his loyalty, quick intellect and resourcefulness. It was these very qualities that had kept him alive during the realignment, rising to become the head of Arabian Military Intelligence and now commanding Special Operations and Planning. And it was because he held such an important role that he was now being jolted around inside a helicopter as it raced across the moonlit desert. The pilot's voice crackled in his headphones.

'Five minutes.'

Mousa looked across at the elderly man opposite him and spread his fingers in a five gesture. The man, flanked by two large and heavily armed bodyguards, smiled and nodded. He was dressed in a simple dark robe and wore a traditional Arab *shemagh* on his head. His grey beard was neatly trimmed, framing his heavily lined face, and a pair of round spectacles rested on the bridge of his hooked nose. Through his fingers he ran a continuous pattern with a simple band of prayer beads. Mousa pulled his safety belt a little tighter, smiling inwardly. The man looked like any other elderly Arabian gentleman approaching his seventy-second year; a slight, unremarkable figure who would otherwise be seen chatting outside a mosque or playing chess in the park. Even though the soldiers on either side of him dwarfed his diminutive frame, Mousa knew that one glance, one word or gesture from this quiet man would have his bodyguards shaking in their boots. For the man opposite Mousa was His Holiness the Grand Mufti Mohammed Khathami, the chief cleric and supreme ruler of Arabia.

The Black Hawk slowed its forward air speed and banked to the left. Below them, bathed in the moonlight and scattered amongst the crumbling remains of an ancient desert fort, Mousa glimpsed the tents, nestling beneath the palms of a large oasis. In a cloud of sand, the helicopter settled a short distance from the old fort. Mousa, always keen to be first man out, slid the door open and kicked over the folding stairs. He held out an arm, which the cleric took, and they headed past the decaying fort towards the oasis, where two men waited in the shadows for them. Mousa recognised them as the Arabian defence minister and the foreign secretary. The men bowed deeply as Mousa's party approached.

'Your Holiness. An honour as always,' cooed the defence minister. Both men kissed the cleric's outstretched hand.

'Is everyone here?' Khathami enquired. The defence minister nodded in the affirmative. 'Then lead on.'

The party continued through the trees, the path lit by flame torches on ornate stands, until they reached a small clearing where several tents had been carefully erected beneath the dark green canopy of palm leaves. Inside the luxurious Bedouin marquee that commanded the centre of the clearing, several men waited, raising themselves off the expensive couches arranged around a stone fire pit. Mousa's eyes were drawn to small, almost imperceptible movements in the gloom. The other bodyguards, he noticed, were loitering in the deep shadows round the marquee's periphery. With so many powerful and influential men meeting this night, an assassin could have a field day and Mousa's career would last about as long as a camel in the Arctic Circle if such a criminal got to within a hundred kilometres of this place. However, the location was remote, with the surrounding desert monitored by thermal cameras, UAVs and heavily armed patrols. He'd planned well, as always.

As Khathami moved towards an empty couch, Mousa waved his bodyguards into the shadows and took a seat behind the Holy One. Through another awning several more men ducked inside the marquee. As Khathami made himself comfortable, they approached him one by one, bowing deeply, kissing his hands and expressing their joy at the great man's presence. They took their seats on the remaining couches alongside Khathami's defence minister and foreign secretary. They were wearing a mixture of civilian and military uniforms and Mousa recognised them as the heads, or their deputies, of the former countries of the Middle East and North Africa. These were the Area Protectors of Arabia, powerful men in their own right and personally appointed to their current positions by the grand mufti himself. The atmosphere was charged, despite the fussing over tea and coffee and the small talk around the fire. The Holy One focussed everyone's attention with his customary throat clearance.

'It is fitting that we should meet like this, beneath the stars, as in the custom of our forefathers. They smile down upon us tonight, for our people have witnessed a level of co-operation unknown throughout the history of the Middle East. Our enemies have become cautious, wary of our growing material wealth, our political influence and combined military power. The time has come to deliver Europe unto Islam, to embark on our own crusade. History in reverse, if you will.' Khathami smiled, crossing his thin legs beneath the black robe. 'Now, I wish to hear your final readiness reports. Let us start with our Turkish brothers. Mustafa, if you please.'

Mousa eyed Demir Hassan, vice president of the Turkish Federation and the real power behind the throne in Ankara since the president had suffered a debilitating stroke. A strategically crucial ally and a powerful military force, the Turks had finally duped Brussels into inviting their nation to become a full member of the European Union. Since then, the Turks had sent thousands of sleeper agents westward. Now, with an army of over a million men, Turkish forces would be at the spearhead of the initial push into enemy territory on the eastern front. Nothing in the region could stop their advance.

'Everything is in place, Your Eminence,' began Hassan. 'Our role is threefold. Firstly, we have twenty-two tank divisions positioned along the Greek border, ready to advance at the specified hour. Our Special Forces will seize all border crossings, and artillery and rocket troops will bombard Greek defensive positions and military bases that pose the biggest threat to our advance. Our forward observation teams are already on Greek soil and they report no increased alert status on that side of the border. As far as they are concerned, our recent troop movements are all part of our annual military exercises.'

Hassan cleared his throat and continued, glancing occasionally at the briefing documents in his hand.

'Secondly, the strategically important island of Cyprus. All along the NATO dividing line defensive bunkers, observation posts and watchtowers have been targeted by Turkish artillery and missile batteries. We also have four thousand paratroopers on standby at Diyarbakir airbase ready to drop into the Greek Cypriot sector as soon as the attack commences. They will be supported by our Eastern Mediterranean fleet, which is being fuelled and loaded with three armoured divisions as we speak. We anticipate the neutralisation of Cyprus within two to three days. Resistance there will be crushed quickly.'

Mousa smiled at that one. Lucky for the Turks that the British, after a long and bitter political campaign, had been forced to pull its troops out of Cyprus a couple of years ago; otherwise, they would have a far tougher fight on their hands. As it was, two battalions of Swedish infantry on NATO duties were all that stood between success and failure.

Referring to his notes, the Turk continued. 'Thirdly, we have twenty-eight civilian merchant vessels currently steaming towards their destination ports around the French and British coasts. Each ship is over forty thousand tonnes and carries a fully mechanised battalion including tanks, armoured personnel carriers and supporting infantry. The ships are presently disguised as normal cargo vessels flying under a flag of convenience. At the given moment, destination ports will be seized by amphibious forces aboard the ships or by sleeper units on the mainland. Trained personnel will be on hand to unload the cargo and each battalion commander has been issued with marshalling points and military objectives for the initial forty-eight-hour period. The men are ready and the final orders have been issued, Your Holiness. We await only your signal to commence operations. Until that time, all units are observing a complete radio blackout.'

Next, it was the turn of the Russian, who nervously dabbed a handkerchief around his thick neck. Mousa silently revelled in the man's obvious discomfort, mindful of the appalling treatment meted out to Russia's Muslim population by the former regime. But the Russians were now bankrupt, the sudden and inexplicable failure of the oil and gas fields in the Barents Sea basin the catalyst for their economic downfall.

Then there were the food riots, the ominous rumblings of discontent within the armed forces, all forcing the new regime in Moscow to do business with Arabia. The cleric had bailed them out to the tune of billions and that kind of money bought power and influence, particularly where greed and moral corruption were part of everyday life. Now the Russians were heavily in Arabian debt and the time had come to pay up. Besides, reasoned Mousa, they'd been given the task of invading Germany and there was a lot of historical precedent there. Ordinarily, the Germans would have been tough nuts to crack, even given the element of surprise, but Germany, like the rest of Europe, would have enough to cope with once the sleeper teams went active.

And so it went on, around the table. Mousa's eyes began to feel heavy. He'd heard the plans thousands of times, thrashed them out with the other Arabian generals in dusty living rooms, abandoned airfields and even in parked cars on motorways, where curious eyes could not see them or inquisitive ears overhear them. Security was everything. Hundreds had died, some probably innocent, to protect that secret. The result was that eighteen regional army groups stood ready, comprising almost a million troops, thousands of tanks, aircraft, artillery pieces, bridging equipment, logistics support – and only the men in this marquee, plus seven hundred and fifty other trusted individuals, knew the real reason for all the military exercises, the preparations and the sacrifices. One week from today and we'll know if the plan was a solid one, decided Mousa.

For a further three hours the operation was picked apart, every detail analysed and reanalysed, dissected and debated. In the weary silence that followed, all eyes turned to the cleric as he sipped his dark, bitter coffee, lost in thought. Eventually he leaned forward and placed the cup on the low table in front of him.

'It is clear that you have all worked long and hard to ensure our success. Much blood has been spilt, much more will be spilt, yet only God, peace be upon him, can judge if our sacrifices have been worthy of his name. So be it. Operation Swift Sword will commence one week from today. Ensure your forces are ready.'

A fitting name, decided Mousa. It was the Prophet himself who once said: *Swords are the key to Paradise. He who draws his sword in the path of God, swears allegiance.* Yes, a fitting name indeed.

The cleric flicked his wrist and the occupants of the marquee scrambled to their feet. One after the other, they paid their respects and left, bodyguards in tow. Already Mousa could hear the distant whine of helicopters beyond the ridgeline as engines were fired up and rotors began to chop the night air. Khathami invited Mousa to sit beside him.

'Everything appears to be in place, General Mousa. What is the latest word from our people in Europe?'

Mousa extracted a sheath of intelligence briefing papers from his pocket, handed to him shortly before their flight into the desert.

'Your Holiness, the financial crisis in Europe continues, its cities plagued by civil unrest and industrial action, fuelled by our socialist allies across the continent who have answered the call for direct action. In addition, converts in many European countries have infiltrated right-wing groups to stir up hatred against our people, resulting in mosque burnings and physical attacks on our Brothers and Sisters. Many crave vengeance, and it has been difficult to suppress retaliation, particularly in France, where we are strongest. However, the message is loud and clear: Muslim communities across the continent are under threat and demand action. Key political operatives within European governments report a sense of fear amongst those in power, yet no administration has the courage to mobilise their armed forces to counter the escalating violence. It's being viewed as a temporary aberration, a symptom of the continuing recession and widespread strike action, and sympathetic legal assets plus our own ambassadors are mounting pressure on local administrations to protect Muslim communities. In the meantime, our joint military exercises go on, practically unobserved. Western security agencies are being monitored and almost universally the intelligence focus is domestic. The infidels simply fail to see the storm that is brewing on their horizon. Allah has truly deafened the ears and blinded the eyes of our enemies.'

The cleric nodded his head respectfully at the mention of the one, true God. 'What about the Americans?'

'Their spy satellites over Europe have still not been replaced after the remote detonation of the Chinese communications satellite ten weeks ago.'

'Why not?' queried the Holy One.

'The nature of the explosion and the loss of a Keyhole bird has given Washington pause for thought,' replied Mousa. 'They have yet to re-task another spacecraft. Clearly, they suspect foul play but their diplomatic efforts are focussed in Beijing. Again, our military build-up can continue unhindered.'

'Good. And our French brothers?'

'The nuclear codes will be secured within the first hour of the attack. Military imams and senior Muslim officers will appeal directly to the French forces, over a third of whom are Brothers and Sisters of the faith. Their loyalty, like all Muslims, will be to their faith first. With the president assassinated and a Muslim-heavy administration waiting in the wings, France will fall quickly.'

'Excellent,' breathed Khathami. 'Come, we must return to the city.' He rose and headed across the marquee. Mousa followed closely behind, reaching for his personal radio and quietly ordering the Black Hawk to fire up its engines. As they walked back through the trees, the cleric spoke softly.

'What does your heart tell you, Faris? About the success of the operation? You may speak freely.'

Mousa considered the question. It wasn't often the Holy One used his first name, and normally only when his counsel was sought on matters of a delicate nature. He knew his opinion was valued by the man before him and he weighed his words carefully.

'We simply must succeed,' he began. 'Despite their expulsion from our lands and the oil embargoes against them, somehow the Americans continue to advance technologically. Their economy survives and shows signs of strengthening. There are rumours from our people in Washington.'

'What rumours?'

Mousa shrugged. 'Rumours of a new energy source. The details are sketchy, but our mole reports a sense of some excitement amongst Defense Department officials.'

'We cannot concern ourselves with rumours, Faris. Do the Americans pose a threat to the operation?'

Mousa shook his head. 'No, not yet. It's possible they may come to Europe's aid in some way, but the speed of our operations will leave them little time in which to counter our forces. That may change in the future, and for that we must be prepared. Europe has to be conquered quickly for us to consolidate our positions.'

'And the Chinese?'

'Co-operative, because they need our oil,' Mousa sneered. 'But they have no love for westerners, or anyone for that matter. Yes, they destroyed the spy satellite for us and they will be interested bystanders as the operation unfolds, but they are untrustworthy, godless pigs. They will study our tactics, probe our battle plans for weaknesses. There will be trouble in the future.'

'I agree,' nodded the cleric, 'but for now they remain allies. And Europe itself?'

'The economic depression has crippled their military forces, as predicted. Islam is strong everywhere, particularly in northern Europe, and our people cry out for justice. Yes, in my heart I believe we will succeed. But we must strike hard and fast.'

In the shadows of the old fort, moonlight glinted off the cleric's glasses, the brown eyes behind burning brightly.

'It will be so, Faris. In my meditations I have seen the future of Europe, and the flag of Islam flies above its capitals. The eleventh day of June will indeed be a day of liberation.'

Beyond the fort the helicopter waited, its rotors lazily chopping the night air. Khathami stopped short and turned to face a puzzled Mousa.

'Your Eminence? Is something the matter?'

'I've decided to relieve you of your duties, General Mousa.'

Mousa's blood ran cold and his eyes instinctively darted to the bodyguards, their weapons held tightly to their chests. His mind raced back over the previous weeks with the Holy One. Had he caused some offence? Imparted some slight?

Khathami's yellowed teeth glowed in the darkness. 'Relax, Faris. As much as you would have me believe that your place is at my side, I know that the soldier inside you craves the roar of battle.' He raised a bony finger. 'I trust those paratrooper wings on your tunic are more than a soldier's vain decoration?'

Mousa was both relieved and perplexed. He offered a slight bow. 'I am at your service, Your Eminence.'

'You will command an airborne unit that will seize control of Whitehall in London,' Khathami explained. 'When we return to Baghdad you will organise transport on to Cairo, where you will be met by your new liaison officer, a Major Karroubi. He will brief you on the details.' Mousa began to speak, but Khathami cut him short with a raised hand. 'Do not concern yourself now, Faris. The mission plans have already been rehearsed many times. Your new men will not disappoint and Major Karroubi has come highly recommended. What is important is that I have your eyes and ears on the ground in England.' Khathami paused, his voice suddenly quiet as he gazed up at the stars in the night sky. 'It is a strange land, Britain. Although we are strong there, I believe the infidels have the potential to resist us. That's why I need you there, Faris, my best and most gifted warrior.'

Mousa felt the weight of responsibility on his shoulders, the Holy One's words triggering strong emotions.

'I will not fail you,' he breathed, taking Khathami's offered hand and kissing it reverently. The old man smiled briefly and turned towards the waiting helicopter. Mousa followed behind, exhilaration coursing through his veins. He was going to war against the infidels, about to become a major player in events that would see the maps of Europe redrawn, a witness to Islam's resurgent history. It was once said that the Holy One could see into the minds and hearts of men, to know their private thoughts and feelings. For a brief moment Mousa almost believed those peasant superstitions.

As they boarded the Black Hawk, Mousa ran through a mental checklist. At forty-four, he was still in good shape, but a five-mile run every morning for the next few days wouldn't hurt. Some refresher parachute jumps too, and time on the weapons ranges. As the rotor blades reached full speed, Khathami gestured to Mousa, tapping his headphones. Mousa dialled in his own headset to the internal comms channel.

'You will never make a politician,' Khathami chuckled, his voice crackling through the headphones. 'It is plain to see the joy in your heart. You are ready for the task ahead?'

Mousa's brief surge of excitement had passed and now his professionalism took over. He spoke with quiet determination. 'Whatever it is, I will ensure its success, Your Eminence.'

'I do not doubt it, General Mousa. It shall be written. In one month, the continent of Europe will no longer exist.'

'Insha'Allah,' smiled the general.

Crisis Management Centre
11th June: 10.44 a.m.

Harry Beecham, the British prime minister, shifted impatiently in his chair and glanced at the men and women around the conference table, wondering if they detested this room as much as he did. Lately he seemed to be spending far more time in the fortified bunker beneath Downing Street and he didn't like it. In fact, if truth be known, Harry was a little claustrophobic.

He glanced up at the reinforced concrete ceiling as the discussions continued around him. Twenty-seven feet above was the rear garden of Number Ten. Twenty-seven feet. It was like being in a tomb – a modern, high-tech tomb, of course, with direct subterranean access to Downing Street and the Ministry of Defence, but a tomb nonetheless. Harry had been reliably informed on his first visit that the complex, constructed in great secrecy in the 1960s, could withstand a nuclear attack in the ten-kiloton region. Harry was more sceptical. A tower block in Poplar had collapsed some years ago, killing over two hundred people. That had also been constructed in the sixties, Harry had pointed out to the bemused aide. He smiled at the memory, then refocussed his mind to the business at hand.

The COBRA Intelligence Group breakfast meeting had been a long one and, despite copious amounts of coffee and croissants fuelling the heated debate, it was beginning to show on the tired and strained faces around the air-conditioned room. The CIG was made up of representatives from MI5, MI6, GCHQ, the Joint Intelligence Group, Defence Intelligence Staff and Special Branch and each and every agency had taken the opportunity to demonstrate their own specialist insight into what was fast becoming a national crisis.

Over the last eighteen months, the economic recession gripping Britain had developed into a full-blown depression, plunging Harry's administration into a state of permanent crisis and the country into despair. Despite the bailouts and intervention from Brussels and the IMF, nothing seemed able to halt the slide of the pound, the rise in interest rates and double-figure inflation.

Harry had ordered a programme of sweeping financial cuts, prompting a campaign of industrial action that plagued the public and private sectors. Schools and hospitals had begun to close, while mountains of rubbish piled up on the streets and power cuts rolled across the country. On strike days, public transport ground to a halt and every week more and more people took to the streets, the seemingly endless demonstrations resulting in ever rising levels of violence. Britain was being crippled by militant action, stirred up by thousands of hard left agitators, anarchists and general troublemakers. With unemployment pushing the five million mark, people were desperate. Harry understood their frustration – the skyrocketing fuel prices, interest rates heading towards twelve per cent and the cost of food production that triggered long queues at supermarkets. Recently, in his darker moments, Harry had begun to wonder where it would all end. The chants were getting louder, the newspaper headlines more hysterical, his own car pelted with missiles every time he left Whitehall, the twisted faces of hate that screamed for his head – any head – on a pole outside Downing Street. The same despair had also gripped Europe, the scenes of public protest and violent disorder mirrored right across the continent, where many had been killed in clashes with the police and security forces.

As the meeting wore on it was clear that the CIG attendees were pretty unanimous in their conclusions. Hard times called for hard measures and the use of water cannon and tear gas, emergency arrest and detention powers, even a partial military deployment, had been debated around the room. Harry, feeling increasingly isolated, had refused to invoke such measures. This wasn't South America, he pointed out. Not yet, as someone from defence had grimly noted. But if the thin blue line crumbled, if the mobs turned uglier, then all the measures discussed this morning might be unavoidable. And once they went down that road the country would never be the same again, Harry realised. A way forward had to be found, and found quickly. The people needed hope, enough to calm the palpable frustration on the streets. But hope was in short supply.

The economic depression had been triggered by the Russian energy field failures, the Arabians using the opportunity to ramp up the price of gas and oil to previously unimaginable levels. They had insisted it was due to production problems, but Harry wasn't buying it. Meanwhile the Chinese, always ready to take advantage of a Western crisis, waited in the wings to become Europe's biggest creditor as they sought to buy up the ever rising mountain of European debt. Quiet diplomacy, once the soothing balm of British foreign relations, wasn't working either. If Harry didn't know better he'd probably entertain the anti-Western conspiracy theories being bandied around the room, but to do so would invoke a siege mentality within the administration and that would be bad for everyone. Besides, he argued, what good was a broke and busted Europe?

So the meeting had ended, grim looks in evidence as the attendees left the room. Harry left too, his communications director, David Fuller, hurrying behind him. As they made their way back upstairs into Number Ten, Harry's thoughts turned to the forthcoming dinner that night with the US ambassador. After years of Eurocentric governments in Whitehall, Harry had focussed significant diplomatic efforts in rekindling long neglected

Anglo-American friendships.

The US economy, in difficulties for nearly a decade, was now beginning to show signs of a marked recovery. After the Gulf and Afghan withdrawals, and the Arab Spring that had eventually given birth to the Arabian Super-state, America had been badly let down by her allies in Europe. No one had fought her corner when Grand Mufti Khathami had decided to cut off oil exports to North America, when the same economic woes had gripped the US as they had here in Britain and, as a result, Washington had pursued a somewhat isolationist foreign policy. Harry didn't blame them for that, and had often felt ashamed at the almost unbridled joy exhibited by many fellow politicians at America's downfall.

But things had changed recently; in the last few months, US exports had risen, the dollar had been slowly strengthening, the power cuts that had bankrupted the state of California and affected every major US city had ceased almost overnight. Something was going on across the pond and Harry was glad that he'd reached out to Washington in his first months as prime minister, offering a hand of friendship that was tenuously accepted. Relations were still fragile, but Harry believed he was considered a friend in Washington, and right now that friend needed help. Tonight, at dinner with the ambassador, he'd find out if help was forthcoming.

In the lobby of Number Ten, Harry dismissed Fuller and made his way upstairs to his private apartment on the top floor. Anna, his wife, was working on her laptop in the kitchen when he entered.

'Missus B,' he chirped, brushing her blonde hair back and pecking her cheek.

'Hi,' smiled Anna, tapping away at the keyboard. 'How was the meeting?'

'Tedious,' he sighed. His wife knew about the CIG meetings, was aware of the type of topics discussed in the deep level bunker below ground. And it frightened her. Harry could hear the edge in her voice, saw the lines that creased her forehead, remembered the fear in those pale blue eyes when the paint had splattered against the car window, when she came face to face with the baying crowds beyond the shields and the barriers. She'd changed in the last year, and Harry had seen her strength and confidence falter in the face of mob violence, of class hatred, at becoming an establishment hate figure alongside her husband.

The thought of exposing his wife to such animosity made Harry's stomach churn. His marriage was important to him, more than anything, but he also had a duty to the country, to all those people out there who were suffering similar strains and pressures. Anna knew that, accepted it, but wasn't coping as well as she might. She was a good person, decent, caring. She didn't deserve this. The bloody job was making them both old, Harry fumed.

He forced a smile as he watched Anna close her laptop and move it to one side.

'Can we leave town this weekend?' she asked. 'I don't want to be around for this bloody march.'

'Of course. I can work from Chequers.' Harry poured them both a coffee and sat down at the kitchen table, loosening his tie. A siren suddenly wailed on Whitehall and he saw anxiety cloud her eyes again, the worry lines around her mouth deepen. He took her hands in his. 'Hey, it's probably an ambulance.'

Anna squeezed his fingers, then brought them up to her mouth and kissed them. 'I know, I'm being stupid. Just spooked again, that's all. A weekend in the country will do us both good.'

'You bet.'

'What's on for the rest of the day?'

'I've got that school thing in Greenwich, remember? The wing opening?'

Anna frowned. 'I thought you were going to cancel? Because of the dinner tonight?'

'I'd love to. But, as David rightly reminded me, I made a personal commitment. Besides, the developers are significant party donors.'

'They'd understand, Harry. What's more important – preparing for a dinner that may reap considerable rewards for the whole country, or a school wing opening?'

Harry frowned. 'You're right, I know. It's tricky, that's all.'

'Then cite security concerns, the march, whatever. Or send someone else. What about Kay Fleming?'

Harry thought about his barrel-figured minister for education, her negative reaction to an abrupt change in her schedule, her famously abrasive manner.

'No, Kay's all wrong for this. Like I said, it's more of a personal commitment. I made a promise, when they broke ground, in front of the board, the parents and pupils. I went to school there, remember?'

Anna laid her hands on the table. 'In that case, I'll go.'

Harry shook his head. 'No way.'

'Yes,' Anna insisted in a calm voice. 'It's only Greenwich, and it'll be more personal if I go. Anyway, I'm beginning to feel like a prisoner here. It'll be nice to do a bit of meet-and-greet, take my mind off things. Who knows, it might give the polls a little boost too.'

Harry thought quickly. True, it was a short trip, made even shorter in a ministerial car that didn't stop for anything across town. He'd insist on a larger police escort too, strong but subtle, just to keep Anna reassured. And maybe she was right, maybe the media would spin it in a positive light.

'You're sure?' asked Harry, squeezing her shoulder.

'Certain.'

'You've saved my life,' he smiled, scraping his chair back and kissing her cheek. 'I'll speak to David, get things organised with the governors. Can you be ready by three? The unveiling's supposed to take place after the final bell, give the kids and parents a chance to see the ceremony.'

Anna nodded. 'Sure.'

'You're an angel. Thanks.'

He turned, closing the apartment door behind him, and headed downstairs.

Morden, South London
3.03 p.m.

Danesh Khan's knees cracked painfully as he got to his feet and made his way stiffly out of the prayer hall and into the adjoining atrium. He took his trainers from the cubbyhole and slipped them on, continuing along the carpeted hallway to the busy entrance foyer. There he joined a throng of other worshippers browsing the trestle tables stacked with Islamic books and pamphlets. Feigning interest, he engaged one of the mosque workers in a brief conversation about the latest goings-on in Arabia, all the time keeping a watchful eye on the hallway.

After a minute or so, the wait was over. There he was. Khan headed for the exit, keeping a small group of worshippers between himself and the object of his surveillance, the man known simply as Target One. He eyed the individual through the crowd as the target bid farewell to two other men, then made his way out into the street.

The mosque was situated just off the A24 Morden Road in south-west London, a rather uninspiring structure as mosques went, but Khan thought it was one of the more interesting buildings in this drab suburb on the borders of London and Surrey. Target One walked out of the main gate and turned right towards Morden town centre, no doubt making for the bus stop that would take him home to Mitcham, assumed Khan.

'Target One on the move,' he mumbled into his tiny microphone secreted under his shirt collar. His hidden earpiece hissed in reply.

'Copy that, Kilo Whiskey Seven. Fifty metres from the Tube station.'

Khan let Target One drift slightly ahead. As a Muslim operative for MI5, he was one of only a small handful of intelligence officers whose sole task was to infiltrate British Islamic society and investigate potential links to terrorism. Historically, Western intelligence agencies had difficulty infiltrating such closed communities, but Khan, a British Pakistani and former practising Muslim, had little difficulty blending in. His well-rehearsed cover story was always watertight, his natural discretion and unobtrusive manner lending itself perfectly to the painstaking task of intelligence gathering. But there was little real success.

During an eight-year career, his undercover work had led to many arrests, but those had been mostly for immigration or counterfeiting offences, a fair amount of drug seizures and benefit fraud. Peanuts, as far as Khan was concerned. What he wanted was a major terror bust to improve his case figures; but this wasn't like the old days, when young radicals wore their loyalties on their sleeves and the targets were easy to identify. No, things had changed in the last decade. As the years passed, the firebrands had ceased their recruitment drives, the foreign imams no longer spreading their messages of hate in the mosques and madrasas of Britain. The jihad had gone dark.

There used to be plenty of Muslims who spoke quietly about taking up arms and fighting for the Islamic cause, even the so-called moderates, who quietly supported the fighters and performed their own brand of jihad. In the early days, Khan had heard their whispered conversations, watching, listening, until all he was left with were words. No plans ever materialised, no operations were ever given the green light. It was as if the word had come down from on high: 'No more talk of Holy War, of struggle and sacrifice. Let the infidels be deafened by our silence.'

Khan didn't believe it. The conflict had lasted for over fourteen hundred years, an enduring state of mind, the raison d'être of an ideology that just couldn't be switched off overnight. Along with other operatives, Khan had warned his superiors, understanding only too well the practice of *taqiyya*, the cloak of deceit that the Qur'an permitted in order to fool unbelievers. But politics prevailed, the mindset of appeasement that permeated the corridors of power in Whitehall stalling fresh lines of investigation, of surveillance and tracking. The rise of the Muslim brotherhood across the Arab world, culminating in the formation of the state of Arabia, was directly linked to the scaling down of Islamic-related terror investigations. Khan had viewed the move as foolish.

Target One was a case in point. Khan was under increasing pressure to justify the man-hours and expenditure for continued surveillance on a subject that had yet to yield anything of any significance. Target One had come to the attention of the security services some time ago, a raid on his house producing a computer filled with jihadist video files, large amounts of cash that couldn't be accounted for, blank passports and credit cards found hidden under floorboards in an upstairs bedroom. Target One's lawyer had argued successfully that the property was a halfway house for overseas travellers, that Target One couldn't be linked to the cash or passports, and that his computer had been used by others, now long gone. He'd walked, as Khan knew he would. But the trips to Arabia continued, final destination unknown, MI6 being virtually redundant in the Holy State.

Target One was in his thirties, like Khan, with a slim build and a short-cropped beard. There was something wrong about the man, Khan's gut instinct told him, but his superiors were tiring of Khan's hunches, and had given him a month to produce evidence – hard, concrete evidence – or else the plug would be pulled. So Khan had worked for the past eight days straight, desperately seeking something that would tip the balance of the investigation back in his favour. If unsuccessful, Khan's team of watchers would move on to other operations. Right now, the focus was on hard-left agitators, subversives and other anarchists, all seemingly hell-bent on bringing down the government. They were the priority, Khan was told, not so-called Muslim terrorists. The jihad was dead, and Arabia had risen from its funeral pyre, a phoenix of stable government, of strengthened diplomacy and economic prosperity. It was a mistake.

Khan shook off his thoughts and concentrated instead on the immediate task, following from a distance as Target One sidestepped a mountain of bin liners that spewed rubbish across the pavement, and jogged over the main road. A van drew up alongside Khan, the side cargo door sliding open. Khan jumped in as another watcher, Spencer, hopped out, taking up the surveillance on Target One.

The driver, Max, studied Khan in his rear-view mirror. 'Well?'

'Nothing,' Khan shrugged. 'Prayers as usual, a quick chat with a couple of older guys I've never seen before, and then he left.'

Max exhaled loudly. 'Dammit. Any luck with the wiretap?'

'Judge threw it out. Unwarranted, bordering on harassment she said.'

'Stupid cow,' cursed Max. 'So, we're back to square one again. Let's face it, we're going to have to cut this fucker loose.'

Khan opened his mouth to reply, but then paused, frowning. 'Wait. There was one odd moment, just before I left the mosque.'

A sharp rap on the passenger window drew their attention outside. A traffic warden stared sullenly at them from beneath the peak of his cap, his wide black face locked in a permanent snarl.

'No parking,' he ordered. 'Move.'

Max reached into his jacket, produced a Metropolitan Police warrant card. 'Fuck off.' The warden sloped away, muttering under his breath. Max turned back to Khan. 'Go on.'

'Yeah, the others, the older guys. They kissed.' Max screwed his face up. 'They what?'

'They kissed our boy, on the cheeks, respectfully. I caught it just before he left the foyer.'

'Is it significant?'

Khan thought about it for a moment. The embraces were warm, the kisses from the older ones courteous, respectful. No, almost reverential. One of them had even bowed his head slightly. It was out of the ordinary, a parting that held some significance for all three men. It was a scene that most human beings had witnessed or experienced themselves at some time in their lives, usually at airports or train stations, and Khan suddenly realised the importance of the moment.

'I think they were saying goodbye.'

Target One walked swiftly towards the station, his heart racing. Finally, the day had arrived. He had prayed at the mosque for the last time, washed and shaved, and recorded a final message to his family, which would be delivered after the operation was complete. Target One was prepared. But despite the honour he felt at being selected for such a mission and the comforting embrace of his faith, he was also quietly terrified. That was why his heart raced, why his skin felt clammy, why his armpits sweated profusely.

He passed the bus stop, his usual stop, resisting the sudden urge to wait with the other sour-faced infidels and take the bus back to Mitcham. But he couldn't, of course. He'd been chosen, educated and trained, his place in paradise already assured, and he clung to that thought as he continued across the road into the Tube station, swiping his travel card at the passenger barrier. The station was quiet and a train waited on the platform as Target One headed toward the front carriage.

Employing his anti-surveillance training, he stopped suddenly and turned around, doubling back. There were two people behind him on the platform. One was an old woman laden with shopping bags, puffing her way on to an empty carriage. The other, a white man in his late twenties, continued down the stairs towards him. He wore a baseball cap, jacket, jeans and running shoes. Target One made a show of checking his watch against the passenger display above his head. The man veered off and hopped aboard the train halfway up the platform. Good. Target One continued towards the front of the train and entered the empty carriage behind the driver's compartment. He took a seat facing the platform and presently a computerised voice announced the train's imminent departure. After a moment, the doors hissed shut and the train lurched forward, accelerating into the tunnel.

Target One glanced to his right, searching the rows of empty carriages as they rocked and swayed from side to side through the darkness. He noticed the man in the baseball cap, two carriages down, staring at an advertising display above his head. Target One pulled out a battered copy of the Qur'an from his trouser pocket and leafed through the well-thumbed pages. He wracked his brains, trying to work out what carriage Baseball Cap had got on. He was sure it wasn't as far up as he was now. He must have used the interconnecting doors to work his way towards the front of the train. If that was the case, then he might have a tail. Or he could just be paranoid. But the anti-surveillance training he'd received in the desert had taught him to be paranoid. Everyone was a possible infidel agent.

He mulled over what he knew about the man, gleaned from a momentary glance on the platform. He was white; not that many white people in Morden any more, but there were some. Baseball cap and jacket, possible disguise. Remove the hat, reverse the jacket, now you're someone else. Jeans and running shoes; common enough clothing to go unnoticed, yet running shoes were good for pursuit. So, a possible tail. I'll know soon enough, he decided.

The train continued on its journey, rattling beneath the densely populated suburbs of south-west London, the carriages becoming more crowded with each stop. The carriage intercom hissed and crackled.

'The next station is Clapham Common. Customers requiring the Clapham Junction Eurostar terminal please change here.'

Target One stood up. He stumbled slightly with the motion of the carriage, reaching for the handrail above his head. He glanced to his right. Two carriages down, Baseball Cap was also on his feet. The train hissed to a stop at Clapham Common. Target One got off, noting that Baseball Cap had got off too. He silently cursed. The man's behaviour was displaying all the characteristics of a tail; he had to lose this tail or abort his operation. And that would mean he had failed. There was no alternative.

Target One walked slowly along the platform, keeping his head down, shuffling towards the stairs along with the other passengers who had just alighted. From the corner of his eye, he saw Baseball Cap move to the southbound side of the platform, as if waiting to board a train travelling in the other direction. Now he was almost certain the man was an infidel agent. Moments later, Target One drew parallel with Baseball Cap, who suddenly feigned interest in the advertising displays on the curved wall of the opposite tunnel. At that moment, the door closure signal beeped, echoing around the concourse. Target One cut quickly through the crowd and stepped back on to the northbound train, squeezing himself behind a large black man and peering over his shoulder out on to the platform. The doors hissed closed. He saw Baseball Cap casually turn around, trying to locate his mark. As the train began to move, he saw him frantically searching the crowds and then move swiftly towards the stairs. He didn't look at the carriage once.

As the train continued towards Clapham North station, Target One found a seat and pondered his predicament. Yes, he was being followed, and by the Security Service no doubt, but for how long had he been followed? Not that long, probably a routine operation, he decided. Target One had lived a simple life, employing the same habits and schedule for most of the time, with only a single brush with the law to his name. Besides, he was only being followed by one man. If he wasn't, then Baseball Cap wouldn't have panicked, wouldn't have run for the stairs, a sure sign he was operating alone.

The train slowed, pulling into the next station. Target One took out his mobile phone and jammed the device between the seats, pushing his travel card after it. He stood up, waiting for the doors to open. When they did, he moved further up the platform and re-boarded the train.

So far, so good, he smiled.

Khan pointed through the windscreen as the van weaved through the traffic towards the station at Clapham Common.

'There he is!'

Max swung the wheel to the left and slid into the kerb. Spencer jumped aboard.

'Lost him,' he puffed. 'Carried out an area search, but nothing. Sorry.'

'Forget it,' Khan said. 'Who knew he was going to take the bloody Tube? This is my fault. He put us to sleep.' The alarm bells were ringing urgently now, his gut feeling that something major was in progress becoming stronger by the minute. He keyed his radio.

'Control, this is Kilo Whiskey Seven, requesting immediate surveillance assistance, over.'

Overhead, the speaker hissed back.

'Copy that, Kilo Whiskey Seven. Wait. Out.'

Wait. Out? Khan keyed the radio again. 'Control, Kilo Whiskey Seven, surveillance target may be operational at this time. Requesting assets for priority reacquisition, over.'

The speaker crackled, the controller's voice laced with irritation. 'Kilo Whiskey Seven, Control, message received, standby.'

Khan shared a look with Max and Spencer. What the hell was up with Control? Didn't they understand the urgency of the situation? Khan was about to key his radio again, when another voice echoed inside the van.

'Kilo Whiskey Seven, what's your location?'

'Outside Clapham Common Tube station.'

'Where did you lose your target?'

'Down on the platform. Target was travelling northbound. How soon can I get those assets?'

'You can't,' the voice replied. 'Seventeen targets have just gone active in the London area. We're swamped.'

Khan stared at the speaker, his blood suddenly cold.

At Stockwell Underground station, Target One left the carriage and made his way up the escalator to the ticket hall, his eyes scanning the concourse... there. A tall Arabian man wearing a hooded sweatshirt waited near the gate line. Target One veered towards him, pushing through the crowd.

'Easy, bruv!'

He glanced over his shoulder. He'd cut across the path of a black man, the same one he'd hidden behind on the train. He mumbled an apology and moved towards the Arab who, seeing Target One approach, palmed him a ticket. They moved quickly out of the station and into the bright sunlight, turning left into Binfield Road. The Arab set a brisk pace.

'Your journey was okay?'

'I was followed,' confessed Target One.

The Arab slowed his pace, glancing over his shoulder. 'Explain.' Target One recounted the details of his journey, leaving nothing out. 'You are certain that is all?'

'Yes, I...'

A voice boomed behind them. 'Wait up, bruv!'

Without slowing, both men glanced behind them. The black man from the station was advancing quickly towards them.

'Yeah, you!'

The Arab slipped a hand under his sweatshirt. He turned to Target One.

'I will deal with this. Say nothing.'

They stopped and turned as the black man marched up to them. He was in his early twenties, over six feet tall and roughly two hundred pounds, nearly all of it muscle. And he was angry. Without breaking stride, he planted both hands on Target One's chest and shoved hard, sending him stumbling backwards on to the pavement. The Arab stepped sideways to distance himself, caught off guard by the sudden attack. The black man ignored him, loomed over Target One and jabbed a thick finger in his face.

'You dissing me? You know who I am, ya piece of shit?'

Target One's eyes blazed with anger. This infidel had laid his unclean hands on him, had disgraced him with his physical assault. Target One could smell the man's disgusting breath on his face as a fine spray of spittle dampened his cheek. He tried to get up, but the black man raised his fist.

'I'll beat ya down, get me? Teach you some fucking–'

Target One saw the tiniest flicker of confusion in the black man's eyes as the barrel of the pistol touched the side of his head, just before the flash and crack of the ten millimetre round blew out a hole above his left ear. He toppled over into the gutter, the wide rent in his skull pumping blood on to the road. The Arab slipped the gun back under his sweatshirt and grabbed Target One's hand, dragging him to his feet. Behind them, a scream split the air.

'Move!'

The Arab shoved Target One forward, who smiled as he stepped over his assailant's lifeless body. They reached the junction of Binfield Road and Lansdowne Way, crossing quickly into Guildford Road and dodging the early-evening traffic that blasted their horns at the men's reckless passage. The Arab pointed to a battered Ford saloon car parked along the street. There was a man behind the wheel, the engine running.

'Get in,' commanded the Arab. Target One slid into the back while the Arab jumped into the front passenger seat. The car accelerated away from the kerb and turned down another side street, heading in the direction of the city. In the distance, they heard the rising wail of a police response vehicle.

10 Downing Street, London
4.33 p.m.

Harry was seated alone in the Cabinet Room, lost in thought as he pored over his notes in preparation for the evening's engagement with the US ambassador. Although he had his own private office in the building, the Cabinet Room exuded a certain gravitas that sharpened his mind for the task at hand. He took a moment to glance around the room that never failed to impress him. A rather flattering oil painting of Sir Robert Walpole, the man considered to be England's first prime minister, hung above the fireplace; the chairs, which were arranged around the large antique table, had been used in this room since the reign of Queen Victoria. How could anyone fail to be impressed by these surroundings?

For Harry, being prime minister was more than just the pinnacle of his political career. He understood the responsibility of office completely, could feel the weight of history bearing down on him, yet it didn't make him uncomfortable. When he thought about the men – and, of course, Mrs Thatcher – who had all occupied the seat he was now sitting in, well, it made him feel quite humble. And it gave him a determination to be worthy of the post of prime minister of Great Britain. His thoughts were interrupted by a tap at the door. David Fuller entered the room.

'David. What is it?'

'Sorry to disturb you, Harry, but something's come up. An urgent security matter.'

'Really? What kind?' asked Harry without looking up, sifting through the papers before him.

'Intelligence reports a number of their surveillance targets have suddenly disappeared. They think it could mean something.'

Harry put down the papers. 'What targets?'

'SIS has all the details. They believe it's significant.'

'When did this happen?'

'In the last hour. They've collated some preliminary information and prepared a report. They'd like to brief you at five in the CMC.'

Damn it, cursed Harry privately. He was running out of time and he still had a lot of work to do. He stood quickly, gathering his papers together.

'Fine. Get Peter over here, too.' Peter Noonan was the deputy PM, a competent politician with a cool head in any crisis.

'Peter's giving a speech, at the Press Club in Mayfair,' replied Fuller. 'Do you want me to pull him out?'

Harry thought about it for a moment then shook his head. 'If he was anywhere else I'd say yes. What time is he due to finish?'

'Five thirty.'

'Get a message to him, discreetly please, David. I want him over here as soon as he's done.'

Fuller turned on his heel, pulling out his mobile phone. Harry followed on behind, pausing to retrieve his own phone and speed-dialling his wife's number. After a few rings her voice clicked on the line.

'Hi, darling. How are things at Greenwich?'

'Fine. Everything's going very smoothly.'

In the background Harry could hear the hubbub of conversation and the scrape of china crockery. He smiled. 'You're better at this than I am.' Making an effort to keep his tone casual, he continued. 'Look Anna, something's come up.'

'What?'

'Nothing to be concerned about, just a security matter. What time are you finishing?'

'Twenty minutes. Thirty tops.'

Harry checked his watch. 'I've got a brief in ten minutes. Can you call me in an hour? Let me know where you are?'

There was a pause on the line, then Harry heard the first traces of concern leaking into her voice. 'Should I be worried, Harry?'

'Jesus, no. Look, it's probably nothing. Twenty minutes, did you say?'

'Maybe thirty.'

'Call me, okay?'

'Sure. See you soon.'

'Anna? Can you put Matt on the line, please? I'd like a quick word.'

There was a pause as the phone was passed to Matt Goodge, a tough Geordie and a detective sergeant in Anna Beecham's security team.

'Sir?'

'Hi, Matt. Look, a possible security situation has arisen.'

Goodge's voice was all business. 'Any specifics, sir?'

'None yet. I'm probably overreacting, but just get Anna back here as soon as possible. Take all the usual precautions, but don't alarm anyone. And I don't want you whisking her out of there before she's finished. Just make sure that you waste no time getting her home.'

'Of course.'

Harry flipped his phone closed, ending the call. He wasn't sure if telling Goodge was a wise idea. He had no information about this so-called security situation and sometimes a little knowledge can be dangerous. All of Anna's bodyguards carried weapons. What if someone popped a balloon or slammed a door too hard? Those guys operated on a hair trigger at times. He shook his head, chastising himself. He was being stupid. They were professionals, for God's sake. He glanced at his notes, an untidy scrawl of talking points and information to be memorised. He'd try and delegate this security matter and wrap the meeting up as quickly as possible. As far as Harry was concerned, kick-starting Britain's economy was the real issue.

Anything else could wait.

Hammersmith, West London
5.15 p.m.

Alex Taylor left his motorcycle in the garage on Ravenscourt Road and decided to walk the mile or so back to his apartment in Chiswick. It was a beautiful afternoon and he was looking forward to a couple of days off. Not that being a firearms officer in the Metropolitan Police was tremendously taxing – most of his operational time was spent driving around in cars or on a firing range somewhere. But the job could be stressful at times and it was nice to get a break every now and then, especially when it was quiet. And it had been quiet for weeks. True, London's gangland was still blowing lumps out of each other but, apart from that, it was relatively peaceful in London and Alex hoped it stayed that way.

He'd left the station in Southwark at five, weaving his BMW tourer across London to the garage in Hammersmith for its annual service. After chatting with the mechanic for a few minutes, Alex hefted his small rucksack over his shoulder and set off towards the river.

When he got home he would grab his gym gear and go to the club for a workout, he decided. After that, he'd wander down to the pub, where he'd enjoy the rest of the evening sipping beers by the river. And who knows, maybe Kirsty would join him.

Kirsty Moore lived on the top floor of his apartment block and Alex had been well and truly smitten since the first day he'd set eyes on her. That was a few months ago now and he'd been trying to find the right opportunity to ask her out on a date, but fate had often played a hand and screwed the timing up. They'd pass each other in the hallway, Kirsty pounding down the stairs, hair wet and late for work, or Alex would be heading off to Southwark for an evening shift, just as Kirsty arrived home from her job in the city.

What little contact they enjoyed was casual; they'd smile and enquire after each other's health before going their separate ways, but Alex felt that there was a connection there and he was almost certain Kirsty felt it too. It wasn't anything obvious, just a glint in her deep brown eyes, a subtle look over her shoulder as they passed; not much to go on, but Alex saw them as positive signals. So, the time had come to bite the bullet and make his intentions known. If Kirsty was home this evening, he'd ask her to join him down the pub on a date. If she wasn't home he'd scribble a note and pop it through her letter box. Either way, he'd make plain his interest and take it from there. Alex smiled to himself. The thought of asking her made him a little nervous.

He crossed over into King Street and headed south, cutting through the subway under the A4 arterial road that carried traffic in and out of West London. At this time of day, the road was very busy in both directions and the sound and smell of the crawling vehicles soured his mood slightly. He watched the traffic as he strolled towards the river, feeling sympathy for the sweating drivers trapped in their cars and vans, the impatient horns, the revving engines, the thumping music, all overlapping into a cacophony of headache-inducing noise. Thank God he rode a bike. Still, even on a road like the A4 a bike could sometimes be a chore, too.

He turned down a side street and reached the riverbank a few minutes later, taking the towpath alongside the slow-moving waters, the sudden peace and tranquillity a world away from the river of metal behind him. Technically, the towpath was a longer route home, but he wasn't in much of a hurry and he felt like walking, anyway. He was in good spirits as he checked his watch: five twenty-five.

Deep inside his rucksack his work phone remained unanswered, the four missed calls drowned out by the crawling traffic beyond the rooftops.

Clapham, South London
5.31 p.m.

In a side street off Clapham High Street, Khan was pacing up and down the pavement when Max beckoned him over to the van. He pulled the side door open and jumped in.

'What is it?'

'Got something on the Met band.'

Khan activated the communications panel in the rear of the van. He tapped the police icon on the screen and a series of incidents began scrolling downwards. Only two events in the area were flagged as serious; one was a road accident fatality involving a cyclist on Brixton Hill, but the other had him reaching for the radio.

'Direct patch to OCC, please.'

The OCC was the Met's Operations Command Centre, a high-tech communications hub located several floors beneath Scotland Yard. His headset reverberated with digital clicks and warbles. Seconds later, a female voice announced, 'OCC.'

'Supervisor, please,' said Khan. After a moment another voice came on the line.

'Superintendent Greenwood, Duty Operations Controller. How can we help?'

'Designate my call sign Kilo Whiskey Seven,' replied Khan. The OCC needed to identify him somehow and they'd know he was MI5.

'Roger, Kilo Whiskey Seven. Go ahead,' acknowledged Greenwood.

'Superintendent, you have a shooting incident logged adjacent to Stockwell Tube station. Can you upload the footage?'

'Sure. It's probably a Trident gang job, though. Victim is a black male in his twenties, single shot to the head. Standby while I get it routed through.'

Khan bit his lip as the seconds ticked by and the download bar crept across his screen. Then the CCTV footage was streaming inside the van.

'It's him! It's Target One,' Khan declared, stabbing a finger at the monitor. He keyed his mike again. 'Superintendent, the man on the left of the picture is one of our surveillance targets. This isn't a local job, it's a national security issue. We need to pick him up ASAP.'

'They decamped in a vehicle,' Greenwood replied. 'No description or index number yet, but we're trawling the local CCTV and ANPR systems. It's a matter of time before we get a hit.'

Khan kicked the side door in frustration. 'Okay, thanks. If you get any more info, patch it straight through, please. We've got to find this guy as quickly as possible.'

Now what? fretted Khan. One thing was clear: an operation was in progress and it didn't just involve Target One. There were others out there, all of whom had managed to shake their surveillance.

'Get in touch with Control,' he ordered Max. 'See if they've got an update. Something big is about to kick off and we're sitting here with our thumbs up our arses.'

Chiswick, West London
5.37 p.m.

Kirsty Moore wasn't sure whether it was the car tyres crunching up the gravel driveway or her insistent bladder that woke her from her nap. She pulled her knees up and shifted position on the sun lounger, wrapped in the warmth of the early evening sunshine that bathed her balcony, but her bladder was refusing to co-operate. She still felt tired, even after several lazy hours on the sofa, but after yesterday's drinking session she wasn't at all surprised.

Her weekday morning had started as it always did, with the chirping of the alarm clock at six fifteen. After ten minutes and two clumsy attempts to connect with the snooze button, Kirsty had dragged herself out of bed and headed for the shower, making a conscious effort to avoid the mirror on her way past. Not that Kirsty was unattractive. With her shoulder-length black hair, olive skin, huge brown eyes and a figure most girls would kill for, Kirsty drew admiring glances wherever she went, and was considered a top catch at Fisher Brown Finance in Holborn where she worked. As an internet marketing company it was a relaxed and occasionally fun place to work and the night before was no exception.

Her friend, Annie, was celebrating her twenty-eighth birthday and, after work, they went to a nearby bar with most of the office turning out in support. From there, things got out of control; a mad two hours in a karaoke bar near Oxford Circus, a Chinese meal in Soho, cocktails at Zoo, and dancing (shoes in hand) until three. When Kirsty eventually arrived home, at around four in the morning, it was almost light and she was feeling decidedly worse for wear. Not good, considering she had to be up in two and a quarter hours. Still, she'd done it before. She was only thirty, young enough to get away with a good night out and turn up for work the next morning. Or so she thought.

Showered and dressed, but feeling very fragile, Kirsty had made her way downstairs to the street. Her apartment block was situated in Chiswick, West London, which wasn't the most convenient of locations for getting into the city, but the fact that she had an apartment overlooking the river more than made up for the hassle of commuting. And besides, the rent was dirt cheap. Her older brother, Bruce, who lived in Slovenia, owned the place and let his baby sister stay there indefinitely. A two-bedroom apartment overlooking the Thames, no room-mates required, thank you very much.

Exiting the building, she made her way towards Chiswick station, her bleary eyes hidden behind sunglasses. A bus roared past as she waited to cross the main road, belching a thick cloud of diesel fumes in Kirsty's direction. Her head spun as she breathed in a lungful and she groped at a traffic light post to steady herself. She really wasn't feeling too good...

It was at that moment that last night's alcoholic indulgences decided to manifest themselves. Clutching her mouth tightly, she turned and stumbled across the pavement to an overflowing waste bin outside a newsagent. Other pedestrians turned their noses up in disgust and the occupants of a passing van jeered and hooted with laughter. Kirsty threw up until her stomach was empty, and then her body dry retched for another minute just to be sure. No way was she going to the office today.

She had walked home on wobbly legs and spent the rest of the day watching daytime TV, drifting in and out of sleep. At around four in the afternoon, she made herself scrambled eggs on toast, after which she began to feel a little more human. She grabbed a book, a trashy chick-lit novel that she'd been sucked into, and settled down in her favourite lounger on the balcony. After a few pages her eyelids began to feel very heavy and the words on the page began to blur. Kirsty was soon asleep.

But now, the combination of her insistent bladder and the sound of the vehicle in the driveway below had woken her. She was puzzled and a little irritated. She wondered who it could be and considered having a quick peek over the balcony, but the call of nature was becoming more persistent and wouldn't be ignored. Well, she needed a shower anyway. She slapped her novel down on to the balcony deck and padded across the lounge to the bathroom. As she passed the kitchen, Kirsty glanced at the clock on the wall.

It was almost twenty to six.

Crisis Management Centre
5.41 p.m.

'So, what do we do now?' Harry asked, leaning back in his chair.

He'd been in the CMC for over forty minutes and the information contained in the confidential handout was really rather thin. No, that was unfair, Harry corrected himself. The security services were doing their best with what they had, but his impatience was beginning to bubble to the surface. Islamic terrorists, for God's sake? Like everyone else, Harry had thought that that deadly phenomenon was far behind them all.

His eyes drifted along the walls, past the huge plasma screens that linked to various defence and intelligence agencies, until he reached the political map of the world at the end of the room. Harry studied it as the debate continued around the table, his eye drawn to the huge swathe of green that represented the Islamic state of Arabia. It dominated the map, curling around the Mediterranean and dwarfing the myriad of politically fractured countries around it.

Like most politicians the world over, Harry was impressed with the enormous achievements that Arabia had made over the last ten years. The rebirth of a caliphate had certainly assuaged the anger of Muslims worldwide, and that was something they all had to be thankful for. However, Arabia's stranglehold on the world's oil markets was bankrupting Europe. Baghdad had complained about contaminated wells and problems with their offshore pumping facilities, but privately no Western leader believed it. Europe's nuts were in a vice and the Arabs were twisting the handle. But why?

It was a topic discussed at every European summit over the last year and the same conclusion was always reached: find an alternative energy source and find it quickly. Harry would have laughed if the situation wasn't so serious. Wind farms and electric cars, sacred touchstones of the Green movement and championed by their most fervent disciples, just weren't going to cut it, not if Europe's economies were to thrive once more.

But the Americans, well, there was a mystery. California, arguably America's most power-hungry state, once bankrupt, was now quietly enjoying sound economic growth and stable power supplies. How? And could Harry persuade the US to share some of its new-found prosperity? He thought he could, but sitting down here in this drab bunker wasn't going to make that happen, despite the urgency of the meeting. Time, in that case, to wrap things up. He cleared his throat loudly and the arguments died away, the CIG attendees lapsing into silence.

'Time is pressing, ladies and gentlemen. Recommendations, please.'

'Prime Minister, losing a subject isn't unusual, but in the last few hours we've witnessed multiple disappearances,' the head of SIS reminded the room. 'They all appear to be pre-planned. This isn't mere coincidence. An operation is under way.'

'So, what do we do?' asked Harry.

The senior Defence Intelligence Staff officer, Brigadier Giles Forsythe, leaned forward and clasped his hands together on the table. All eyes turned to the man in the green uniform.

'Prime Minister, I agree with my colleagues. Our alert status should be raised across the board in both our civil and military forces. As SIS has pointed out, a planned operation looks increasingly likely against–'

'Nonsense!' Around the room, heads swivelled sharply towards the suntanned, balding pate of the foreign secretary, Geoffrey Cooper. 'Prime Minister, I really think that we may be overreacting here.' The brigadier shot him an icy look. Cooper ignored the glare and concentrated on Harry. 'Yes,' he continued, 'I agree with our colleague from SIS that the circumstances are rather unusual. However, the subjects in question are all Muslims and I think that this raises a very important issue.'

'Explain,' ordered Harry, glancing at the clock on the wall. He could see that Cooper was in his element, the focus of attention in the room. A small, dapper man in his early fifties, Cooper exuded an air of annoying self-importance and not a small degree of arrogance, qualities that seemed to have manifested themselves only after his appointment as foreign secretary. As a result, Harry had quietly pencilled Cooper in for a demotion in the next cabinet reshuffle. He wasn't a vindictive person, but Cooper had a habit of getting under everybody's skin, which was bad for business and bad for the country. Harry was curious to see if a stint in transport would deflate that ego.

'As you know,' began Cooper, 'I have spent some time working with the present Arabian administration with whom I have been able to forge some very productive diplomatic ties, ties that have directly benefited this country. Now, it's a fact that since the state of Arabia came into being, Islamic terrorism has melted away across the globe, something that–'

'Get to the point, Geoffrey.'

Cooper visibly reddened. 'My point? Quite simply, why are we watching these people? What evidence do we have to warrant this potentially illegal surveillance? The Commissioner here says that none of them have criminal records and most of them are taxpaying voters. The fact that they've visited Arabia on several occasions and are on some vague watch list doesn't mean they're guilty of anything. I'm sure I don't have to remind anyone in this room that the diplomatic implications of these clumsy intrusions could be severe.'

'They're British citizens,' Harry reminded Cooper. 'This is a domestic issue.'

'Have we learned nothing over the years?' the foreign secretary countered. 'My time in Arabia has taught me many things, not least that for people of the faith their loyalty is towards Islam first. It's offensive to suggest otherwise. And we all know Arabia can be very unforgiving if it feels its people are being persecuted.'

Further along the table the SIS official bristled. 'Foreign Secretary, there are some in the Intelligence Services who believe that the threat posed by Islamic extremism still exists, despite the ambient diplomatic temperatures we've become used to. And with these particular subjects there is some history, their citizenship notwithstanding. Right now the evidence is clear; a timetable is almost certainly being followed and anti-surveillance methods employed. This is no time to consider diplomatic niceties. This is happening on our streets, right now.'

Cooper barely glanced at the man, instead focussing his attentions on Harry. 'Prime Minister, if we start arresting Muslims on the whims of our Intelligence Services it could prove both provocative and inflammatory. The adoption of a domestic anti-Islamic stance could have severe repercussions in Baghdad.'

The Metropolitan Police commissioner nodded in agreement. 'Sir, the Foreign Secretary has a valid point. We also have a legal responsibility to ensure that what we're doing doesn't contravene our race and religion bills. We've spent years trying to rebuild relations between our communities after the problems we've experienced in the past. I'm sure nobody wants to see all that good work undone.'

'Quite right,' agreed Cooper.

Harry pinched the bridge of his nose between thumb and forefinger. Cooper's condescending tone was getting on his nerves and the commissioner had just played right into his hands. The policeman himself was more or less a political appointee and had assured his lofty position after a career that was without controversy, lacking any real-world experience but with all the right political connections and ideology. Harry pushed his chair back and stood up, a signal that the meeting was at an end.

'I understand everybody's individual concerns,' he began. 'However, I think we must err on the side of caution and go with the general consensus. SIS will continue their efforts to reacquire the subjects using any means possible, and I want alert levels raised across the board. Commissioner, I expect your people to handle any subsequent arrests or detentions with the utmost professionalism. And Geoffrey, you will prepare something for the ambassador, just in case things do turn nasty. I want to be kept fully abreast of any developments, day or night, is that clear? Brigadier Forsythe, you have my authority to raise the military alert level. It won't hurt to test our responses to intelligence briefs.'

The brigadier nodded curtly. Cooper, he saw, flushed red with anger.

'No press statements on this one,' Harry warned. 'We keep everything in-house for the time being. Let's raise our guard without raising fears.' As the meeting dispersed, Harry pulled his phone from his pocket and punched his wife's number. After two rings he was connected.

'Hi, Harry.'

'Hi, love. How did it go?' Harry glanced up to see a stern-faced Cooper hovering nearby. 'One second.' He held the phone against his chest. 'Be kind enough to wait outside, would you Geoffrey? A private call, you understand.' He turned his back and lifted the phone to his ear. 'Sorry about that.'

'Let me guess,' Anna chuckled. 'Geoffrey Cooper?'

'Bingo. Where are you?'

'Nearly home. Matt seems keen to get me back to Whitehall in record time. He thinks we'll arrive around six or thereabouts. It all went very well, by the way.'

'Good. I owe you dinner. A very expensive one.' Harry checked his watch. 'Look, I have to talk to Cooper and there are a few other things that need taking care of. I'll see you upstairs when you get back.'

'Okay, darling.'

Harry slipped his phone back into his pocket and made his way out into the corridor, where David Fuller was trying to placate his simmering foreign secretary.

'Prime Minister,' puffed a red-faced Cooper. 'With the greatest respect, I feel that my experience in matters concerning Arabia should be given greater consideration.'

'And in spite of that influence, your friends in Baghdad aren't doing us any bloody favours at the moment, are they Geoffrey?'

'They've had their own problems,' spluttered Cooper, 'all well documented. Look, I'm not buying that oil conspiracy rubbish and, furthermore, this so-called security situation could jeopardise future relationships at a time when we need them most.'

Harry glanced at his watch again and moved past Cooper. 'Sorry Geoffrey, I haven't got time to argue with you on this one. I suggest we leave security to those who know best.'

'Those who know best?' the portly minister blustered, his anger booming along the corridor. 'SIS are a bunch of public bloody schoolboys, singularly misplaced to judge the ramifications of–'

Harry stopped in his tracks and spun around. 'Geoffrey, you will retract that remark or I'll have your resignation on my desk within the hour. Is that clear?'

Cooper's nostrils flared, his breath coming in angry snorts. 'Very well. I apologise for–'

'Accepted,' Harry barked, turning smartly on his heel and trotting up the steps to Number Ten. Maybe the next reshuffle was too long a wait, he mused. He'd sleep on it and make his decision in the morning.

Cooper's eyes burned into the prime minister's departing back, the quiet rage spreading through his chest. Humiliated, and in front of that arse kisser Fuller too. In fact, Fuller seemed to take some pleasure in Cooper's embarrassment, smiling as he looked down at the rotund foreign secretary.

'Come on Geoff, you know Harry is under some pressure right now. We all are.'

'It's Geoffrey. How many times do I have to remind you?' snapped Cooper, realising they were quite alone in the corridor. 'You're a fucking weasel, Fuller, you know that?' he hissed. 'Harry's little golden boy. All the perks, all the authority, none of the responsibility. You're not even a minister, for God's sake.'

Fuller's smile widened. 'Geoffrey, please. There's no call for insults, is there? We're both grown men with jobs to do, and I'm afraid I've neglected mine for too long, today. Now, if you'll excuse me, I have to prepare some press papers. I'll see you later.'

With that, Fuller turned and made his way up the stairs. Cooper couldn't resist a parting shot.

'What if all this is a false alarm? Imagine the flak from the Muslim Council, the Islamic Congress in Brussels. Who has to clear up that diplomatic mess, eh? Me. Not you, or your precious prime minister. So you run along, Fuller. I'm going to put out this fire before it takes hold.'

Fuller paused at the top of the stairs. The smile was gone, his words laced with caution. 'Don't do anything rash, Geoffrey. You should discuss this with Harry in the morning.'

'Who are you to advise me?' scoffed Cooper. 'You're out of your depth, Fuller. Now piss off.' He watched the director of communications disappear up the stairs into Number Ten. The anger still coursed through him and he chastised himself for losing his temper. It was a foolish thing to do, particularly for a man of his standing and importance.

And right now there was so much at stake.

The Foreign Secretary

Geoffrey Cooper knew he'd made a few mistakes during his tenure as foreign secretary, but no more than previous holders of the post. His lack of experience and occasional political naivety had embarrassed Harry, and Cooper had been forced to grovel apologetically on several occasions. He knew his job was on the line. And it was a job that Cooper took the greatest of pleasure in. He enjoyed the status, the chauffeur-driven cars, the sumptuous banquets, the first-class trips abroad. And he particularly enjoyed his relationship with the Arabians.

He'd worked hard on that front, eager to make a name for himself as the first British foreign secretary to bargain the Arabians down. He'd managed a few small concessions, but it wasn't much. No, he felt real progress had been made on a more personal level. His relationship with the Arabian ambassador in London was excellent and had started when Cooper was trade secretary. He'd been to the embassy many times, a beautifully renovated Georgian building near Kensington Gore, and enjoyed their superb cuisine and well-stocked wine cellar, an indulgence reserved only for Western guests. Cooper smiled as he recalled availing himself of some excellent grand cru on several visits.

Yes, Geoffrey Cooper enjoyed a close, personal relationship with his Arabian friends. They listened to him, really listened. And, after too many glasses of the embassy's equally impressive burgundy, he impressed upon them his political ambition; to be granted a private audience with the supreme ruler of Arabia himself. Harry wouldn't think him incompetent then.

Cooper's involvement with the Arabians had started just after Harry had come to power; at the time, Cooper had occupied the post of international secretary for trade and industry. He'd flown to Egypt for a Euro-Arabian trade conference, landing at Cairo International, the only airport in the whole of Arabia that serviced direct flights from the West. Visas into the state were extremely hard to acquire for westerners and all travellers, no matter where they were headed in the Gulf region, had to pass through Cairo and continue their journey aboard the state airline.

Not that there were many holidaymakers anyway. Since being assimilated into the new Arabia, the tourist sites at Luxor, the Pyramids, the magnificent hotels in Dubai, the Great Temple of Petra in Jordan and many other holiday destinations had been closed to non-Muslims indefinitely. Essential maintenance and architectural preservation programmes to combat the damage caused by endless tour parties were the initial reasons, but the truth was that Western travellers were not welcome any more, their dollars and euros no longer needed in the prosperous and unified Islamic state of Arabia.

Cooper interpreted these actions another way. He saw all this religious and nationalist posturing as the predictable growing pains of a new empire. He prided himself on his ability to gain the trust of the Arabians and, after some initial contact, felt that they, in turn, warmed to his obvious charm and sophistication.

But his ambitions didn't stop at what he knew to be low-ranking Arabian delegates. No, the pinnacle of his career would be to gain an audience with the supreme ruler of Arabia, the Grand Mufti Mohammed Khathami himself. There was a possibility that, given the right circumstances and enough time, this secretive and powerful man would grant him, Geoffrey Cooper, a personal audience. Since his rise to power, Khathami hadn't received a single Western diplomat on any official state visit. All meetings, appointments, state banquets and every other facet of diplomatic life were handled by emissaries, local dignitaries or other representatives. The man was a virtual recluse.

It was rumoured that Khathami lived in an ancient Arabian fort by the azure waters of the Persian Gulf. Another rumour spoke of a desert palace in the hills of Jabal Sawda, in south-western Arabia. Or that he enjoyed a home in the marble city that was the newly rebuilt Baghdad. In reality, no one really knew. Invitations had been extended to him and his ministers by foreign governments, Britain included, and all were attended by the cleric's closest aides; the cleric himself had always politely refused.

His Holiness would see no one, his responsibilities to his people and to the state were too demanding. But international diplomatic relationships were important. Why would he not see foreign representatives? The man had a dream for his people, his aides would answer. The moral and religious fibre of some Arabian states had been corrupted and westernised over the years. They'd lost their way. The cleric was out there somewhere, deep in the desert or by the shores of the sea, spending his time in quiet contemplation or with other holy seers. He would be reading and interpreting the holy scriptures, forming new laws, new religious guidelines that would lead Arabia from out of the dark days of their recent past and into a bright future of Islamic brotherhood. For not only was Khathami a great leader, but he was also a learned scholar and holy man. He didn't soil his hands with the grubby business of politics on the world stage. His only concern was for the Islamic state and the future of its peoples. Everything else was unimportant.

As Cooper travelled around Cairo, he saw the grand mufti's image everywhere. His face adorned posters plastered on roadside hoardings, was lovingly painted in glorious colour on the sides of buildings, or found in cheap picture frames behind shopkeepers' heads. The slight, bespectacled

Khathami, head held high in profile, looking bravely into the future, or maybe gazing benignly downwards, head tilted and hands clasped together in divine compassion.

However, since his rise to power, he'd rarely been seen in person. The man was an enigma, a mystery, the key to Cooper's future. As trade secretary he travelled to Cairo often, officially on government business, but unofficially to ingratiate himself with the Arabians, to become their friend. It was during his fifth trip to the region that Cooper realised his growing importance to the powers that be.

At a multinational conference in the port city of Alexandria, he'd given a speech outlining the importance of Arabia, its spreading influence across the globe and the desire of Western governments, particularly Britain, to extend the hand of friendship towards the Islamic state. His Arabian hosts had responded well and Cooper was invited to extend his stay in Arabia, a guest at the palace resort of Sharm el-Sheikh, where a banquet was to be held for important friends of Arabia. Cooper was over the moon. Finally!

In a carefully worded call to Harry in London, Cooper had dismissed the invitation to the desert resort as a possible stunt, but felt that a refusal may offend. Harry had agreed and Cooper could barely conceal the excitement in his voice. He was whisked by limousine to Cairo airport, where he boarded an executive helicopter, along with his secretary and personal aide. Despite his protestations, Cooper's bodyguard was ordered to stay behind at the embassy by Cooper himself. Couldn't have a potential snitch in the group, reporting back every little conversation to Harry. Besides, the Arabians had guaranteed his security and Cooper had simply glowed with self-importance.

The helicopter travelled south-east under the hot sun. Their destination was paradise, or so the rumours went, located a few miles inland from the old tourist hotels and dive beaches of Sharm el-Sheikh, where the Gulf of Suez emptied into the Red Sea. But the tourists had long gone, the coastal hotels demolished, the ground bulldozed and returned to nature. In the rebuilt harbour, erstwhile tourist dive boats once again trawled the warm waters for fish.

Looking beyond the pilot's windscreen, Cooper's heart beat a little faster as he caught a glimpse of the huge oasis up ahead. The helicopter landed a few moments later, settling on to a raised helipad above the trees. As the rotors wound down, Cooper and his party were escorted by a small welcoming committee into an elevator that took them down to the oasis floor, where they boarded a large electric buggy.

The British party were very excited, none more so than Cooper. So, this was where the favoured friends of Arabia were taken, he mused happily as the buggy hummed along snaking asphalt paths beneath the trees. It was beautiful, and Cooper watched with delight as colourful birds flitted between the palms, diving and swooping around the cool waters of gurgling streams and deep rock pools. Cooper had met one or two European diplomats who'd been here before, but he was the first Briton. In the past, he'd had to sit and listen with gritted teeth as the Italian and German ambassadors had both waxed lyrical about their own visits and expressed mock sympathy at Cooper's continued exclusion. Cooper had been quietly furious and he burned with envy, but now the boot was on the other foot. While his European comrades baked in the Cairo heat, here was Geoffrey Cooper at the palace of Sharm el-Sheikh.

Presently, the buggy left the shade of the trees as the path carried them through the ornate gardens towards the splendid marble palace ahead of them. Cooper was impressed. It was every bit as magnificent as it was rumoured to be – a seven-storey circular marble building with a huge, ornate brazier at its pinnacle, the natural gas flame that burned inside said to be visible for fifty miles. The grounds that surrounded the building were perfectly manicured and alive with flora and fauna of the most vivid colours. Designed and built specifically for the accommodation and entertainment of selected diplomatic guests of Arabia, the palace was the pinnacle in luxury without the decadence of Western avarice, a place where the real business of Arabian politics was carried out, away from the superficial posturing of Cairo. An invite here meant that the Arabians wanted to do business. Cooper had arrived, in more ways than one.

The British party was met by a large group of Arabian officials in the towering glass and marble atrium. Palms were pressed, photographs taken and Cooper was shown to his private penthouse. The suite was a sumptuous, ornate affair, the huge bed and furnishings bedecked in the finest silks and fabrics and woven in the richest colours. The bathroom was enormous, encompassing a walk-in bath, whirlpool and the most wonderful multi-jet shower that Cooper had ever experienced. Outside on the balcony, Cooper towelled himself dry as he admired the view, the surrounding oasis giving way to the Red Sea that shimmered in the distance under the warm rays of the setting sun.

After dressing in the traditional silk gown provided, Cooper made his way down to the atrium. He was ushered out across the ornate gardens where dinner was being served in the balmy night air. The meal was an informal affair and Cooper mingled happily with the twenty or so businessmen and politicians already there. Some he knew, others he did not. They sat around a low wooden table, propped up on mounds of large silk cushions. As the shadows lengthened, huge candles bathed the gardens in soft light and the exotic night call of birds could be heard from nearby palm groves. A quartet of musicians played quietly in the background whilst, overhead, a billion stars created an ambience that bore no comparison. As he looked around, Cooper thought the scene quite surreal, almost magical in its composition.

They ate from the finest china and feasted on curried soups, roasted chickens, succulent fish, sweet potatoes, green salads and vegetables, all washed down with crisp white wines and deep, fruity reds served by attractive young women in traditional Arabic dress. Unlike most of Arabia, the palace was not alcohol free. In fact, to further facilitate an atmosphere of conviviality, it was positively encouraged, the Arabians skilfully managing the meal and the conversation, neither singling out nor ignoring any particular guest, ensuring that stomachs were full and glasses continually topped.

After dinner, Cooper found himself engaged in an interesting debate with a Turkish businessman and a low-level Spanish diplomat. The Turk was baiting the Spaniard about his government's historically harsh policies towards immigrants from North Africa and Cooper was keen to hear the official Spanish line. Immigration was a sensitive issue in Western Europe and Cooper was always keen to get a new angle on things.

'Would you like a refill, sir?'

The moment he turned around, Cooper decided she was the most beautiful woman he'd ever seen. Her eyes, so warm and brown, her long eyelashes and sensual lips, her face perfectly framed by a cascade of dark ringlets, all combining to form a vision of exquisite female splendour. Her smile was genuine, disarming, and her skin, lit softly by the myriad of candles, was tanned and flawless. Cooper held out his glass, speechless in the presence of the vision before him. As she leaned over to fill his glass, his eyes darted to her deep, full cleavage. She smiled at his indiscretion and he averted his gaze.

'If there is anything else you need, please don't hesitate to ask,' she smiled.

Cooper stared into the dark pools of her eyes and was hopelessly lost. He mumbled something unintelligible as she drifted away, tending to the other guests, but stealing an occasional glance towards Cooper. For him, the conversation was no longer important. It became background noise, a muted hum that failed to distract him as he focussed on this spectacle of Arabian beauty. He stumbled through the rest of the evening, barely socialising with his fellow guests, whilst watching her every move. And then she was gone. When he looked for her again, the girl had disappeared. He retired for the evening and, despite the comforts of his suite, found sleep elusive. When he did eventually slip into unconsciousness, the girl invaded his dreams and he slept fitfully.

The next day, the palace guests took a coach to the coast, visiting a desalination plant and a local farm that had been built using reclaimed land and operated on advanced irrigation technology. All very impressive, admitted Cooper, but he was utterly bored. At midday, as the temperature climbed to the low forties, they were thankfully whisked back to the comforts of the palace, where they enjoyed an exquisitely prepared lunch. The afternoon itinerary was flexible and some of the more active guests played tennis or swam. Cooper decided on a walk through the gardens.

He was deep into the oasis, where the sunlight was filtered by the huge palm fronds above, when he saw her again. From the corner of his eye he caught a movement, a vivid splash of colour, and there she was, crouched in a small clearing, picking flowers and placing them in a basket. For a moment Cooper hesitated, a sudden dart of uncertainty tempering his excitement, the setting suspiciously contrived. Then she turned, her face lighting up with a broad smile. Cooper's heart galloped away from his intuition.

'Hello again.'

The girl nodded, her smile radiant. 'Sir.'

'My name's Geoffrey. Geoffrey Cooper.'

'I know who you are,' the woman smiled. 'I'm Aleema.'

Cooper was totally captivated. He spent the rest of the afternoon with the girl, describing the paths their lives had taken and what had brought them both here to Sharm el-Sheikh. He learned that she was twenty-seven years old and had worked at the palace for a year, that she'd studied English at school and secretly listened to Western radio stations, a practice that she made Cooper promise never to reveal.

She also knew that Geoffrey Cooper was an intelligent and powerful man. She'd seen him many times on the news networks and realised he was an important figure in his country. He was also very handsome. She enjoyed the company of older men, she admitted, more so than men of her own age. They were just so childish. Boys, really. When the time came for them to part, her fingers brushed lightly along his arm. It was the most delicate of touches, yet Cooper felt the electricity almost crackle between them and, from that second, he was lost. No, more than that. For the first time in his life, Geoffrey Cooper had fallen deeply in love.

At dinner that night, as the object of his desire flitted between the other guests, Cooper cursed the ambition that left him, after two messy divorces, without a wife. When Aleema palmed him the note during dessert his heart raced. The horses were supplied by a friend at the stables and Aleema led Cooper out into the desert, far from the watchful eyes of the palace.

She was an expert rider and she guided them to a distant ridgeline out in the wilderness, where they built a fire and enjoyed hot sweet tea under the black dome of the night sky. They held hands and Aleema kissed him with a passion he'd forgotten existed. She too felt the same love, she explained breathlessly. She gave herself to him that night and afterwards he held her tightly under a blanket, gazing at the stars in the sky. If there was a heaven, Cooper decided, this was it.

Packing his suitcase the next morning, Cooper felt almost physical pain as Cairo beckoned. Aleema was nowhere to be found and he didn't dare look for her. He thanked his hosts for their gracious hospitality and waved goodbye, a smile frozen on his face, but inside his heart was breaking. His eyes roamed the balconies of the palace, the ornate gardens, the sun-dappled clearings amongst the palms, but Aleema was nowhere to be seen. They eventually reached the landing tower and, with a heavy heart, Cooper boarded the waiting helicopter. Twelve hours later he was back in London, utterly dejected.

As the weeks went by, his mood only worsened. He felt totally depressed and threw himself into his work to escape the memories of Aleema that invaded his consciousness. So, four months later, when the foreign secretary died of sudden heart failure and Cooper was subsequently promoted to replace him, he was simply overjoyed. It was a sign, he decided; fate had brought them together once and now it would keep them together.

His immediate priority on taking office was to renew his friendship with Arabia, albeit in a more senior capacity. A diplomatic trip was planned, destination Cairo, and it wasn't long before a trip to the palace at Sharm el-Sheikh materialised. Cooper could barely contain himself and that very afternoon he found himself, once again, circling the helipad above the oasis. At dinner there was no sign of Aleema, and his heart ached at the thought that she may have moved on to pastures new. Maybe tomorrow he would make a discreet inquiry. If he dared.

After dinner, Cooper bid his hosts goodnight and retired early. He got undressed and slipped between the cool sheets of his emperor-sized bed. Sleep evaded him as he lay there, listening to the night breezes that hissed through the palms beneath his private balcony.

It was just after midnight when he heard the quiet tapping. He slipped on a robe and opened the door, his heart nearly bursting from his chest. Aleema put her finger to her lips, pushing past him into the room. Cooper quickly closed the door and swept her into his arms. They embraced silently for a long time and then, without a word, Aleema led him to the bed. For Geoffrey Cooper, it was the night of his life. For a young girl, she displayed a surprising wealth of expertise between the sheets and Cooper made a mental note to get back into the gym. As the sky in the east slowly paled and the first rays of the sun streaked across the horizon, they both succumbed to a deep sleep. He awoke a couple of hours later to find her gone. On the pillow was a handwritten note: *Meet me in the oasis at noon. By the waterfall. Love, A.*

Thankfully, the mid-morning meeting he was due to attend in the conference centre had been cancelled. As casually as he could manage in the blistering midday heat, Cooper wandered across the gardens and followed the paths to the waterfall. He reached a clearing amongst massive, slate-coloured rocks where a crystal-clear stream cascaded twenty feet into a deep pool below. It was a magical setting. Aleema appeared from the treeline and they kissed passionately. Suddenly she pulled away, the tears running down her cheeks.

'What's the matter, my love?'

'I have a confession,' Aleema admitted, staring at the ground.

Cooper's heart skipped a beat. 'What? What is it?'

'I'm not who you think I am. I'm not a waitress. I work for the Foreign Ministry and I'm here because of my language skills. My job is to listen to the conversations of our foreign guests, to gather information and report back to my superiors.'

'A spy?' Cooper whispered. His face slowly drained of colour and he sat down heavily on a flat rock.

'No, not really,' Aleema protested. 'It's just small things. You know, opinions, ideas, enough to give the ministry an insight, something that might give them an advantage in negotiations. Every country does it.'

Cooper's political instincts screamed at him to walk away, to leave this desert paradise and never return. But his emotions held him prisoner, as if he were chained to the very rock he sat on.

'So I was your target?'

Aleema shook her head, the delicate black ringlets whipping across her face.

'No, Geoffrey. You remember the Spaniard? On your first trip?'

Cooper vaguely recalled the man, the debate with the Turk about immigration. 'Sort of.'

'He was my assignment.'

Cooper's eyes flashed. 'You slept with him?'

Aleema's face darkened. 'Is that what you think, Geoffrey? That I'm a whore?'

She turned away from him and Cooper went after her, spinning her around.

'Wait, Aleema! For God's sake, I don't know what to think!'

She took his hands in hers and squeezed them gently, her deep brown eyes searching his. 'I'm in love with you, Geoffrey. Don't you realise that?'

Cooper thought he was going to faint. Was it possible? Could a girl like Aleema seriously want to be with someone like him?

'How do I know you're telling the truth? That I'm not a target?' He could tell his words were like knives, stabbing at her heart. The tears rolled down her cheeks and her hands trembled in his. No, that level of emotion couldn't be faked, not even by an Oscar winner. 'I'm sorry,' he blurted. 'I take that back. It's just so confusing, so much to–'

'I want to go to London,' Aleema declared, the words tumbling from her lips. Cooper looked at her uncomprehendingly. 'That's right, London,' she repeated. 'That's where I really learned English, as a teenager. I fell in love with the city, with the people. But most importantly I fell in love with the freedom.' She guided Cooper back to the flat rock and sat down, snaking her arm in his. 'Do you know what it's like to be a woman in Arabia, Geoffrey? To be told when you can and cannot speak, to be unable to drive a car, to walk behind men in the street, to never feel the sun on your skin outside of this palace?'

Cooper nodded silently. As a diplomat, he'd trained himself to ignore the shackles of sharia under which Arabian women lived, the surreal streets of Cairo where every woman was draped head to toe in black, the frequent looks of despair behind the veils that kept them prisoner.

'I'm supposed to be married now,' Aleema continued.

Cooper's head snapped up. 'Married?'

'Twice. And twice I've faked a barren womb, so the man my father had chosen for me would find another. I don't want to live like that, Geoffrey. I want a man to love me for who I am, not to be traded like a goat at the market. I want to be free, with you. In London.'

Cooper's stomach churned with excitement at the thought, his mind racing ahead. He'd have to resign of course, but he'd find something else, something lucrative in the private sector. That was the way in government, a considerable civil service pension pot, topped up handsomely by a six-figure salary in consulting. Easy money. And Aleema, she'd be with him every step of the way, living together in Wimbledon, holidaying in the south of France, her nubile body soaking up the warm rays of a Mediterranean sun…

'How?' he blurted. 'How can you travel? To London, I mean? Once you get there I can process your asylum application, get the ball rolling. I know a decent lawyer.'

Aleema sighed and shook her head. 'It's not as simple as that. I can get to Cairo, but my job forbids foreign travel.'

'Then how do we do this?'

Aleema stared at the ground. 'There is a way, but it is one you will certainly disapprove of.'

'Go on,' Cooper urged.

'There's a man in London. His name is Ali. He works at your passport office.'

Cooper couldn't help himself. 'Who is he? An ex-lover?'

Aleema chuckled, gently stroking Cooper's chubby face. 'No, my love. A second cousin, on my mother's side. If you approve, then he will deliver a passport to you, in my name. The next time you visit us, here at the palace, you will give it to me. I will then travel to Cairo and board a plane for London, using my new identity. It's the only way.'

Cooper thought about the proposition. What she was asking wasn't that much, merely smuggling a passport in a diplomatic bag. Better still, Cooper would carry it on his person. But the passport was faked, a crime in itself. No, when Aleema got to London they'd destroy it once she was through customs, do things the right way. The main thing was getting her on to British soil.

'What about an entry stamp, into Arabia? They'll check at Cairo.'

'Ali will take care of that.'

'Resourceful chap, this Ali.'

'You must get together. How about your private office in Whitehall?' Aleema suggested. 'Can you meet him there?'

'Of course,' scoffed Cooper. 'No one questions my authority there. In fact, the office is probably the best place to meet. People coming and going all day. I'll keep it informal, get Charlotte to put him in my diary. All very low-key.'

'Really?' gushed Aleema. 'Does that mean you'll–'

Cooper lunged forward, planting his wet lips on hers. 'I'll do it. As long as we're together.'

'Oh, Geoffrey,' sighed Aleema, returning the kiss. 'My God, my heart is beating so fast. Here, feel.' She brought his hand to her breast and Cooper felt the firm flesh beneath the thin material of her sari. 'Together, in London,' she exhaled happily. 'It's like a dream.' Then the smile slipped from her face, unease clouding her eyes. She took his hands in hers and gripped them tightly. 'My future, my whole life, rests in these hands. Without you I am lost.'

Cooper looked into those brown liquid pools and his head swam. 'I won't let you down, Aleema. Ever,' he breathed.

Cooper met Ali three weeks later, at an informal reception inside the Foreign Office building in Whitehall. He was a slim, bearded Asian in his early thirties, good-looking in a well-cut navy suit. Cooper was instantly jealous. They shook hands. Ali's grip was firm, his voice low in Cooper's ear.

'Foreign Secretary. Your friend in Sharm el-Sheikh sends her fondest regards.'

Cooper could have cried out with joy. Instead, his face remained a mask of formality. 'Good to know,' he muttered. 'No problems with security, I trust? You gave them the right name?'

'Of course.' He gave a small, amused bow. 'Ali Omar, junior trade delegate from the Indian High Commission, at your service.'

Cooper took an instant dislike to Ali, but he couldn't decide if it was his good looks or his overconfident manner that rubbed him up the wrong way. He expected Ali to be a typical low-level civil servant, intimidated by Cooper's status and cowed by the opulent surroundings, but this Ali was neither. He shrugged off the feelings and concentrated on the real issue; getting Aleema to London.

'You've brought the item?'

'Let's talk in your office,' murmured Ali.

Cooper led the way, slipping out of the reception room and upstairs to his private study. He closed the door and invited Ali to sit, taking a seat behind his own desk.

'I'll stand,' Ali said. 'Listen, there's a problem with the passport.'

'Shh!' Cooper ordered, a finger to his lips, his eyes darting towards the door. 'Keep your voice down.'

'Relax, Geoff, no one can hear us,' smiled Ali. 'That door's a foot thick.'

Yes, too assured by half, observed Cooper.

'It's the entry visa,' Ali explained. 'Cairo have just changed their stamp. It's going to take a while before I can get one and replicate it in Aleema's passport.'

Cooper sighed heavily. 'How long?'

'A month. Maybe two.'

'Shit. Bloody shit.' Cooper helped himself to a large brandy from a decanter on the desk and leaned back in his chair. 'Sorry, would you like a drink? You can't rush off straight away. It'll look suspicious.'

'Thanks. Ginger ale.' Ali slipped into a chair, crossing his legs.

Cooper picked up the phone and punched a number, quickly slamming the phone back in its cradle. 'Bloody hell, Charlotte's downstairs. Wait here. I'll get it myself.'

The moment Cooper left the room, Ali got to his feet and went to the computer on the desk. The back of the machine had eight USB ports, two of them already in use. He fished an object from his pocket, a tiny device that, when plugged in, was barely noticeable. Rearranging the mess of cables to further disguise the minuscule device, Ali crossed the room and sat back down. He wasn't a technical man, he couldn't tell if it was working or not, but someone, somewhere, would let him know if the exercise had been successful.

Two kilometres away across the Thames, on the fifth floor of a commercial office building in Waterloo, two men sat patiently behind a large desk watching a single, lifeless computer screen. In the corner of the screen, a cursor blinked slowly, the only sign that the system was actually drawing power. Each man had in front of him a powerful notebook computer and their eyes flicked occasionally between both systems as they continued their vigil.

The office suite was empty, hired through a bogus front company on a long-term lease, and consisted of a single desk, two chairs and a telephone. There was food and water in the small kitchenette and, in the corner office, two sleeping bags lay spread out on foam roll mats. They shouldn't have to wait long, their superior had informed them. An hour, maybe two. And so it had proved.

The computer screen suddenly sprang into life and lines of coded information began scrolling down it at a rapid rate. Both men reacted quickly and launched into their pre-planned tasks as fingers flew across keyboards. They watched with satisfaction as they uploaded the sophisticated software program that burrowed in past the remote system's defences undetected and began its discovery program, mapping out the file structure of the massive, integrated governmental and defence systems across the river in Whitehall.

One of the men smiled. A brilliant and gifted software engineer, he'd worked on some of the most sophisticated systems in the world – and cracked them all. The device plugged into Cooper's workstation was an encrypted transmitter that held on its tiny hard drive an undetectable software program that allowed the men in Waterloo to gain high-level access to the British government's computer networks. Once past the firewall and system defences they would be able to navigate anywhere, roaming between the myriad of server clusters and packet routers, through LAN side security firewalls and across floor hubs. In fact, they'd be able to go anywhere that Cooper's software profile gave them access to, and a lot more besides. Including the Ministry of Defence systems.

Within hours, the software program had hacked and cracked several top-level passwords, gaining undetected access to defence's most secure data areas. Terabytes of secret data began humming across the river; defence budgets, strategy documents, war plan scenarios, briefing papers, naval and air assets, civil emergency planning, troop deployments, manning records, reservist quotas, infrastructure, munitions deployments… the list went on. And the data flowed eastwards.

The weeks turned into months and Geoffrey Cooper's mood darkened. There were problems with the passport, the visa, Ali was sick, on holiday, couldn't meet because he thought he was being followed, and all the while Cooper brooded, his temper slowly fraying, his nights sleepless, his suspicions deepening. He was desperate for contact with Aleema, desperate for her to finally escape her degrading existence and join him in London. Desperate for the love of a beautiful young woman. And so he did nothing, and waited.

Meanwhile, the device attached to the foreign secretary's computer continued its program, squirting enormous amounts of sensitive information to its host in Waterloo and, from there, on to military planners in Arabia.

Geoffrey Cooper stood in the lower basement of Downing Street and cursed his bad luck. This bloody ham-fisted surveillance and raising of the security alert levels could ruin everything. And he was so close. A few more days, Ali had finally promised him. He couldn't afford to upset the Arabians now, couldn't risk a diplomatic incident that would negate a trip to the palace in Egypt. He had to try and nip this thing in the bud, use his influence to diffuse the situation. He felt suddenly frightened, dreading the thought of never seeing Aleema again.

In a worst-case scenario, Cooper would get Aleema to the consulate and process an asylum application from there. It'd be messy, and questions would be asked, but what the hell. Fucking Ali wasn't seeing his end of the deal through, anyway. The bastard was stalling, Cooper was convinced of that now. Probably wanted Aleema for himself. Not a chance, old son.

Feeling a little more confident, Cooper trotted up the stairs and walked out of Number Ten. When he got back to the office, he'd email the Arabian ambassador to try and organise a trip to the palace. Shouldn't be too difficult, as long as the shit didn't hit the fan in the next few days.

As he slid across the soft leather seats of his waiting limousine, Cooper realised he could use Harry's meeting with the Yank ambassador as leverage for private talks at Sharm el-Sheik. He'd hint at a new, warmer climate of Anglo-US relations, thawing the frosty association that had existed for the last few years. Yes, the Arabians would be very interested in that, knowing their distrust of America. And he'd apologise to Harry, in person, tomorrow. Once he was on his good side he'd enquire about that dinner, how it went, what was discussed, pass it all on to the guys at the palace. Meanwhile, passport or not, he'd tell Aleema to head for Cairo. Either way, she was getting out.

Yes, he smiled to himself, things were starting to look a little rosier now he'd taken matters into his own hands. He reached for his mobile phone to check messages. Four missed calls, number blocked. That was Ali, no doubt. The passport must finally be ready.

Things really were looking up.

Whitehall
5.55 p.m.

Target One sat in the cab of the UPS van, gripping the steering wheel hard to try and stop his hands from shaking. Seven minutes earlier, he'd pulled up outside Richmond House, the Department of Health ministerial building on Whitehall, and hopped out on to the street, looking every inch the UPS employee in his smart brown uniform and cap. The package he was delivering to the DOH civil servant was genuine, as was the UPS delivery note and handheld scanner, thanks to a contact at the depot in Southwark. He made his delivery in the foyer of the government building, obtained the necessary signature and walked back to the van where he now sat, repeatedly glancing at his watch.

He looked across the road, towards Downing Street, his primary target. Pretending to study his paperwork, he peered over the top of his clipboard and studied the famous cul-de-sac that was home to the British prime minister. The tall security gates loomed large and unauthorised traffic was forbidden, but Target One only had to get close to inflict the required devastation. Part of him wanted to witness the glorious day of victory, to see the planes fly overhead, to hear the sound of gunfire thundering across the city, but mostly he longed for paradise. It was just the transition from this life to the next that troubled him, the pain he might feel, the prospect of failure, or maybe even a sudden, inexplicable urge to live that would turn him from the path he had chosen. No, he consoled himself, nothing would go wrong and today would be the day he died. And that was the reason his hands shook so badly.

Buried beneath the cardboard packages that filled the rear of the vehicle was a one-thousand-pound bomb. In addition to the explosives, the cavities of the van's side panels and doors had been filled with a deadly mix of nuts, bolts and nails. All Target One had to do was to drive the bomb as close as possible to Downing Street and detonate it. This is what he'd been chosen for, he reminded himself. This was his destiny.

Still, his hands shook with the enormity of what he was about to do. But he wouldn't be alone, oh no. He was reassured in the knowledge that, at that very moment, there would be others like him around the country, watching their own targets and checking their own watches. Target One took comfort in the fact that they would all meet in paradise in a very short time.

He glanced at his watch again. Time was short now. He reached down between the seats and retrieved the detonator, a small plastic cylinder with a metal pressure switch on top. A fibre-optic cable attached to the bottom snaked away into the device at the rear of the vehicle. Once armed, it worked much like a hand grenade. If he maintained pressure on the switch the bomb was safe. As soon as he released the pressure, the switch would close and complete a small electrical circuit, detonating the device. He twisted his wrist and watched the minute hand of his watch creep towards the top of the hour. It was nearly time.

Whitehall was busy. The pavements thronged with commuters and tourists, the roads thick with rush hour traffic. With a deep breath, Target One reached under the dashboard and punched a button, simultaneously depressing the trigger switch with his thumb. A small red LED glowed in his palm. The massive bomb beneath him was now armed.

With his free hand he started the van's engine, while his lips began to move in silent prayer.

Foreign and Commonwealth Office
5.56 p.m.

The phone rang again as Cooper climbed out of his vehicle, the number blocked. Ali. He breezed past security and climbed the staircase, answering the phone on the fifth ring.

'Yes?'

'Ah, Foreign Secretary. It's me, Ali.'

Cooper looked around, his voice a harsh whisper. 'For God's sake, I said no names.'

'Relax, Geoff,' Ali chuckled.

Cooper almost exploded with anger, but he still needed Ali on side. He took a deep breath. 'You're right. Sorry. Busy day, that's all. You have some news?'

'No, not really. Where have you been, anyway? I've been trying to reach you for the last hour.'

Ali sounded faintly amused. What was going on here? Cooper decided right then to cut Ali out of the loop, get Aleema to Cairo, to the consulate, claim asylum. This guy was a waste of bloody time.

'Well, if you've no news then why are you ringing me?' He tried and failed to keep the irritation from his voice.

'Listen, you don't have much time, Geoff. I've sent you an email. You should check it, before it's too late.'

Cooper froze, a cold wave of fear suddenly washing over him. 'What do you mean? What the hell are you talking about?'

'It's over, Geoff. You, Aleema, everything. You've played your part. Now check your email.'

The line went dead. Cooper stood frozen on the staircase, unable to comprehend what had just happened. He'd been cut adrift, that much was clear. But the manner of it, the tone, seemed so... final. He began to sweat profusely, sick to his stomach, gripped by a sense of impending disaster. He took the stairs two at a time, slamming the door to his office.

An email icon flashed intermittently on his workstation terminal. His mouth dry, he touched the icon and a digital movie file began to play. Confusion twisted Cooper's face. What was this? It was a home movie, two kids playing on a beach somewhere, azure-blue waters washing gently on white sands behind them. The Gulf, Cooper realised, dabbing at his neck with a handkerchief. The children looked young, maybe five or six, dark-skinned, Arabic. Who the hell were they? Suddenly, the camera panned to the right and his heart skipped a beat. Aleema. She was still beautiful as ever, but her beauty no longer filled Cooper with longing and excitement. Instead, he felt dread. This wasn't the Aleema he knew and loved.

The delicate make-up was gone, along with the flowing silk robes. In their place, Aleema wore an unflattering military uniform, a baggy desert-patterned camouflage shirt and trousers tucked into high-legged boots, her dark tresses scraped back into a tight bun. She stared into the lens, a blank expression on her face. No, not blank, Cooper realised, simply emotionless. One of the children ran to her and grasped her legs and she bent down, suddenly beaming that familiar, perfect smile.

A man entered the frame and scooped up the child. He was roughly the same age as Aleema, dark and handsome, also dressed in combat uniform. They embraced and Cooper felt a sharp stab of jealousy as he watched them, watched the way Aleema looked at the man, how she stroked his face and laughed, the love, the admiration in her eyes impossible to ignore. They were a couple, that much was obvious, the children theirs, by-products of their love for each other.

In the top corner of the screen Cooper noticed the date stamp. Two days ago. His fingers stabbed at the keyboard, Aleema's beautiful face frozen on the screen. It was a message, plain and simple; farewell to the fool called Geoffrey Cooper. For a long time he just stared at her image, his emotions ranging from utter despair to fear and rage. Then, with a cry of frustration, he picked up the display and hurled it across the room where it shattered on the floor. All the strength left his legs and he slumped into his chair. He felt totally crushed, his hopes and dreams as shattered and irreparable as the computer screen lying in pieces across his ornate office. What had she done? What had he done? He'd been baited and caught, like a fish in a net. But for what purpose? So what if she was a spy? He'd said nothing, passed nothing to her that could incriminate him. What the bloody hell was going on?

He refused to accept the fact that Aleema felt nothing. Those special times they'd enjoyed together, the words of love exchanged between them, her pain at their parting. All a ruse? Impossible. The game was up, though. He knew this would come out. Maybe that's what Ali meant when he said something about being too late. Maybe the press had got hold of it. In that case he was ruined, his career gone. Cooper slid deeper into his chair. On swift reflection he realised he didn't care. He was no spy. Besides, when all was said and done, it was only losing Aleema that really hurt. Without her he had nothing. In his mind he'd included her in his life, his future plans. Now she was gone forever.

Cooper opened a desk drawer, retrieved a glass and bottle and poured himself a generous brandy. He took a large gulp, the liquid burning a fiery path down the back of his throat. There was a knock at the door and his stern, middle-aged secretary Charlotte, entered the room. She observed Cooper splayed in his chair, drink in hand and tie askew. She tut-tutted under her breath and took a step forward, looking down in alarm as her shoe crunched on the wreckage of the computer screen.

'Foreign Secretary? Is everything all right, sir?'

Without looking up, Cooper tipped the contents of his glass down his throat and refilled it. 'Be a good girl Charlotte, and fuck off. I've had rather a day of it.'

Speechless, his secretary backed away, closing the door behind her.

Chiswick, West London
5.57 p.m.

Fresh from her shower, Kirsty Moore was towelling her hair dry when she suddenly paused in mid rub; a car door slammed below and again she wondered who might be down there. There were six flats in her block and the gay couple opposite her were the only ones who owned a car. They were presently on holiday somewhere in the Greek islands, so it couldn't be them. The other five flats were all single occupancy and none of those people had a vehicle either. Except one.

Yes, maybe it was Alex. Kirsty finished drying her hair and hurried back to the balcony in her bathrobe. Now, he was worth being woken up for. He was a bit older than Kirsty, mid-thirties maybe, but handsome with grey flecks in his dark hair. But she'd always gone for older men, anyway. Not too old, of course, but something with a little bit of mileage on the clock, as her friend Annie would say. She'd seen Alex many times since he'd moved in a few months ago, but she really hadn't spoken to him that much. He worked odd hours and that made it difficult to 'accidentally' bump into him. Still, he always flashed her a smile and exchanged a few pleasantries when they did meet and, as far as Kirsty knew, he hadn't brought another girl home since he'd been there. Maybe there was hope after all.

She slipped on to the balcony and lay back on the sun lounger, keen to play it cool. Didn't want to look too eager. She'd glance over the railing, a subtle cough to attract his attention, a wave maybe. Hi, Alex. Nice night, huh? Fancy a drink later?

It was very quiet down there. What was he doing? If she moved now she'd probably scrape the lounger, then it would look like she was spying on him. She didn't want to look foolish or desperate; but then again, he might leave in the next few seconds and she may not get another opportunity for a while. It was then she noted the approaching whine of aircraft engines. That was nothing new for Kirsty, or anyone else who lived in West London, residing as they did under a major flight path into Heathrow. But the noise of the aircraft would give her cover, a chance to stand up and have a peek below. She'd give it a minute, when the noise was louder, and chance it then.

Clever girl, she smiled.

'Roger Speedbird Two-Niner-Seven, you are cleared to land, runway one-one-four.' Captain Lewis Ainsworth sat a little straighter in the cockpit seat of his double-decked Airbus A380 and gently pulled back on his central control thrusters, easing the three-hundred-and-eighty-five-tonne giant back several knots.

Another few minutes and he'd be on the ground, thank God. It had been a long trip; London to LA and then on to Hong Kong for a two-night layover. From Hong Kong, he'd flown the twin-decked superliner via Moscow, skirting Arabian airspace, as was the norm these days. It meant flying a roundabout route, crawling north-eastwards up the spine of the Himalayas and across the western Siberian plain into Russian Federation airspace.

Unusually, Moscow air traffic control then routed them north again, much to Ainsworth's annoyance. The quickest route would be due east into Polish, then German airspace, but the Russians had other ideas. After repeated requests for information, a Russian air traffic controller had informed him that there had been a security incident near the Polish border involving some kind of surface-to-air weapon and all civilian traffic was being rerouted away from that particular sector. Fair enough, he thought. If there was one thing that could give a pilot the jitters it was the thought of some nut brandishing anti-aircraft weapons around. Best keep well out of their way. The Russians had passed the Airbus into Finnish airspace, whose controllers very kindly vectored them south-west to London. By now, Ainsworth had had enough of this particular trip and was looking forward to getting the aircraft on the ground.

He was due a little time off. He would take Jessie away for a few days, he decided, down to the cottage in Devon, or maybe up to Scotland. A trip to the Highlands, like last year. They'd have a chat about it over dinner when he got home. If the traffic was light on the M25, he could be there in under an hour.

The twinkling runway lights beckoned in the distance. Captain Ainsworth touched his foot pedals, slipping the aircraft a fraction to the right. Nine hundred feet below, the River Thames snaked its way westward, a sparkling ribbon under the warm summer sun.

Alex cut away from the river and strolled along the residential side street, a short distance from the apartment block. He hoped Kirsty was around, confident she'd say yes to a few drinks. He'd take her down to the Wheatsheaf, the one by the river; then, if things went well, maybe a bite to eat later on. That'd be a nice touch. And it was going to be a beautiful evening, too. Gorgeous girl, lovely weather, day off tomorrow; life was looking pretty good right now, Alex smiled.

He felt the rumble deep in the pit of his stomach. His smile faded as he turned to see a British Airways Airbus on final approach into Heathrow.

Alex shielded his eyes and watched as the huge aircraft swept low overhead. Wouldn't catch me on one of those things, he thought. Look at the size of it. Alex felt he could almost reach out and touch it, it looked so low. Optical illusion of course, but still.

Be nice to move away one day, he thought, out of London and away from any flight paths. Day in, day out, hundreds of planes flying overhead, yet there'd never been a major accident, thank God. But Alex believed in the law of averages. So many flights a day, the airspace over London becoming increasingly tighter; the media had speculated about the possibility of a major disaster for years. Surely it was only a matter of time?

One of these days, he thought grimly.

From her position on the sun lounger, Kirsty craned her neck to see what was going on down below. The driveway between the apartment blocks led straight to the gardens at the rear and, beyond that, the towpath and the Thames itself. Sitting up a little straighter, Kirsty could make out the roof of a vehicle. It looked like a minivan or something similar, parked just behind the buildings. Not Alex, then. Damn. So who the hell was it? The driveway was private property, residents only, but that didn't stop some people who wanted a quiet place off the street to get up to all sorts of nonsense. She heard the sound of feet crunching on the gravel and low voices. She slipped off the lounger and peered carefully over the balcony.

Thirty feet below, three men dressed in fatigues were unloading long green tubes from the back of the minivan. Kirsty instinctively pulled her head back, unaware of what was going on, but knowing that whatever it was it didn't look right. Very slowly, she leaned forward and stole another glance. The men were all Asian or something, dressed in baggy combat trousers and T-shirts. And the tubes, they were green with black stencilling on the sides. Two of the men were bent over them doing something, and the third man kept looking upwards into the sky. She could hear them talking, urgent barks more like, but it was getting harder to hear because there was a bloody plane coming and... Oh God.

In that moment, Kirsty realised what these men were about to do, but the horror of it rooted her to the spot. Below, two of the men clambered quickly on to the roof of the minivan, the other passing up the surface-to-air missile launchers. The men rested the weapons on their shoulders, swinging them around and aiming into the summer sky. Kirsty stood transfixed on the balcony, unable to move, her hands gripping the rail and her mouth moving soundlessly in silent terror.

Europe
5.58 p.m. GMT

All across the continent they waited. The moment they had trained for was nearly upon them and each cell, each group, each individual had planned their operations meticulously. Some had been preparing for years, receiving their briefings in the desert lands, moving to the countries of the West, assimilating into local communities, infiltrating their target organisations, securing employment, identifying the personalities, mapping the infrastructure, absorbing and planning the finer details of their operations and briefing their own assault teams. Other individuals and groups had received target-only instructions weeks, days and, in a few cases, hours before. Hidden weapons had been distributed, explosives obtained and targets reconnoitred. Twenty-four hours earlier, they'd received the 'go' signal from their handlers; there would be no going back.

Final checks were made, wristwatches and other timepieces synchronised with atomic clocks across the continent. Last-minute recesses were organised and conducted, equipment and weapons were checked and vehicles fuelled and readied. Nothing was left to chance. From the Baltic coast to the toecap of Italy, thousands of individuals and assault teams all across Europe moved into their positions. The countdown had begun.

At air, land and sea control points, computer systems were logged into and powerful software codes secretly executed. Security guards at targeted locations were lured away and neutralised, or simply wandered from their posts, leaving them unguarded. Intruder alarms and CCTV systems suddenly developed 'faults' or were shut down completely. As the minutes ticked away, other teams took up ambush positions around their targets, their weapons loaded and ready.

Transport infrastructure was a paramount objective. Railheads and major junctions, marshalling yards, airports, air traffic control centres, motorways, trunk roads, bridges, tunnels, crossing points, ferry ports, cargo docks and the Channel Tunnel itself were all targeted with specialist teams, whose tasks were to secure and hold with the minimum of damage. Laser designators were activated and placed in the grounds of buildings and installations that were targeted for military action. Their unique signals were detected by Arabian aircraft patrolling high above the Mediterranean Sea. Locations were plotted, co-ordinates fed into targeting computers and downloaded into fuelled and prepared missiles that waited silently in darkened silos.

Around the coastlines and docks of Europe, combat troops and their supporting tanks and armoured vehicles waited in the rolling gloom of cavernous cargo holds. Sailing under false papers and flags of convenience, the ships had arrived at their target ports over the last twenty-four hours. The troops inside these ships peered cautiously out through hidden viewing ports at the activity on the docks below them and the landscape beyond. This was to be their battleground.

Across Arabia, under the harsh desert sun, hundreds of thousands of fighting troops and support units made final checks to their weapons and equipment whilst they waited in huge, sprawling camps, airfields and assembly points dotted around the coast from Turkey to Morocco. Twenty thousand paratroopers and their airmobile support units were already airborne, their aircraft transponders identifying them to air traffic controllers across Europe as simple cargo or passenger planes. They flew criss-cross patterns over Eastern Europe and the Southern Mediterranean, adhering to well-rehearsed schedules and air traffic lanes.

On the ground, another one hundred and ten thousand paratroopers sweated inside their aircraft as they waited for the 'go' signal that would send them across the skies into Europe. The wait would be short as the minutes ticked away.

An operation that had been over two decades in the planning was about to be realised. Years had become months, weeks had become days, the hours, minutes. The military might of Arabia was poised, about to unleash itself upon the West in a show of force not seen since the beginning of man.

Chiswick, West London
5.59 p.m.

Kirsty heard the roar of the aircraft overhead and her eyes were drawn upwards. Several hundred feet above, a huge Airbus thundered over the rooftops of Chiswick on its final approach into Heathrow. She turned back to the men below her, gripping the balcony rail until her knuckles turned white. The horror of what was about to happen numbed her senses. As the plane passed overhead, the men below fired their weapons almost simultaneously. In a blast of white smoke, the high explosive missiles streaked away towards their targets, the superheated engines of Speedbird Two-Niner-Seven.

Kirsty finally found her voice and screamed, an ear-splitting, high-pitched wail that cut through the roar of the plane's engines and the launch of the missiles. The men on the ground spun around. On seeing Kirsty, one of them reached into the van and retrieved an automatic weapon. He shouldered it and took aim.

It was over mercifully quickly for Captain Ainsworth, his crew and the five hundred and eleven passengers of British Airways flight Two-Niner-Seven. The moment the Stinger missiles bored their way into the starboard engines they detonated, igniting the remaining fuel in the wing. It literally separated from the body of the aircraft.

Ainsworth's world turned upside down as the instrument warning panel lit up and the plane banked violently to port. In that hideous moment, the experienced pilot knew they were doomed. With an audible groan, its engines screaming, the huge aircraft flipped over completely and plummeted towards the ground at nearly two hundred miles per hour.

At that time of day, Mortlake Road was heavy with traffic in both directions. People were making their way home, eager to escape the heat of the city. A muffled boom and a steadily increasing roar drowned out the noise of the traffic and the blare of horns. In nearby shops and homes, the televisions, radios, adults' conversations, children's laughter and babies' cries seemed to fade away as a sudden pressure began to build in the air around them. In local streets, people stopped what they were doing. Something was about to happen, something terrible. The sky darkened. For those that saw it coming there was no time to react, no time to warn others. A dreadful scream filled the air as three hundred and eighty-five tonnes of aircraft ploughed into the busy junction of Cumberland Road and the South Circular, destroying everything in a four-hundred-metre radius.

Kirsty Moore cowered in terror behind her sofa. Her balcony was littered with glass, her sun lounger torn to shreds, its stuffing still drifting lazily in the air. She had instinctively pushed herself away from the balcony rail when the man below had fired, tripping over the patio door frame and landing on her backside on the lounge carpet. It had saved her life. The balcony had exploded with bullets, the rounds shattering glass and brick and stitching a wild pattern into the ceiling above her head.

She crawled across the living room and scrambled behind the sofa. There she lay, hands clamped over her ears, her heart hammering in her chest, her body paralysed by fear.

Alex instinctively ducked when he heard the roar of the missiles as they rocketed upwards from behind his apartment building. He watched in horrified fascination as the Stingers homed in on the aircraft overhead and obliterated the wing. The plane lurched in the sky and disappeared from view, a stain of black smoke hanging in the air above West London.

He heard a scream and a long burst of automatic fire. Momentarily, Alex's thought processes shut down. Just a few moments ago he'd existed in another world, a world where the sun shone warmly, and there was the promise of a cold beer and a pleasant summer evening ahead with a pretty girl. But that world had gone, turned dark. Even the sun seemed to have lost its heat.

The ground shook beneath his feet, a deep rumbling that he felt in the pit of his stomach. Alex knew it was the plane hitting the ground, and that's when his training took over. He drew his service pistol hidden in his rucksack, a ten millimetre Glock automatic, and chambered a round. He found his mobile phone, noted the missed calls and speed-dialled his unit in Southwark. No signal. He yanked a police armband up over his arm and advanced quickly past the glass foyer to his apartment block. He reached the corner and peered around the brickwork.

He saw a dark-coloured minivan, shrouded in a thinning cloud of white exhaust smoke. The three men climbing aboard did so almost casually, one of them clutching a black rifle. The minivan's engine roared into life and it crunched along the gravel drive towards the street. Their apparent lack of urgency was what struck Alex the most, what chilled him.

They'd just taken out an airliner, for God's sake, and killed hundreds. There was no time to call for backup – these scumbags had to be stopped. He brought his pistol up as the van eased along the driveway between the apartment buildings. That's when he stepped out from cover.

'Stop! Armed police!'

The driver saw the pistol and accelerated, swerving towards him. Alex fired twice, hitting the driver through the windscreen. He slumped over the wheel, the van veering to the left and colliding with the wall of the opposite building, grinding along the brickwork. Alex stepped back behind cover and, as the van drew level, he fired twice at the front passenger. The van roared past and careered across the main road, where it crashed into the side of a parked vehicle with a loud crunch of metal. The engine roared for another few seconds and then died.

For a moment an eerie silence blanketed the street. Then Alex heard a rough curse and he saw the third man, the one with the gun, scrambling to get out of the van. Alex ran across the road, just as the side door was wrenched open. He dropped to one knee, levelling his pistol. The man in the minivan stumbled out and spun around. Seeing Alex, he brought his weapon up, his face contorted with rage. Alex shot him twice in the chest and the man flopped to the road, the gun clattering to the tarmac.

He moved forward carefully, weapon extended in front of him. They were all dead. He would have preferred to take at least one man into custody, but these boys weren't coming in quietly. Besides, even dead men can offer up clues as to who and why, but a quick search of the bodies revealed nothing to confirm their identities. He picked up the automatic weapon from the ground, a Heckler-Koch 416 assault rifle, and unloaded it, shoving the magazine and two spares into the waistband of his trousers.

He ran to the block of flats, pulling his mobile phone from his pocket; still no signal. He flung open the glass door, weapon at the ready and announced his presence. It was deathly quiet. He fumbled for his keys and entered his apartment, heading for the phone in the kitchen. The line was dead. He marched into the bedroom. At the back of the built-in wardrobe was a false panel, which he quickly removed. Behind that was a large steel gun cabinet. Alex unlocked it and placed the rifle and magazines inside. He ran back out to the hallway and up the stairs. When he reached Kirsty's door, he heard sobbing inside.

'Kirsty, it's Alex, from downstairs. Are you okay?' The sobbing stopped. Alex stepped away from the door. Maybe she wasn't alone. 'Kirsty, can you come to the door?' Still no answer. 'Kirsty, it's me, Alex. I need to know you're okay. Open the door, please.'

He heard movement inside and the door was unlocked. He pushed it open and stepped inside. Kirsty was behind the sofa, back against the wall, clutching herself tightly. Her body shook with fear. Alex took a quick look around, holstered his weapon and marched into her bedroom. He returned with her duvet and wrapped it around her shoulders. Kirsty leaned into him and then the floodgates really opened. For several minutes her body shuddered with sobs. Alex held her tight, noting the damage to her apartment. Lucky, bloody lucky. No wonder the poor girl was terrified. He held her tighter, listening for the sirens of the response vehicles that must surely be on their way.

'It's alright, Kirsty. It's over now.' He checked his wristwatch: six o'clock. 'It's over now,' he repeated.

Alex had no idea that across Europe it was just beginning.

Whitehall
6.00 p.m.

It was time. The final minutes seemed to have stretched into hours, but now the moment had finally arrived. Target One, bomb armed and pressure switch in hand, eased the UPS van away from the kerb.

At Parliament Square, the armoured black Jaguar carrying Anna Beecham, flanked by her two-vehicle police escort, swept past a mob of placard-waving protesters. Anna tried not to look but couldn't help herself, saw the obscene hand gestures, heard the muffled filth that poured from the protesters' twisted mouths beyond the bulletproof glass. What had she ever done to these people? She had asked herself that question a thousand times. There was no answer, other than the fact that they hated her for reasons of their own.

As they turned into Whitehall, Anna knew she'd made the right decision in going to Greenwich. It'd felt good to get out, to escape Westminster and have a civilised day with decent people, meeting the parents and children. But now they were back in town, her raw nerves were exposed once again. They turned left into Whitehall, and Anna noticed that the driver had eased off the accelerator as they approached the black gates of Downing Street. Even her protection officers were glad to get behind that formidable barrier these days.

She was looking forward to a shower and a few moments with Harry before this evening's dinner. They'd take a holiday soon, she decided, when Parliament goes into recess, perhaps the villa in Italy for some Mediterranean sun. Harry could certainly use a break and Anna longed to leave the pressure cooker of Britain behind them for a while. Or maybe longer, God willing. She reached down for her handbag as the Jaguar slowed for the turn into Downing Street. She pulled out her mobile phone, tapped the text message and hit send: *I'm home xx*.

Target One turned the wheel to his left and touched the accelerator, cutting across the westbound traffic. Dead ahead, across the wide expanse of Whitehall, a three-vehicle convoy was turning into the security gates of Downing Street. A gift from Allah, Target One realised. If he was quick he might be able to get in behind them, drive the bomb into Downing Street itself...

In a moment of cold clarity, Target One realised the enormity of the task he was about to undertake and it filled him with an aching pride. Gone were the nerves and the shaking hands. The fear he'd felt only minutes before had slipped away, like the removal of a heavy coat. A calm descended upon him then, a calm unlike anything he had ever experienced before. Or would again. Muttering his last prayer, he floored the accelerator and powered the vehicle across the street, a cacophony of angry car horns trailing in his wake.

At the entrance to Downing Street, Anna saw the police constable on duty take a few steps towards the security post to activate the gate release. A sudden blast of car horns brought his head around and Anna turned too, her heart rate suddenly increasing. Something was happening behind them, something that had the police officers around the Jaguar scattering in all directions.

'Get that fucking gate open!' Matt Goodge suddenly roared from the passenger front seat, a pistol in his hand. Anna nearly leapt out of her skin and the next moment she was dragged to the floor of the limousine by the police officer next to her, his weight pinning her to the carpet. Rifle shots echoed across Whitehall and Anna shrieked involuntarily. She buried her face deeper into the carpet, her hands covering her ears as the sounds of screaming and shouting, of gunfire, and the growing roar of a vehicle engine tore away the thin veil of composure she'd struggled to maintain for so long. She drew her knees up and closed her eyes, the litany whispered through trembling lips.

'Please God, I can't take this anymore. I can't take this anymore...'

Target One had kept as low as possible on his final journey, peering just over the dashboard to keep the truck straight. The bullets had cracked through his windscreen but all had missed. Death was seconds away. He sat up then, flooring the accelerator as hard as he could. He had not failed! He screamed, a scream of pure exultation that was cut short as a bullet took him through the throat. Target One's head snapped backwards, his body slumping to his left. The pressure switch dropped from his hand.

The van hit the rear of Anna Beecham's Jaguar and exploded in a white-hot blast. The detonation pulverised buildings, cars, buses, people, shredding everything with a million shards of metal and a wave of heat and fire that punched across Whitehall, destroying everything in its path. Smoke and dust blanketed the area and alarm klaxons began to wail over the shattered rooftops, battling for supremacy with screams, alarms and sirens.

A massive crater, several feet deep and filling rapidly with water from a cracked main, marked the spot where Target One had died achieving his deadly goal. Everything around it was gone, The Cenotaph cut in two by the blast, its flags and wreaths scattered and charred to dust. In Downing Street itself, every window was blown out and a large part of the façade of numbers ten and eleven had caved inwards, exposing the shattered interiors. Roofs had collapsed into the street, black railings twisted and buckled. There was rubble everywhere and smoke from scores of fires billowed into the sky.

One of the prime minister's domestic staff staggered out into the street, blood streaming from several wounds, his once-white shirt blackened and shredded. He looked around at the devastation, his eyes wide in shock. He staggered a few more steps, determined to get help, but his legs failed him and he collapsed on to the smoking rubble. He dragged himself into an upright position and sat there, his legs splayed out before him. No matter, help would be here shortly.

No sooner had the thought entered his head when the alarm klaxons that split the early evening air with their ghastly wail suddenly fell silent.

10 Downing Street

Harry picked himself up off the kitchen floor, grimacing in pain. The palms of his hands were scalded where a pot of steaming coffee had hit the floor tiles and blood ran down his face from a gash on his skull. He felt dizzy and nauseous and his ears rang with a persistent, high-pitched tone.

He looked around what was left of the kitchen. Part of the ceiling had collapsed and the wall that overlooked Downing Street was completely gone. Harry scrambled backwards. Exposed power cables swung lazily from the shattered ceiling and roof tiles scraped down from above, sailing past the huge hole and crashing to the street below. The power was out and he could smell gas. That wasn't good. Harry's first thought was a gas blast.

His mind reeled as he tried to piece together the last few moments. He'd been pouring a coffee when a huge flash had lit up the kitchen, followed by an ear-splitting bang. Harry had felt the floor drop away only to rush back up and meet him, then the air filled with choking dust. The contents of the coffee pot had washed over his hands causing him to howl in agony, yet curiously the pain helped him to focus.

As the ringing in his head faded, he became aware of the sound of breaking glass and falling debris. He thought he heard sirens, too. Getting slowly to his feet, Harry grabbed a tea towel from the shattered kitchen worktop and clamped it to his head to stem the blood flow. He could still smell gas. That must have been the cause of the explosion.

He stumbled out of the kitchen and into the hallway where the air was thick with dust. He picked up the wall phone. Nothing. He made his way out of the apartment and headed downstairs, staggered by the damage around him. The whole building seemed to have taken a terrible hammering, as if some huge hand had picked it up and shaken it violently. Nearly every photograph that lined the staircase had been ripped from the walls and Harry's feet crunched on the broken glass that littered the carpet.

As he stepped over more debris on the first-floor landing, he heard someone coming up the stairs and David Fuller stumbled into view. Harry stared, open-mouthed, in shock. Fuller's normally immaculate appearance was gone. His face was covered in black soot and his thick, well-groomed hair was almost completely singed off. What hair he had left stood up in small clumps across a skull that bled from various cuts. His suit was shredded, a shoe was missing and his left foot was covered in blood. When he saw Harry, a mixture of relief and pain swept over his face. Harry was rooted to the spot.

'Jesus Christ, David, what happened?'

Fuller tried to speak, then coughed deeply for several seconds, steadying himself on the banister. Harry rushed to his side and grabbed his elbow. He saw blood on his lips.

'Take it easy. We need to get you some help.'

Fuller, gasping for breath, shook his head. 'Not yet, Harry. First we have to get you to safety.'

Harry heard more shouts downstairs. Several black-clad police officers brandishing automatic weapons had entered the shattered lobby of Number Ten. One of them looked up and saw Harry on the staircase above. He charged up towards them.

'Sergeant Morris, Met Police,' he panted. 'There's been a bomb, at the entrance to Downing Street.' He tapped the radio clamped to his Kevlar vest. 'Afraid that's all I know. All comms are down.'

Harry was dumbfounded. A bomb? Where the hell did all this come from? And where was Anna? She'd texted him only...

'Jesus Christ! Anna!'

Harry pushed passed him and charged down the stairs, running out into Downing Street. What he saw stopped him dead in his tracks. The security gates at the end of Downing Street had simply disappeared, along with large corners of both the Cabinet and Foreign Office. On a devastated floor above, a large conference table hung by two of its legs from severed timber joists. As Harry watched, the timbers groaned and gave way, sending the table crashing to the ground in a cloud of dust and rubble.

A gigantic crater marked the entrance to the street and water from a broken main arced into the air, showering a curtain of mist halfway across Whitehall. In the surrounding buildings, fires were beginning to take hold and the road beneath Harry's feet was buried under a carpet of rubble. Amongst the debris he could make out a body, crushed beneath a collapsed wall. He turned away in revulsion – and saw the wreckage of a car buried in a wall at the far end of Downing Street. Harry stumbled towards it, ignoring the shouts of the police officers behind him. All that was left of the Jaguar was the front axle and a blackened engine block, overturned and half buried in rubble, the remaining wheel with its distinctive emblem still alight and dripping burning rubber. Was it hers? Was Anna inside?

She was gone. He knew it then, felt it deep inside; a sudden, gaping hole in his heart that hadn't been there before. I'm home, his mobile had chirped only moments before the blast. He reached out towards the twisted metal, but Morris and another police officer grabbed his arms and pulled him back from the flames. Morris's face was an inch from Harry's.

'Prime Minister!' he shouted. 'We have to get you out of here, now! No arguments! We may be under attack!' As if to emphasise his words, a distant explosion echoed around Whitehall, followed by several gunshots.

Harry stared uncomprehendingly at Morris. 'What the hell's happening?'

'No idea, but we have to get off the street! Let's go!'

Harry found himself being bundled back to Number Ten. Across Whitehall, he saw the façade of the MOD building, windows broken and stonework peppered by the blast. He flinched as another volley of gunfire split the air and then they were back inside the remains of Number Ten.

He felt breathless, numb, no fear, no despair, just numb. First a car bomb and now more gunfire. A coup, his inner voice warned him, this must be some sort of coup, and Harry shuddered at the thought. This wasn't the way things were done in Britain. This was a civilised country, where policies were robustly debated on national TV, where people queued quietly to cast their votes in libraries, schools and church halls.

But things had changed, he knew that; the level of anger across the country building daily, the public's patience wearing thin, his own administration failing to deliver on a number of fronts. Is that what they were witnessing here, a new form of British rebellion? Harry didn't think it possible. Surely things hadn't got that bad, that quickly?

As the police officers formed a protective cordon around him, Harry wondered that if a coup was really in progress then who was behind it? Who out there, amongst his many political rivalries, amongst an angry and desperate electorate, would possess the means and the motivation to engage in such a deadly course of action? To kill so many? To kill his wife?

Harry clamped a blood-covered hand across his mouth to stifle the wail of despair that threatened to erupt from his throat.

Foreign and Commonwealth Office

Geoffrey Cooper regained consciousness slowly, his vision wavering between darkness and a blurred nightmare. Cooper preferred the darkness. It was somehow warmer, more comforting, but a sharp pain in his lower abdomen was denying him the beckoning shadows. He gradually opened his eyes, cuffing away the dust that clogged them. After several confused moments, he realised he was lying face down on the floor of his private office. How on earth did he get here? Had he fallen? He shifted his head around to the right. There was his computer screen, the one he'd thrown earlier, lying in pieces on the floor. There was something about that screen, a suspicion that it was somehow key to his present condition.

Slowly, painfully, he rolled over on to his back. The ceiling above was scarred and pitted, the large crystal chandelier that hung from the centre of the room gone. Cooper raised his head slightly. The wall was gone too. How could that be? In its place was a huge, jagged hole through which he could see all the way across Whitehall. Above him, the damage reached up into the shattered ceiling where the plaster had been blasted away and large, wooden floor joists hung dangerously low. A few feet away, the floorboards were torn and ripped at crazy angles, creating long, jagged splinters.

Very much like the one in his stomach, thought Cooper. A thick wooden stake, about eight inches long, had penetrated his abdomen close to his left hip. It was bent all the way over, presumably where he had lain on his stomach in the gentle embrace of unconsciousness. Cooper was too dazed to be horrified. Instead, he looked at the wound with a detached fascination. There didn't seem to be much blood, which was good. Blood was so difficult to remove and the shirt was handmade from Savile Row. And I'll probably need a tetanus shot, too, he realised.

It bloody well hurt, but the pain ebbed and flowed and Cooper briefly considered pulling the stake out. He'd seen it done in films and suchlike, the hero extracting whatever sharp implement had skewered him, normally followed by some sort of wisecrack. But this wasn't the movies. Cooper gently unbuttoned his shirt and opened it around his plump waist. Ugh. The skin around the wound was a deep bluish-purple and from the wound itself seeped a steady flow of thick dark blood. Cooper felt sick. No, he'd better not attempt any amateur surgery. Better leave it to the experts.

He let his head rest back on to the rubble-strewn carpet. There was another pain too, niggling at the back of his mind; a bad memory that bubbled just under the surface. Something to do with his computer…

Aleema's message. That's when he'd first felt the pain, far worse than the wood in his gut. Cooper closed his eyes, trying to recall the details that led to this nightmare. Dammit, what was it? He slowly opened his eyes and there it was, just a few feet away, lying amongst the rubble. Its slim, metallic case was cracked and covered in dust, but it was unmistakable. His computer terminal. That's when Cooper saw it, the small device plugged into the back. With considerable effort, he crawled across and removed it, studying its tiny black case with a suspicious eye. No asset tag, no serial number or manufacturer's stamp. He'd never seen it before, the use of such hardware being forbidden in government departments.

Ali.

It had to be. He was the obvious suspect. The device was some sort of bug, he knew that now. Whatever its intended use, Ali's call and Aleema's gut-wrenching movie had confirmed the success of whatever espionage mission they were on. Buried beneath the thick layers of his ego, Cooper had half suspected he was being used, the odd fleeting thought that had piqued his conscience, but the promise of a life with Aleema had smothered his better judgement. At the CIG meeting a short while ago he'd berated the others, treating their views with contempt. Now look. My God, what a naive fool he'd been. A stupid, naive fool. All this devastation, somehow it was all his fault. *There isn't much time*, Ali had warned, or something like that. That information had to be important to someone.

He could hear the wail of sirens but they sounded a long way off. Where the hell were his staff, the police and ambulances? This was Whitehall, for God's sake, filled with important people like him. Surely they should have responded by now? Cooper wasn't certain how long he'd been lying there, but it seemed like quite a while. Where was everybody?

To hell with it, he'd find help himself. Maybe he could make it the few yards to Downing Street. Harry had to be told, of course, about Aleema and that greasy bastard Ali, about Sharm el-Sheikh and the bug in his computer. And he'd get medical help too, get this awful piece of wood removed. It was really beginning to hurt now.

Cooper leaned against the wall, pushing himself to his feet. His head swam and he suddenly felt the bile rise in his throat. He leaned over and vomited, splashing a late luncheon over his shoes. When he had finished retching, he wiped his mouth with his shirtsleeve. Now, that can't be good. Blood in his vomit. Better get a move on.

He made it to the landing and staggered down the stairs, gripping the handrail fiercely with both hands. There didn't seem to be much damage down here, or even in the small courtyard that led out into King Charles Street, but he didn't see a single person. He looked at his watch, but the face was cracked and the hour hand rattled loosely inside. Dammit. A Tag

Heuer too, bloody expensive. He squinted to focus, swaying on wobbly legs. Well, it was gone six, anyway. Most people would have left for home by now. Good. The fewer casualties, the better.

He stumbled out into King Charles Street, through the arched portico and past the deserted security gate. He turned left and shuffled the few yards to the junction of Whitehall, where he leaned heavily against the white stone façade. He looked down and discovered his trousers were wet with blood. Fear gripped him then. He might actually die if he didn't get help soon. He raised his head and, despite the growing pain, Cooper's mouth dropped open as his eyes took in the full scale of the devastation around him.

The Cenotaph was cut in two and there was a sea of rubble that stretched across Whitehall. He looked up above him, to his first floor study where he had been lying moments before. He could see the huge hole and his blackened ceiling beyond, the wrecked floors above his own. The whole front of the building had been blasted away. Further up the street, a deep crater marked the entrance to Downing Street and a burst pipe sprayed water high into the air. Falling masonry from surrounding buildings rumbled and collapsed into the street in clouds of dust. Cooper could see fires too, crackling and spitting amongst the rubble. A bomb, a huge one, he realised. Cooper's head spun with the enormity of the scene. For God's sake Geoffrey, what have you done?

Summoning his failing strength, he pushed himself off the wall and headed towards Downing Street, veering into the road to avoid the worst of the damage and the falling masonry. He picked his way amongst the rubble, stumbling over the debris, but the effort was proving too much and he fell several times. He vomited again, only this time the fluid seemed more like blood than anything else. It took Cooper nearly every ounce of strength just to stand upright. He had to get to Downing Street, but the pain was really starting to take hold now and he was feeling very weak. Maybe he'd take a quick rest, gather his strength.

He sat down heavily, leaning against the remains of The Cenotaph, and looked across the road. What little he could see of Downing Street was in bad shape. There were fires down there too and he couldn't see a single person moving. And those lifeless rags there, they looked like bodies. When all this was over, when the dead had been buried and Whitehall rebuilt, when all the investigations had been completed, his reputation would be in utter ruins. He would be branded everything: traitor, murderer, lovesick puppy. Spy. But he was beyond caring now.

He felt faint and let his body slump sideways, lying prone against the base of the monument. Even being here, in this spot, felt wrong. The Cenotaph was a monument erected to commemorate those who'd died in the First World War, an annual focus for solemn remembrance and national pride. Not a place for selfish, reckless fools like Geoffrey Cooper.

His eyes clouded over and the darkness called him again. He felt relieved. He'd succumb this time. The pain in his stomach had gone, to be replaced by the pain of remorse, betrayal... and unrequited love.

He opened his eyes and he held her again, under the cool canopy of the oasis, her beautiful face, her warm smile, a smile that embraced and caressed him. She slipped away from his arms and he reached out after her. She laughed, dancing from his grasp as she flitted between the trees. He chased after her but she pulled further away, her voice echoing amongst the palms. Then she was lost in the shadows.

Cooper looked up through the treetops. It was night, but a night so dark that it momentarily frightened him. There were no stars and no moon, and the darkness seemed to be descending like a black ceiling, swallowing the tops of the palms as it sank towards him. Then it swallowed him completely and suddenly he didn't feel afraid any more. The darkness felt warm and comforting, a place where he could forget everything that had ever been, except the love of a beautiful woman.

He closed his eyes and then there was nothing.

10 Downing Street

Sergeant Alan Morris had been sitting inside a police van on Birdcage Walk, just a few hundred yards from Whitehall, when the bomb detonated. Morris and his six-man rapid response team had been enjoying a break under the leafy canopy of St James's Park when suddenly their radios went dead. Seconds later, the ground shook beneath them as the Downing Street blast thundered across Central London. As the debris cannoned off the roof of their vehicle, Morris had seen the smoke billowing above the rooftops and ordered the driver into Whitehall.

Parliament Square was in chaos. Scores of civilian cars had been damaged by bomb debris, while others had careered into each other, causing a huge traffic jam. Many drivers had abandoned their vehicles and were running away from the immediate vicinity, whilst other police units were desperately trying to clear the road to make way for the emergency services that were surely on their way.

Whitehall itself was littered with rubble, so Morris had ordered his team out of their van and double-timed it along the wide avenue. They skirted the huge, smouldering crater at the entrance to Downing Street and sprinted along the cul-de-sac to Number Ten. As Morris ran, he'd tried frantically to radio his controller but all he heard was static. Thankfully they'd found the prime minister alive. The Downing Street police detail were nowhere to be seen, no doubt killed in the blast and buried under the mountains of rubble. Morris shuddered.

Now, as he stood outside the most famous front door in the world, he could hear gunshots. Some were single reports but he heard automatic fire, too. A siren wailed in the distance only to be drowned out by a series of large explosions in quick succession. To Morris, it sounded like war had broken out, but he had to ignore what was happening elsewhere and concentrate on keeping the immediate situation under control.

He heard crackling above his head and looked up to see thousands of burning embers swirling in the air. The fires in Number Ten were starting to take hold. He had to move the PM soon, but where to? Where was safe? He couldn't take him up Whitehall, it was chaos up there and there may be other explosive devices, not to mention the shooting. He had to find another way out. The PM would know, surely? He must have rehearsed Downing Street evacuation drills a dozen times.

When Morris re-entered Number Ten, he saw that Beecham's aide had been carried down into the lobby, his wounds being attended to by one of his team. The prime minister was there too, holding the man's hand. Mac, his most senior officer, pulled him to one side. He kept his voice low.

'Most of the domestic staff were at the rear of the building when the bomb went off. They legged it out into the garden and a couple of the lads are out there keeping an eye on them. There's a few missing but, as far as the survivors are concerned, there are no major injuries, just shock and a few cuts and bruises. I thought I'd leave them out there for now. Might be too dangerous to take them out the front.'

Morris nodded. 'Good job, Mac. How's he doing?' indicating the casualty in the lobby.

'That's David Fuller.'

Morris was shocked. He'd seen Fuller many times on TV, an instantly recognisable figure. Now he was a mess of blood and burns. 'Jesus Christ. How is he?'

Mac lowered his voice. 'Not good. Deep shock, internal bleeding, blood pressure's way down. Unless we get proper help soon he won't make it.'

'Where was he when the bomb went off?'

'In the Cabinet Room. Part of the wall collapsed but he managed to dig himself out.'

Morris looked around the lobby. There was debris everywhere and smoke was starting to drift in from the street. 'Okay Mac, here's what we're going to do. We've got to move the PM to a secure location. Don't ask me where, I haven't figured that out yet, but we can't take everyone. Tell the lads in the garden to stay with the staff until help arrives. Try and salvage some blankets, cushions, curtains, anything to make them comfortable. And get some water, too. Make sure they're kept as far away from the building as possible. I don't know what the fuck's going on, but I've a feeling the fire brigade might be very busy tonight.'

'I'm on it.'

'Another thing. Try and find a phone, a radio, anything. See if you can find out what the hell's happening.'

Mac hurried away and Morris walked over to the prime minister who was kneeling down, gripping his injured friend's hand. Fuller wasn't looking good at all. His face was pale and drawn, sweat beaded his forehead and thick, dark blood had pooled around his badly injured leg. The police officer treating the wound caught Morris's eye. Subtly, he shook his head.

Harry, talking quietly to Fuller, missed the exchange. 'You're going to be fine, David. Just hang on,' he soothed.

Fuller turned his head towards Beecham. His eyes were horribly bloodshot and his voice rasped heavily as he spoke.

'Don't feel too good, Harry. Something inside me... feels all wrong.'

His voice trailed away and his eyelids began to close.

Harry gripped his shoulder. 'David, listen to me. I need you to stay with me. Try to stay awake. Help will be here soon.'

Fuller's eyes flicked open. 'Where's Anna? She should have... been back here by now. The dinner, tonight...'

Harry bit his lip hard. Fifteen minutes ago, the world revolved at its usual pace, routine, predictable even. Now it had turned upside down and, in that short space of time, Harry had become a widower. And, by the look of things, he was about to lose his best friend too. He fought to keep his voice from cracking.

'She's gone, David.'

With a supreme effort, Fuller squeezed Harry's hand. 'Harry, I'm so...'

A spasm of pain wracked Fuller's body and his hand went limp. Harry's eyes flicked to the police medic and saw the resignation in his eyes. This can't be happening.

'Surely there's something we can do? Where the hell are the emergency services?' he whispered urgently.

Morris stepped in, laying a hand on Harry's shoulder. 'Sir, we don't know what's going on out there. It's chaos.'

Harry's face paled. 'You said we were under some sort of attack.'

'Without doubt. That's why we've got to move as quickly as possible.'

'Where to?'

'Well, I was hoping you could tell us. I think it's too dangerous to evacuate into Whitehall. Is there another way out of here?'

Harry looked down at Fuller. 'What about David?'

The police medic finished taping a large bandage around Fuller's leg wound.

'He needs immediate surgery, Prime Minister. All I can do is try and make him comfortable.'

Harry leaned over Fuller, whose eyes were closed. 'David. Can you hear me?'

Fuller's eyes flickered open. He tried to smile through a mask of pain. 'I may be injured, Harry but... I'm not deaf. You have to... leave me here.'

'No David, we won't do that.'

Fuller coughed, a deep wet hack, speckling his lips with blood. Harry pulled out a handkerchief and wiped Fuller's mouth. As he did, Fuller clamped his hand weakly around Harry's wrist.

'You've been a good friend, Harry. I–' He cried out as another spasm of pain rippled through his broken body. When he spoke again his voice was little more than a faint whisper. 'I can't feel anything. You need to get out, now. Go, please.'

Harry held Fuller's hand tight. 'I'm sorry I couldn't do more, David.' His voice cracked then. He was watching his best friend die, right in front of him.

'Help me get him outside,' he ordered Morris.

Gently they carried Fuller out to the garden, laying him down on the grass away from the building. Gunfire and sirens filled the air. The Downing Street staff were there too, huddled together against the far wall. Harry bent down, covering Fuller with a blanket recovered from the house.

'Is there anything else we can do for you, David?'

Fuller's face had taken on a grey pallor. He could barely talk. 'Just… something for the pain… anything,' he whispered.

Harry glanced at the police medic, who led him a few yards away. The policeman kept his voice low. 'I've got a couple of ampoules of morphine, sir. He won't feel a thing.'

Harry nodded grimly. 'Do it.'

Morris decided to give the prime minister a moment with his dying friend. He hurried across the grass to where the staff were gathered near the garden wall. Two men were stood against the wall, one balancing on the other's shoulders. Morris called up to him.

'What can you see?'

The man look down, fear etched on his face. 'There's shooting across the park, coming from the direction of the barracks. I can see lots of smoke and flashes. What the bloody hell's going on?' he cried.

Morris knew that all the civilians were on the verge of panic and he had to calm them down somehow. 'First things first, get down from there.' The man jumped down and the staff gathered around Morris. 'Look, I know as much about what's happening as you lot. The best thing you people can do right now is stay put. The emergency services will get here, but it may take them a while. In the meantime, stay away from the building and keep together.' Morris jerked a thumb over his shoulder. 'I'm leaving two of my guys with you. They'll look after you.'

'Where are you going?' asked a portly middle-aged woman in chef's whites. 'Our priority is to get the PM away from here and I haven't got the manpower to take care of all of you. As soon as we get to a secure location I'll send someone back for you.'

'How long will that be?' a younger woman wailed.

'Shouldn't be long. And no more peering over walls, okay?'

The staff grumbled begrudging agreement. Morris felt a twinge of guilt at deserting them, but his priority now was the PM. He trotted back to Harry who was gently pulling the blanket over Fuller's face. He stood up as Morris approached.

'I'm sorry,' Morris offered.

Harry looked down at Fuller's lifeless body. 'He was a good man. A good friend.'

'Sir, we have to move,' urged Morris.

Harry shook his head. 'I can't leave him here like this.'

'I'm afraid we'll have to,' said Morris gently. 'We can come back for him later, when things settle down.'

Harry took another look at his departed friend, now covered with a cheap grey blanket. It didn't seem right to abandon him, but he knew they had no other choice. Besides, if David were alive he would be more concerned about Harry's safety than his own.

'What now?'

Morris saw Mac jogging across the grass towards him. 'What's the word on the comms?'

Mac shook his head. 'Can't raise a soul. Everything's down, including the civvy phone network.'

'Shit.' Morris turned to Harry. 'You must have some sort of secure room, an emergency location or–'

'Crisis Management Centre,' Harry cut in, 'down in the basement. There's also a tunnel that runs beneath Whitehall, leading directly to the Ministry of Defence building.'

Morris thought quickly. 'Sounds like a plan. And we can use the tunnel to evacuate everybody out of here and into the MOD building.' For the first time since it all began, Morris began to breathe a little easier. He turned to Mac. 'Round up all the civvies. When we get downstairs, I want you to take them straight through the tunnel. Once you're in the MOD building, stick them in a room away from the windows. I'll stay here and try to establish comms. Once we've organised a way out of Whitehall we'll come and get you. Okay?'

In a few moments, the civilian staff had been safely herded together. Morris turned to Harry. 'That's everybody. Lead on, sir.'

With a final glance at his dead friend, Harry turned and led the group across the garden and back into Number Ten. The smoke inside had thickened and they could all hear the crack and spit of flames as the fires began to take hold on the upper floors. The group continued quickly through the building until they arrived at a short corridor, at the end of which was a large steel door marked Secure Area – Authorised Personnel Only. With a sharp twist of the handle, Harry led them through the door and down into a wide stairwell.

'Mind your step,' he cautioned. They made their way down several flights of concrete stairs and found themselves in a long, brightly lit corridor. On the right was the CMC. Harry stopped outside and pointed towards the end of the corridor.

'Turn right at the end there and the tunnel will lead you into the MOD building.'

Morris nodded to Mac who set off immediately, taking the civilian staff with him. As they filed past him, Harry reached out and shook a hand here and there, trying to sound as optimistic as possible. His voice trembled slightly.

'Good luck. I'm sure everything will turn out okay. Just do what the police tell you.'

Harry watched them go. They were good people, dedicated in their duty to the office of prime minister. The irony was that he didn't know half their names and he felt rather guilty about that. He watched the last of them disappear around the corner, then turned to Morris.

'As you can see we've got power down here, thanks to an emergency backup generator in that room over there.' Harry pointed to a steel door on the other side of the corridor. It looked the same as the main door to the basement; government grey, with two large locking handles and adorned with yellow signs that warned *High Voltage Electricity – Danger of Death*.

'Good,' Morris nodded. 'How about those comms, then?'

Harry led the police officers into the CMC. Morris gave a low whistle when he saw the large amount of electronic maps, LCD displays and high-spec communications equipment scattered around the room. He headed straight for an Airwave comms set, a piece of equipment he was familiar with and the type used across the Met area. He began scrolling through the frequencies.

'Any luck, Sergeant?'

Morris shook his head. 'Can't raise anyone. It's like the whole net's dead.'

'Keep trying.' Harry got up and paced the room. Anna's violent death invaded his thoughts again, the almost physical pain twisting his stomach in knots. He closed his eyes and pinched the bridge of his nose, banishing the images that threatened to overwhelm him. He took several deep breaths, regaining his composure after a few moments. A clear head was needed now, something else to focus on. So what did they know?

An attack on the government had taken place, an attack on a massive scale. No emergency services had arrived, no security forces other than the small police team that now accompanied him, and all communications were down. To cap it all, there were explosions and gunfire across St James's Park. It was all a terrifying, chaotic mess.

He looked up at the bank of monitor screens, some of which were usually tuned in to the media channels. All they transmitted now was a snowstorm of static. What the hell was happening? Short of taking a walking tour of the area, there was no way of finding out. It was clear to Harry that he had to abandon Downing Street. But where to go, and how to get there?

He spun around when he heard footsteps echoing along the corridor. Mac entered the room accompanied by Brigadier Forsythe from the CIG team. The brigadier was dressed in full combat uniform and wearing a camouflaged helmet and flak jacket. On his belt he carried a pistol holster, the flap unbuttoned. Behind him, four heavily armed soldiers also entered the room and fanned out around the walls.

'Giles! Thank God you–'

Without a word, Forsythe took Harry's arm and guided him away from the others. His face told Harry more about the gravity of the situation than anything he'd seen or heard since the whole nightmare had started.

'Prime Minister,' began the brigadier, 'let me start by saying how sorry I am about your wife and Mr Fuller.' Harry looked at him uncomprehendingly. 'The police have briefed me. I was in the MOD building when your staff appeared. I've settled them on the sixth floor, in a conference room. They're safe for the time being.'

'What the bloody hell's going on, Giles?'

Forsythe took a deep breath. 'Here's what we know. At six o'clock this evening a series of co-ordinated attacks took place across the country–'

'Across the country? What do you mean?' interrupted Harry.

The brigadier held up a hand. 'I know it's a shock, but just hear me out. Okay?' Harry nodded soberly. 'The UK, or at least some parts of it, is under attack and what we are experiencing could be the first wave of an even larger operation. Contact has been lost with every major army base and garrison across the country. I was able to speak to a colleague of mine very briefly, a senior commander at Aldershot. He said the garrison had been infiltrated by large groups of armed men and that there were several firefights taking place in or around the vicinity of his particular barracks. Shortly thereafter, the line went dead. So it's not just London. I grabbed some binoculars and went up on to the roof of the MOD. The surrounding area has been devastated and there are smoke plumes right across the horizon. Communications across the board appear to be down, along with all civilian and governmental power grids. This is not a terrorist incident, Prime Minister.'

'A coup, then? The political situation hasn't been–'

'No, I believe these are the opening shots of a much wider conflict. The scale is too large. Our infrastructure, our defences have been deliberately targeted and disabled. This feels like a war.'

Harry's face drained of colour. 'A war? With whom?'

'We haven't got time for speculation. We have to get you out of here.'

'Where to? And how are we going to get out of Whitehall? It's a bloody nightmare out there.'

'Prime Minister–'

Harry cut him off. 'Giles, we've known each other for long enough and, under the circumstances, I think we can dispense with the formalities.'

Forsythe nodded. 'Okay, Harry.' The brigadier cast a look over his shoulder, making sure there was no one within earshot. 'What I'm about to tell you has remained a secret from the British government since work began, many years ago. Quite simply, the situation has never arisen where its use has been necessary.'

Harry couldn't keep the puzzlement from his face. 'What the hell are you talking about?'

'An evacuation plan, one that would be implemented should normal transport and communication channels be deemed to be too risky. Usually, the procedures for a national emergency are clear. You'd be whisked away from your present location and taken under armed escort to an airfield, from where you'd be flown to Alternate One, the command and control complex beneath the Mendip Hills in the West Country. Once there, your cabinet would join you and together you would take control of whatever crisis the country happened to be in the grip of and continue to govern as the situation allowed.'

Harry nodded, familiar with the general national emergency plans. But it was clear Forsythe meant something else, something quite different.

'However,' the brigadier continued, 'it was decided many years ago that there may come a time when events ran out of control too quickly, that the prime minister of the day would have neither the time nor the opportunity to leave Whitehall by the normal routes without putting him or herself in serious jeopardy, even under armed escort. A large-scale nuclear or chemical attack, for example. A time when even a helicopter pickup from Whitehall would be deemed an unacceptable risk. That time is now.'

'Jesus,' whispered Harry.

'Before we go any further I need to send the police back across to the MOD.' Harry started to protest, but Forsythe held up his hand. 'It's just you, me and my security team. They're good boys, all special forces. The police can look after your civilian staff.' A sudden rumble overhead made everyone glance towards the ceiling, the shock wave shaking the walls. 'We're running out of time,' Forsythe warned, signalling to one of his security team.

Harry saw a tall, chisel-faced soldier walk briskly towards them. Like the others, he was heavily armed and dressed in full combat gear. Whereas the brigadier wore a standard-issue Kevlar helmet, this man, like the others, wore a short-peaked cap in the same grey/black pattern as his combat uniform. The man walked with an easy stride, as if he'd done this a hundred times, not a glimpse of tension, not a bead of sweat. Just a calm, self-assured manner, one that Harry found both intimidating and comforting at the same time. Forsythe did the introductions.

'Harry, this is Mike Gibson, my number two. Mike's squad is part of the Sabre Team standby group.'

Gibson held out his hand and Harry shook it, noting the tough skin and firm grip. 'Sir.'

'Sorry, I didn't catch your rank.'

'Technically it's sergeant, but we don't stand much on ceremony in our mob. Everyone's pretty much on first-name terms.'

'Special forces, of course,' echoed Harry, slightly embarrassed. These men operated differently, had their own rules and rituals, their own way of doing things that wasn't always by the book.

Gibson pointed to his comrades. 'Quick introductions then. The big fella is Nasser and that's Brooks. Bloke by the door is Farrell. We've all done this kind of stuff before. You'll be well looked after.'

Harry felt reassured in the presence of this small but no doubt very capable team of professionals. If anyone were going to get him out of this situation, it would be these guys.

Forsythe waved Morris over. 'Time to go, Sergeant. And keep a low profile,' he warned. 'To all intents and purposes we're in a war situation. Find a radio and listen in. Any official broadcasts will be transmitted across the emergency networks. Try and stockpile as much food and water as you can and don't move unless you have to. You might be holed up for a few days.' Forsythe offered a tight smile. 'Best advice I can give you under the circumstances, I'm afraid.'

Morris nodded, shaking Forsythe's hand. 'Appreciate it. Good luck.'

Harry offered his own hand and then Morris and his men were gone. When the echoes of their passage had finally receded, Forsythe ordered everybody out into the corridor.

'Time to go. Follow me.' He took a few brisk steps then came to a halt outside the generator room. Harry nearly collided into him.

'Where are you going, Giles? There's nothing in there.'

'Have you ever been inside, Harry?'

Harry frowned. 'When I first moved into Number Ten, right after the election I was given the full tour as part of my orientation. Impressive if you're an electrical engineer, but I must admit I didn't linger too long.'

'Then let's reacquaint you,' insisted Forsythe. He twisted the two steel retaining levers out of their catches and swung the door open, walking quickly inside. Harry and the others followed closely behind, filing down a shallow concrete ramp.

The room seemed larger than Harry remembered. Against the left-hand wall there were four generators, each about the size of a family refrigerator, humming softly. These were the units that supplied the emergency power to Downing Street, Harry recalled. Against the right-hand wall of the room were the much larger electrical mains cabinets, labelled one to six, which supplied regular power to the Downing Street complex. Each cabinet had a digital display across the front panel next to a numeric keypad and, as Harry looked along the row, he noticed that all the units had a small red light glowing on the display panel alongside the legend *Loss of mains power – Call emergency contact number*. Above their heads, several thick pipes and cables snaked away from the six units into the floors above. At the far wall there was a workbench with some scattered tools and rags on its surface, and a well-thumbed clipboard hung from a small hook on the wall. Harry was even more puzzled. What the hell were they doing down here? Forsythe turned to Gibson, indicating the door to the generator room.

'Mike, seal the door as best you can.'

Gibson looked around and found a thick metal crowbar lying amongst a pile of discarded rags on the workbench. He ran back up the ramp and carefully jammed the bar into the door's mechanism. Satisfied, he leaned on the bar with all his weight but it wouldn't budge. If somebody wanted to open the door from the outside, they'd have to blow it open. Gibson gave Forsythe the thumbs up.

'Well Harry, this is where it gets interesting.'

Harry didn't say a word, confusion etched across his face. Forsythe pulled out a thick plastic card from inside his breast pocket. He snapped it sharply in half, revealing a smaller, thinner card inside. He approached the second mains power unit on the right-hand wall and, reading from the card, punched a code into the small keypad on its front panel. He then slid the card into a slot under the keypad. Harry stepped back in surprise as the bottom half of the unit hissed loudly and swung inwards, revealing a dark recess. Harry crouched down and looked inside. It was pitch black.

'What the hell is this?'

'Our escape route,' answered Forsythe.

'You're joking?' He could tell from the brigadier's expression that wisecracks were the last thing on his mind. 'Small and dark,' noted Harry, standing. 'I'm not good in confined spaces.'

'Don't worry,' said Forsythe getting down on to all fours. 'It's a short crawl of about ten feet to another chamber on the other side of the wall. Torch please, Mike.'

Gibson fished a small MAGLITE from his webbing and handed it to Forsythe, who promptly disappeared inside the hollow unit. While they waited, Gibson took Farrell to one side.

'Stay this side until we call you through. Keep an ear out for trouble,' warned Gibson, pointing to the top of the ramp. 'If anyone tries to force entry, get to the other chamber fast and seal it from the inside, okay?' He took a felt-tip pen from his pocket and scrawled four digits on Farrell's hand. 'Punch that number to lock it and join us as quickly as you can.'

Harry watched Farrell jog back up the ramp. 'We're not leaving him, are we?'

'No. He's just going to watch our backs while we organise things on the other side. Besides, he's got a radio.'

'I thought that all radios were dead.'

'We can use them as walkie-talkies over short distances. He'll be able to give us plenty of warning.'

They both turned at the sound of the brigadier's voice, echoing inside the crawl space. 'Harry! Into the shaft, please!'

Harry got down on his hands and knees and began crawling inside the power unit. He shuffled quickly through and stood up, finding himself in a small concrete room with a steel door in the opposite wall. A single wire-meshed bulb lit the space from the low ceiling above. After a few moments Gibson, Nasser and Brooks had made their way through, dusting themselves off as they stood up.

'Farrell is watching our six, Boss. He's got the code to seal both hatches.'

'Very good, Mike.' Forsythe turned and walked towards a small numeric keypad set into the wall. He punched a sequence of buttons and Harry heard a faint whirring noise then an audible metallic click. He looked up as the bulb above their heads dimmed slightly.

'I'm getting claustrophobic already,' muttered Harry nervously.

'I've got a cure for that. Follow me.' Forsythe took a couple of steps and pulled the steel door open. He stepped to one side. 'After you,' he said, motioning Harry through the door. Harry gratefully complied, finding himself standing on a wide metal gantry. He looked down.

'Jesus Christ.'

The Sleeper

Allah be praised! He was amazed and overjoyed that he'd made it this far, into the very lair of the enemy. It had taken years of hard work, both physical and mental, not to mention the humiliation, the deceit, the loss of his family and friends, the isolation. Shortly, all that would be at an end. The war had begun and soon his Brothers would arrive on the shores of the infidel.

He had engineered his place here with the Sabre Team, hoping against hope that the regimental rotations would place him in Whitehall on this day. They did, and he had thanked Allah profusely. It was a sign, of course; a sign that his mission was a righteous one. And now he was here, standing on the steel gantry, alongside the prime minister. Like the others, he was amazed. It was truly an impressive feat of engineering, something that the infidels had always been good at.

He thrust an innocent hand into his pocket and produced a stick of chewing gum. In reality, he was making sure that his one remaining transmitter pad was still safely tucked away. He'd been issued six of the small devices some years ago, but four had either corroded over time or simply refused to work. Now he had two. He'd just placed one in the generator room, directly above the false panel, innocently bracing his hand on the unit and steadying himself as he crouched to enter the crawl space.

Roughly the size of a coin, the transmitter had a strong adhesive back that would attach to almost any surface. Small and unobtrusive, once adequate pressure had been applied to its coated surface, the pad would begin transmitting a low-frequency signal that his Brothers should be able to pick up with their tracking equipment – if they were quick enough. The signal lasted for only seventy-two hours, after which the tiny battery would be dead and the signal would cease to transmit. No matter, he still had another. This one he would somehow try to attach about Beecham's person. The signal would follow him everywhere and, with luck, he would be detected when his Brothers stormed this underground complex.

But he didn't give it any more thought. It was all about faith, really. Faith had brought him this far, had silently comforted him through the long hours of darkness and through all the hardships of his training. Faith had provided him with the strength to live among these godless people and so faith would deliver him back into the warm embrace of Islam.

A few feet behind him, on the other side of the false panel, the transmitter began signalling its presence. Trooper Nasser had every faith that his Brothers would not be far behind.

Stockwell, South London

The bomb had taken out the top deck of the bus, blocking the junction of Clapham Road and sending terrified commuters running for the side streets. Black smoke spewed from the wreckage, blackened bodies littering the road. There was an ambulance on the scene, dozens of police officers, but still chaos reigned. Comms had gone, dropped out completely, no one talking to anyone else. The screams and shouts from the junction, the sirens, the car horns as traffic began to back up on all directions only added to the chaos.

Khan, Max and Spencer took cover in their van, watching the horror unfold a hundred yards away. The upper deck of the bus was missing and there were several cars on fire around it. Those who hadn't abandoned their vehicles were lying dead or injured inside them. People were running everywhere, along the streets, over cars, trampling others underfoot in an effort to escape. Khan punched the door in frustration, startling the others. Target One had something to do with this. The respectful farewell at the mosque in Morden, dumping his surveillance, a bystander shot in cold blood, just yards from where they were now parked. And now this. It was all beginning to add up.

'Get us out of here, Max. There's nothing we can do. Blues and twos, yeah?'

'I'm on it.' Max fired the engine into life, reaching under the dashboard and flicking on the blue and red emergency lights. It wasn't something they did often, but this was an emergency. Besides, they didn't want to be mistaken for terrorists by a nervous cop armed with an assault rifle. Max swung the van around and put his foot down, leaving the carnage behind them, strobe lights and siren carving a path through the traffic and growing crowds of rubberneckers.

'Where to?'

'Millbank,' Khan said. 'Let's find out what the hell's going on.'

Max swung the van hard around a corner, screeching left on to Lansdowne Way. Almost immediately he began to slow down.

'Shit. Look at this.'

A multiple-vehicle pile-up was blocking the junction of Wandsworth Road, pedestrians running in all directions. Khan saw a group of people hiding behind a low wall, bodies piled on top of one another. *What the hell...?*

'Go around,' he barked. The van reached the junction and mounted the pavement, swinging around the pile-up and into Wandsworth Road. Max stamped heavily on the brakes and Khan fell forward against the dashboard.

'Bloody hell, Max!' he shouted.

Max pointed through the windscreen. On the road, as far as they could see, scores of vehicles had been abandoned, their doors hanging open. Several were burning as other vehicles tried to weave through the smoke and wreckage, hampered by the obstacles and bodies scattered across the road. Further down towards Vauxhall, a petrol station was burning, a huge wall of flame licking hungrily around the overhead canopy. Through the flames, Khan could make out the incinerated shells of several vehicles, and a column of black smoke boiled into the air.

Something clanged off the van's bodywork. Khan flipped off the van's emergency lights.

'We're taking fire! Turn around, find another way!'

In his haste, Max stalled the vehicle. Another round ricocheted off the bonnet. 'Shit!'

'C'mon Max!' screamed Khan. He registered movement from the corner of his eye and saw a figure emerge from a convenience store on his left, not more than twenty yards away. The man was walking quickly towards them, wearing a desert pattern combat jacket and black jeans. The weapon he was bringing up to his shoulder was a black assault rifle. Before anyone could react, the man opened fire. Khan just made it, ducking below the dashboard as the side window and windscreen exploded in a shower of glass. The noise from the weapon was deafening. Bullets hammered the van, ricocheting off the Kevlar-lined walls and burying themselves into anything that would yield to their deadly velocity. Like Max.

Khan, pistol in hand, suddenly realised that Max hadn't got down in time. His eyes travelled upwards. Max's face was unrecognisable, as if it had been stoved in with a giant hammer. Surprisingly, there was very little blood, but Khan could see wisps of smoke rising from the wound in his face. He turned away quickly. The gunman was probably closing on them, carefully skirting the van. Maybe he'd seen Khan duck down and was just waiting for an opportunity to empty another magazine in his direction. Maybe he had already walked away, in search of his next victim. Or maybe not.

Khan didn't move a muscle, straining to filter out the sounds around him and pinpoint the shooter's position. In the distance, he could hear a siren wailing and the roar of the petrol station blaze. Closer, he heard the pop and tinkle of glass exploding and the dull thump of vehicle petrol tanks igniting. He realised he couldn't hear any human sounds at all – no shouts, no screaming, no crying. It felt like he was alone in this nightmare. He couldn't even hear Spencer in the rear of the van and he dare not even whisper to him. No doubt he too, was trying to stay as quiet as possible.

There. The crunch of glass underfoot, very close. Khan was down in the passenger footwell, his head below the window and his back pressed against the passenger door. He heard the scrape of a foot directly outside the van and twisted his body around as quietly as he could manage. Khan knew he had to use deadly force and the thought of killing suddenly made him feel nauseous, but he had no choice. This was one of those 'kill or be killed' situations they'd discussed during his training. The instructors had spoken about it on the weapons ranges and in the classroom, and some of those guys had had to make that fateful decision once or twice during their careers. There was no set procedure for it in the manual, but it didn't matter in this case. Khan knew that the gunman would shoot him in an instant.

He twisted his head around, looking upwards through the shattered passenger window. He could see the flat roof of a building above a row of cheap grocery shops and off-licences. Not the nicest area of town, remembered Khan. Then he saw something else, a figure in the driver's wing mirror, getting larger.

The shooter was only a couple of yards away, carefully inspecting the van. Khan could see his head turning but the weapon was out of sight, no longer on the man's shoulder. He seemed almost relaxed. Maybe he assumed the threat had been eliminated and was–

Suddenly the side door was wrenched open, light flooding into the rear compartment. Khan reacted immediately. He grabbed the door handle and threw himself out, landing hard on the ground. The shooter spun around, catching the barrel of his rifle on the door frame. Khan shot him twice in the chest and the man staggered, falling backwards inside the van.

Khan scrambled quickly to his feet, his pistol pointed towards the body. He noticed that the man hadn't released his weapon, and was horrified when the shooter slowly raised himself into a sitting position, coughing and spluttering. Khan watched him in fascination; he was certain he'd hit him. The man looked up and their eyes met. In that instant, Khan saw the body armour under the combat jacket. Both men raised their weapons. Khan fired first, the round taking the gunman through the temple. He flopped backwards into the van, very dead.

Khan quickly scanned the area around him. With all the turmoil going on, he figured nobody had seen what had just happened by the van. One thing was for sure, this guy wasn't working alone. Khan pulled the body out and let it drop to the ground. He climbed inside the van and knelt down beside Spencer. It was obvious he was dead. The floor was slick with blood and Khan noticed the single bullet wound to the chest, probably hit by a ricochet.

He spun around and peered over the driver's seat. To his right he could see a sprawling housing estate that ran for half a mile along the Wandsworth Road towards Vauxhall Cross. As he watched, he saw flashes coming from several windows overlooking the main road and automatic gunfire rippled the air. The only people he could see were dead, scattered along the road. Nobody seemed to be taking any undue interest in him or the van, which was now obscured by a veil of smoke that swirled around on the light summer breeze.

Khan slid back out on to the road, crouching down next to the gunman's body. He quickly searched the corpse. No ID card, no travel pass, no money, nothing. Khan studied his features. Dark curly hair, thin beard framing his jawline, high cheekbones, slight build; possibly from one of the North African states. Arabian, then. He was dead, so no chance of a roadside interrogation. But dead men could still prove useful.

Khan holstered his pistol and stripped off the man's body armour, strapping it tightly around his own torso. He picked up the AK-84, checking the magazine and making sure a round was chambered. He rifled the man's pockets, finding two more magazines. He weighed the AK-84 in his hands, getting reacquainted with its feel. Satisfied, and feeling better able to protect himself, Khan turned his attention to his immediate dilemma.

He still had a major problem and that was how to get to back to the office at Millbank. Any further progress eastwards along Wandsworth Road could prove deadly. The gunmen in the tower blocks had the road covered, and from their high elevation could easily pick off anyone stupid enough to attempt passage. No, he'd have to wait until dark. He checked his watch. That was in three and a half, maybe four hours. He'd have to find a bolthole somewhere, keep off the streets.

Scanning the buildings to his left, Khan searched for an escape route. There, an alleyway between two shopfronts. It may be a dead end but, then again, it may be just the hiding place he was looking for. He checked the street again. There was sporadic gunfire, but thankfully it seemed to be coming from much further up the road. Behind him, the Wandsworth Road continued westwards which, apart from a few hastily abandoned vehicles, looked relatively unscathed. But it was east that Khan needed to go.

As if on cue, the wind shifted slightly, drawing a curtain of smoke across the street. Khan used it as cover, running to the side of the road and ducking between two parked cars. Keeping his head low, he checked the pavement in both directions, but it was empty. He turned his attention to the alleyway. It was maybe five or six yards away to his left, sandwiched between an Internet café and a shopfront with steel shutters protecting its façade. Khan slowly scanned the area in all directions as smoke drifted silently overhead. He held his breath and dashed into the alleyway.

It was narrow, about thirty feet long, with a wooden gate at the far end topped with razor wire. Khan ran quickly along its length, his footsteps echoing loudly in the tight passage. He tried the handle; locked.

He glanced up at the razor wire. It was rusted, thickly curled and vicious looking. Khan didn't fancy trying to climb over that, not in his light summer trousers and short-sleeved shirt. He tried the gate again, forcing it with his shoulder. It gave a little, but not much. He couldn't risk shooting the lock out in case it attracted unwanted attention.

Two or three shots rang out close by and Khan spun around in alarm, raising his rifle. Smoke carried on the breeze, obscuring the end of the alleyway. Khan imagined figures behind it, armed, angry, searching him out. He was trapped like a rat in a pipe. He turned his attention back to the gate and carefully reached over the top, threading his hand between the coils of razor wire. He groped around and found a deadbolt on the other side, sliding it quickly backwards. He tried the handle again and, to his relief, the gate swung open. Khan went through quickly, closing it behind him and securing the bolt.

He found himself in a small backyard. High walls surrounded him on three sides and the ground was covered with rubbish and discarded building materials. There was a door to his left that led into the rear of the steel-shuttered store, secured with nothing more than a hasp with a thin piece of wood jammed into it. Khan removed the wood and stepped inside. He stood quite still, listening. There were no other sounds apart from muffled noises coming from the street outside.

In the dim light, Khan noticed that the walls had been recently plastered and decorated. There were two small rooms to his left and ahead of him a large empty space with a few bags of plaster and some building debris piled in the middle of the room. There was no glass frontage or door entrance, just a wide aluminium shutter separating the newly renovated store from the street outside. Light pierced the shutters, illuminating a billion dust particles drifting lazily on the air.

Khan breathed a little easier. It was just an empty retail shell, obviously still in the process of being renovated, but it would give him the temporary shelter he needed until darkness fell. He made his way out into the rear yard. There were several heavy bags of concrete lying amongst the debris and Khan dragged a few over to the gate and piled them against the foot of it.

He returned to the shop, securing the back door with a piece of discarded wire and a plastic chair wedged under the handle. It wasn't perfect security but it would alert him if somebody tried to gain entry. He found a spot at the front of the building and lost himself in the deep shadows. Although it offered him short-term sanctuary from the anarchy outside, Khan knew he was effectively trapped, but he needed to lay low for a while. If he stayed here, hidden away in this empty store, the trouble outside might just pass him by. Later, he would make his move.

Of course, the darkness held its own dangers; any friendlies out there would have little or no time to react before they realised that the dark-skinned man with the flak vest and assault rifle was actually a British intelligence operative rather than a terrorist, but it was a chance he'd have to take. So what the hell was going on out there? Khan shivered involuntarily. Was this happening elsewhere around the city? And what about the rest of the country? There would be a lot of terrified people out there tonight and the emergency services would be completely overwhelmed.

Fleetingly, he thought about Salma, the bright, attractive legal secretary he'd met a few weeks ago on a rare day off. Things had been going well, and they'd enjoyed a few dates together. She lived near Brick Lane in an outrageously priced one-bedroom apartment, where Khan had spent the odd night sleeping on the couch. Salma was not one to rush things and Khan respected her for that. Besides, he didn't want to blow his chances.

He wondered where she was right now. If she was still at work she'd be able to see the fires from her office in the city. Khan tried to remember what floor she worked on. The forty-second, that was it, although he got the impression that the height bothered her. Or maybe she was already at home, watching it all on the news. He hoped so.

Khan had told her he was a civil servant working for a dreary government department in Whitehall, a well-paid but uninteresting position, prompting no further curiosity on her part. How would she react if she saw him now, holed up in an empty shop with an automatic rifle across his lap? For the first time since he got out of bed that morning, Khan managed a thin smile.

She'd probably have a fit.

At that precise moment, Salma Nawaz was fighting for her own life. She pushed and clawed to no avail against the unyielding mass of shouting and screaming bodies that had her pinned against the floor-to-ceiling window on the forty-second floor of the Hanson building. As she twisted her neck and looked out across the city, the chaos on the streets below only heightened her terror.

At six p.m., Salma had been working in the data centre, one floor down from her desk at Lewison, Butler and Partners, the prestigious city law firm where she worked. She'd been sitting in front of the large display screen, dragging and dropping electronic documents around the company's file structure, when she heard a deep boom and the floor shook beneath her two-inch black heels. Then, all the lights in the room went out and the display in front of her died. A wave of panic gripped her and she'd stumbled out into the corridor, where the emergency lights had flicked on. She made her way up the fire escape stairs, emerging on to the forty-second floor, where the first thing she noticed was that all the desks were empty and every computer screen was lifeless. The power must be out up here too, she realised.

She heard loud voices, then shouting. Salma thought she recognised some of the voices, but they sounded different, shriller and high pitched. There was a commotion coming from the other side of the large, open-plan office. She walked quickly between the desks, seeing most of her colleagues crowded against the east-facing windows. What on earth were they looking at?

Salma didn't like to get too close to the windows. Heights scared her, although she didn't mention that in her interview and had struggled to keep it a secret since she'd been at Lewison Butler. Sometimes, whenever something of interest was happening outside, people would loiter near the windows to watch, particularly if it was a lightning storm or a light show over at the Dome. Salma always stayed on the periphery, away from the windows. She imagined that the slightest pressure against them would make the glass crack and break. Irrational, of course, because during her building induction she'd been told the windows could withstand squillions of pounds of pressure and the glass was coated with super strength epoxy something or other, but none of that was any consolation to Salma. The only statistic she remembered was that here, on the forty-second floor, she was standing five hundred and forty-six feet above the streets of London. And that thought alone made her feel sick.

Against her better judgement, Salma made her way towards the windows. There were maybe sixty or seventy people gathered there, nearly everyone in the office, looking out over East London. Everyone seemed to be shouting and pointing. What on earth was going on? She saw several others break away from the crowd and bolt for the staircase. The first pangs of real fear began to gnaw at Salma then, but curiosity was the stronger emotion. She climbed on to a desk and stood up, looking out over the heads of the crowd. The scream rose in her throat and she stifled it with a fist.

Above the urban sprawl to the east, a giant airliner circled the sky, two of its engines ablaze and trailing black smoke. Salma watched in horrified fascination as the aircraft turned slowly towards them. She suddenly recalled the attacks on the World Trade Center, many years ago. She hadn't even been born then, but the footage she'd seen had always chilled her, the images of those plunging to their deaths, the crowds below watching, unable to help. She'd imagined herself there, trapped on a shattered window ledge a thousand feet above the ground, a curtain of smoke and flames behind her, those around her screaming, crying. Jumping.

More people broke away from the crowd and bolted for the lobby, but Salma found herself rooted to the spot, transfixed, as the crippled aircraft lumbered around the sky. She jumped off the desk and made her way to the window, drawn to the macabre spectacle. It was an Atlantic Airlines Airbus, a double-decked, five-hundred-seater. She could see it quite clearly now. It wasn't heading directly for them, she could see that also, but it was going to be close. The pilot seemed to be fighting for control as the wings dipped and swayed and the aircraft yawed from side to side. She could see that the tail fin was also damaged, the upper half shattered and blackened, trailing ribbons of twisted aluminium. The aircraft loomed closer.

One of the senior partners suddenly cannoned into her, sprinting for the lobby. She scrambled to her feet and swivelled back to the window. The aircraft was almost upon them. One moment it seemed far away, but then the office darkened as the huge airliner filled the sky in front of the building. It thundered past the windows, slightly below her, the wing tip barely fifty feet from the glass. In its wake, the whole building shook to its foundations. Pictures sprang off the walls and everything rattled violently as terrified employees clung to anything they could to steady themselves.

Salma just stood there swaying, her hands clamped over her ears as the winged monster screamed past the building. She followed its path as it headed towards the centre of London, knowing it was going to crash. She lost sight of it as it banked to avoid another high building, the turn abnormally steep. Moments later, a towering fireball mushroomed into the air over the West End. Salma was paralysed with horror. She'd just witnessed the final, terrible moments of hundreds of people. Nausea churned her stomach and made her head spin. She staggered away from the window.

She had to get out, get away from the horror that threatened to overwhelm her. She had to get home. She was about to run to the stairs when another sound stopped her in her tracks. It was like rumbling thunder, growing louder with each passing second. Suddenly, the fire escape doors burst open and scores of people spilled out into the office, shouting and screaming, tumbling over desks and sprawling on to the carpeted floor. Then smoke started belching into the room, thick black smoke, travelling quickly across the ceiling, filling the air above them.

Salma ran down the corridor towards the kitchen. The crowd surged after her, seeking a way out, charging like a herd of panicked wildebeest. She found herself lifted off her feet and hurled forwards. Her head cracked sharply against something hard and her vision swam. She scrambled upright and fought to stay on her feet as the bodies closed in around her. Her vision blurred momentarily, but her face pressed against a smooth surface, cool and comforting under her skin. Like glass...

Salma's eyes regained focus as she realised she was pinned against the kitchen window. She twisted her neck painfully to see what was going on. Down the packed corridor she saw a group of men desperately trying to block the gaps beneath the fire doors, their hands clamped over their mouths as the smoke continued to pour into the office. Then the realisation hit her: they couldn't get out. The fire was below, leaping up the stairwells, the building shafts, burning, melting...

She felt herself crushed against the window as the crowd sought refuge away from the choking curtain of smoke. She screamed with all the power in her lungs, pushing backwards with her bottom, but the pressure was too much and her voice was lost in the crowd. She was pinned against the glass, her arms above her head.

And that's when she heard it. Above the shouting and screaming, Salma heard an audible crack. She twisted her face upwards and her blood froze. There. A small fissure had appeared at the top of the huge glass pane and, as she watched, the jagged finger reached downwards another few centimetres. It was the plane, she thought. The near miss had rattled everything, weakened it somehow, and now everybody was herded into this tiny kitchen and the pressure against the glass was making it crack.

Salma tried to turn her body, but she was pinned fast by the writhing mass against her. Her chest hurt and it was getting difficult to breathe. Then she felt it; the crack had worked its way down to her fingertips. At the top of the window frame, she could see a fine dust sprinkling down from around the surrounding concrete. The crack up there was wider, deeper, working its way past her fingers and across her cheek. With every ounce of strength she possessed, Salma tried to wriggle her way out, but the wall of bodies pressing against her had her trapped.

She watched with mounting horror as the fracture widened near the top and more concrete and plaster rained down. The man next to her suddenly became aware of the danger and shouted in alarm. Others around her joined in the sudden chorus of desperation and tried to push their way forward, shoving and punching their colleagues in front of them. They managed to make some progress and Salma felt the pressure on her body ease slightly. But it wasn't over.

The men near the fire escape doors were suddenly engulfed in flames as one of the doors buckled and flew inwards in a rush of boiling air. The crowd surged backwards again, desperate to escape the fire. For the damaged window, the renewed pressure proved too much.

Salma was slammed against the glass and this time she felt it move, watched in terror as the top sill was suddenly wrenched out of its concrete housing. The window tilted outwards a few degrees and held there. Screaming filled the air. Salma felt her eyes drawn upwards. A single steel bolt seemed to be holding the frame in place and she watched in horrified fascination as it slowly buckled under the pressure. Her life was being measured out by a thin metal bolt; as long as it held, she would live. But she knew it would not – could not – hold. The tears streamed down her face and she tried desperately to push herself away from the window, but it was no use. The bolt bent to almost fifty degrees, the concrete around it fracturing and crumbling. And then it was gone.

The window buckled outwards and fell away beneath her body. Salma Nawaz, along with forty-four other employees, plunged five hundred and forty-six feet to their deaths.

Firestorm

Elsewhere across Europe, confusion reigned.

As in Britain, major European cities experienced widespread power outages moments before hostilities commenced. In city centres and surrounding suburbs, traffic-signalling systems suddenly failed, causing many accidents and huge jams. Subway systems, trams and trains glided to a halt, powerless. For a few moments, people reacted in a manner typical of the long-suffering commuter. Many complained loudly about the state of the public transport system, while others merely shrugged their shoulders and took it in their stride. Some closed their eyes and settled into their seats or buried their noses in books and newspapers, resigned to the delay. Many reached for their mobile phones to call friends and loved ones and were puzzled by the sudden loss of signal.

In transport control centres across the continent, worried staff frantically tapped the keypads of dead telephones and lifeless computers as, one by one, all of their control and monitoring systems shut down. Panic increased further as emergency power systems failed to kick in. After several minutes, commuters packed inside stranded carriages began to feel uneasy. For others, trapped in subway tunnels deep underground, fear had already taken control as passengers clawed at doors, windows and each other to escape the claustrophobic blackness.

In residential suburbs across Europe, people tinkered with televisions, checked telephones and repeatedly flicked the switches of lifeless air-conditioning units and household appliances. Frustrated and confused, they joined their neighbours to shrug shoulders and complain light-heartedly about the sudden loss of power. The comforting routine of everyday life had suddenly been turned upside down but things would return to normal very soon, they reassured each other.

And then, without any warning at all, the chaos began.

Kastanies Border Crossing, Greece

Nico Panayides, his hands expertly flexi-cuffed behind him, sat on the car park asphalt with twenty-two of his colleagues and watched in horror as column after column of Turkish battle tanks rumbled through the rocky canyon and surged across the border into mainland Greece. Above them, attack helicopters nosed ahead of the armour, seeking out targets.

Panayides felt he was living inside one of his nightmares. As senior Greek customs officer at the Kastanies international border crossing, it was he who was ultimately responsible for the security of this section of the Greek frontier. Here, in the steep valleys and jagged peaks of the Rhodope Mountains, Greek customs officials fought a continuous battle against cross-border infiltration, people smuggling, drugs and weapons offences and all manner of illegalities and infringements. The border with Turkey was marked by sharp, rocky slopes and the fast-flowing Evros river, as it meandered for approximately two hundred and forty kilometres from the Bulgarian frontier in the north to the Aegean Sea in the south. It was tough, dangerous country, but Panayides and his vigilant team of experienced officers had seen it all before at this busy border crossing.

Busy. That was a word that, remarkably, didn't apply that morning. In the four years since Panayides had been in charge at Kastanies, he'd seen hundreds of vehicles pass every single day in either direction, from huge articulated lorries to single mopeds and every size of vehicle in between. Every day, day in, day out, for the last four years. Except today.

A few hours earlier, Panayides had been sitting in his office and checking the daily figures on his computer terminal. Since eight o'clock that morning, one hundred and forty-four Greek-registered vehicles had crossed into Turkey and seven had crossed from Turkey into Greece. Seven.

Normally, the Greek checkpoint would expect to see at least two to three hundred vehicles pass in both directions through the border. But seven? He checked the terminal again. None of the Greek vehicles had returned, either. Now that was odd. Panayides picked up his binoculars and walked to the window. From his first-floor office he could see the Turkish customs post, a mile further down the road. Beyond the distant fences and barbed wire, the Turkish flag hung limply in the still evening air from the roof of the administration building. There was no queue of vehicles waiting to cross into Greece, no people bustling around the car park; it seemed extremely quiet, which was most unusual.

Beyond the customs post, the ground rose steeply and the road disappeared, twisting around the foothills into Turkey itself. What was going on behind those hills? wondered Panayides. Despite Turkey's entry into the European Union and the continual protests from Ankara and Brussels, Greek border controls had remained tight and ever vigilant. Personally, Panayides was only too happy to enforce Greece's commitment to the security of her frontier with Turkey. It wasn't that he felt any personal animosity to the Turks, but it was hard to forget the violent history and bad blood that existed between their countries. It was one of the reasons that the Greek government had resisted Turkey's entry into the EU, but their concerns were ignored. Turkey was rich and powerful, and the bureaucrats in Brussels salivated at the thought of all that Turkish money flowing westwards. But the Greeks remained watchful. It would take many generations before they trusted their old enemy.

Panayides was relaying his concern to Athens when, shortly before 7.00 p.m. local time, business began to pick up. He ended the phone call and went to the window. Several cars had begun to filter across the distant border and he scanned them with his binoculars as they approached Greek territory. The vehicles were Turkish-registered and, after pulling into the empty car park below Panayides' window, the occupants got out. They were all men, some in pairs while others travelled alone. As the rules dictated, they headed towards the customs hall below him. Businessmen, assumed Panayides. They emerged a few minutes later, climbing back into their vehicles and continuing their journey into Greece. Panayides checked the log on his terminal. Still no sign of any Greek vehicles.

Just before eight, a large coach with darkened windows crossed from Turkey into Greece and rolled into the car park. Panayides watched as the passengers disembarked, stretching and rubbing their cramped limbs. They looked like a football team, he thought, all dressed in the same red tracksuits. He was intrigued as to where they were playing and who. Panayides had always been a big soccer fan. He'd played regularly as a young man and had potential, or so he'd been told, until a knee injury forced him to give the game up for good. Now in his late forties, he was too old to play competitively. Too old and too fat, his wife liked to remind him. She could talk.

There were about thirty of them, all Turkish nationals. Panayides watched as the footballers headed into the customs hall beneath him. The younger ones were smiling and joking around and the older guys with them were a little more stern faced and serious. They must be the coaches and support staff. They wore jackets and trousers, but they still looked pretty fit. Just before they disappeared out of view, Panayides saw one of the older guys reach inside his jacket. As he did so, two of the younger men turned to face the car park, their smiles gone, their eyes sweeping the area as if searching for something. One of the younger men said something to the older guy as they filed slowly into the building.

It was at that precise moment that Panayides felt it. What it was he couldn't quite place; a look, a whispered word, something. But it felt wrong. He decided to go downstairs and study the group from the observation room as they filed through the main hall. He picked up his radio and ordered one of his colleagues to run the number plate of the coach. Slipping his cap on to his balding head, he made his way downstairs and along the corridor.

As he reached the door to the customs hall, it flew violently open. Panayides stumbled backwards, lost his footing and ended up on his backside on the tiled floor. He caught a flash of red as several men rushed past him and pounded up the stairs. There were shouts, banging, and glass breaking. Before he could react, he was dragged to his feet and bundled into the customs hall, where somebody spun him around and slammed him against a wall, tying his hands expertly behind his back with a tough plastic tie. After a few seconds, the rest of his men were all similarly trussed up and facing the wall. It was only then that Panayides realised that the football team held weapons and the older guys had produced radios and were talking urgently into them. After a few minutes, Panayides and his colleagues were marched outside and grouped on the ground in the car park. That was roughly thirty minutes ago.

In that time, several military trucks and tracked vehicles had crossed the Turkish border into Greece, while army engineers had dismantled the barriers and bulldozed the chain-linked fences on either side of the road. The Greek flag had also been removed. Panayides saw that the tracksuits of the football team had been replaced by camouflage uniforms. At least his instincts had been proved right.

The ground beneath them began to rumble. Greek heads swivelled as the noise increased and echoed around the steep canyons. In the distance, accelerating past the Turkish border post, a column of armoured vehicles roared towards them. Panayides sat on the ground and watched the seemingly endless convoy snake its way past in a cloud of dust and continue on into Greece. He was filled with a mixture of fear and rage. Were they at war? How the devil did it happen? And why?

The border was now wide open and, as Turkish troops jeered from the turrets and cabs of their vehicles, Nico Panayides wondered if he'd live to see the dawn of a new day.

European Air Space

While the surviving governments of the West screamed for information, undercover sleeper teams and deep infiltration units of the Arabian forces went to work. Using human assets working on the inside, or through sheer surprise and deadly force, transport control centres and major road and rail junctions were seized and secured by thousands of small but heavily armed groups of men and women. On targeted motorways, vehicles were blocked from joining the carriageways and motorists already travelling on them were encouraged to leave at the next exit, often by the sight of a large tanker or heavy low-loader truck slewed across the lanes and accompanied by bursts of automatic fire. No one needed telling twice. All major road routes across Europe were secured and quickly cleared. The Arabian advance teams were expecting traffic. Lots of traffic.

Meanwhile, inside European air traffic control centres, sleeper agents began their well-rehearsed diversionary tactics. As the power cuts across Europe forced ATCs to switch to emergency generators, smoke flares were thrown into empty rooms and stairwells. Fire alarms were tripped and bomb threats called in. Alarm spread quickly. As buildings were evacuated, air traffic control was hurriedly passed on to other ATC centres and airports, which suddenly found themselves in the grip of their own emergencies. Across the skies of Europe, aircraft were ordered to maintain holding patterns. In most cases, operational personnel inside the ATC buildings followed standard emergency procedures and filed outside, where they gathered in car parks and other designated areas to await staff roll calls. Most were unaware that, as they left their control rooms, their places were being taken by specially trained teams of forward air controllers of the Arabian armed forces.

The FACs settled into comfortable wheeled chairs, slipped on their communication headsets and quickly absorbed the information that glowed on the consoles in front of them. For the next two hours they had only one priority: clear the skies.

In the air, pilots' headsets hissed with new instructions delivered by unfamiliar voices. Despite initial confusion, the urgency of the controllers encouraged them to execute flight plan changes immediately. Hundreds of civilian passenger aircraft were skilfully diverted and landed as quickly as possible at the nearest airport that could accommodate them.

On the ground, at the major airports of Paris, Lyon, Rome, Düsseldorf, Amsterdam and others, police and security units suddenly found themselves embroiled in deadly gun battles that raged around the passenger terminals. Terrified civilians and airport staff scattered across roads and motorways to escape the gunfire as control towers, fuel storage depots and other secure areas were assaulted and seized. The battles were over quickly and had cost half the lives of the sleeper teams. Yet, despite their own losses, they had managed to secure their targets and take up defensive positions inside. Like their Brothers and Sisters at other major airports across the continent, they waited patiently for the main Arabian forces to descend upon Europe.

Paris

Every major European city was rocked by a series of co-ordinated terror attacks that rippled across the continent. Army and civil militia units suddenly found themselves under assault in their own barracks while, on the city streets, police officers screamed for backup over lifeless communications networks.

In the Spanish capital of Madrid, the high-security national police station on the Puerta del Sol was devastated by a huge bus bomb, detonated a few moments after 7 p.m. local time. As survivors staggered out of the smoke and rubble, fourteen Libyan commandos, armed with sniper rifles and dispersed along the high rooftops that overlooked the square, began opening fire. Nearby police and Guardia Civil units that responded to the blast suddenly found themselves in a war zone. Similar scenes were repeated all across Europe but, in terms of violence, Paris was to suffer the most.

Several hundred sleeper agents had descended on the city centre throughout the day, travelling alone or in small teams from the bleak, soulless estates that ringed the French capital. At 7.00 p.m., they created havoc. For the Algerians amongst the sleeper teams, and there were many, it was a night of remorseless revenge. While most hadn't even been born at the time, all Algerians were aware of the 1961 massacre of nearly two hundred of their countrymen by the French police and security forces, most victims either beaten, shot or garrotted to death, while others were thrown into the fast-flowing river Seine. Now, sixty-eight years later, the Algerians would have their revenge.

Nearly every police and civil guard station in the city centre was attacked. In most cases, heavily armed sleeper teams took up positions around the target buildings and bombarded them with automatic weapons fire and rocket-propelled grenades. In others, suicide bombers entered police stations under the pretence of reporting a crime. Once inside, with a muttered prayer or a scream of victory, they detonated their devices. Yet more sleeper teams began their deadly work inside the army and gendarmerie nationale buildings where they were employed. Guards were killed, keys were snatched, doors and gates unlocked, armouries broken into, weapons and vehicles stolen and human targets identified and killed. Anarchy consumed the city.

The fires and explosions across the centre of Paris could be seen and heard for some distance. From the balconies of crumbling tower blocks in the crime-ridden suburbs, the disenfranchised, dispossessed and displaced residents that made up the lowest class of France's social order looked out across the city at the countless pillars of black smoke that towered into the sky and the fireballs that mushroomed above the distant rooftops with every passing minute. But the spectacle did not fill them with fear. What they saw wasn't death, or carnage, or chaos; they saw motive and opportunity. And they sought revenge on a society that had cast them into concrete prisons, both poverty and despair their ever-present jailers. It was time to escape.

At first they were just small groups, maybe ten or twenty youths, stoning panic-stricken motorists on the surrounding overpasses. Soon the numbers grew into hundreds and the hijackings began. Drivers and passengers alike, having escaped the horrors of Paris city centre, now found themselves being dragged from their vehicles and beaten. Some were lucky enough to scramble away from the mobs, their clothes in tatters and their bodies bruised and bloodied, but still able to make good their escape on their own two feet. Others were not so lucky.

Across the Seine, in the western suburb of Nanterre, two quick-thinking girls, both students at the Université Panthéon-Sorbonne, had seen the distant fires and decided to escape the city. Their plan was to make for the forest of St Germain and hide there until they could figure out what the hell was going on. In their small apartment they quickly grabbed a radio, some bottled water, bread and cheese, a torch and two sleeping bags. In the underground garage beneath the apartment block, they unplugged their Renault electric car from its lifeless recharging post and piled in. The power indicator told them that they were good for at least two hundred kilometres.

The car accelerated up the ramp and out on to the street, heading north to intercept the A14 trunk road that would take them out of the city. The girls were terrified as cars roared past them, their occupants crazed with fear. They both screamed as another car overtook them with centimetres to spare, only to take a right-hand turn at high speed and roll, turning over and over until it collided with a shop front and burst into flames.

Instinctively, the driver turned left. She knew that she was headed away from the motorway, but fear now dictated her actions. The girls found themselves driving along a residential street where grimy apartment blocks and graffiti-daubed walls lined their route. They turned left and headed north again, the road leading them deeper into a maze of dilapidated streets. Smoke drifted in the air. As they passed a wide avenue to their left, they saw cars burning fiercely across the middle of the road and a single body lay motionless on the ground. The girls cried in fear, the driver accelerating and wrenching the wheel hard right. As they careered around the corner at sixty kilometres an hour, they found themselves face to face with a thousand-strong mob marching on the city.

A rock bounced off the windscreen and they both screamed. The driver panicked and covered her face, slamming her foot down to brake but flooring the accelerator by mistake. The crowd tried to avoid the speeding vehicle, but it was too late. The Renault ploughed into the mob, tossing bodies high into the air. Some were caught under the front wheels and dragged along the ground, their limbs ripped and torn, their screams drowned by the roar of the scattering crowd.

The Renault shuddered to a halt, its bodywork battered and slick with blood. Desperately, the driver tried to start the car. It was a fatal mistake. In seconds, the vehicle was swamped, the occupants dragged out and beaten. Sensing blood, the remainder of the crowd surged in, trampling some of the injured to death.

In the moments before they died, the girls were savagely beaten then repeatedly raped on the crumpled bonnet of the Renault by a frenzied mob, urged on by jeering hordes that couldn't see what was happening, but could sense the power that emanated from an unstoppable force in a lawless environment.

After a few painful minutes a man stepped forward, pushing his way purposefully through the crowd. He was tall, dark-skinned, in his mid-thirties. The shouts and screams died away and a hush fell over those immediately gathered around the vehicle. There was something about this man, a sense of importance, a seriousness and conviction that commanded respect. He drew a short, curved knife from his belt. Without warning and with shocking expertise, he moved quickly between each girl, cutting their throats. There was stunned silence for a moment and then one or two half-hearted cheers rang out. The two girls slipped limply from the bonnet of the car and flopped on to the road where they lay, side by side, their eyes wide with shock and pain. Moments later they were dead.

The man sheathed his knife and slipped back into the crowd that parted in respectful silence. For him, it wasn't an act of cruelty. What was cruel was the way the girls had been treated in the last few moments of their lives. The crowd had beaten them and forced themselves inside the two women. That was the behaviour of animals. But what did he expect? The crowd were mainly infidels from a variety of cultures. They had gathered together and now existed as a single entity that had only one purpose: destruction.

For the time being the man would stay with them. He had their respect and they would do his bidding. He would direct them against the surviving French police and army units until they were either all killed or captured. When it was over, when the violence had abated, he would await the arrival of his Brothers and round up the survivors of this rabble. They would be punished for their act of brutality.

As he strode to the front of the mob, the Renault was set alight. The pack had a leader now, a man who urged them onwards towards the centre of Paris. In less than two hours, the City of Lights had descended into a land of barbarism and death.

Pause

At H-hour plus three, the terror attacks stopped. In major cities across Europe, the sleeper teams broke off their engagements and melted away into the side streets, leaving their dead and wounded where they lay. The element of surprise had been invaluable and a large percentage of military and police forces across the continent had been decimated. Those that survived tried to re-establish some semblance of order amid the chaos, but it was too late. The chain of command had broken down and, with it, any hope of an organised response to what was now becoming a conventional war on a huge front. The destruction of European life was under way and the governments of the West were powerless to do anything about it.

For the Arabian intelligence officers on the ground, the reports coming back were almost too good to be true. Over eighty per cent of military targets had been hit successfully. Over sixty per cent of power and utility targets had been captured intact and the main motorway and high-speed rail routes were all secured. Reports from forward air controllers reported that the skies were now clear. Only Schiphol airport in Holland had suffered major damage when a Japan Airlines Boeing 787 Dreamliner collided on take-off with a FedEx cargo plane on final approach. Burning wreckage had severely damaged one of the main runways and several planes on the ground. For the next twenty-four hours, Schiphol would be out of service.

Meanwhile, preliminary contact reports were collated from each sector of operations and uplinked via UHF radio to the senior Arabian intelligence officer in Europe. He, in turn, sent the encrypted data east via an Arabian military communications aircraft orbiting high above the Mediterranean Sea. The data was checked and rechecked. Europe was reeling, like a tired boxer leaning against the ropes, bloodied and breathless – but still dangerous. Her scattered forces retained the ability to fight back, if they could somehow regroup and reorganise. To the east, Turkish troops were already deep inside Greek territory and naval units had bombarded the city of Athens. The war had been under way for nearly three hours and it was now time to commit the main body of Arabian forces. The orders were encrypted and beamed to a thousand field commanders waiting in command and control centres dotted across the Arabian continent, where they were decoded and verified.

The first shots had been fired, the first blows had been struck. Now it was time to finish the fight. The order was given.

Invade.

Invasion

Thousands of aircraft, circling high over North Africa and Turkey, finally received the signal. Following pre-planned flight paths, they dipped their wings and increased power, bringing their aircraft around to new headings. These were the Pathfinder units, numbering tens of thousands of paratroopers, light infantry, small armour, engineering, communications and intelligence troops. All had a multitude of tasks and objectives. The main priority for the paratroopers was to secure the airfields, bridges, road, rail and other major transportation junctions and control centres and relieve the sleeper teams that held them. In sticks of twenty, the planes trimmed their engines and began a slow descent towards the European mainland. Below and ahead of them, squadrons of Arabian F-22 Raptor fighter jets went to full afterburner, their APG-77 active-element radars scanning the skies before them.

Above the Spanish mainland, six Eurofighter Typhoons of the Ejército del Aire de España had managed to make it airborne, although only three planes had working missile systems beneath their wings. The others had been in such a hurry to get away from their besieged airbase that the ground crews had been unable to deploy their weapons. Now they patrolled the skies above the city of Granada, desperately trying to contact a command network that had failed to respond. Below them, in the city centres, huge plumes of black smoke funnelled up into the evening sky. A few minutes ago, an unknown voice had broadcast over the military comms net ordering them to land their aircraft, immediately, at the civilian airport at Málaga. Were they mad? The pilots had politely, yet firmly, refused.

Eight Arabian Raptors approached the Spanish coastline from the south. Their beyond-visual-range weapons systems alerted them to the presence of the Eurofighters and each aircraft launched a single AIM-160 guided missile from its internal weapons bay. The missiles dropped from beneath the bellies of the Raptors, falling six metres until the solid-fuel rocket motors ignited, rapidly accelerating the weapons to Mach three and streaking them towards their oblivious targets.

The Spanish pilots, scanning the ground below them, jerked their heads around when on-board threat detector systems suddenly lit up and electronic alarms screamed inside their helmets. For three of the pilots, their flight careers ended abruptly when their aircraft disintegrated under the impact of the powerful air-to-air missiles that seemed to come from nowhere. For the remaining three pilots, training and instinct had momentarily saved their lives. On hearing the alarms, each pilot had either banked, climbed or dived for the ground, punching out masking flares and chaff to distract the missiles. Yet, despite their well-honed skills and swift reactions, none of them made it.

The first fighter banked hard to the north and went to full afterburner. The missile caught him six seconds later and obliterated his fighter from the sky. The second pilot pulled back on his stick and pushed his thrusters to the stops, sending the plane into a near vertical climb. At eight thousand metres, just before the missile exploded behind his starboard wing, the pilot noticed his radar light up to the south with hundreds of surface returns.

The third pilot, on hearing the cockpit alarms, immediately banked hard to port and headed for the ground. He pulled up a mere twenty metres above the jagged peaks of the Sierra Nevada mountains and continued south-east at top speed, crossing the coastline above Roquetas de Mar at an altitude of fifty metres and over two thousand kilometres per hour. Four kilometres out to sea, the missile lost its track and dived into the blue waters of the Mediterranean.

Madre de Dios, that was close, gasped the pilot. He looked down at his threat display. There was something else out there...

Two F-22s thundered past the Spaniard's wing tips at a closing speed of over Mach three. The turbulence tossed him around the sky and he desperately fought for control of his aircraft, until he glanced out of the cockpit and saw his port wing shredded. One of the planes must have fired his cannon before the Spaniard had even registered him. He noted the fuel leaking from the twenty-millimetre shell holes and knew that his crippled Eurofighter was dying beneath him. Alarm buzzers rang in his ears and a glance at his instrumentation confirmed the worst.

With practised ease, he slowed the aircraft and eased it into a shallow climb. Reaching down between his legs, he pulled the ejection system handle, which exploded his canopy upwards and fired him out of the cockpit, his parachute deploying in less than two seconds. As he drifted down towards the blue waters a hundred metres below him, he wondered how long it would be before he was picked up. The emergency transponder would already be transmitting so it shouldn't be too long. Then, maybe he would find out who Spain was at war with. The pilot's question was answered sooner than he thought.

The parachute spun him around to face due south towards the North African coast. Several kilometres distant, hundreds of ships of all shapes and sizes dotted the sea, their wakes clearly visible even as the sun dipped towards the horizon. And they were all headed north.

The sea rushed up to meet him and he splashed down, his buoyancy aids immediately deploying and the water around him staining with red marker dye. As he bobbed up and down on the surface, he saw an inflatable powerboat bouncing across the waves towards him. Well, at least he wasn't going to drown. He watched as the boat drew closer and he thought of his wife and daughter at home in the small town of Albaicín. He closed his eyes and wondered what was happening there. Maybe this was all a very intense dream. In a moment, he'd wake up next to his sleeping wife and their precious daughter gurgling away in her cot. He'd get up, make some coffee and sit on the shaded terrace that overlooked the old Arab quarter and he would thank the Lord, as he did every day, to have blessed him with such a life. He heard the boat's engines wind down and his eyes snapped open.

As the inflatable slowed alongside him, the Spaniard looked up at the hard, unsmiling faces of the Arabian marines. So, it wasn't a dream after all. Strong hands reached over and pulled him roughly into the boat and he found himself staring down the barrel of a machine pistol. At that moment, the Spaniard doubted he'd ever see his family again.

In northern Europe, sixty Russian armoured fighting divisions with close-combat air support swept across the Polish border and headed for the German frontier. The Poles, a proud but militarily weak nation, were swept aside. The German town of Cottbus, forty kilometres from the Polish border, was one of many frontier towns that had been bombarded with long-range Russian missiles. The tactic was to induce terror, confusion and chaos. With no power, no phones, no TV or radio, the terrified civilian population sought cover in their own homes as German police and army installations came under ferocious attack from sleeper units. To compound the turmoil, long-range missiles launched from the east began to rain down on strategic targets all along the border as German resistance to the onslaught began to crumble. The Arabian tactic had worked.

Terror reigned.

On the outskirts of Nicosia on the Mediterranean island of Cyprus, Greek Cypriot farmers looked up in curiosity and then with mounting disbelief as waves of Turkish planes droned overhead and the sky filled with blossoming white canopies. Rooted to the spot, they watched as heavily armed paratroopers began dropping into the fields around them.

With the help of their large Muslim populations, the Balkans were quickly swallowed up and the Italian ports of Bari, Pescara and Ancona lay in the path of the advancing Arabian warships and troop transporters. On the Italian west coast the ports of Naples, Civitavecchia and Livorno were also hit by sleeper units, who blockaded the vehicle entrances to the ports and engaged Italian security forces with small arms, grenades and rocket fire. They had been briefed that their wait would be relatively short. Hold the port for twelve hours. Arabian naval forces would arrive before then.

At sea, the flotillas of ships carrying troops, supporting armour and heavy weapons changed course and steamed at full speed to their destinations. Initial reports were good; all the target ports had been secured and were being held comfortably. With the continuing attacks across the continent, any organised opposition would be tied up elsewhere. It would only be a matter of time before all resistance collapsed.

Chiswick,
West London

As quietly as possible, Alex peered around the bedroom door and checked on Kirsty. Thankfully she was still sleeping and, as he watched, she murmured something unintelligible and rolled over. After a few moments, she settled down again.

When he'd failed to ease her frantic sobbing, Alex had gone back down to his own flat and grabbed a sleeping pill from the small supply he kept in his medicine cabinet. It was a mild dose, something Alex used for those times when his shift pattern at work robbed him of the ability to get some decent sleep. He'd given her the pill and Kirsty had gulped it down with a glass of water. Shortly afterwards, she had begun to calm down and Alex had helped her to her bed and covered her with a quilt. The sedative wouldn't keep her under for long, but at least it would give Alex time to find out what the hell was going on out there.

Since he'd been inside Kirsty's apartment, Alex had heard a myriad of different sounds. The one he expected was the reassuring wail of a police patrol vehicle making its way at speed to his location, followed by the paramedic teams and even the Met helicopter. What he hadn't expected was a complete and total lack of response. His mobile phone was dead, the phone lines to the apartment block down. Add to that the loss of power and an airliner being shot down with surface-to-air missiles and things weren't looking too rosy.

So he stayed in Kirsty's flat, comforting her as he waited for backup. He'd heard some sirens, but they seemed distant and eventually they, too, had stopped. Alex didn't understand it. He knew that large numbers of emergency personnel would be attending the crash site, that the street outside should be crawling with police and counter-terror units. Instead, nothing. He was worried about the contamination of the crime scene outside. Would there be civilians trampling all over the place, poking around, disturbing evidence? Alex had pleaded with Kirsty to let him go and check, but she'd wrapped her arms around him like a vice and wouldn't let go. So he'd sat there behind the sofa, listening to the sounds of a city descending into chaos.

He'd heard shouting from outside in the street and then screaming. He'd heard car horns being hammered and vehicle alarms being tripped. Somewhere – Alex thought it might be from the elevated section of the M4 motorway at Brentford – he heard the screech of tyres and sickening crunch of multiple high-speed vehicle impacts. He'd heard shots too. He couldn't make out where they were coming from, but it didn't seem that far away.

There was something else: aircraft. He hadn't noticed any other traffic on final approach to Heathrow. Obviously, the shooting down of the airliner had an impact on flight security procedures, but the Airbus couldn't have been the only plane in the sky on final approach. There had to have been scores of others. Surely Heathrow hadn't been completely shut down? Not all five terminals? He'd wanted to get up and find out what was going on, but Kirsty had held him tighter and begged him not to leave. Against his better judgement, he'd relented, staying by her side. Some first date, he thought.

Now, with Kirsty still in the grip of a fitful sleep, Alex decided to recce the immediate area. He closed the apartment door quietly and went out on to the darkened landing. He drew his pistol and walked slowly down the stairs, his back tight to the wall. Keeping to the lengthening shadows, he moved silently until he reached the main lobby. Outside, through the glass entrance doors, he could see the terrorists' minivan and their bodies still lying on the road. Alex watched carefully for several minutes but the street appeared lifeless.

It was getting dark, the sun already dipping below the horizon. Alex was about to step outside when a sharp light washed across the road. A car was approaching. Maybe it's a patrol car, thought Alex. Encouraging though the thought was, he decided to stay put. After the events of the last few hours, Alex had no doubt that his colleagues in uniform would be operating on a hair trigger.

He watched as the lights grew brighter, heard the soft purr of powerful engines. Then they came into view, moving slowly from left to right, a three-car convoy of BMW saloon cars. The windows were down, the occupants all young black men, weapons brandished in their hands. They cruised past slowly, assuredly, and Alex noticed the cars had no registration plates. Stolen then, probably from a dealership.

Music thumped on the air as the convoy cruised slowly past the minivan and the bodies. Brake lights glowed in the mounting darkness. He heard doors open, voices, then laughter as the bodies on the ground were picked over for items of interest. There were maybe a dozen young men gathered on the street now, jeans and T-shirts, pistols jammed into low-hung jeans. Gang-bangers, Alex realised, taking advantage of the chaos.

He stayed where he was, hidden, watching and listening. The laughter was coarse but Alex noticed the men were fully alert, their heads swivelling around the street, hands resting on pistol butts. Whatever had happened out there, there was no one to stop them and they knew it. Worse still, Alex got the impression that if challenged there'd be a fight. He waited a while longer, until the men got bored and moved on to more lucrative pastures.

Eventually Alex ventured out from his hiding place. He stood in the dark, head cocked to one side, listening for the slightest sound. Nothing. He wondered how far the trouble extended, or was it just West London that was suffering? And what about the power cuts? Again, were they just local? He had to find out what was going on.

He climbed the stairs and went back into Kirsty's apartment, peering around the bedroom door. Kirsty was still sleeping, the gunfire outside unable to fully penetrate the double-glazed bedroom window or her pill-induced slumber. He crossed the living room floor, crunching broken glass underfoot, and stood on the balcony, careful to avoid the splintered wooden decking. He looked out across the darkness of the river. Huge flames lit up the area where the plane had hit, the fires still raging unchecked. Even from a distance the devastation seemed enormous. But what he needed to do was to get higher, to see how far the chaos had spread. He had an idea.

On the top floor was a padlocked access door that led up to the roof. A minute later, with the aid of a crowbar from his toolkit, he found himself on top of the building.

Outside, the air carried the tang of burning aviation fuel and a pale moon bathed the darkened suburbs in a silvery glow. He walked towards the edge of the building and stopped, looking east towards the city. A chill ran through his body. As far as Alex could see, the whole of London was blanketed in darkness, lit only by the fires that seemed to rage around the horizon. To the south and west just emptiness, the moonlight glinting off the rooftops as they marched into the distance. Fire and darkness. Closer, he could make out the elevated section of the M4 motorway where vehicles burned unchecked.

The sky over Hammersmith suddenly lit up in a pulse of intense white light, followed by a huge fireball and a shower of sparks. A low rumble reached Alex's ears. Jesus Christ! Another flash lit up the skyline to the east, followed quickly by three more. Seconds later, several dull thunderclaps rumbled around the horizon. Alex felt his legs go weak. In that moment he realised that, for some reason beyond his comprehension, the country had been plunged into war.

Southampton Docks, England

Inside his armoured command vehicle, General Yar Al-Bitruji, commander, invasion forces (Britain), stood over the command console and watched the battlefield information scrolling down the screen. By his side Colonel Farad, his second in command, studied it intently.

'Resistance?'

'Light, disorganised,' Farad explained. 'The chain of command has been broken and their forces are in disarray. Their command communications relay hubs have been captured and shut down or have been destroyed. The same applies to their landline, mobile phone and subsurface networks. Their spy bases at GCHQ and Fylingdales have also been neutralised and major military bases have all been attacked by sleeper teams with a high degree of success. Surprise has been the key and it has worked remarkably well. We have also captured the major radio and television stations at the BBC and various commercial broadcasters. The pre-recorded message is beginning to be transmitted across the country. So far the plan seems to be working.'

The general looked at his subordinate, his eyebrow arched quizzically.

'Of course,' Farad continued quickly, 'there are some rogue units that continue to operate. A troop of tanks has managed to escape from its barracks near the garrison town of Tidworth. They were last seen headed on to the military exercise area on Salisbury Plain. A small number of aircraft also managed to survive and have engaged some of our fighter jets, but their lack of resources and methods of resupply will curb their overall effectiveness.'

'I need a cigarette,' muttered the general in reply.

He swung open the rear door of the multi-wheeled vehicle and jumped down. He reached for a pack of crumpled cigarettes in his trouser pocket and lit one. Two bodyguards fell in behind him as Al-Bitruji strolled past a column of command vehicles parked alongside a warehouse in Southampton's western docks. Fifty metres away, in the darkness of a car park, an anti-aircraft vehicle squatted motionless, only the hum of its electrically powered turret bristling with surface-to-air missiles giving away its position.

Al-Bitruji and his escort climbed a metal staircase that led to a gantry on the roof of the warehouse. From there, he enjoyed an unrestricted view over the dockyards where huge container ships were bathed in the harsh glow of portable arc lights. Hundreds of logistical personnel swarmed all over the dockside, unloading tonnes of equipment and guiding thousands of troops to their designated marshalling points, as cranes swung continuously from ship to shore and back again, their cargo nets bulging with military supplies. Out in the darkness of the Channel, many more ships waited for tugs to guide them into the docks.

What a lovely target this would make, thought Al-Bitruji. Let's hope none of those rogue British fighters decide to take a look along the south coast. The skies around Southampton docks were swept continuously by SAM crews located both on shore and at sea, and it would be a foolhardy pilot indeed that would dare run the gauntlet of a bombing run up the Solent. Still, this was a critical time. A successful air attack now could be disastrous.

Al-Bitruji, along with his battle group, had sailed from Port Said on the Egyptian coast three weeks ago, hidden inside a huge container ship that was now being unloaded a short distance away. From its cavernous hold, thousands of tonnes of military hardware were being delivered to shore before being checked off and mated with waiting crews. As the general watched, attack helicopters were carefully lifted by crane from the hold and lowered gently on to the quayside. Maintenance crews waited nearby to tow them to specially prepared assembly areas, where they would attach the rotor blades and load the magazines before beginning pre-flight checks. The scale of the operation was enormous and Al-Bitruji silently thanked Allah that the docks had been captured so easily, allowing the ships to dock without losses. But how long would it last? He flicked his cigarette over the rail and made his way back to the command vehicle.

'Get me the chief landing officer,' he ordered Farad. Within minutes, a middle-aged man in naval uniform climbed into the back of the mobile command centre. He saluted the general smartly.

'How long before the equipment is unloaded?' Al-Bitruji demanded without preamble. The naval officer's gaze never wavered. Not intimidated by a general, then, he thought to himself. Maybe I'll get an accurate assessment.

'Every berth from here to the Ocean Village Marina is occupied by one of our vessels, General. The ships transporting your spearhead battalions and their equipment are almost unloaded, maybe an hour at the most. There are still twenty-four vessels waiting to berth and dock space is tight, but we should accomplish this in forty-eight hours or less. The ammunition ships are already unloaded and the munitions have been dispersed around the dockyards. However, I recommend that they be moved immediately. We have many more ships en route from the Mediterranean and any damage to the docks would seriously hinder our operations.'

Al-Bitruji nodded in agreement. 'Indeed. The forward units have been issued their ammunition and the rest is being moved to a more secure area on the northern borders of the city as we speak. Have no fear, Commander, your docks will be secure. You are dismissed.' The naval officer snapped another smart salute and left the vehicle. Al-Bitruji turned to Farad. 'Where are the recce units now?'

'Holding station at the junction of a couple of motorways. Early reports indicate that the roads are relatively clear.'

'Send them towards London as planned. Form up the mechanised units and get them moving to their jump off points.' Al-Bitruji's eyes were fixed to the system console and its three-dimensional map of the surrounding area. 'Redeploy these SAM units at my marks. Get those ships unloaded as soon as possible with priority given to any stores required for the helicopters. I want my air assets covering that convoy. And order two security battalions into position and tell them to begin patrols in the surrounding area. I want these docks sown up tighter than an ass's backside.'

The general stepped out of the vehicle and lit another cigarette. Farad joined him a moment later.

'All orders confirmed, General. Spearhead mechanised units are headed towards the motorway jump off points. ETA, ten minutes.'

'Good. Let's get moving.' As he was about to climb back into his command vehicle, the general stopped in his tracks. Farad collided into him.

'General, my apologies, I–'

Al-Bitruji held up his hand for silence. Slowly, he walked a few steps away from the armoured vehicle, his head cocked to one side.

'What is it, General?' Farad whispered.

Then they heard it, the low droning noise that grew in volume, high above their heads. The airborne phase, Al-Bitruji realised, scores of tactical transport aircraft, each one capable of carrying over a hundred fully loaded paratroopers and their equipment. Al-Bitruji saw them then, silhouetted against the moonlit sky, their turboprop engines throbbing gently. The general rubbed his neck. Somewhere up there was his nemesis, streaking ahead of him towards London.

'Get the command vehicle moved up to the outer orbital motorway as soon as possible. If a helicopter becomes available before then, get it to pick us up en route. Let's move.'

'At once, General.'

Farad barked at the operators hunched over their screens inside the command vehicle. Seconds later, Al-Bitruji watched with satisfaction as the long line of armoured vehicles beside the warehouse roared into life in a cloud of grey exhaust fumes. Armoured doors were slammed shut and secured and top hatches clanged open as vehicle commanders waited for the order to move. Farad signalled to the commander of the lead vehicle. The multi-wheeled armoured beast lurched out of line towards him and rocked to a halt a few metres away. The vehicle commander threw up a salute.

'Awaiting your orders, General,' he yelled above the noise.

'We move on London,' Al-Bitruji said, climbing back inside his vehicle. 'At last,' grinned the commander.

The Tunnels

Harry Beecham found himself back in Downing Street. He was in the kitchen sipping a cup of coffee when he heard his wife calling his name. It seemed to be coming from outside in the street. He stood up and walked across to the kitchen window, looking down into the devastated cul-de-sac. To Harry's surprise Anna was there, along with Matt Goodge and her other close-protection officers. David Fuller was there too, and they were all looking up at him, waving. Harry was confused. What did they want? His wife was beckoning silently. She couldn't speak because something black was oozing from her mouth, some kind of disgusting, treacle-like substance that dripped in thick clumps on to her blouse. Then Harry saw something from the corner of his eye. Fire.

A sheet of flame was moving slowly towards the group below him, approaching them from behind. They seemed unaware of the danger, still grinning and waving, Anna still vomiting that strange-looking substance. Harry wanted to warn them, tried to open the window, but he couldn't shift it. He started hammering on the glass and pointing, his shouts becoming louder and louder, but still they waved and smiled. The fire crept closer until it was right behind them and then it stopped. Harry screamed at them to run, but they just carried on waving, oblivious to the danger. Then the fire swept back and rose up like a huge, burning wave. Harry was rooted to the spot, horrified, as the flames hung menacingly over them. The tears coursed down his cheeks and his voice suddenly failed him. All he could do was watch.

Then, the wave of fire crashed down, engulfing the smiling, waving group below.

Harry screamed.

'Prime Minister, wake up!'

Harry sat bolt upright on the sofa, his shirt bathed in sweat and a blanket tossed to one side. It took him several seconds to realise where he was.

Brigadier Forsythe took a step back. 'Are you alright?'

Harry retrieved a handkerchief from his trouser pocket and shakily dabbed his sweat-soaked face. 'Yes. Just give me a minute.'

Forsythe filled a plastic cup from a nearby water cooler and offered it to Harry, who gulped it down greedily.

'Are you sure you're okay, Prime Minister?'

'I'm fine,' Harry snapped. 'Just a bad dream. It's nothing,' he lied. He pushed himself off the sofa and stood, rubbing his face. 'God, I could use a shower.'

'Well, I think we can accommodate you there,' replied the brigadier. Harry wasn't surprised.

When he'd crawled through the false panel in the generator room, Harry envisaged scrambling through small, dark tunnels for the next few hours. He couldn't have been more wrong. He'd found himself standing on a steel gantry looking down upon a large cavern, the concrete floor a good forty feet below him. Above his head, halogen lights hanging from the ceiling illuminated the small-gauge railway tracks that disappeared into the blackness of two wide tunnels in the far wall. An underground railway station, directly beneath Downing Street! Harry was astounded.

He continued down the steel staircase, his footsteps echoing around the concrete walls, Forsythe and his SAS team following on behind. The tunnels were lit by small green lights recessed into the smooth walls and seemed to head off in different directions. Harry wondered where they went. He turned around. Several rooms had been cut into the face of the cavern, the largest of which boasted a glass wall that looked out over the small platforms. To his right, Harry noticed a corridor that led off somewhere else and he counted several doors along its length. Yet, despite the tunnels, the tracks and the small platforms, there were no trains to be seen.

'Well, Harry, what do you think?' Forsythe and his men were all looking at him, sizing up his reaction. Harry began to say something but words failed him. 'Impressive, isn't it? I was pretty speechless when I first saw it, too. Hard to imagine that this sort of thing could be built in secret without anyone upstairs knowing about it. But there you have it. This way please, Harry.'

Forsythe led them into the large glass-fronted room, which turned out to be a high-tech control centre. There were numerous display panels on the surrounding walls and a small bank of consoles with several swivel chairs in front of them. Forsythe turned to Gibson.

'Comms, please Mike. Quick as you can.'

Gibson nodded and left the room, while Nasser and Brooks moved off to make a quick recce of the cavern and tunnel entrances. Harry watched them go.

'What the hell is this place?'

Forsythe rolled a chair across to Harry. 'It's an emergency transport system, for use by the prime minister, his cabinet and members of the royal family. It was built in secret over many years using state-of-the-art tunnelling techniques. Above top secret, all this.'

Harry was suitably impressed. 'Where do the tracks lead?'

Forsythe pointed through the glass to the tunnels across the cavern. 'The left-hand line turns due west and runs beneath Buckingham Palace. There's a smaller platform facility there, located directly under the rear gardens. From the palace the tunnel turns north-east, where it terminates in Kensington Gardens. Access to ground level there is via a staircase leading to a seemingly disused but very secure Royal Parks police office. From there, you have quick and easy access to the M4 and M40 motorways and there's also a designated area close by for helicopter landings.'

'Is that the plan, Giles? Leave London by helicopter?'

Forsythe leaned forward in his chair. 'If this is an all-out shooting war, then we need to get you out of the city, to the emergency control facility at Alternate One in the West Country.'

'How do we get there?' asked Harry.

'There are two options. One, we take the left-hand tunnel, travelling beneath the palace and rendezvousing with a helicopter in Kensington Gardens, which will fly us out under cover of darkness. Or two, we take the other tunnel to Mill Hill in North London. That one terminates inside a nondescript Ministry of Defence storage depot. From there it's a short drive to Northolt, then air transport to Alternate One.'

Harry glanced towards the dark tunnels, their curved walls washed in a pale blue light. At least they would be protected from the horrors on the surface.

'Where's the power coming from?'

'Direct spur into Dungeness Nuclear Power Station. The actual amount of electricity drawn is very small, so we don't even register on the main grid.'

'What about communications?'

'Good point,' replied Forsythe. 'Let's see if Mike's had any luck.'

The brigadier led the way through a glass door into the adjacent comms room. Here, several telephones and computers were arranged on a central table along with two military-spec radios. Mike Gibson, headphones on, was listening to one intently while stepping slowly through the airwaves. Across the table, Brooks and Nasser had returned from their patrol and were thumbing through directories and punching telephone numbers. Gibson looked up as Forsythe entered.

'Anything, Mike?'

The sergeant shook his head. 'Can't raise anybody, Boss. Evac teams are not answering, there's no acknowledgement from Mill Hill and I can't raise any air assets at Northolt at all. Alternate One is also off the air. It's like the whole network's down. I'm running through all the frequencies now, both civilian and military.'

Forsythe looked over at Brooks, who shook his head. 'I've tried every number in the emergency directory. Nothing.'

'Keep trying,' urged Forsythe. He turned to Harry. 'If we can't raise anyone then we have zero chance of getting you out of here using the pre-planned procedures. Can't call up a chopper, you see. It also means that no one knows you're alive and that could have its own consequences. Who takes over in the event of your incapacitation?'

'Deputy PM,' explained Harry. 'If not him, then the Home Secretary. If that's not an option, then the Foreign Secretary.'

'All of whom could be dead,' Forsythe speculated. 'I'd feel far more confident if people knew you were alive. The civilian population will be panicked, frightened. They'll need reassurance and the only way to do that is to get you on the air. Alternate One is still our best option I think, so we have to try and get you there. In the meantime, you should make use of the facilities while we try to establish communications. Come, let me show you.'

A few minutes later, Harry was sitting at a small table nursing a hot cup of tea. The kitchen was small but it had fresh running water, cooking facilities and boxes of canned and dried goods stacked high along one wall. Forsythe was eating something from a tin that looked decidedly unsavoury to Harry.

'It's going to take a while to power up the train and run through the checklists,' he said. 'Then we can get moving.'

'Don't let me keep you, Giles.'

'There's a rest room next door, with a sofa. Why don't you sit down for a while, try and relax? It could be a while before we're ready to move and you'll need the energy when we do. Things could get rough.'

'Good idea,' said Harry, getting to his feet. 'Call me if you hear anything.'

'Of course.'

Harry wandered into the rest room and slumped on to the sofa. What had caused all this? Was the country really at war? Or was it a series of terrorist attacks? If so, why and by whom? The heat of the room leaked into his limbs and Harry's eyelids began to droop. He felt absolutely drained, the adrenaline that had coursed through his body for the last few hours taking its toll. He tried to fight his drooping eyelids and failed.

In the darkness of sleep, Anna haunted his dreams.

The radio hissed and crackled, then a cold voice echoed around the room.

'Your attention, please. This is a public safety message broadcasting on all frequencies. Due to the ongoing emergency, members of the public are advised to remain in their homes. Martial law is now in effect and all public services, including transport networks, have been temporarily suspended. I repeat, all civilians are to remain in their homes or alternative places of shelter. Stay tuned to this station for further information. This ends this public safety message.'

'Jesus, it's really happening,' whispered Forsythe.

Harry let the shower jets wash away the last vestiges of tiredness. The nightmare had been a bad one, but nightmares happen and he'd just lost is wife. All perfectly natural, he tried to reassure himself.

He turned off the water and towelled himself dry. Forsythe had left some fresh clothes for him, scrounged from a storeroom packed with military supplies and equipment. Harry wasn't sure that baggy black trousers and a combat jacket were particularly fitting for a prime minister, but they were an improvement on his shredded suit and bloodied shirt.

Freshly attired, he made his way out into the main cavern. Through the glass of the comms room, Harry could see Forsythe, Nasser and Brooks gathered around Mike Gibson. He saw Mike's mouth move, speaking into the wrap-around microphone that framed his jaw. They'd made contact, thank God. He walked quickly into the room. Forsythe looked up and raised his hand for silence.

'Roger that, Alpha Two-Zero-Niner. Next transmission in three-zero minutes. Out.' Gibson slipped the headphones off.

'What's going on?' asked Harry.

'Alternate One is up and running,' Forsythe explained. 'Due to signal jamming they've been transmitting on one of the more obscure UHF bands in the higher ranges. They're changing frequencies every half hour. We've got the pattern.'

'That's excellent news.'

'There's more,' the brigadier continued ominously. 'Mike found something else, on the civilian network. It's still transmitting. Mike?' Gibson flipped a switch and held the headphones out to Harry, who clamped them over his ears. At first, all he could hear was the hiss of empty ether.

'Your attention, please. This is a public safety message...'

Harry stood tight-lipped as the broadcast finished. He slipped off the headset. 'Who the hell is it?' he asked incredulously.

'No idea,' Forsythe shrugged. 'It's on every civilian frequency. Anybody with a working radio out there will hear it.'

'If we're not broadcasting it, then who is?'

Forsythe folded his arms, a deep frown creasing his forehead.

'Sounds like an attempt at a power grab.'

'A coup,' Harry breathed.

'Sounds incredible I know, but to all intents and purposes that's a government-sanctioned message. The word will spread quickly. People will believe control is being restored. From an enemy perspective, it keeps casualties down and makes it easier for their troops to move around without columns of potential refugees blocking the roads.'

'For God's sake Giles, you make it sound as if we are being invaded.' Harry's voice cut short. He suddenly realised that Forsythe was describing exactly that.

'Alternate One have filled in a few blanks. At approximately eighteen hundred hours GMT, they started registering comms failures at our Joint Services nodes–'

'English, please Giles.'

'That means the military network started to fail. Satellite comms, telephones, computers – everything. Before it failed, operators managed to record a series of garbled messages that began swamping the networks. The reports told of armed men taking control of buildings, shootings outside various military establishments, a truck bomb at an army base in Colchester and numerous other incidents. One by one, all of our major military bases started dropping off the air. Same for the police, but not before they received a deluge of incident reports; bombings and shootings across the country, attacks on dockyards on the south coast and even reports of two airliner crashes, one in West London and one near Tottenham Court Road. It would also appear that many essential services have been hit. Water supplies have been cut, along with gas and electricity across most of England and Wales, and the civil emergency services are no longer functioning. It's a planned strike, Harry, without any doubt. A series of co-ordinated attacks designed to cripple our military and police forces and keep the civilian population out of the picture.'

Harry sat down heavily in a chair, the information bearing down on him like a physical weight. 'Jesus Christ.'

'Alternate One believes it can only mean one thing.'

For the first time since hostilities had begun, Harry thought he detected the tiniest note of despair in the brigadier's voice.

'They think that these are the opening moves of a full-scale military invasion.'

'Arabia,' said Harry.

'Correct.'

Why on earth would Arabia want to initiate a war against Britain? Relations had been good over the last decade. Granted, they were never cosy, but there was a mutual respect there. Besides, there were over eight million Muslims in England and Wales. That was nearly fourteen per cent of the population. Surely that bought the government some leverage with the Holy State? And Geoffrey Cooper – he'd made good progress with their diplomats, had been their guest several times both at the Arabian embassy and out in Arabia itself. Things had been going so well. If the slightest hint of trouble had been brewing he would have known about it. And their military build-up. Surely that would have been noticed? Harry found it hard to believe, but this wasn't the time for an in-depth analysis.

'Who's in charge at Alternate One?' he asked.

'Major General Julian Bashford is co-ordinating the Joint Services' response. There are several other key personnel, plus one or two of your ministers who were ferried there by helicopter. The surrounding area is secure and under heavy guard and they've had no trouble to deal with as yet, although I suspect that'll change. The intelligence types have been sifting through what little information there is available, but they believe that the main threat appears to be from the south-east of the country. They're ordering any military units that are still operating to head to the West of England or north to Scotland, whichever's closest; but they have to broadcast that message using Morse and clear speech. It looks like the general is shortening his defence line, which doesn't bode well for the rest of the country.'

No, it bloody well doesn't, echoed Harry silently. He tried to focus on the positives. At least there was a functioning command and control centre manned by experienced personnel.

'What happens to us? How do we get to Alternate One?' he asked.

'Well, Northolt airfield is out of the question. We've been advised to take the train into Kensington Gardens. Once there, we're to make radio contact again. Our priority now is to get out of Whitehall. Mike?'

'Boss?'

'Let's get that train down here ASAP.'

Assault

They approached from the west at just over four hundred kilometres per hour. Eighty kilometres from their target, they descended from two thousand metres to level off at one hundred and fifty, quickly reducing their airspeed.

In the lead aircraft, the jumpmaster, listening intently to the instructions crackling inside his headset, gave the thumbs up signal to an airborne forces officer, who barked a command. The airborne troops, laden with heavy battle-order equipment and bulky parachutes, struggled to their feet. They were glad to be finally up and moving after a flight of nearly six hours. Their journey was almost at an end and no paratrooper enjoyed waiting inside a fat, heavy transport plane in a combat zone. They stretched their limbs to get the circulation going and carried out final equipment checks.

The night air whistled around the cargo bay as the huge tailgate of the A400 transport plane was lowered on hydraulic arms and locked into its jump position. Below them, the ground passed quickly under the silver light of a new moon. This was when the aircraft was at its most vulnerable. Although the pilots had been informed enemy air activity was negligible, they had also been advised to stay alert. There were rogue fighters still out there, looking for targets. On the ground, forward air controllers reported empty skies above the drop zones, but the pilots sweated in their green jumpsuits anyway. They'd rehearsed this mission many times, both in simulators and in actual field exercises, but the real thing was always different.

There were ten aircraft in all, flying in two sticks of five planes just under a mile apart, carrying a mixture of paratroopers, light armoured vehicles and jeeps. There were hundreds of other aircraft in the sky that night, all heading towards their various targets across southern England and the Midlands. Their job was to secure and protect the airfields, clear the runways and bring the rest of the invasion force in along safe air corridors, guided in by FACs in captured air traffic control centres.

At eight kilometres to target the paratroopers shuffled forward, dragging their parachute harness hooks along thick static lines secured to the aircraft's fuselage. They watched for the green indicator light, their eyes occasionally flicking to the ground rushing below them. If death waited for them down there, then so be it. They were ready.

Behind them, aircrews rigged pallets and checked running rails, ensuring that vehicles, supplies and munitions would be deployed safely and correctly behind the disembarking troops.

Over the drop zones, pilots activated green lights. One by one, the paratroopers stepped off the ramp and were plucked away into the night sky. When the last man had jumped, the equipment pallets were shoved off by tethered aircrews. As each plane disgorged its load, the pilots applied full power and climbed for altitude, turning on a southerly heading for the coast.

At Heathrow Airport, on the outskirts of West London, hundreds of paratroopers floated to the ground. They released their harnesses and quickly formed into units, racing for their prearranged rendezvous points. Each unit had a specific objective and the paratroopers achieved them with quiet, determined professionalism. Within thirty minutes of the first landings, all five terminal buildings at Heathrow had been secured. Elsewhere, the airports of Gatwick, Stansted, Luton, and Birmingham were also captured without major incident and their main runways swept by combat engineers of the Arabian airborne forces. The path was now clear for the main invasion force and, within minutes of the confirmation order, transport planes and their fighter escorts began to lift off from military bases all across the Arabian Peninsula.

There were four other planes in the sky that night, on a wholly different mission. These aircraft flew north-eastwards across southern England, each carrying a detachment of specialist Pathfinder airborne forces. Over the darkened suburbs of London, the four transport aircraft swept in low towards their target. They approached from the west, their path lit by the fires that raged across the city skyline. Inside the aircraft were the elite of the Arabian airborne units, four hundred men specially chosen for this most important of missions. Even the aircrews were hand-picked, the most skilful and competent pilots, navigational experts and jumpmasters in the Arabian Air Force. The pilots scanned their instruments as they jinked their aircraft up and down, left and right to avoid the blaze of light and updraughts from the fires below.

The timing had to be right. It was to be an extremely low-altitude opening for the paratroopers, only sixty metres, using a recently developed low-deployment system. Each soldier had trained continuously for the last three months, the aircrews even longer. Precision flying was called for and, with it, no small amount of courage.

Their drop zone was The Mall, the wide, tree-lined avenue that ran from the front gates of Buckingham Palace to Admiralty Arch at Trafalgar Square, a ceremonial route used by British royalty for the last two centuries. Just under a couple of kilometres long and thirty metres wide, it was going to be very tight, but the men were well trained and the mission was an important one. The risk was acceptable.

With four kilometres to go, the planes bounced up and down in the roiled air over South Kensington and then banked left to avoid a huge fire close to Victoria Station. The pilots lined up on their target and pulled back on their throttles as, one by one, the transport planes roared over the roof of Buckingham Palace, The Mall directly below them. In the cargo bay of each transport, a green light blinked on. The planes disgorged their troops then clawed for height, thundering out over Admiralty Arch towards the Embankment and the River Thames.

He was first out of the lead aircraft, as he should be. His chute deployed perfectly and its layered ram air configuration stopped his rapid decent towards the ground below with a few metres to spare. He stepped lightly on to the tarmac and unhooked his harness, racing towards the cover of St James's Park. In less than a minute, all four hundred of his men had made it to the ground and were moving swiftly through the shadows towards Horse Guards Parade. All that remained of their passage was the faint hum of the departing transports and the soft rustle of hundreds of discarded parachutes, as a gentle night breeze swept along the deserted Mall.

Squadron Leader Robert Howarth searched desperately for a target for his final AIM-120 advanced medium-range air-to-air missile, slung under the port wing of his F/A-18E Hornet fighter jet. He'd got one kill already, an enemy fighter that had blown his wingman out of the sky before either aircraft had a chance to react. What had started out as a standard training mission over the Thames Estuary had turned into a fight that had already claimed the lives of most of his squadron and half of his ground crew at RAF Mildenhall in the eastern county of Suffolk.

The attack had started at six o'clock that evening, when a car bomb had been driven through the gates and detonated. After that, three or four vanloads of armed men had entered the base and attacked the buildings and personnel with automatic weapons and grenades. Luckily, a company of RAF Regiment soldiers had been queuing up outside the base armoury after returning from a live fire exercise at the Thetford Forest training area. The soldiers were quickly issued with fresh ammunition and deployed to counter the threat. They succeeded, but not before many of the squadron's planes were destroyed and most of the Royal Air Force ground crew killed. The base had been saved but it had been touch and go for a while. Howarth had been one of the lucky ones.

The squadron leader banked his plane, bringing the nose around to head due south over London. It was a surreal sight. From the air, the city normally shimmered like a carpet of a billion lights. Now only darkness lay before him, punctuated by hundreds of fires below and a moon above that ducked in and out of some high-level cloud. Howarth thought the scene reminiscent of the German air raids on London during the Second World War. He cruised at an altitude of four hundred feet, his air-search radar shut down to avoid announcing his presence to enemy fighters. Only his threat receiver was fully active and this was his third pass over London without a target. And Howarth desperately wanted a target.

About an hour ago, a call sign had responded to his repeated transmissions and given him a quick brief of the military situation; all British units had been ordered to disengage and regroup either north of the border in Scotland or west beyond Salisbury Plain. After confirmation of the transmission, Howarth had declared his presence, indicating his rough position and fuel state. He was ordered north to Scotland, but not before he carried out another mission. Using his on-board systems, he was tasked to fly to London with strict instructions. Gauge enemy strength and air assets, check for ground forces, major structural damage, enemy movements, then head back to Mildenhall. The base was being wound down and everything useful that couldn't be moved was to be destroyed. Howarth was to refuel there and then head north. The remaining troops and ground crew would be leaving in a blacked-out convoy at twenty-three hundred hours.

As he approached the centre of London, Howarth visually scanned the ground ahead. He was flying in a south-easterly direction, four hundred feet above the Edgware Road. Below and slightly to his right lay Paddington Green Police Station. Or what was left of it. Fires raged on every floor and, down on the ground, Howarth could see a huge mob surging beneath the A40 overpass. The darkness of Hyde Park slipped under the nose of his fighter as Howarth mentally mapped out his route. Head for the Whitehall area, check for distress signals, flares, anything that may indicate that there were high-level military or civilian survivors down there, then follow the River Thames east to Tilbury, turning north-eastwards back to Mildenhall. Straightforward enough, but he certainly wouldn't feel safe until his wheels hit the runway of a secure air base... Bingo! Three – no, four – targets had suddenly appeared a mile in front of him. Howarth could see that they were slow-moving transport aircraft climbing for altitude, and their IFF transponders identified them as distinctly unfriendly. Howarth lit up the lead aircraft with his search radar and thumbed the launch button of his one remaining missile. It would be an easy kill.

Inside the lead troop transport, the pilot was reflecting on the success of the parachute drop on The Mall when his co-pilot shouted in alarm. The cockpit threat receiver was indicating that their aircraft had suddenly been illuminated by an enemy aircraft. Behind him, the other three aircraft in the formation also detected the powerful emissions and began to fire off chaff pods. The huge cloud of tiny aluminium strips would surely confuse any incoming missile. If one had been fired.

Howarth swore in frustration as his computer display registered a launch failure on his missile. He advanced his throttles and chased the slow-moving transport planes, arming his twenty-millimetre cannon. They were in a nice, tight formation. Perfect.

Carter Whitman was losing the battle to keep his wife calm. For over three hours they'd been trapped inside a Perspex capsule high over the River Thames and she was slowly coming apart. Carter hadn't wanted to go on the London Eye, but his wife had promised to send the folks back home her goddam digital movies, live and uncut. Of course, she didn't stop to think that people in the States would have to drop everything in the middle of a workday to watch her stream her footage over the Internet, but that didn't worry her, no sir. And good ole Carter would be there too, smiling like a dummy for the camera and waving hi to her supersize clan back in South Carolina.

Hours earlier, Carter and his wife had queued up with the rest of the tourist sheep, paid for their exorbitantly priced tickets and boarded the rusting, thirty-year-old attraction, squeezing into a stuffy plastic bubble that creaked and groaned its way to the top. Goddam Brits. Couldn't build a case of haemorrhoids worth a damn. Not that Carter disliked England. In fact, he loved all the castles and old buildings, the sheer goddam history of the place. He'd made the trip over the Atlantic many times on business, but now he was retired he thought he'd seen the last of London. But oh no, his dear wife had dragged him over the Atlantic for one final holiday, and that was the reason for his mounting anger and frustration. Because Carter Whitman knew he'd never see home again.

When the capsule had shuddered to a halt, he hadn't been unduly worried. As a regular visitor to Britain, Whitman was used to the dirty streets, the dilapidated and potholed roads and the decaying and overcrowded public transport systems that would be considered a disgrace in the Third World. And he was almost used to the rude and aggressive people and a customer service ethic that was so bad, Whitman imagined he was trapped inside a giant theme park dedicated to indifferent attitudes and bad manners. And no asshole seemed to speak English any more.

So the rusting, iron ring had popped a cog, so what? Being England, it would probably take some jerk-off an hour just to attend the call. He'd looked down at the ground where a crowd had gathered and several of the lower capsules were being evacuated. Of all the goddam luck. Couldn't have crapped out when their shitty capsule was near the bottom. Oh no, had to be here, right at the fucking summit, four hundred and fifty feet above the goddam river. He forced a grin at his worried wife and contemplated a couple of hours in a packed, sweaty capsule overlooking the dirtiest, most expensive capital city in the Western world. Shit.

But then came the explosions. They'd seen some, like the one that detonated somewhere along Whitehall across the river. Whitman had watched in horror as the explosion sent tiles, bricks and other debris spiralling into the air above the rooftops. The detonation had rattled the wheel and people had begun to scream. They'd seen the flames reach high into the sky all around them. Whitman had heard the volleys of automatic fire too. That was some serious shit. Occasionally smoke drifted across the canopy, obscuring their vision. Then night fell and panic swirled around the packed pod. Nobody had come to their aid. No cops, no fire department, nothing. It was anarchy out there.

Whitman slipped a comforting arm around his wife and held her tight.

'Enemy aircraft! Seven o'clock.'

The flight leader was about to issue evasive manoeuvre orders to the other aircraft when two hundred rounds of explosive ammunition ripped through the skin of the fuselage and detonated around the cockpit. With both pilots dead and its controls shattered, the huge transport aircraft lurched to the left, losing height rapidly. Behind it, the pilot of the second aircraft flinched as the laser-like tracer rounds appeared from nowhere, shredding the plane in front of him. He also banked to the left. That was his first mistake. His second was to increase power as he craned his neck and scanned the night sky over his port wing. As the lead plane stalled, the pilot of the second aircraft accelerated through its tail fin, destroying his cockpit on the starboard side. The lead A400 military transport, its tail disintegrated, nosedived towards the huge steel wheel below.

Whitman heard the thunderous ripping sound and saw the tracers flying over their heads. The capsule rocked as people finally gave way to their panic, screaming and pushing in sheer terror. He saw the sparks and flames in the sky above them. In the blackness he heard the roar of aircraft engines and the sound of screaming metal. He watched with mounting horror as a huge, burning aircraft loomed out of the darkness and headed straight for their capsule.

Whitman held his sobbing wife tight and chastised himself for his feelings of anger. The plain truth was, he loved her deeply, always had done, from the moment they had met. He was angry because fate had decreed that their lives would end in a dirty, piss-stained plastic box rather than in their beachside home in Santa Barbara that they both loved so much.

Carter Whitman squeezed his eyes shut and kissed his wife gently on the cheek. His last thought was of the cool, blue waters of the Pacific Ocean.

Squadron Leader Howarth watched in horror as the aircraft crashed into the London Eye, its turbofan propeller blades scything through several of the uppermost observation capsules. The remaining wreckage deflected off the top rim and hurtled to the ground, severing the steel backstay cables and exploding in a massive fireball. A huge sheet of flame blossomed around the giant A-frame supports, engulfing the London Eye in thick smoke. Jesus Christ, he hoped there weren't people down there. Howarth banked his fighter around. One down, one severely damaged, two to go. The remaining transports had broken right and headed south on full power, screaming for fighter support.

Howarth closed the distance, the targets bright in his head up display. Just as he was about to squeeze the trigger, he stopped. If he fired now, he could send both planes crashing into residential areas south of the river. He could kill hundreds, not just the aircrews in the transports. He slipped his fighter to the left and fired a short burst after the planes, the tracer rounds zipping a bare hundred feet past the port wing of the nearest transport. Howarth smiled grimly. The sight alone should make the bastards think twice about venturing over the capital. He brought the fighter around and headed back up the Thames towards the city. There was still a wounded transport out there.

He thought it was an optical illusion at first, so he pulled a tight turn above Vauxhall Embankment and came around again. It was no mistake. Howarth's blood ran cold. The London Eye, burned and twisted with half its capsules shattered or missing, swayed drunkenly on its massive steel feet. And there were people in there, too. Howarth could see scores of pale faces pressed up against the Perspex of several capsules. As he watched with mounting horror, a capsule near the top swung free from one of its retaining rings and crashed against the steel framework, pitching its occupants through the broken Perspex. Some hit the water far below, while others cannoned off the structure and disappeared into the flames. But the destruction wasn't over.

The London Eye had stood on the south bank of the Thames for nearly thirty years. In that time, the river had ebbed and flowed and seeped through the walls of the riverbank, soaking into the deep foundation piles. Far below the embankment pavement, the compression foundation was slowly being reclaimed by the murky waters of the Thames. In time, the whole structure would have become unstable and the attraction itself unsafe. The arrival of seventy-nine tonnes of free-falling military transport aircraft just speeded up the process. The few remaining backstay cables sheared away from the structure and, for a few moments, the huge wheel just stood there, swaying ever so slightly.

Underground, the twin factors of water erosion and the impact of the aircraft combined to fracture several piles at once. Without its retaining cables a pendulum effect quickly ensued, as the Eye swayed back and forth in the darkness. Seconds later, the huge retaining bolts broke free from their crumbling concrete housings and sent nearly two thousand tonnes of steel toppling into the dark waters of the Thames.

'For the love of Allah, pull up!'

The pilot of the second transport gripped the control yoke with all his might, fighting the dying plane around him. When he'd punched through the tail of his flight leader's plane he'd automatically increased power and tried to gain height, activating the fire suppression systems as alarm buzzers screamed inside what was left of the cockpit. The co-pilot was gone, along with his seat and a whole swathe of instruments. Sparks fizzed and spat from severed power cables and his own instruments were covered in a thin film of hydraulic fluid.

He banked the plane around, desperately trying to gain height. He only needed a hundred metres or so, just enough to bail out. Of course, that meant trying to keep the plane level while he tried to extract the chute from under his seat and put it on, but he'd deal with that when he had height and airspeed. He realised he had only a few seconds before the aircraft failed completely.

He was headed due east now, right over the Thames. Two of the plane's engines began to cough and splutter. He eased back on the yoke, the wind screaming around him. Ahead, the twin columns of Tower Bridge were silhouetted against the night sky.

Half a mile behind, Howarth had the transport plane neatly bracketed in the gunsights of his F/A-18. He could see that the plane was damaged, thin plumes of white smoke trailing from both starboard engines. He'd wait until it had cleared the city before firing. The plane would hit the river and, with any luck, the only casualties would be a few fish.

The transport plane was losing height fast. The pilot couldn't lose any more airspeed for fear of stalling so, with one hand on the yoke, he reached for his parachute. He had a plan of sorts. Slip the chute on, pull the plane up as high as possible and jump through the gaping hole where his co-pilot once sat. Not the best of plans, but the plane was on its last legs. He glanced at his altimeter. It spun crazily around the dial, first one way and then the other. Useless. He'd have to get a visual reference. The canopy in front of him was cracked like a spider's web and the window to his side was covered in hydraulic fluid. He had to hurry. He could feel the nose of the aircraft dipping rapidly. There was a fire to the south-east, but it was too far away to give him any idea of how high he actually was...

'Jesus!' Howarth cried. The transport plane in front of him disintegrated in a ball of flame as it struck the northern column of Tower Bridge. The tower itself crumbled, sending hundreds of tonnes of Portland stone crashing on to the roadway below. It was too much to bear. The road bridge arches gave way, twisting and falling into the river below. The southern tower, now fatally weakened by the loss of its sister, wrenched itself free and fell forward on top of the already submerged wreckage of the road, the collapse causing a huge wave to wash over the riverbanks along the Thames.

In the space of a few minutes, two of London's most famous landmarks had ceased to exist.

Squadron Leader Howarth advanced his throttles and turned north-east for Mildenhall. He was tired, completely drained. The adrenaline of combat had sapped his energy. Not only that, he'd also witnessed awful destruction across the capital and the subsequent loss of life. He knew the images would haunt him for the rest of his days.

He glanced out of his cockpit at the dark earth below. His thoughts turned to the people down there, on the ground. What must they be feeling? Fear, of course; panic, uncertainty... and pain. He didn't even want to think about casualties. As his aircraft skimmed low over the Essex border, Howarth resigned himself to the fact that his country was at war and he had no idea why. All he knew was that many people had died today. He had no clue as to what the future held or even if he'd make it through the night. But if he survived the trip to Scotland, and if there was a decent airbase with a well-supplied armoury, and if there were spares for his F/A-18...

If; the biggest word in the dictionary. But if all those things came to pass, well, he'd try and even up the odds for the people down there.

The paratroopers had assembled quickly into their designated units and fanned out across the shadows of St James's Park. Each unit had its own objective. Several moved east towards Horse Guards Parade. Their job was to secure the northern end of Whitehall and for that task they were armed with anti-tank weapons, mortars and heavy machine guns. Another unit did the same at the southern end, taking up position at the junction of Parliament Square. A short distance away another small detachment, laden with specialist equipment, stayed out of sight in the darkness.

From the leafy fringes of the park, the main assault force sprinted across Horse Guards Road and ran up the wide, stone staircase into King Charles Street. They formed into two columns, each moving quickly up either side of the street, leaping over the broken timbers and rubble that littered the road. Above their heads, fires had taken hold in both the Treasury and Foreign Office buildings. The flames bathed the area in an orange glow, sending showers of sparks and burning embers drifting down on the night air.

At the junction with Whitehall, one column sprinted across the road and took up defensive positions along the wide avenue. The other column of paratroopers turned left, scrambling quickly through the deep bomb crater that marked the entrance to Downing Street. Without pausing, they picked their way quickly through the rubble and raced towards the most famous front door in the world, now scorched, splintered and hanging from a single brass hinge.

The assault team discharged several flash bang grenades into the entrance and adjoining rooms and followed them in, weapons raised, trigger fingers poised. Moments later, the ground floor was pronounced clear. More assault teams hurried inside and began clearing the remainder of the building floor by floor. After several minutes, the all-clear signal was given.

From the darkness of the park, the small detachment of paratroopers waiting under the tree canopy made their way quickly into Downing Street. Striding purposefully through the entrance to Number Ten, a dozen or so figures, some laden with black, shockproof cases, walked briskly into the reception hall, where other paratroopers were already clearing rubble and broken furnishings from the floors under the pale glow of temporary lamps. Above them, the muted roar of fire extinguishers could be heard as more personnel tackled the flames on the upper floors. As they filed into the reception hall, the leader of the group stopped abruptly.

He gazed around the once-grand house that had received and entertained world leaders for over two hundred years. And now here it was, scorched and wrecked beyond recognition. A pity. He would have liked to have seen it in all its glory. Still, no matter, there was work to be done.

General Faris Mousa continued into the Cabinet Room along with his command group personnel. The famous cabinet table was swept clear of debris as Mousa's staff immediately began cracking open their foam-lined cases and setting up their communications equipment. A captain approached.

'General Mousa, we've found a body.'

'Is it Beecham?'

'No, General.'

'Where is this body?'

'Rear of the building, sir.'

'Show me.'

The two men made their way out into the garden. Other airborne troops were already out there, sweeping the grounds and establishing a security perimeter. The body was lying near the rear wall, a grey blanket draped over the still form. General Mousa squatted down and pulled back a corner to reveal a waxen corpse. He looked up at the captain, who was flipping through a sheaf of index cards. After a moment he handed one over.

'I believe it's this man, General.'

Mousa studied the picture on the card and compared it to the face lying at his feet. 'David Fuller, director of communications. Have the body removed but kept separate from other casualties.'

'Yes, sir.'

Mousa returned to the Cabinet Room, already a hive of activity. Cables snaked their way around the floor and electronic data flowed across several screens that had been quickly set up by their operators, who now sat around the cabinet table, headphones clamped to their ears as they digested the information on the monitors before them.

'Status report, Major Karroubi.'

A short but very broad-shouldered major limped heavily across the room. 'Voice communications are up and running. Battlefield command system is online and we are active on the divisional network. We've uploaded our initial mission report and status. We have received verification from General Al-Bitruji and from High Command. Both await our next update.'

'Our troops?'

'Whitehall is sealed at both ends and we are about to send in the assault teams to clear and secure the various buildings along Whitehall.

The Treasury building and Foreign Office are both on fire and have sustained heavy damage. The Ministry of Defence across the street will be dealt with last. Our spotters report movement on several floors there. I thought it prudent to secure the rest of Whitehall before sending in a probing team.'

'Good. The surrounding area?'

'I have ordered four teams of recce troops to observe and report anything in the vicinity of our location. Our sleeper teams have successfully quashed all local threats and we have taken many prisoners.'

'Reinforcements?'

'Travelling towards London as we speak. The security battalion assigned to Whitehall should arrive within two to three hours. Reports indicate that resistance has been light across the country.'

'Allah preserve us, that was close!'

Both General Al-Bitruji and Colonel Farad brushed the dirt off their clothes as they surveyed the burning wreckage of their command vehicle from the relative safety of a drainage ditch beside the M3 motorway.

The British Apache attack helicopter had appeared from nowhere and managed to loose off a couple of missiles before anyone had had a chance to react. Their driver had swerved to avoid the armoured vehicle in front of them, which had taken a direct hit, but they'd clipped the rear of the burning vehicle and spun to the left, crashing into another vehicle travelling parallel to them. The second missile screamed out of the darkness and roared over their heads, hitting a troop truck and sending it spinning into the air. Instinctively, their driver had slammed on the brakes. Behind them, scores of other military vehicles began to swerve and brake to avoid the carnage ahead.

Al-Bitruji had seen the danger and grabbed Colonel Farad by the collar, dragging him out of the rear door before his subordinate knew what was happening. They made it to the ditch, just in time to see a white-hot stream of twenty-millimetre explosive rounds cut through the armoured skin of their command vehicle. Several rounds found the fuel tank and the resulting explosion destroyed another two vehicles and several more personnel. The rounds continued to chew up the column of vehicles and then stopped abruptly.

Al-Bitruji saw the dark silhouette of the attack helicopter as it hovered above the road two hundred metres ahead of them. It swivelled under its rotor blades and banked away, roaring up a wide firebreak cut amongst a forest of pine trees that flanked the motorway. A single SAM missile flew wildly above the trees in its wake.

'What the devil happened?' asked Farad as both men scrambled back on to the road.

'Panic. That's what happened. This is the first time many of our troops have been under fire,' replied Al-Bitruji, trying hard to control the tremor in his own voice.

'The infidel could have inflicted far more damage than he did. Why did he break off the attack?'

The general had been asking himself the same question. Their massive convoy had started off well but, as the distance to London dwindled, so the vehicles had begun to bunch up. It must have been a target-rich environment for the Apache pilot. He could have fired more missiles or used his cannon to far greater effect, but he'd broken off the attack and made good his escape. Maybe it wasn't an organised ambush. Maybe the helicopter had run into the convoy by chance. Maybe he was low on fuel or ordnance. And maybe he would be back.

'Never mind, we need to get the convoy moving again. And where the devil are our own helicopters?'

'Still being assembled in Southampton,' Farad explained. 'It seems that there has been a problem with the rotor couplings on the first batch that has kept them grounded. They should be in the air within two hours.'

'Always the details,' Al-Bitruji muttered under his breath. 'Get on to the air force,' he barked. 'Tell them we require air cover for this convoy. We may not be so lucky next time.'

'Yes, General.'

Al-Bitruji was pleased to see that vehicles were already on the move. Men waving fluorescent traffic-control wands were diverting the long column of vehicles around the wreckage, whilst other teams tackled the fires and cleared bodies from the road. A heavily armed Humvee pulled up alongside them and both officers climbed aboard. Al-Bitruji turned to his second in command.

'Have the gap between each vehicle increased to a hundred metres. Every fifth vehicle will carry two troopers with portable SAMs, and vehicles are to travel in groups of no more than ten. Everyone is to observe strict light discipline. We can't afford to lose more men or equipment.'

Farad grabbed a radio headset and began to issue orders while the general contemplated his next move. He had his own orders to carry out. He studied the command console for a moment. So, Mousa was in Downing Street already. No doubt the arrogant bastard would gloat when they saw each other again. Al-Bitruji was no admirer of his fellow general and thought the paratrooper a pompous ass. But he was close to the Holy One, a position that Al-Bitruji himself would have given anything to be in. Still, maybe the tide would turn in Al-Bitruji's favour.

There was no mention of resistance. The general smiled at the thought of Mousa desperately fighting for his life in a rubble-strewn Whitehall. If he failed – if he was killed, or captured – then what? The Holy One would've lost his golden child, eventually seeking the counsel of another perhaps, someone who had proved his loyalty, who waited patiently in the wings to serve at the cleric's right hand. Someone who might discover Mousa's bullet-ridden body in Whitehall or save the arrogant bastard's skin with his own troops. Either way, he had to get to London quickly.

The general slapped the driver on the shoulder and the Humvee lurched forward, racing towards the head of the convoy.

10 Downing Street

'Any news on Beecham?' demanded General Mousa.

He was holding conference with his senior staff in the Cabinet Room while around the walls, heavily armed troops stood sentinel and the air crackled with continuous radio chatter.

Major Karroubi studied his notes. 'Our intelligence puts him inside Number Ten at eighteen hundred hours. We've found the bodies of dozens of high-value casualties both in this building and the surrounding area, but not Beecham. There are additional remains that have yet to be identified, but due to their condition it's likely they were victims of the truck bomb. There's blood on the floor of Beecham's private apartment and footprints in the dust up there.'

'He's still alive,' muttered Mousa.

'It looks likely,' agreed Karroubi. 'Someone must have carried Fuller's body to the garden and more footprints down here indicate that several people have been moving around the lower levels after the explosion.'

'Which means there's another way out,' reasoned Mousa.

'As you know, the access tunnel below us leads to the Ministry of Defence building across the street. It's highly likely the prime minister has fled there. Our assault troops are in place, ready to storm the building.'

Mousa thought about the opportunity that had presented itself. A captured prime minister, paraded before the cameras, urging his fellow citizens not to resist, surrendering the country to a victorious General Mousa.

'Give the order to advance, Major. And I want Beecham found. Alive.'

'Yes, General.'

Wandsworth, South London

The shooting had finally died down. It had been some time since Khan had heard any gunfire outside and what little he could hear sounded like it was some distance away. But as he waited for darkness to fall, Khan heard other sounds too. Harsh, urgent voices close by, shouting in both English and Arabic, although it was difficult to tell what was being said. He'd heard screaming too, ear-splitting screams of anguish that made the hair on the back of his neck stand on end. Later, a car had approached at high speed, its engine roaring and its tyres screeching in protest. Then, an almighty bang followed by a deathly silence.

At one point, Khan had scrambled to his feet as several people ran past outside, their shadows flitting across the walls and their footsteps pounding the pavement. The metal shutters crashed and rippled as a body cannoned off them. Khan stood frozen, heart hammering, the rifle clasped tightly in his shaking hands, but the commotion had quickly passed and he'd slumped back down against the wall. For the last hour the only sounds he'd heard were the fires crackling and spitting outside in the street.

Now the shadows had lengthened and Khan moved carefully towards the shutters, peering between the metal slats. There were scores of burning vehicles out there, most of them now blackened shells. The smoke was still thick, hanging in low clouds that drifted across the darkening streets. He saw the surveillance vehicle about twenty yards away, the windscreen peppered with bullet holes but still relatively intact. He could also see Spencer's legs splayed out in the rear of the vehicle and Max was still in there too. The fact that he had to leave them there made Khan feel nauseous.

He moved away from the shutters and back into the shadows. He wondered how far this chaos had spread. Was it confined to a few square miles in South London or was it part of a larger, more well-planned operation? He ran his mind back over the events of... this morning? So much had happened since then that it seemed like another time and place. Without doubt, Khan was caught in the middle of a major terrorist attack. But how far had it spread and where were the police cordons? Well, if anywhere, they'd be towards the bridge at Vauxhall.

He doubted that the SIS building at Vauxhall Cross had been hit. In the event of any major incident, dedicated police units would be on standby to secure the whole area, effectively sealing off Vauxhall Cross itself from vehicular and pedestrian traffic. In addition to that, the building had its own formidable defences, including bombproof gates, reinforced concrete walls and steel window shutters over bulletproof Plexiglas on every floor. Yeah, Vauxhall Cross, Khan decided. That's where the police cordons will be.

He headed back through the shop towards the rear of the building. He threw the bolt on the rear gate and found himself in a darkened back street tucked behind the Wandsworth Road. The street was empty, the sky glowing red above the rooftops to the east. He made his way towards Vauxhall, keeping to the shadows. The houses on his left soon gave way to a chain-link fence and Khan quickly realised he was looking at the darkened sprawl of New Covent Garden Market. It was a massive warehouse complex, certainly one that had seen better days, but the seemingly deserted site boasted a multitude of loading bays with towers of wooden pallets stacked every few yards under the dark shadows of wide, overhead canopies. It was the perfect place to get off the streets and close the distance to Vauxhall Cross.

He scaled the fence and headed across the empty market towards Nine Elms Lane, a wide commuter road that ran east along the Thames towards Vauxhall Cross. Maybe there was a police roadblock there. He was more cautious now as he left the cover of the market complex, ducking under the vehicle entrance barrier and heading towards the main road. What he saw momentarily stopped him in his tracks. In the darkness, Nine Elms Lane was a graveyard of vehicles. Some displayed signs of collision damage, while others looked surprisingly intact. Most had their doors open, an indication of a panicked exit. The abandoned vehicles stretched far into the distance where, above the roofs of the residential buildings at Vauxhall Cross, a huge fire consumed everything and set the night sky ablaze.

Khan's head spun in shock. Everything he'd gone through tonight had convinced him that he was involved in a major terrorist operation of a scale never seen before. But he'd been mistaken. It wasn't just confined to a small area. He spun slowly around and, for the first time, Khan noticed that the sky around the horizon glowed red from a multitude of fires, a scene made more noticeable by the fact that the whole city was blanketed in darkness. The sky, usually so busy with the dull roar of jet engines, was eerily quiet. He didn't see a single aircraft.

Khan looked up and down the road. Where were all the people, the countless emergency service vehicles that should be swamping the area? Events like this usually brought the curious and the troublesome out on to the streets, but Khan didn't see a single person. It was as if everyone had disappeared. He sat down behind a low wall, his legs feeling suddenly weak. A massive intelligence failure, of that there was no doubt. Of course, the intelligence services had their surveillance operations, such as the one in the Morden mosque, but who could have imagined it would lead to this?

They hadn't had a single sniff of an attack. Why not? An operation of this magnitude should have surely turned up the odd whisper. But no, nothing. Khan didn't bother to speculate who might be behind it.

It was Arabia, of course. This kind of op called for meticulous preparation and timing. The power cuts, the weapons, the lack of any co-ordinated response – an operation planned at the highest level requiring the best minds and an intelligence network of the highest calibre. Who else but Arabia would have the means and the motive? We should have seen it coming, realised Khan. Old hatreds died hard, especially religious ones. His gut instincts were right all along.

He got to his feet. As he did so, a sudden movement caught his eye. A short distance away, a large DIY warehouse squatted across several acres of land alongside New Covent Garden. Khan saw scores of pale faces staring back at him from behind the glass of the main doors, melting back into the shadows when they caught sight of the automatic weapon in Khan's hands.

He inspected the area more carefully. There were dozens of cars and vans in the forecourt and he saw movement inside some of them too, just a glimpse of a head or glow of a cigarette. Civilians; caught out in the chaos, too scared to move, waiting for help that might never come. By their movements and their sudden withdrawal from view he guessed he'd been marked down as a bad guy. This identification business was going to be a problem, Khan realised. Sooner or later someone would mistake him for a terrorist. Then again, if he acquired some kind of official uniform, something that people would recognise as being friendly, then the bad guys would see him as a target and he'd be in more trouble. So, what to do?

Going east towards Vauxhall Cross was clearly out of the question. He needed to get to Millbank, where his MI5 colleagues would be working the crisis behind the deceptively secure walls of Thames House. He needed to report the deaths of his colleagues, to recover their bodies, be part of a team again. But first he had to get out of the area and across the river.

North then, via Chelsea Bridge. But what lay in wait for him on the way? He could see the glow of fires in all directions, a sign that danger lurked at all points of the compass. It could be even worse over the river, but that's where the professional organisations were – Scotland Yard, Whitehall, the MOD. Right now they would be co-ordinating some kind of response, deploying their forces, executing well-prepared emergency plans and rescue efforts. As he moved towards the bridge, an idea suddenly came to him. If he needed to recce his route across the river, what better place than one of the best viewing platforms in West London: Park Heights Tower.

The Park Heights complex was the result of a huge regeneration project that had transformed the crumbling site of Battersea Power Station into a twenty-first-century development. It had everything: shopping malls, conference suites, hotels, cinemas, plush apartment blocks and even a marina. But it was the tower that Khan was most interested in. Park Heights was a thirty-storey, circular glass and steel structure that rose up from the middle of the power station floor, creating a fifth tower that stood over four hundred feet high, dominating the four original chimney stacks. It would be a long climb but it would be worth it. From up there he would be able to see the extent of the attacks and how far the power cuts had spread. It would also give him a good indicator of where he could find help.

The complex was deserted when he arrived. There were several abandoned cars on the access ramp that led to the mezzanine level, but thankfully no bodies. At the top of the ramp was an abandoned security station, its red and white striped barrier blocking vehicular access to the upper level. Khan ducked under the barrier and headed towards a set of large glass doors.

Inside, he found himself on a wide walkway, fifty feet above the deserted mall floor below. He turned his gaze upwards and saw the tower looming above him in the darkness. Khan had seen it many times from a distance, but up close and blacked out it took on a foreboding quality that made him apprehensive. He pushed on regardless. The reception area was empty and undamaged and Khan moved quickly to the fire escape, finding himself inside a smooth-walled concrete tube with a circular steel staircase that wound up into the darkness above. It was going to be a long climb.

He doubled back to the reception area and rummaged beneath the security desk until he found a torch, slipping it into his pocket. Back inside the fire escape he began to climb. By the tenth floor Khan's body confirmed that he was badly out of shape. By floor twenty-two, he had to stop for a five-minute break while his lungs gasped for air and his heart hammered loudly in his chest. Thirty minutes later, an exhausted Khan finally reached the elevator maintenance and electrical storerooms on the thirty-second floor.

The sign on the door at the top of the stairs warned of high winds and safety lines. Khan unbolted it and pushed it open, finding himself on a circular gantry at the very top of the building. The wind whipped his hair and clothes and Khan's hands gripped the rail tightly. But it wasn't the height that bothered him – it was the vision of hell around him that made his tired legs weaken further.

London was completely blacked out. For as far as he could see, the city was blanketed in darkness, punctuated by the glow of fires dotted around the horizon. He steadied himself and shuffled further around the gantry, his hands gripping the thick steel rail. He concentrated on the east, towards Vauxhall Cross and Whitehall, where dozens of buildings were on fire, the flames dancing and leaping into the air, bathing the sky above in a red glow.

He moved further around the gantry and looked north across the Thames. Directly over the river, Khan could see another large fire had engulfed several waterfront buildings and, further west, there were other conflagrations, their flames climbing into the night sky. Fear suddenly gripped him. This was like something from a nightmare. No lights, no communications, no signs of order, no rescue services; only chaos. And if the seat of power in London could be disabled and plunged into such chaos, what about the rest of the country?

He heard shots below him. From his lofty vantage point, they sounded more like hollow pops drifting up on the night air, but Khan wasn't fooled. He made his way around the gantry until he overlooked the dark spread of Battersea Park and Chelsea Bridge Road. Below him, Khan saw the bridge itself had been blocked by cars, with armed men standing behind the makeshift barrier. Despite the distance it was clear they weren't police or army. As he watched, two flatbed trucks, their headlights piercing the darkness, peeled away from the bridge and headed towards the complex. He could see men clinging to the backs of the trucks, armed men, swaying in unison as the vehicles turned into the access road that led to the mall below him. He headed for the staircase as fast as he could.

Chiswick
West London

When he returned to the apartment, Alex was relieved to find Kirsty awake. She still looked pretty spaced out, but she was up and moving and in the process of getting dressed when Alex entered the bedroom. Instinctively, Kirsty pulled the sweatshirt she was holding to her chest.

'Alex!' she protested. She tried to sound suitably outraged, but the attempt was half-hearted. Naked or not, she was glad that Alex was there with her.

'Sorry Kirsty, but we haven't got much time. Get dressed quickly and I'll explain everything.'

Alex went out into the living room. Grouped in the centre of the coffee table were some decorative candles and a box of matches. Alex lit one, illuminating the room with its flickering glow. The light was not very bright but it was enough to see by; besides, Alex didn't want to draw attention to the apartment. He wandered out towards the balcony. Across the river, the darkness took on a blood-red hue, silhouetting the trees that lined the riverbank and beyond. Alex guessed that the airliner still burned over there somewhere. He shuddered at the thought of the carnage.

A faint noise caught his attention and his eyes were drawn towards the river. There it was again, the sound of water splashing. As his vision adjusted to the darkness, he thought he could see a slight luminescence on the surface of the dark waters. Something moved in his peripheral vision, an object that seemed to glide across the gloom below him. As it passed through a watery patch of moonlight, Alex suddenly realised what it was: a rowing boat. He could make out a figure aboard, rowing gently upstream towards the bend in the river at Kew Bridge. He watched it for several minutes until the boat slowly faded from view. The boat's passing had an almost dream-like quality, a vision of serenity while all around the city burned. A thought suddenly occurred to Alex and, in that instant, he'd formulated a plan.

'Alex?'

Kirsty was standing in the middle of the living room, her hair askew, dressed in jogging pants and a baggy sweatshirt, her arms wrapped protectively around herself.

'You okay?'

Kirsty nodded, a thin smile cracking her pale face. Alex grabbed an arm of the overturned sofa and righted it. He patted one of the torn cushions, inviting Kirsty to sit down. She did so gratefully, the effects of the sleeping pill still causing her to feel groggy and heavy limbed.

'Alex, what's happening? Those men with guns, and the plane…' Her eyes clouded over. 'Oh my God, those poor people.'

Alex knelt down in front of her and grabbed her arms tightly. Neither of them needed the hysterics again. 'Look Kirsty, I don't know what's happening here, but London seems to be under some kind of attack. I don't know who by, or why or anything like that, but I do know that we can't stay here.'

Kirsty paled. 'Attack? But I don't understand. Can't we ring somebody? Surely the TV or the radio will tell us what's going on? What about you? You're a bloody policeman, for God's sake. Aren't you supposed to know?'

Alex tried to keep his voice calm, his manner reassuring. 'Everything's down. I can't raise anybody, not even my own team. And there's not a single light across the whole of London. I went up on to the roof and had a look. It's bloody eerie.'

'This can't be real,' Kirsty mumbled.

'It is, believe me.'

'What are we going to do?' Kirsty's voiced trembled as she spoke.

Alex had to keep her calm, keep her mind occupied. 'Do you know anyone who has a boat?'

Kirsty frowned. 'A boat? No, I… surely you're not going to…'

'Yes, we've got to find a boat, get out of the city. Whatever crisis this is, it's big, big enough to shut down London. People are dying out there and no one's coming to help. Right now the best course of action is to get out, while we still can. Christ knows what's going to happen next, but I'm betting it won't be good. We've got to move, and move quickly. The roads aren't safe, that's for sure. That's why we need a boat.'

Kirsty shook her head. 'We can't just leave. What about my job? My friends, my mum and dad?'

'They'll be fine. They'd want you to be safe.'

'Leaving doesn't sound very safe.'

Alex got to his feet. 'I can't force you, Kirsty. I could stay too, try and head into work, find out what's happening, but the phones and radios are all dead and people are getting killed out there. Fact is, I probably wouldn't make it. Tell me, have you heard a single police siren in the last hour?' Kirsty shook her head. 'Exactly. And how long can you stay here before you run out of food, before somebody starts nosing around this block? I've already seen one gang outside. It won't be long before others turn up. You want to be here when they do?'

Kirsty clambered to her feet, her brown eyes wide with fear. 'You're scaring me, Alex.'

'I'm trying to protect us.'

'Where would we go?'

'My brother Rob lives on a farm in the West Country, quite isolated. Him and his wife are eco-nuts. They've got solar power, a wind turbine, chickens, pigs, a freshwater well – you name it. We'd be safe there until all this dies down. But if we don't go now, while it's dark, we could be trapped here. Right now a million people are wondering whether to make a move or to stay put. A lot of them will try, sooner rather than later. We've got to go before every escape route is blocked.'

Kirsty took a deep breath and nodded. 'You're right. Just until things get back to normal.' She brushed past Alex into the kitchen, returning with a couple of litre bottles of mineral water.

'We'll bring these. What else do we need?'

'Warm clothes. I know it's summer, but it can still get cold at night. Have you got a rucksack or a backpack?'

Kirsty disappeared out into the hallway. After a moment, she returned with a large backpack complete with sleeping bag. She stood there, bathed in the soft glow of candlelight, a tired smile on her face, and just for a moment the crisis was the furthest thing from Alex's mind.

'Right, er, pack some spare clothes and a waterproof jacket. We'll need food too, soup, dried cereal, peanut butter, anything like that. And make sure you wear dark clothes. We don't want to attract any unwelcome attention. I'm going downstairs, get my own gear. Back in five.'

'Okay. Hurry up.'

Alex closed the door and crept slowly down the stairs, alert for trouble. On the ground floor he clicked on a small torch and entered his own apartment, where he stripped off his shirt and slacks and changed into police-issue black tactical trousers and jacket. He grabbed a rucksack from the spare bedroom and packed clothes and several other items including another torch, batteries, water, a compass, some tinned foods and a small hexamine cooker. He was ready to go in less than three minutes. But there were just a couple more essential items to pack.

From the gun cabinet in the bedroom, Alex retrieved the assault rifle and magazines. If he was going to have a weapon it might as well be a good one. All in all, he had one hundred and twenty 5.56 millimetre rounds for the Heckler-Koch and five pistol mags totalling eighty rounds. Not great, but not bad either. The trick would be to avoid contact, not look for it. Fully kitted and ready, Alex locked the front door of his apartment. Leaving his rucksack in the hallway, he trotted back upstairs where Kirsty was in the process of hefting her rucksack over her shoulders. Her eyes widened when she saw the weapons.

'Jesus Christ, Alex.'

'Just for protection, that's all.'

They made a final check of the flat, locking the doors and shutting off the gas and electricity.

'I'll get on to the insurance people as soon as I get back,' joked Kirsty. Alex watched the tears roll down her face. He put an arm around her shoulders and gave her a gentle squeeze.

'Everything'll be okay, you'll see. We'll probably laugh about all this in a year's time.' He could see she didn't believe him. They crept downstairs to the lobby doors and peered out into the night. Nothing moved. Silently, Alex pulled the door open and moved outside. After a few moments he motioned Kirsty to join him. He leaned close to her and whispered in her ear.

'Move around the side of the building and keep to the shadows. When you get to the gardens at the rear, head for the bushes near the towpath and keep low.' Kirsty nodded and headed off.

Alex watched her go, listening to the soft crunch of her feet as she crossed the gravel driveway between the apartment blocks. He waited for nearly a minute before he was satisfied that she hadn't been seen or heard. He let the main door swing softly back into place, where it relocked itself with an audible click. The doors wouldn't last two seconds against a mob intent on looting and Alex despaired that he'd not see his flat in such good condition when he returned. If he returned, he corrected himself.

Making a final visual sweep, Alex moved off into the shadows. He found Kirsty crouched down behind some bushes. Beyond the shrubbery was the towpath itself. If he was going to find a boat he was certainly in the right area.

'Where does he live, your brother?' whispered Kirsty.

'Near a village called South Lockeridge, in Wiltshire. I reckon the river could take us as far as Reading, maybe further if we're lucky. It's about thirty-odd miles from there, so even if we had to walk it would only take us three days at the most.'

'Walk?'

'The roads might not be safe, so we may have to cut across country. Don't worry, I've packed a tent and we've got enough food and water to last us for a couple of days. And it's summer, so the weather's on our side. In the meantime we find a boat. Let's get on the towpath, start heading towards Kew Bridge.'

'What if we don't find one?'

'We're bound to. Look, don't worry, okay? Now, when we move off I want you to stay a few yards behind me. If I hold up my hand, just freeze and keep as quiet as possible. Have you got a torch?'

'Yes.'

'Good. Don't use it unless I say so. Your eyes'll get used to the dark quite quickly, so we'll rely on our night vision. And no talking.'

Kirsty took a deep breath. 'Okay.'

'Let's go.'

Alex cut through the shrubs until they were on the towpath. The moon shone brightly in the sky, revealing the damp, gloomy trail along the riverbank.

'Keep close and keep quiet,' whispered Alex.

Kirsty smiled weakly and gave him a thumbs up. They made their way slowly towards Kew Bridge.

10 Downing Street

General Mousa watched impassively as the badly beaten figure of the policeman was dragged unceremoniously out of the CMC, a thin trail of blood marking his departure along the corridor. As a rule, Mousa didn't normally soil his hands with the messy business of torture as a means to extract information, but it had proved necessary in this particular case. And the information Sergeant Morris had rasped through broken teeth was exactly what he wanted to hear. Beecham was still alive.

The invasion plans had called for the elimination of the various heads of the EU states. A country suddenly robbed of its political rulers while at the same time plunged into chaos and armed conflict would rapidly become disorganised, leading to political indecision and communications failures. In the meantime, any mobilisation by military forces would be hindered by a lack of credible political guidance save for their own senior officers, who would be unable to act without the necessary civilian authorisation. And so it proved to be the case.

According to the latest reports, Arabian forces were streaming into Western Europe against scattered and disorganised opposition. In some areas they had advanced virtually unopposed, their enemies defeated before they knew what had happened. The Italian, Dutch, French, Spanish and Belgian leaders and several of their high-ranking cabinet members were all reported killed or missing. Only the German chancellor had escaped, a last-minute change to her schedule saving her life and avoiding the suicide bomber who had detonated his explosives in the lobby of the Reichstag building in Berlin. Her helicopter had been found abandoned an hour ago by Soviet forces outside the city of Rostock on the Baltic coast. She probably made for Denmark, assumed Mousa.

Strategically, the elimination of state leaders had proved to be successful. Devoid of any serious opposition, the Arabian forces were seizing their objectives with minimal casualties and, more importantly, the towns and cities were suffering far less damage than they would normally endure in a long, drawn-out campaign.

But now, an opportunity had presented itself. As a nation, the British people were normally slow to anger and demonstrated a blind faith in their politicians, something that Mousa fully intended to exploit. A captured Beecham could be used as a political pawn, forced to address the nation and declare an end to hostilities. The Holy One himself was concerned by the potential for resistance in Britain. If Mousa could negate that resistance, sap the will to fight from the populace, it would be a considerable personal coup. And afterwards, when the nation had been suitably subjugated, Beecham would be removed, quietly but permanently.

The omens boded well. Beecham had survived the truck bomb intact and was somewhere in the locality. According to the policeman, he'd been joined by others, a small detachment of soldiers tasked to protect him. But where would safety lie? The policeman, nursing his third broken finger, had recalled through gritted teeth a whispered conversation in which he'd overheard the phrase 'tunnel system'. Further interrogation of the other prisoners had revealed nothing of any significance. They were telling the truth, or what little truth there was to be told. So, Beecham was probably still hiding close by. But where?

Mousa stepped out into the basement corridor, deep in thought. The Downing Street complex had been searched thoroughly and, apart from one or two civilians hiding amongst the rubble, it had proved to be deserted. Which left only one conclusion: there was another tunnel right here beneath Number Ten. Where else would it be?

He stopped pacing and looked once again at the heavy steel door to the generator room. He reached out and grasped the topmost handle, pulling it down. It moved less than an inch and held fast. Mousa pulled down harder, but it wouldn't move any further. He grasped the handle with both hands and used his body weight to try and shift it, but it remained locked solid. He bent down and tried the other one, heaving it upwards with all his might. Mousa prided himself on his physical prowess, but to his surprise and, mounting anger, he couldn't move the handles any further. He straightened up, slapping his hands clean.

'Major!'

Karroubi emerged from the CMC and hobbled out into the corridor, his right lower leg wrapped in a field dressing. 'General?'

'Get the combat engineers and a SERTRAK team down here as quickly as possible.'

'You think that–'

'Yes, Major Karroubi, I think they went behind this door. It's the only place we haven't looked and the door appears to be jammed.'

Mousa balled his fist and pulled it back, about to crash it against the door in frustration. He stopped in mid-air, suddenly mindful of the possibility of booby traps. Instead, he gently rested an ear against the cold steel, his voice barely rising above a whisper. 'And the devil himself must have sealed it from the inside.'

Four inches away from Mousa's left ear, Trooper Farrell also had his head pressed against the steel door. He'd heard movement outside, had leaned in close to try and improve the acoustics, then nearly jumped out of his skin when the handles had been forced from outside. But the steel bars jammed into the mechanism, preventing any further movement. He heard low, muffled voices but it was impossible to catch what they were saying. It didn't matter anyway. Whoever was outside wanted to get in here, and that meant it was time to get moving.

Farrell moved quietly away from the door and trotted down the ramp. He ducked through the false panel and sealed it from the other side, punching in the locking code. A minute later, he was down on the cavern floor.

The Tunnels

'What's the problem?' demanded Brigadier Forsythe as he entered the control room, Harry following close behind.

'Train carriage won't move,' Gibson replied. 'We've got a green light on the panel but it's just not moving.'

'Keep trying.'

Through the glass wall they saw Trooper Farrell running towards them.

'We've got movement in the basement corridor,' he panted. 'Someone's trying to get access to the generator room.'

'Could it be civilians? Stragglers maybe?' offered Harry. He was horrified at the thought that there may be people trapped below Downing Street with all that destruction raging above them.

Forsythe shook his head. 'Doubtful. No one knows about the tunnel system apart from a very small group of people with the highest clearance.'

'Well, maybe it's one of them?'

'There's one way of finding out.'

Forsythe flipped the power on a monitor built into the control desk. Harry and the soldiers gathered around the screen, which was split into numerous smaller images transmitted from the underground cavern and its tunnels.

'This complex and parts of the tunnel system are covered by surveillance cameras. There's even one in the generator room above us.'

'There's the train, Boss. Number four,' said Gibson pointing to one of the images.

The brigadier touched the screen and the picture instantly filled the monitor. They could all see a large, open train carriage with enough seating to carry about twenty people.

'Picture looks rather hazy,' observed Harry.

'That's smoke,' said Gibson, peering closely at the black and white image.

'Let's try calling the train down again.' He punched a command into the console. On the screen more smoke began to rise from beneath the unmoving carriage.

'Something must have burned out underneath. Maybe the electric motor.'

'We'll have to move out on foot,' declared Forsythe. 'Let's have a look at that generator room.' He touched the screen again, returning it to its multi-camera view. He found the right screen and enlarged it. The room was empty, the camera set at a high angle facing the steel door at the top of the concrete ramp.

'Seems quiet,' observed Harry.

Forsythe shrugged. 'Even if they did get in, they'd have to know about the tunnel system. I wouldn't worry too much, Harry. I think we're pretty safe down here for the time being.'

'Detonate!'

The combat engineer, wearing thick headphones, clamped his eyes shut and depressed the rubberised switch on his remote-control unit. The generator room door had been quickly and expertly assessed by the senior officer of engineers, a powerful charge rigged and the corridor cleared. Inside the CMC, Mousa crouched against the wall with his hands over his ears, while all around him his paratroopers did the same. The resulting explosion shook the ground beneath their feet and the loud blast echoed around the basement for several seconds. With the corridor still thick with dust, Mousa ordered the first assault team inside with orders to clear the now accessible generator room.

'Jesus!'

Harry almost jumped out of his skin as the screen turned to digital snow and the overhead explosion rumbled around the cavern. After a few seconds, the picture returned to normal. In the upper centre of the screen, what could only be the entrance to the corridor showed up as a white rectangle, throwing a shaft of pale light across the ramp. More thin shafts of light appeared, bouncing around the screen.

'Assault team,' warned Gibson. Several armed men charged into the room, torches slung beneath the barrels of their weapons, and took up defensive positions along the walls as the dust slowly began to settle. On the screen, another soldier entered the room.

It was clear from his poise and authority that this new arrival was a senior officer. Harry and the others watched in silence as the shadowy figure made his way slowly along the line of electrical power units as if he were inspecting a squad of troops, pausing here and there to glance behind a unit or leaning forward to read a display panel. He seemed to be taking an undue interest in the room, as if he were searching for something. Harry swallowed, the hairs rising on the back of his neck. The figure carried on past the power units and approached the workbench beneath the surveillance camera. He absently fingered the tools and rags on its surface and then glanced upwards, straight into the camera lens.

'Busted,' whispered Gibson under his breath.

'Major Karroubi!' bellowed Mousa, and seconds later his subordinate limped down the ramp. 'Look.'

Karroubi followed his superior's pointed finger and saw the small camera mounted near the ceiling below some overhead pipework. 'A camera, General.'

Mousa looked sideways at his deputy. 'Indeed. Why do you think someone would install a camera in a room such as this?' Karroubi pondered the question.

'For observation purposes. Safety reasons maybe?'

'I think not,' replied Mousa. He turned away from the camera, inviting Karroubi to do the same. 'Over there is a sophisticated alarm panel and there are smoke detectors along the ceiling. Why bother with a camera with such equipment in place?' Mousa turned back to the camera. 'Observe the angle of the lens. Does it point towards the electrical equipment on that side of the room? No. Its position and angle give it only one purpose.'

'It points towards the door. A surveillance camera?' answered Karroubi.

'Correct. There is a hidden entrance to the tunnel system in this room. Get the engineers in here and rip this place apart. I want it found, Major, and quickly. Where is the SERTRAK team?'

'On their way. Fifteen minutes out.'

'Good. Have them standing by.'

Karroubi nodded curtly – salutes were forbidden in a combat zone – and hobbled up the ramp. Mousa wandered back to the far wall and looked up at the camera, staring hard into the lens.

Forty feet below the general's boots, Harry and the others watched the frantic activity taking place behind the man who stared into the lens. Combat engineers were tracing pipes and cables, tapping the walls and floors for hidden or false panels. As they watched, the Arabian officer's hand obscured the lens briefly. When it cleared, all they were left with was a view of the workbench. Forsythe straightened up. Harry saw the look on his face and his pulse began to rise.

'Time to leave. How's your fitness, Harry?'

He gave the brigadier a tight grin. 'With those bastards up there on our tail, I think I'll have all the incentive I need to keep going. How did they get here so quickly?'

'Their equipment and insignia mark them out as paratroopers. They probably landed close by, maybe Hyde Park.'

'Paratroopers? Landing in London? How the bloody hell is it possible?'

'Hard to believe I know, but you've seen the evidence for yourself.

Those are Arabian troops up there and, judging by the speed and significance of their arrival, I'm guessing that you're their target. We've got to move quickly.'

'Jesus Christ,' breathed Harry. The realisation that he was the target for a foreign military power chilled him.

'It's all about speed and distance, now,' Forsythe continued. 'We've got to get to that radio in Kensington Gardens as fast as possible.'

Harry gulped. With the train carriage out of service they were limited to how fast he could run, and that certainly wasn't going to be fast enough. It was just over half a mile to the Buckingham Palace interchange and one and a half miles from there to the disused building in Kensington Gardens. It would be tough going.

'Let's get on with it then,' declared Forsythe. He reached behind the console and began snipping at the coloured wires with a multitool. Video feeds suddenly failed, and lights went out across the control panel. 'No sense in letting them know where we've gone, is there?'

Harry nodded in agreement. 'Why don't we just destroy it all?' he asked.

'Better to leave some of it working. They might try to figure it all out, get the trains running or the monitors to work. It could buy us a bit more time.'

Out on the platform, Forsythe gathered the soldiers around him. 'We've got to slow them down, create a diversion, so we can put some distance between them and us. We'll need to split up. Mike, you and I will escort the PM, plus one other.'

Gibson pointed to Farrell. 'You're with us. Get upstairs and set a couple of booby traps, quick as you can.' Farrell raced away towards the staircase.

Forsythe turned to Nasser and Brooks. 'You two will have a tougher job, I'm afraid. You'll need to leave a trail, lead them away from us using the other tunnel. When you get to Mill Hill, head west to Alternate One, any way you can. You've got the grid reference. Good luck, Godspeed.'

Gibson slapped Brooks on the arm. 'Off you go, lads.'

Nasser turned to Harry. 'Just wanted to say good luck, Prime Minister.' He stepped forward and held out his hand. Without thinking, Harry took it. The soldier clamped both hands around his own and pumped it warmly. 'See you out west.'

'Good luck,' Harry echoed, faintly embarrassed by the gesture.

'Get moving,' barked Gibson.

With that, the two soldiers disappeared into the mouth of the northbound tunnel. After a minute or so they were swallowed up by the darkness.

Forsythe turned to Harry. 'Ready?' Harry nodded. 'Then let's go.'

Gibson led the way, towards the westbound tunnel. At the entrance, he turned and gave a short whistle. Harry looked up and saw Trooper Farrell crouched on the gantry forty feet above them. Gibson keyed his radio headset. 'We're leaving.'

Farrell made his way down the staircase, taking the steps two at a time, and jogged over to the tunnel entrance. 'I've rigged a small, shaped charge in the room up there, connected to the light switch. It's not massive, but it'll scare the shit out of them when it goes. The other one is big, a pressure switch set under the gantry. More than three people on that landing and it'll blow large.'

'Nice work,' confirmed Gibson. 'Now, all of you get going up the tunnel. I'll catch up.'

Forsythe nodded. 'Let's go, Harry.'

They set off at a brisk pace, somewhere between a fast walk and a jog, with Farrell taking point. Gibson watched them disappear around the bend and headed back to the control room.

He found the electrical fuse box that served the cavern lighting and, one by one, began popping the fuses, the large banks of ceiling lights going out above him, one after the other. As he pulled the last fuse, the whole complex was plunged into an inky blackness. Across the cavern, Gibson could barely make out the tunnel entrances, dimly lit by their faint blue lights. He made his way towards the westbound tunnel and disappeared into its dark mouth.

10 Downing Street

'Well, anything?'

Mousa was growing increasingly impatient. The engineers had been searching the generator room for over thirty minutes and still they'd found nothing. He felt certain the escape tunnel was here somewhere, but so far they'd drawn a blank. The combat engineer captain standing before him shook his head nervously.

'My apologies, General. Wherever the entrance is, it's extremely well hidden. We'll find it, though. It's just a matter of time.'

'Then don't let me delay you,' snapped Mousa, and turned on his heel.

The corridor beneath Number Ten was packed with heavily armed assault teams. They parted like the Red Sea as Mousa walked through them, none willing to meet his stern gaze.

Mousa took a seat in the CMC and lit a cigarette, studying the portable command console on the conference table before him. Al-Bitruji had made it to London. He saw that the general was setting up his headquarters in Buckingham Palace. A wise choice. It would be hard for any Englishman to order an attack on such a culturally significant landmark.

'The SERTRAK team is here,' announced Karroubi, limping into the room. Mousa crushed his cigarette underfoot and went out into the corridor. There wasn't much room in the tightly packed space and he was about to order half the assault team out, when a hush descended over the paratroopers. Mousa turned towards the stairs and saw the first SERTRAK man enter the basement. SERTRAK (search and tracking) teams were feared above all others in the Arabian forces. Drawn exclusively from Afghan units, SERTRAK personnel were trained to seek out, track and kill in areas where their enemies would least expect them to live, let alone do battle. Some of the original members were veterans of the War on Terror at the turn of the century. Living deep in caves beneath the Tora Bora mountains in Afghanistan, the insurgents, as they were labelled back then, would crawl from their lairs at night to attack government and allied forces, engaging them on snow-capped rocky outcrops above three thousand metres or on the desert floor, where they would lie for days in man-sized 'spider holes' to ambush their enemy. They were experts in fighting in dark and confined spaces, lethal with guns, knives and their bare hands.

As the war against the infidel occupation continued, the resistance became more organised and their leaders formed the fighters into specialised units. They were given a new name, SERTRAK, and the unit had gone from strength to strength after a number of successful operations across the Middle East. After the rise to power of the Grand Mufti Khathami, they were absorbed into the Arabian Special Forces. These were men that would perform the impossible tasks, the men that would operate in places that regular troops would fear to tread. They had proved themselves to be tough, capable and intelligent fighters, and that was why Mousa needed them now.

The paratroopers assembled in the corridor watched the new arrivals warily. SERTRAK's reputation had spread far and wide amongst Arabian forces over the preceding years and, although the soldiers that lined the walls considered themselves the elite, the men passing them now were a different breed entirely. The paratroopers were excellent soldiers, but soldiers nonetheless, trained and conditioned to operate in predictable ways. But the Afghans? Some said they were cold-blooded killers sent by the devil himself and the gruesome details of their operations, filtered down through the armed forces grapevine, left nobody in any doubt of their murderous prowess.

As the SERTRAK team made their way through the packed corridor, the airborne troops moved out of their path. They numbered fifteen altogether and their uniforms consisted of various mixtures of modern battledress and traditional Afghan clothing. Despite the summer weather they wore heavy, full battle-order webbing and backpacks from which hung an assortment of gear including ropes, clamps and various other items. Each man carried at least two weapons, ranging from small arms to man-portable mini missile launchers. However, what most paratroopers noticed were the deadly array of knives that each man wore about his body. The knife was the weapon of choice when operating in darkness and the SERTRAK teams were experts in their use. Unconsciously, the paratroopers closest to the passing Afghans moved a little further back.

The SERTRAK leader was tall, well over six feet, his bearded face heavily scarred. He wore a sleeveless sheepskin jerkin over a US-issue combat jacket and trousers and cradled an AK-84 in his muscular arms. He saw Mousa in the doorway of the CMC and followed him inside. Out in the corridor, a murmur rose from the paratroopers as the last Afghan disappeared from view. Mousa smiled to himself. These men always created a stir wherever they went.

The leader introduced himself as Captain Haseeb and Mousa quickly briefed him on the situation. When the tunnel entrance was found, Haseeb was to enter first and capture the infidel leader alive. The military escorts were believed to be British Special Forces. Haseeb could do what he wished with them.

Mousa watched as the big Afghan briefed his team. Of all the people in the basement, Mousa was the only one not intimidated by these fierce mountain men. It was universally known across the Arabian armed forces that Mousa held close council with the cleric himself, and this fact alone made him equally as intimidating, if not more so, than the hardened killers gathered before him. After a few moments, Haseeb turned to Mousa.

'General, my men are ready. If it pleases you, I have one or two operational requests.'

'Go on,' invited Mousa.

Haseeb outlined his wishes and Mousa nodded agreement. Major Karroubi was dispatched into the generator room, where he quickly cleared out the combat engineers. Still no luck, Karroubi reported. Haseeb barked an order and one of his men stepped forward with a small black box.

'What's he doing?' Mousa asked.

'He uses a multiband receiver, to scan for sleeper transmitters. Our teams in France have had much success in finding government bunkers with this equipment.'

Mousa could have kicked himself. The transmitter issue was one concept he had initially approved during the earliest planning phases, but problems were encountered with their operation. The plan was quietly shelved but not before hundreds had been issued to deep-cover agents. He followed Haseeb and his team into the generator room, while the Afghan with the receiver unit extended a short aerial and walked slowly down the ramp, waving the instrument from side to side. A few metres behind, Haseeb turned to Mousa.

'It is possible an agent may have secreted a transmitter in this room or its locality.'

'Unlikely,' Mousa countered.

An audible beep echoed around the room. The Afghan with the transmitter walked slowly towards one of the electrical cabinets; the volume and rapidity of the electronic signal suddenly intensified. Haseeb turned and nodded.

Mousa's pulse quickened. A deep-penetration agent in Number Ten? No, he knew of all of the high-level agents. Someone else then, a sleeper who had somehow gained access to the tunnel system. The chaos of the terror attacks could certainly produce such a scenario. So maybe the signal was genuine? He ran his hands over the cabinet, tapping, probing, feeling the joints for any abnormality. He summoned Karroubi with a loud bark.

'I want this unit taken apart, now!'

Minutes later, Mousa watched with satisfaction as an ingeniously disguised crawl space was exposed at the base of the unit. Shortly afterwards, the engineering team reported the existence of a small room on the other side. Mousa ordered the crawl space cleared and turned to Karroubi.

'Captain Haseeb has a request. Is there a penal squad close by?'

Major Karroubi had an answer within thirty seconds. 'Yes, General. There's one under guard less than a mile from here.'

'Their crimes?'

'Most are being held for looting. Some for rape.'

'Have them brought over here immediately.'

Twenty minutes later, fourteen terrified Arabian soldiers trooped down into the generator room under armed guard. Their weapons and webbing had been stripped from them and they were forced to wear the black armbands and epaulettes of penal troops.

Mousa could barely look at them, such was his contempt. He waved a dismissive hand. 'They're all yours, Haseeb.'

Several of the penal squad watched in barely concealed horror as the big Afghan stepped out from the shadows. Haseeb picked out two men, gave them a torch each and ordered them inside the crawl space. One immediately dropped to his knees and began crawling. The other looked the Afghan squarely in the eye and refused point-blank, claiming his presence in the penal squad had been a mistake.

With amazing speed that surprised them all, Haseeb drew a short, curved knife and slit the man's throat as he protested his innocence. A look of surprise came over the prisoner's face as Haseeb holstered the blade and pulled him out from the group, shoving him roughly across the room. The man dropped his torch and reached up, his surprise turning to shock, then fear, as warm blood ran freely over his hands, splashing down the front of his combat jacket. By the time he crumpled to the floor, another volunteer had scurried quickly into the crawl space. Mousa tried to keep the look of surprise off his own face at the speed and skill of the knife attack. A shout from inside the cabinet refocussed the general's attention.

'We're in a small room,' echoed the voice. 'There's another door here, a big steel one. Wait... I've found a light switch.'

The explosion rocked the floor beneath them, sending everyone diving to the ground. A cloud of smoke and debris billowed from the crawl space and filled the generator room. When the dust had settled, Captain Haseeb bundled another penal squad member inside. He reported back a few minutes later, covered in blood and what Mousa presumed to be pieces of human tissue.

'A cavern?' Mousa repeated.

'Yes, General,' the soldier stammered. 'And more tunnels, large ones.'

'Get down there, quickly!' he ordered the Afghan.

As the remainder of the penal troops disappeared from view, another explosion rocked the floor beneath them. Mousa cursed the delay as Haseeb's team were forced to drop flares down on to the cavern floor and rappel their way down on ropes. Mousa watched from above as the two surviving penal squad members, moaning in agony beneath the twisted wreckage of the gantry and staircase, were swiftly and expertly released from their pain. Next to Mousa, Haseeb listened to the team's radio chatter through his headset. After several minutes he turned to the general.

'It's some sort of transport system. There are two small-gauge train tunnels, one heading north, the other west. The complex appears to be deserted.'

Mousa fumed silently. No doubt Beecham had been here, and recently; but the tunnel was far more complex than he'd imagined. Speed was what they needed now. Mousa fired off his orders.

'Major Karroubi, get the assault teams down here now. Captain Haseeb, split your men into two groups and send one up each tunnel. Tell them to look for signs of recent passage. And get the engineers down there. I want power and light as soon as possible. I also want three companies of infantry on the surface at my disposal. Have them assemble in St James's Park with their vehicles. I want to be able to cut off the infidels' escape once we find out where they're headed.'

Haseeb's headset crackled again. The Afghan listened intently for a few moments and turned to Mousa. 'General, we have acquired another transmitter signal, broadcasting on the same frequency as the one in the generator room. It's faint, but it's there.'

'Where?' demanded Mousa.

'The westbound tunnel.'

Mousa thought quickly. He turned to Karroubi. 'My orders stand. Get it done immediately.'

'Yes sir.' The major limped away.

'Captain Haseeb, send your men into the westbound tunnel as quickly as you can. We may be right behind them. Remember, the prime minister must be taken alive. Go!'

Battersea,
South London

It had taken Danesh Khan almost half an hour to climb the fire escape stairs inside Park Heights. On seeing the trucks loaded with armed men approach the complex below him, it had taken him less than fifteen minutes to get back down to the lobby.

He took a moment to catch his breath, then made his way outside on to the mezzanine level, peering carefully over the railing. The armed men were already inside the mall, milling around the deserted shops and restaurants. Khan did a quick headcount. Twenty, maybe more, and in no apparent hurry to leave the scene. Their voices drifted up towards him, the sound echoing around the darkened complex. It wouldn't be long before they began to move up to the mezzanine level, maybe check out Park Heights Tower itself. He had to get out of there.

Keeping low, he made his way outside the building. His instincts told him he would be safer north of the river, to cross Chelsea Bridge and disappear into the streets beyond. It wasn't the best plan ever, but it was all he could think of at that moment. He took a quick look outside and headed towards the security hut and the ramp beyond.

The approaching headlights blinded him, the roar of the trucks deafening as they thundered up the ramp towards him. Every fibre in Khan's body screamed at him to run until the truck tooted its horn as it approached the barrier. In that instant, Khan knew that the driver had mistaken him for one of their own. He forced himself to relax. The trucks slowed, hissing to a stop. The driver in the first truck leaned out and shouted something to him over the sound of idling engines.

Khan could see the silhouettes of two figures on the back of the lead truck, leaning on the roof of the cab. The driver shouted again, beckoning Khan towards him urgently. Khan began to back away, very slowly. Although he spoke fluent Punjabi and Urdu, he couldn't understand this man's dialect. Now one of the men on the back of the truck joined in, beckoning Khan impatiently. Khan replied in Punjabi, telling them he was going to get help to lift the barrier, hoping the ruse would work. He'd almost reached the mezzanine entrance when a loud crack sent him hurtling through the doors, the bullet smashing through a glass pane less than three feet from his body. He slid along the floor on his stomach, scrambling for cover. He stood up and peered around the shattered door. The first truck had crashed through the barrier and was approaching fast.

Khan looked along the mezzanine level to the staircase at the other end of the complex. Two hundred yards at least, and no cover – he'd never make it.

He took a quick look over the railing to the floor below. The men down there had scattered at the sound of the shot and Khan saw several running up the dead escalators to the mezzanine level. It left him with only one possible course of action.

He lifted his weapon and, as the first truck rumbled to a halt outside the glass doors, Khan swung around and fired at the men behind the cab. The long burst sent them tumbling from view and Khan switched targets to the driver, punching several holes through the passenger door and window. The truck lurched forward and stalled, the driver slumped dead over the wheel. Khan turned his attention to the second truck and fired several rounds through the windscreen. The driver ducked and pulled the wheel to the right, saving himself but exposing another man on the back of the truck, who held on with both hands as it veered across the road. Khan shot him and the man screamed, falling from the accelerating vehicle. The truck roared onwards and disappeared down an exit ramp. Khan fired a few more rounds to encourage the driver to keep going.

The darkness of the distant riverside complex beckoned. Khan kept to the shadows of the building, cutting across the moonlit car park just as the first bullets zipped past him. He turned to see a dozen bad guys spread out across the road in pursuit. Ahead of him, several large buildings squatted near the river, seemingly dark and deserted. And that meant lots of hiding places.

With bullets cracking overhead, Khan leapt over the bonnet of an abandoned car and headed north towards the River Thames.

Somewhere Beneath St. James's Park

In the westbound tunnel, Harry slowed from a reasonably paced run to a jog, then a walk. Finally he stopped, resting his hands on his knees while he took in huge gulps of air. He felt like vomiting. Despite his determination to keep up, despite the rumble of explosions behind them, Harry would rather face the prospect of capture than run another step. His head spun and he sank to his knees, retching loudly. Nothing came up except bile.

He heard Gibson order Farrell back down the tunnel to cover their rear. It was clear from the tension in the soldier's voice that progress had been far too slow and Harry was in silent agreement. They'd only just passed the broken train carriage, which was less than a mile in. Still, once they got to the terminus beneath the palace another train carriage should be waiting. Hopefully, that one would be in working order. If it wasn't, they could all be in serious trouble. Harry stood up, cuffing his mouth dry as Farrell returned.

'Sounds like somebody's on our arse already. We've got to speed up,' the soldier said, his eyes flicking toward Harry.

The PM raised his hand. 'Didn't realise how out of condition I was. I don't think–'

Forsythe cut him off. 'Let's keep moving.' He headed up the tunnel without waiting. Harry took a deep breath and followed on behind. Farrell disappeared in the opposite direction.

'Where's he going?'

'He'll try and delay our pursuers. Just keep moving,' urged Forsythe.

They'd covered another few hundred yards when Gibson raised his arm for the group to halt. As Harry tried to catch his breath, Farrell returned.

'Two claymores, all set,' the soldier announced.

Gibson nodded. 'Sweet. Let's take point and recce the platform.'

It was only then that Harry noticed a pale light, its faint glow illuminating the curved wall of the tunnel ahead. Thank God, he breathed silently.

A few minutes later, they were jogging up a sloping ramp and on to the brightly lit platform beneath Buckingham Palace. Harry noticed the cavern here was much smaller than the Downing Street complex, just one platform with several metal benches along its length and a single steel door built into the rough stone wall. Gibson observed that their footsteps created dusty footprints on the platform floor, which meant no one had been down here yet.

An open train carriage waited invitingly halfway along the platform and they piled in quickly, Gibson settling behind a set of uncomplicated controls that consisted of a few digital read-outs and a single lever. He slapped Farrell's arm.

'How many claymores you got left?'

'One.'

'Rig it in the tunnel behind us.'

While Farrell got to work, Gibson turned to Forsythe. 'What happens if we get to Kensington Gardens and the comms equipment is buggered?'

'If we're unable to contact Alternate One, we may have to commandeer a vehicle and head west.'

'Drive through London with all this going on? I wouldn't give much for our chances.'

'It may be our only choice. We have to get clear of the city while we still can.' Forsythe checked his watch. 'It's after midnight. As long as we're away by first light, we may have a chance.'

Harry pointed a finger at the ceiling. 'What about the people up there? I know the king and his family are at Balmoral, but the palace staff?'

The brigadier shook his head. 'We can't save everyone, Harry. Our priority is getting you to Alternate One.'

After another minute or so, Farrell came running up the platform and scrambled aboard the carriage. 'All set.'

'Hold tight, then,' warned Gibson.

He pushed the control lever forward and the carriage began to move slowly away from the platform. Comfortable with its action, he pushed it further, and the carriage accelerated into the dimly lit tunnel deep below Hyde Park Corner.

The Tunnels

General Mousa blinked several times, as the main cavern was suddenly flooded with light.

'Power is restored, General.'

Mousa shot the combat engineer a look. All around him, engineering troops had exposed wiring cabinets and ducting panels, and were busy ferreting away inside them. Mousa stood and left the room. He'd only be in their way. Outside the control room, a company of his paratroopers were assembling on the platform area. Behind him, a continuous stream of soldiers abseiled down on nylon ropes rigged from the room above.

'Captain Haseeb!' The big Afghan was standing at the entrance to the westbound tunnel, a radio clamped to his ear. On Mousa's command, he hurried over. 'Well?'

'My men have discovered a transportation carriage, General. They are inspecting it now–'

Two loud explosions reverberated around the cavern, sending everybody diving for cover. Only Mousa and Haseeb remained upright. Seconds later, a large cloud of dust billowed out of the westbound tunnel. Haseeb's radio crackled. He nodded quickly as he listened to the report and then barked another order. He turned to Mousa.

'More booby traps, claymores this time. I have three dead, one badly wounded. Have we any more penal troops, General? I cannot waste more of my men.'

Mousa gave him a hard look. 'There's no time for that. The British prime minister may be just ahead. You are the experts at this type of warfare. Send your men on!' Haseeb hurried away, barking orders into his radio.

'Major Karroubi!' bellowed Mousa, his voice echoing around the cavern walls. The major, busy organising the rapidly growing number of paratroopers, limped over.

'General?'

'Send two platoons into the westbound tunnel to support the SERTRAK team. Stay out of their way and let them do their job, but tell them to secure any prisoners and send them straight back to me.'

'Yes, General.'

'What of the other tunnel?'

'It heads north, more or less. Apart from the odd curve, the tunnel runs almost straight. I've sent a squad to recce it. No contact so far.'

For Mousa it confirmed what he already believed. 'Call them back.

Where are my surveillance drones?'

'On their way, General. They should be here in minutes.'

Mousa took a few paces towards the mouth of the westbound tunnel, momentarily lost in thought. Al-Bitruji had set up his command post in Buckingham Palace. What was it about that place? He turned to Major Karroubi.

'A map of the area, quickly.'

Karroubi snapped his fingers and a waiting orderly complied. Mousa unfolded the map and laid it on the floor, studying it carefully. After scrutinising it for several seconds, he tapped the document with his finger.

'The westbound tunnel, it leads to Buckingham Palace, I am certain of it. If the infidels would go to such lengths to evacuate a prime minister this way, the same would surely apply to their royal family, which means that this system can be accessed from underneath the palace. Get General Al-Bitruji on the radio. Tell him there is a tunnel entrance somewhere beneath him. It must be found, quickly. We may be able to get ahead of them.'

Karroubi turned to a waiting signaller, who was already hailing Al-Bitruji's command post. After a hurried three-way conversation, Karroubi reported that the surveillance drones had arrived and were being brought down to the cavern along with their operators.

'I'm going to Al-Bitruji's command post,' Mousa announced. 'Have transport waiting for me in Whitehall and call me when the drones are ready to fly. Stay close to the radio, Major. I may need you to move quickly.'

'As you wish, General.'

Mousa secured himself inside a small harness and was winched up to the room above. There was still blood on the walls where the explosive light fitting had detonated, but Mousa was pleased to see that the false electrical unit and the wall behind it had been removed completely, allowing Mousa to pass unhindered into the generator room. Two paratroopers fell in alongside him as he made his way out into a rubble-strewn Whitehall. Smoke hung like a heavy curtain across the street and distant gunfire echoed on the night air. A Humvee waited, engine idling. Mousa hopped aboard with his escort and the vehicle swung around, heading towards Parliament Square.

The jeep turned right into Birdcage Walk, then right again into Horse Guards Road. Mousa watched as hundreds of prisoners, their hands clasped above their heads, shuffled slowly forward towards Parliament Square, guarded by Arabian soldiers. By the look of most of them they were office workers, maybe government personnel. Many wore shirts and ties, and some wore clothes that were torn and bloodied. There were others mixed among them, wearing uniforms; soldiers, police officers, surrendered or captured. Mousa didn't give much for their eventual fate.

The vehicle hummed along The Mall, the driver weaving left and right to avoid the hundreds of discarded parachutes that drifted across the road. When they reached the gates of Buckingham Palace, Mousa saw that the black iron barricades had been wrenched from their concrete plinths and lay twisted on the parade ground. In their place, two armoured fighting vehicles had taken up position either side of the entrance. Mousa watched as their forty-millimetre guns tracked the Humvee as it approached. A soldier waved a fluorescent wand and the vehicle whined to a halt.

Mousa's identity was confirmed and the Humvee was quickly waved through. It continued under the arched portico and entered the central courtyard of the palace, where the driver found a space amongst the numerous vehicles already there. Mousa glanced up, noticing the camouflage netting that had been draped overhead. An orderly approached and gave a small bow.

'General Mousa, an honour, sir. General Al-Bitruji is in the command post. I will escort you there immediately.'

With his bodyguards in tow, Mousa followed the orderly along the red-carpeted hallways of Buckingham Palace. He was pleased to see it untouched. Looting by Arabian troops was strictly forbidden, although Mousa had to admit that the temptation to pick up a souvenir here would be hard to resist. They made their way through several rooms into what was obviously a staff corridor. They passed a room that housed several easy chairs, an old plasma TV screen, and piles of newspapers and magazines scattered on a heavily stained coffee table.

After several more twists and turns through the palace kitchens, Mousa followed the orderly down a flight of smooth stone steps to the palace basement. There was much more activity here, with communications and power cables running along the floor. The cables snaked their way into a large, low-ceilinged storeroom and it was here that Al-Bitruji had sited his command post. A good choice, Mousa had to admit: underground, easy access to the floors above and, if he was not mistaken, an exit to the grounds of the palace itself. A corridor opposite the command post had a heavy blackout curtain across it and a sign ordering the observation of light discipline. Soldiers scurried to and fro. The place was a hive of activity.

Inside the command post, a large battlefield command screen was being monitored by a dozen operators. Mousa noticed an air defence detachment lining one wall, their air-search consoles glowing in the darkened room. No doubt the roof of the palace bristled with anti-aircraft batteries and troops with handheld SAMs. General Al-Bitruji looked up from a large-scale map as Mousa entered.

'Ah! General Mousa! Good to see you!'

The overweight Al-Bitruji crossed the room and shook Mousa's hand, kissing him lightly on each cheek. They had known each other for many years, each man's steady rise up the ladder mirrored by the other. But there the similarities ended. Although both held the rank of general, it was Mousa who had unrestricted access to the cleric. Technically, there was no difference in their status, but the reality was somewhat different, as both men knew. It was for that reason that Al-Bitruji tried to humour the tough paratrooper before him. He gently steered Mousa by the elbow out of earshot of the command post staff.

'So, Faris. Still jumping out of planes with the young bucks, eh?'

Mousa smiled thinly. 'General Al-Bitruji, the mission I have been given is one of the highest importance. This is neither the time nor the place for frivolity. You received my message?'

Al-Bitruji's dark eyes darted left and right. Only Mousa's bodyguards had heard the rebuke.

'Yes, of course, your message. Come.' He smiled through gritted teeth, leading Mousa over to the command screen and barking orders at the operators. The display changed to a large-scale representation of Buckingham Palace and its immediate area. Mousa watched as a row of coloured dots moved upwards across the screen. Al-Bitruji pointed to the slow-moving icons.

'Those are combat engineers, spread out across the grounds of the palace. They're carrying imaging equipment that can detect heat sources deep underground. They can also detect large voids and cavities beneath the surface. I have other teams searching every basement and cellar in this building. If there is a tunnel here, we'll find it.'

Mousa nodded. Al-Bitruji had deployed his troops well. Maybe he'd been a bit hard on his fellow general. 'How goes the invasion?' he asked, softening his tone.

Al-Bitruji gave another order and the screen changed to show an overhead view of England and Wales. Arabian forces were represented by green icons and the southern half of England showed large concentrations of them, particularly in the south-east and the Midlands.

'The invasion is going exactly as planned,' replied Al-Bitruji, clearly eager to please. 'All preliminary targets have been seized. Our ships are docking unopposed and offloading supplies as we speak. Apart from a brief contact with an enemy helicopter, our own convoy made it here virtually unopposed. The second convoy from the port of Southampton is on its way. That one is made up of heavy armour, tanks and fighting vehicles. In fact, it has almost reached the outskirts of the capital.' Al-Bitruji pointed to a long line of icons that stretched along the M3 motorway.

Mousa's eye drifted down towards the city of Portsmouth, situated on the south coast. 'What is happening here?' enquired Mousa, pointing at a cluster of red dots.

'British marines on the naval base, digging their heels in. Two of our cargo ships have also been sunk by a frigate. They also have air defences. One of our helicopters was shot down with a SAM.'

The pale light of the basement failed to mask the sheen of sweat on Al-Bitruji's brow. Mousa knew he only had to file one bad report, plant a single seed of doubt about Al-Bitruji's abilities, and the portly general's career would be over. He would be shipped back east, to serve out his time in some flyblown posting in the desert. An inglorious end to a long and distinguished career. He kept his face neutral, deriving some pleasure from Al-Bitruji's obvious discomfort.

A junior officer approached, flicking up a hand in salute.

'Yes, what is it?' demanded Al-Bitruji.

'General, we have found the entrance to the tunnel system.'

'Show me,' interrupted Mousa, barging past Al-Bitruji. They marched along a short corridor and out into the gardens at the rear of the palace, making their way quickly across the manicured lawns towards Constitution Hill, where the trees and shrubbery were thickest. Close to the boundary wall and adjacent to a woodland path, Mousa saw several soldiers in a clearing. They were gathered around a small blockhouse, expertly dressed in ornate flowers and vines and partly shielded from the path by thick bushes. Even in daylight it would be hard to spot. As he approached, the soldiers parted silently. Mousa's guide pointed beyond the heavy wooden door.

'It leads down to a train platform, General.'

Mousa took the stairs two at a time. At the bottom he found himself in a cavern similar to the one under Downing Street but much smaller. Several engineers were already inspecting the platform area along with some of Al-Bitruji's combat troops. To his right, the tunnel disappeared around a curve. Mousa jumped down on to the tracks. The smooth concrete between the rails was spotted with oil. Mousa dipped his finger into a small stain and rubbed it between thumb and forefinger. Fresh. So, they had missed them. They must have found another train and continued on into the tunnel. Where that led was anyone's guess.

As if to rubber-stamp his hypothesis, Captain Haseeb and his SERTRAK team appeared in the mouth of the eastbound tunnel. They were panting hard, trying to make up for the lost time that the claymores had cost them. Haseeb approached, cocking a thumb over his shoulder.

'We've defused another booby trap, but this one was clumsily sited. We cannot be far behind them.'

A low humming noise from the tunnel caused everyone to stop what they were doing and turn to face the growing sound. The humming increased in volume and the object glided gently into the cavern. As it reached the centre of the platform area it slowed and hovered quietly in the air, bouncing and swaying two yards off the ground. Mousa reached for his radio.

'Major Karroubi!'

Karroubi's voice crackled in Mousa's earpiece. 'General! I have you on audio and visual.'

Mousa saw the surveillance drone turn and dip its nose towards him. It was grey in colour and just over two metres in length. Shaped like a cigar with two small wings, the drone sported two high-powered cameras in its nose and a directional microphone that could pick up normal human conversation at fifteen metres. It was powered by four small multidirectional electric motors, and the built-in helium cells along its toughened plastic body gave it lift. It was very quiet and very fast. Mousa pointed to his right.

'Continue up the tunnel, Major. Find them!'

The drone's nose dipped again and its small motors swivelled around and thrust it forward, its low hum echoing off the tunnels walls. Mousa turned to the big Afghan.

'Follow the bird but do not engage the infidels, do you understand?'

The Afghan bowed his head. 'As you wish.'

Haseeb and his team set off after the drone at a fast pace. Mousa watched them disappear around a bend in the tunnel and turned quickly on his heel, making his way back up the stairs to the palace gardens.

Battersea, South London

Khan ran for his life towards the River Thames. Behind him, the sounds of deadly pursuit echoed across the night air. There were at least a dozen bad guys behind him, maybe more, and they were coming up fast. He veered right, cutting across the dark expanse of an open car park. He heard a shout and glanced over his shoulder. His toe caught a raised kerb and he tumbled across the concrete, rolling painfully over the weapon slung across his back. He lay still, peering beneath a parked car as he caught his breath. Several figures had reached the edge of the car park, spread out and alert, their weapons sweeping the darkness ahead of them. Khan rolled away and crawled towards a grassy slope, dragging himself down the short bank. Back on his feet, he headed east along the riverbank.

A short distance away was Battersea Harbour. Like its nearby cousin in Chelsea, Battersea Harbour was a luxury hotel and residential complex that boasted a private marina, with low-rise apartment buildings forming an expensive boundary around its wooden jetties. Khan headed straight towards the marina. He forced his way through the landscaped shrubbery and found himself on a wide footpath overlooking the man-made harbour.

Now he had two choices; one, keep moving and double back on himself, losing his pursuers in the labyrinth of apartment blocks, walkways and streets between the river and Nine Elms Lane. But that would mean heading back to where he started, trapped on the south bank of the river. Or two, find an empty apartment or hotel room amongst the many hundreds in the area and hole up inside, where he'd stand a good chance of avoiding detection until his pursuers eventually gave up their search. But for how long could he stay hidden? Without food or water it wouldn't be long before he'd have to venture out on to the streets again. But maybe there was a third choice, staring him right in the face.

Keeping low, Khan headed towards a flight of stone steps that led down to the marina. He stepped over a chain from which dangled a small sign that read 'Private' and headed down to the wooden jetties. There were numerous boats tied alongside their moorings, ranging from sailing boats to luxury motor cruisers and rigid inflatable craft. Sailing boats were out; too much effort to get moving and far too slow. He dismissed the motor cruisers too; a gleaming white craft would make an excellent target out on the dark waters of the river. No, he needed something else and, as his eyes swept the small harbour, he spotted the very thing. He moved quickly along the jetty.

The twenty-four-foot Targa was tied off between a single-masted yacht and a small skiff. Khan gave it the once-over. It looked like a workboat, its dull grey paint flaking and its sides blackened by the constant rub of jetty tyres, but if she would start she would be perfect. He noticed that the mooring lines had been tied expertly around the cleats. Whoever owned this vessel obviously possessed a fair degree of seamanship, which was a good sign.

She was called *Kingfisher* and she wobbled on the water as Khan jumped aboard. He moved forward into the small wheelhouse, which had a two-berth cabin immediately below it. Khan hissed a quick 'hello' just in case there was anyone aboard, but thankfully the boat was empty.

He looked around quickly, familiarising himself with the layout as best he could in the darkness. There was a small chart table to his left with what looked like several river maps clipped to its surface. He pulled himself up on to the helm seat and acquainted himself with the controls, searching the immediate area for an ignition key. Nothing. He went out on to the aft deck, removed the hatch cover of the engine compartment and found what he was looking for. Strapped to the underside of the cover was a small tool roll. He unfurled it on the deck and found a medium-sized screwdriver.

Back in the pilot house, he jammed the blade into the ignition slot and forced the barrel. Khan was relieved to see the ignition lights glow red and watched with mounting satisfaction as the fuel needle crept up to the full mark and the oil pressure gauge levelled out. Even the battery was fully charged. As Khan had suspected, the *Kingfisher* was well maintained.

He turned the screwdriver another notch and the small but powerful inboard engine rumbled into life. Outside, Khan replaced the engine cover and untied the mooring ropes. He held his breath. Above him he could hear the shouts of his pursuers echoing around the car park. Soon they would head towards the marina and that would be that.

He jammed his foot against the jetty and pushed off, drifting out into the oily waters of the harbour. He scrambled into the wheelhouse and eased the throttle forward a notch. The propeller bit into the black water and the *Kingfisher* began to make headway. Ahead of him, he could see the open gates of the harbour entrance and the darkness of the river beyond. He muttered a silent prayer of thanks that the tide was high enough.

The moon had slid behind a bank of cloud and visibility was momentarily restricted. He kept the revs low, passing the harbour gates and drifting out on to the river. Almost immediately the current caught the bow and turned the small boat downstream. Khan increased power and turned her back to port, his eyes scanning the riverbank above him. Nothing.

Ahead of him in the darkness were two bridges. The first was Grosvenor Bridge, the crossing used by commuter trains heading in and out of Victoria station north of the river. Almost immediately after that was

Chelsea Bridge, the span used by motorists. Khan couldn't detect any movement on either crossing, but from his position on the water it would be difficult to spot anyway. He had to risk it.

The *Kingfisher's* engine echoed off the damp walls of the Grosvenor Bridge pier as the boat slid under the wide, iron span above. Khan cut the revs to idle to keep the engine noise down, but the strong current threatened to turn the bow and drag him back towards the marina. He had no choice. Khan pushed the throttle to the stop and the water at the stern turned to white foam as the *Kingfisher* surged forward. Anyone on the riverbank above would surely hear the boat's engine, but it was time to put some distance between himself and the danger behind him.

Moments later, Khan was relieved to see Chelsea Bridge pass above him as he headed further out towards the middle of the river, cutting the power back once he had cleared the bridge. Behind him a flare arched into the air and popped high overhead, the river suddenly bathed in a green phosphorous light. The illumination wavered and flickered, casting the dark, looming towers of Park Heights into sharp relief. The flare fizzed and hissed beneath its tiny parachute as it drifted out over the water. Khan instinctively ducked when he heard a long burst of automatic fire, but he soon realised it was directed elsewhere and the darkness returned as the flare extinguished itself on the river.

To his left, the shadowy expanse of Battersea Park drifted by and Khan breathed a small sigh of relief. He had escaped, buying himself a brief respite from the chaos on dry land.

Behind him, the sky over London glowed red. But here, on a small boat on the river, Khan felt cocooned from the violence and carnage that raged around him.

And there was something else, too. He had a plan now, a plan that would take him upriver and out of the city.

Somewhere Beneath Euston Station

The pace had started well enough, but the further north they went, the slower progress became. Tony Brooks was more than a little frustrated, but so far there'd been no sounds of pursuit. Not yet, anyway, but that didn't mean they had to move like a couple of pensioners.

Up ahead, Nasser took the lead, making his way up the tunnel at an almost casual pace. The concrete shaft was lit by small overhead lights, recessed into the curved ceiling and spaced every hundred feet or so. The distance between the overhead fixtures, combined with their low wattage, created pools of gloom in which one trooper and then the other would be momentarily lost as they headed up the tunnel.

Deep in the shadows, Brooks stopped once again, turning to face the way they'd come, a small pair of binoculars clamped to his eyes, his ears alert for the sounds of pursuit. Nothing. The empty tunnel stretched away into the distance, back towards Downing Street. He jogged after Nasser, still strolling along as if he didn't have a care in the world.

'Come on, Naz, let's move it.'

Nasser stopped. He pulled out his water bottle and took a few small sips. 'What's the rush?'

Brooks frowned. 'Is that a joke?'

'We have to leave a trail, you know that.'

'We're wasting our time. No one's after us. Maybe they know the boss has taken the other tunnel,' Brooks speculated. 'We should head back.'

'No,' Nasser ordered. 'We stick to the plan.'

'Bollocks to that. If the lads are in trouble we go back. Besides, we stand a better chance of getting to Alternate One if we can hook up with them again.'

Nasser cocked his chin. 'What's up, Brooksy? Frightened of missing the chopper?'

'What the fuck's that supposed to mean?'

Suddenly Nasser's eyes narrowed. He held up a hand for silence. 'Shh!' He glanced over Brooks's shoulder. 'We've got company.'

Brooks spun around, dropping to one knee. He brought his weapon up into his shoulder, peering through the optical sight. 'Can't see shit,' he whispered.

The flash lit up the tunnel walls and Brooks fell forward. He tried to put his hands up to protect his face, but he was too slow and his head slapped hard on to the concrete floor. Blood began to pool beneath his chin. As the sound of gunfire echoed along the tunnel, Nasser knelt beside him.

'Brooksy, can you hear me?' A thin wisp of smoke curled from the muzzle of his pistol in his hand. He used it to jab Brooks sharply in the back. The soldier grunted, turning his head towards the sound of his colleague's voice. Confusion twisted Brooks's face.

'I've been hit,' he rasped.

Nasser smiled in the gloom. 'I know. Got you right under your body armour. Loads of internal damage, I reckon. Does it hurt?'

Brooks tried to speak again but failed, the pain of betrayal clouding his eyes, blood speckling his lips. 'Why?' he finally managed.

Nasser smiled and shook his head. Why? Such a stupid question. He noticed that Brooks's eyes were beginning to take on the dullness of imminent death. There wasn't enough time to explain why. It was Allah's will, simple as that. Besides, the infidels never understood that a Muslim's duty was to his religion first. Everything else was secondary, unimportant. It was difficult for Nasser to understand the naivety of the infidels, but there it was. They were blind to the threat that existed amongst them and, despite all the security screenings and background checks, all of which failed to uncover his own true allegiances, he'd still made it this far, into the belly of the beast.

Nasser listened to his former comrade's laboured breathing. It wouldn't be long now. He would wait until he'd passed over, then rejoin his Brothers and continue the hunt for Beecham. He hoped the brigadier and Gibson would be captured alive. He hoped to see the shock on their faces when they realised it was Nasser who had betrayed them, who had worked the duty roster to ensure he was on standby this day.

He smiled. Things were working out extremely well. He'd managed to attach the first of his two transmitters to the equipment panel in the generator room, the other one to Beecham's clothing. His Brothers had found the underground complex quickly, probably due to his first transmitter. With the grace of God the other one would ensure the capture of the prime minister. And it would all be Nasser's doing.

He fished inside his webbing and pulled out a green headscarf, wrapping it tightly around his forehead. After all he'd been through, he wouldn't want to be mistaken for an enemy soldier now. He felt a rush of excitement. Soon he would be able to return to his childhood home in the Emirates, to the land he'd fallen in love with as a boy and left in tears as a young man. He remembered the view from his father's veranda well – the sheltered cove, the white sands, the warm waters of the Gulf that lapped against the nearby shore. It was here that he would settle, carve out a new life for himself, reforge his family ties. After almost twenty years away, forced to suffer the immoral existence of an infidel, it was the very least he was owed.

It was time to go, but first he would relieve Brooks of his weapon and ammunition. He had to move quickly now; time was of the essence. He had information, the co-ordinates of Alternate One somewhere beneath the Mendip Hills, information the Arabian high command urgently needed.

He stared into the dull, lifeless eyes of his former comrade. Despite his faults, he hadn't been a bad man. He closed his own eyes and muttered a quick prayer; then, with considerable effort, he grabbed Brooks's webbing straps and stood upright, flipping the dead soldier over on to his back. He heard two sounds, almost simultaneously.

The first came from Brooks himself, a groan that escaped his throat as his body thumped back down on to the concrete. Nasser looked down to see his colleague's blood-covered face grinning up at him. The bastard wasn't dead! The second sound was a metallic zing, and something flew past his leg, caught in his peripheral vision. Instinctively, Nasser knew what it was.

He spun around, desperately searching the gloom behind him, the fear and panic rising in him instantly. Then he saw it, almost at his feet. It rocked from side to side as it settled on the tunnel floor, its fat, green body decorated with stencilled white lettering.

For nine years, SAS Trooper Sami Nasser had lived a secret life, a special forces soldier in the British Army, but one whose true allegiance lay with his Arabian Brothers. At the moment of his death, his years of living in the West, and in particular in the company of elite soldiers, had conditioned the verbal response to his impending doom.

'Oh fuck,' he whispered.

The grenade, along with several others, detonated, shredding both soldiers to pieces.

The Battle of Kew Bridge

For the past hour, Alex and Kirsty had huddled together on the towpath, hidden deep inside a thick clump of bushes two hundred yards short of Kew Bridge. They sat with their rucksacks on, leaning against the tidal wall, while they waited for the soldiers above them to move off.

Progress along the riverbank had been short-lived. They'd barely walked half a mile before Alex had spotted movement on the bridge ahead of them. They'd ducked into bushes alongside the path, watching with mounting alarm as one silhouette became two, then three. Shortly afterwards, a truck growled over the bridge and stopped dead centre, disgorging several more figures. By the headlights of the truck, Alex could see that the new arrivals were soldiers and momentarily his hopes soared. But his elation was fleeting. As he studied the figures on the bridge, one thing became certain: they weren't British troops.

He held Kirsty close as a powerful beam of light washed over the shrubbery that concealed them, lingering for a second before it swept away over the river and the opposite bank. After a few minutes the light was extinguished, replaced with the pinprick glow of cigarettes. Two of the soldiers leaned over the parapet, chatting and smoking, while the others paced up and down the bridge. If they moved now they would surely be spotted.

Alex checked his watch; gone two already. It'd be light in a couple of hours. He felt Kirsty squeeze his hand. She hadn't said a single word, not since she'd followed Alex's pointed finger, saw the soldiers on the bridge, the trucks and armoured vehicles that swept past their hiding place into West London. She shivered in the damp air, her fingers trembling beneath his own. He had to get her out of this godawful mess.

He dropped her hand, his head cocked to one side. He pushed himself into a squatting position, his eyes peering through the foliage and out on to the river. There it was again – the faint chug of a motor that briefly registered above the ambient sound of the river's passage. Was that a boat? He gripped Kirsty's hand again and pulled her quietly to her feet. He leaned in very close, whispering in her ear.

'We're going to head back along the towpath. When I move, you move. Okay?' Kirsty nodded, her eyes wide with fear. Alex eased himself closer to the path.

Up on the bridge, another convoy approached and the smoking soldiers moved out of sight. This was their chance. Alex pulled Kirsty out on to the path and headed back towards the apartment block. After a couple of hundred yards they paused, crouching against the embankment wall. Alex peered into the darkness. There was that sound again, more distinctive now and accompanied by the slap of water against a boat hull. Moments later, he heard the low growl of an engine and an object drifted into his peripheral vision. It glided out from behind the dark bulk of Oliver's Island in the centre of the river, chugging cautiously upstream. Alex had the feeling that whoever was behind the wheel was also trying to avoid contact.

Acting on instinct, he pulled a torch from his pocket. He flicked it on and off, on and off, aiming the thin beam at the pilot house. Come on, willed Alex. Look over here. He kept flicking the switch until his thumb hurt and the boat was almost level with them. Suddenly, the boat's engine died and Alex watched as the bow turned towards them. Slowly the boat drifted into the riverbank. A dark form emerged from the cabin on to the open deck. It was a man.

'Stay low,' Alex whispered to Kirsty. He glanced towards Kew Bridge, where another military convoy rumbled northwards, then stepped carefully towards the water's edge. Alex watched as the man threw a line towards him. Alex grabbed it and began pulling the boat towards the muddy bank. The moon drifted out from behind high cloud and Alex was suddenly alarmed to see that the pilot had a rifle slung across his back. Alex kept his hand close to his pistol just in case.

The boat bumped against the bank as Alex tied the rope off around a bench on the towpath. The men looked at each other in the darkness and Alex suddenly felt the ridiculous urge to shout friend or foe? The pilot smiled and held out his hand.

'Coming aboard?' he whispered.

'Too bloody right. Got room for two?' replied Alex.

'Sure.' They helped a worried-looking Kirsty over the rail, then Alex hopped aboard. The pilot beckoned them into the wheelhouse.

'Thanks for stopping,' Alex whispered. 'Thought you'd miss us.'

'Had to give you the once-over with these.' The man held up a pair of binoculars. 'You're the first friendlies I've seen since all this started. My name is Danesh Khan. Friends call me Dan.'

'Alex Taylor. This is my neighbour, Kirsty. We live in an apartment block back along the river. We're trying to get out of the city.'

'My idea exactly.' Khan indicated Alex's black clothing and weapons. 'Are you military?' he asked.

'No, I'm a police officer. Firearms team.'

Khan dug into his trouser pocket and produced his Security Services ID. 'A spook?' asked Alex.

'Yep. What's your take on all this?'

'I was off duty when it all kicked off. Seems like everything's fallen to pieces.'

Khan nodded in the dark. 'That's about right. What happened to you?'

'Passenger jet got shot down with surface-to-air missiles. It crashed over there.' Alex pointed across the river, where the sky still glowed a deep red. 'The shooters were behind our apartment block. I tried to stop them but I ended up dropping all three. Then things went from bad to worse.'

For the next few minutes, Alex and Khan recounted their experiences of the previous evening. Alex mentioned his plan to hide out at his brother's place in Wiltshire.

'Nice idea.' Khan pointed through the window of the pilot house. 'Looks like the Arabians are consolidating their positions, and it's a fair bet that London isn't their only target. If this is taking place nationwide, then no major city will be safe. Have you seen any military response?'

Alex shook his head. 'Nothing.'

'In that case we're in deep trouble, my friend.'

'So what do we do now?'

Khan sized up the new arrivals. The girl seemed pretty spaced out, but the guy was a cop, one who had weapons, supplies and a plan. In this situation, three heads were better than one.

'Short term? We'll head upriver, get away from the city. Mind if I tag along to your brother's place, until I sort myself out?'

'Sure.'

'Great. Let's go then.'

Alex stepped out of the wheelhouse, untied the line and pushed the *Kingfisher* off the bank. The boat drifted silently out into the dark waters. In the wheelhouse, Khan pointed to the small cabin below.

'Kirsty, why don't you get yourself down there for a bit, just until we clear the bridge?' Kirsty nodded and went below. Khan turned to Alex. 'I'm going to start the engine. When we get to within five hundred feet of the bridge, I'll cut the motor and drift underneath. The tide has turned in the last hour so, with any luck, the current will help us along. We should be able to pass unnoticed, as long as those sentries up there don't take too much interest in the river. If they do spot us, I'm going to make a run for it.'

Alex nodded grimly. 'Just get us under that bloody bridge.'

Khan turned the screwdriver in the ignition on the console and the engine growled into life before settling into a low gurgle. He advanced the throttle and brought the boat midstream, its bow pointed towards the dark mouth under the centre arch. Slowly, they began to advance towards the bridge.

The mob gathered once again beneath the dark concrete towers of the sprawling housing estate. They congregated in silence, herded into position by local gang leaders, men whose reputations for violence were well known. Unlike the first time they'd assembled, this time they were armed. Their weapons were crude: petrol bombs, knives, bats and heavy clubs. The gang leaders carried guns. Their objective was to get more.

They'd all seen the plane crash, the pillars of smoke that rose above the city, the chaos on the streets. As darkness fell and gunfire echoed around West London, the older residents cowered in terror, locked inside their apartments.

But not the young. For them, the anarchy drew them like a magnet, adrenaline the night's drug of choice. They left the safety of their homes, collecting in small groups beneath the concrete awnings and parapets of the housing estate. They were inquisitive, wary, but not frightened. They were accustomed to the random violence of the streets, drip-fed on images of war and bloody conflict their whole lives. Now they were witnessing it at first hand and their blood was up.

Older men arrived in a convoy of vehicles, local men with reputations for drug dealing, violence and intimidation. Some carried weapons, automatic pistols and shotguns. They rounded up the young ones and sent them away.

'Arm up', they said, 'find whatever weapons you can and get back here as quickly as possible.' Some had returned to their apartments, rummaging in bedrooms and kitchen drawers, while others looted the shops around the estate. They were nearly six hundred strong and their targets were the soldiers who guarded Kew Bridge.

They split into two groups. A smaller group, the mob leaders, made their way quietly through the backstreets and scrambled up a steep railway embankment overlooking the area. From here, they had a commanding view of the northern end of the bridge and the intersection at Kew Bridge Road and Chiswick High Road. There, two military lorries had been parked side-on, blocking vehicular access to the bridge from the west. The vehicles were being guarded by several Arabian troops, their demeanour relaxed, almost casual. It was a mistake.

Orders were given and the main group moved quickly, using the unlit backstreets to get into position. They approached to within one hundred feet of the roadblock, bunching behind vehicles and walls. Bodies tense, hearts pounding, they waited for the signal to attack.

The Arabian guards on the bridge passed out another round of cigarettes and relaxed a little more. They had just waved another convoy across and it would be a good half hour before the next one was due. The troops should have been more alert but they were not front-line soldiers, mostly reservists commandeered for traffic duty.

Now that the transport ships had docked along the English coast, the convoys would start to become heavier and more frequent, which meant more work for them. Their officer, who slept soundly in his Humvee in a side street, warned them that things were going to get very busy.

'Enjoy the quiet moments while you still can,' he'd advised them before retiring for the evening. So the soldiers had bid him goodnight and continued their slow pacing up and down the bridge, occasionally shining a torch beam over the dark waters below.

At the northern roadblock by Chiswick High Road, four Arabian soldiers were smoking cigarettes and chatting when the air around them was suddenly filled with flaming torches. The petrol bombs shattered around their feet, engulfing the soldiers in a sheet of flame. The vehicles blocking the road also caught fire, adding to the conflagration.

The guards on the bridge came running towards the roadblock, watching in horror as their comrades screamed and writhed on the floor. That's when the mob rose as one, a blood-curdling crescendo of yelling and screaming, the thunderous stampede of feet. The Arabians spun back towards the bridge.

Encouraged by the fleeing soldiers and eager for a taste of the action, the leaders scrambled down the embankment, advancing carefully towards the fighting. They kept low, hiding in the shadows of a small row of shops, watching, waiting for the right moment. The mob was in full flow now, screaming and pounding towards the rise of the bridge.

The Arabians had managed to organise themselves quickly and spread out across the width of the road. Their weapons began to chatter, every bullet finding a target amongst the charging horde. The first wave fell to the ground, the others immediately behind tripping and stumbling over the casualties. Suddenly, several small explosions detonated in the middle of the crowd and dreadful screams filled the air.

What had started out as a night of action and opportunity for the mob was quickly turning into a horrific tableau of death. Scores of young men and women were cut down, while the wounded desperately tried to drag themselves out of the way, only to be trampled by the suddenly panicked mob. Sensing a sudden loss of momentum, the youngsters at the rear of the mob began to turn and flee.

In all the chaos, no one noticed the dark shape cutting through the black waters below.

Khan nearly jumped out of his skin when the roar of the mob reached his ears. On the still night air it sounded like an express train thundering towards them. He watched as the Arabians were forced back on to the bridge by a howling pack that surged towards them from the northern bank. The trucks at the end of the bridge suddenly exploded, bathing the scene in a fiery glow. A deafening volley of rifle fire rang out across the water.

'Here's our chance!' Khan hissed. 'Hang on!'

Out on deck, Alex clung to a running rail as the *Kingfisher's* engine roared into life, powering the small boat across the flat surface of the river. He crouched low, hands furiously gripping the rail. Above him he could see scores of dark figures, silhouetted against the flames of the burning trucks. It was a scene from hell and the sound of gunfire, punctuated by shouts and screams, was deafening.

A body toppled over the parapet to their right, followed by another. Both hit the water with a loud splash. Khan spun the wheel slightly to starboard, bringing the boat almost dead centre under the middle span. The sound of the engine echoed off the damp brickwork and the boat surged through to the other side, quickly swallowed by the darkness and shielded from the bridge by the bend of the river.

After a couple of hundred yards, Khan eased the throttle back and slowed the boat to a near stop. Kirsty popped her head up from the cabin below.

'You okay?' asked Khan.

Kirsty nodded, her voice a little shaky. 'What the hell was all that terrible noise?'

'Trouble on the bridge. We're past it now. Check on Alex, will you?'

Kirsty stepped out of the wheelhouse and joined Alex on the rear deck.

'Hey,' he said quietly. 'You alright?'

She smiled and nodded, slipping her arm through his and giving him a comforting squeeze. He squeezed back, his eyes locked on the sky that glowed red above the trees.

On Kew Bridge, the mob had finally scattered into the darkness of the surrounding streets. Behind them, littered across the road, over a hundred of their fellow rioters were either dead or wounded. It was the Arabian officer, sleeping soundly in the back of his vehicle, who'd turned the tide of the bloody engagement.

Parked up a small alleyway behind a row of shops on Chiswick High Road, the roar of the mob had sent him scrambling out of the vehicle. Avoiding the high street itself, the officer had approached the bridge via a path near the river. He kept to the shadows and there he saw the charging mob, surging on to the bridge above him. He'd crept forwards, keeping close to the river, lost in the dark shadows of the bridge itself. Above him, the mob were screaming and wailing, the width of the bridge packed with their bodies. Despite their superior weapons, his men were being pushed back. He glanced up to his right. He could see several of his troops running towards the southern end of the bridge in retreat. It was time to act.

One by one, he pulled the pins from each of his six grenades and lobbed them over the parapet into what he hoped would be the middle of the crowd. He didn't stop throwing until all the grenades were gone. The resulting explosions scythed through the swarm of bodies in a wave of deadly metal fragments and scores of rioters were instantly killed or injured. The Arabians continued to fire into the crowd and the mob faltered, suddenly filled with panic – they had never seen such carnage at first hand, and the leading rioters pushed, shoved and beat their way backwards in an effort to escape.

Encouraged by the retreating crowd, the Arabians on the bridge poured fire into an enemy that had lost its appetite for a fight and was now scattering into the surrounding streets. The officer climbed up the bank and on to the road. He ordered his men forward, waving them back over to the northern end of the bridge. In the darkness ahead, the officer saw the mob leaders break from cover and sprint across the street, heading for the safety of the housing estate. He quickly brought his rifle up and opened fire. He was satisfied to see at least three bodies hit the pavement.

The bridge had been retaken, but not without cost. Fifteen of his men were dead and two seriously injured. Nine had been overrun by the mob and were hacked and beaten to death, while the other six had been killed by petrol bombs. Weapons were also missing. The officer was furious. Within one minute he had personally shot dead six mortally wounded rioters where they lay. When he reached the bodies of the mob's leaders, he found that two of them were still breathing. A total of twenty-seven rioters had been captured alive. Apart from the two older leaders, the officer was shocked to see that most were teenagers, some as young as twelve or thirteen. They were bloodstained and scared, shivering where they lay, face down on the road with their hands flexi-cuffed behind their backs.

The bridge was finally secured and the officer called for replacements for his casualties. The new units would be there at sunrise. The officer looked to the east, where the sky had turned from inky black to deepest blue. It would only be a few short hours until dawn. It had been a close-run thing, but his swift actions had turned the engagement and saved the remainder of his men. He glanced along the road. Street lamps, their lights extinguished by the ongoing power cuts, stood sentinel along both sides of the carriageway. On the bridge itself, the officer watched as the broken bodies of his men were lifted carefully out from beneath the piles of dead and dying corpses of the rioters. He looked back at the street lamps and quickly made his decision.

He glanced at his watch. The next convoy was due in seventeen minutes and he wanted the task completed before then. It was distasteful, but it would be an act of deterrence, as well as revenge for his fallen comrades. The order was given.

The rioters lay face down on the tarmac. For most, their earlier bravado had disappeared under the first salvo of Arabian bullets and they sobbed uncontrollably. The older ones cursed their luck for having been caught, but also counted their blessings for having survived their encounter with these angry-looking soldiers. There would be other opportunities for violence and mayhem once they had been released. Or so they imagined.

A young rioter was dragged to his feet by two Arabian soldiers and frogmarched towards a nearby street lamp. Roughly twenty years old, he sneered at his captors. He was a non-combatant, he shouted at them, a civilian. There was nothing they could do to him. He knew his rights. They were all fucking mugs.

By the light of the waning moon, the other prisoners watched in horror as a rope was secured to the street lamp and then quickly coiled about the rioter's thin neck. Before he could register his surprise, he was hoisted off his feet, twisting and kicking, the beginnings of a scream reduced to a strangled gurgle as the nylon noose bit into his windpipe. His face, grotesquely contorted, was a purple mask of disbelief and horror. A stunned silence descended over the detainees as another rioter was quickly hauled to his feet.

Then the real screaming began.

The Tunnels

'Lights up ahead,' Forsythe warned.

Mike Gibson eased back on the control lever, slowing the electric carriage to a crawl. Up ahead, distant lights cast their glow along the tunnel wall. He turned to Farrell, who acknowledged the unspoken command with a curt nod. The soldier leapt out of the carriage and headed up the tunnel. Gibson turned to the prime minister.

'Nearly there. Farrell's checking to make sure the platform is clear.'

Harry nodded. He felt he should say something, perhaps some words of encouragement, but he couldn't think of anything to say. He was tired, and not just because he hadn't slept. It was fear that was making him tired, his sky-high heart rate, the constant flow of adrenaline pumped around his system. And he felt useless, guilty, running from an unseen enemy whilst, above their heads, everyone else was suffering terribly. And then there was Anna.

Her smiling face drifted across his thoughts and he made a conscious effort to cast that image from his mind. It was dangerous to think of her now, to try to comprehend that his life with her was over. The speed of unfolding events had helped, if help was the right word, to focus Harry's mind on escape. But now, as tiredness began to lay siege to his consciousness, his thoughts turned repeatedly to his dead wife. Her body was back there somewhere, broken and burned among the rubble of Downing Street. He'd never recover her, or give her a decent burial. How would he cope?

Harry swallowed hard to stifle the emotion that constricted his throat. He took a deep breath. Don't lose it now, he chided himself. There would be time enough to grieve later. He heard someone approaching and Farrell appeared around the bend.

'All clear. There's a single door on the platform and a staircase that leads to the surface. I didn't go all the way up, but it looks clear. Dust on the floor must be an inch thick.'

'Nice work. I think we–'

Gibson's head snapped around, his eyes searching the tunnel behind them.

It was faint at first, so faint that Harry thought he'd imagined it. But then he heard it again, a low humming that caused the soldiers to share a worried look.

'Shit! Surveillance bird,' Gibson hissed. 'Hang on!' He jammed the lever to the stops and the carriage lurched forward.

'Airborne drone. State-of-the-art piece of kit,' Forsythe explained to a suddenly frightened Harry. 'American design. Light and fast, fitted with cameras and microphones. And it's tough, practically bulletproof.'

'How do you know it's one of those things?' asked Harry, his eyes nervously scanning the tunnel behind them.

Gibson shouted over his shoulder. 'Took part in a Yank exercise in the Mojave Desert a couple of years ago. Escape and evasion drills. We escape and evade, and the Yanks had to try and bag us. We nearly laughed when they gave us a four-hour start. Thought we'd be propping up the bar by the time they caught up with us, but they didn't tell us about the drones. They fly in all weathers and in all conditions, day or night. We could hear them buzzing around us in the dark, but we didn't see them until after we'd been captured. They spotted us from a couple of miles off and the controllers just vectored the hunter groups right on to us. They had us bagged in under six hours. The sound they make, it's very distinctive.'

Harry shrunk down further in his seat, the hairs on his neck tingling.

'We're here,' announced Gibson.

Ahead of them the tracks ended at a set of buffers cut into a concrete wall. Gibson brought the carriage to a stop and they all jumped off and ran for the stairs. Farrell went up first, Harry right behind him. As Forsythe went to pass him, Gibson caught his arm.

'I'm going back, Boss. See if I can disable that drone.'

Forsythe shook his head. 'No point, Mike. They'll know where we've gone. Our only chance is to try and put as much distance between us and our pursuers as possible.'

'True, but the Arabians have no idea how far this tunnel system goes. For all they know it could go on forever, and that surveillance bird is fitted with a GPS. As soon as the operator sees that it's a dead end here, they'll send troops to the grid reference on the surface above us. They'll bag us for sure unless we put that bloody thing out of operation. And we've got to do it before it gets here. That way we might buy ourselves some time.'

'Point taken,' agreed Forsythe. He went back through the door on to the platform, pulling his pistol from its holster. Gibson went after him.

'Boss, what the hell are you doing?'

Forsythe turned. 'No arguments, Mike. It's better if I go. You need to get up top and get on the radio. If not, you're going to have to get the PM out of London another way, so you'll need to recce an escape route. That's your department, not mine. Let's stick to what we're all good at. Now, get going, that's an order. I'll be right behind you.'

Gibson watched as Forsythe went to the platform control panel and flicked a row of switches. The cavern was plunged into darkness, only the lights from the tunnel providing any illumination. Gibson tapped the walkie-talkie attached to the brigadier's chest.

'Radios should work if you're close enough to the stairwell. Let us know when you're on your way back up.' Gibson pointed down the tunnel. 'Wait until it passes you and then try and shoot its rear engine housing. It's the only part of the drone that isn't protected.'

Forsythe nodded and jogged down into the tunnel. Gibson turned and slammed the steel door shut behind him. He took the stairs two at a time.

Forsythe was deep into the tunnel when he heard the low hum of the surveillance drone. He stopped, noticing a dark alcove set into the tunnel wall. It was narrow but fairly deep. A man could hide in there quite easily. Forsythe squeezed his body into the dark recess until he was out of sight.

After a moment or two, the drone's hum got louder and Forsythe's hand tightened around the grip of his automatic pistol. Sixteen rounds meant sixteen chances to disable the drone before its operator discovered that the tunnel was a dead end. A wave of panic washed over him as he realised that he didn't know how fast these drones travelled. What if it shot by him at speed? He'd have no chance of disabling it before it reached the cavern. Damn! Why hadn't he checked with Gibson? He felt a slight vibration in the air as it drew closer and Forsythe cocked his SIG automatic; he may only get one or two shots as it passed. He was a marksman with a handgun; he had no doubts that he could hit it if it travelled slowly enough, but could he disable it? He'd soon find out.

He saw a shadow expand and contract across the curve of the opposite wall and then the surveillance drone hovered into view. Forsythe had never seen one before and, for a moment, he stared at it in amazement. It flew quietly past him, six feet off the tunnel floor, its twin cameras pointed forward like two all-seeing eyes. Forsythe was relieved to see that it was travelling quite slowly and he pushed himself out of the alcove and made after it. This was going to be easy, he thought.

He ran forward and caught up with it within a few strides. He slowed his pace, raised his weapon and fired one, two, three shots directly into the small engine cowling at the rear of the drone. The bullets punched their way through the delicate microchips and sophisticated avionics, one bullet even exiting through one of the camera lenses. The damage was enough.

The drone sputtered and made a sharp left turn, crashing into the tunnel wall and dropping to the ground. Escaping gas hissed noisily and sparks fizzed and spat across the concrete floor. Forsythe smiled in satisfaction. He'd killed his first surveillance bird.

'General! We've lost contact with the drone!'

General Mousa's head snapped up. He marched across the command centre, Al-Bitruji trailing behind him.

'Where?' barked Mousa.

The operator pointed to its last known position on a surface map of London. The flashing red icon was situated west of The Serpentine lake adjacent to Hyde Park. 'North-east of here, just over a mile.'

Mousa turned to Al-Bitruji. 'Inform Haseeb's team. Tell him he could be walking into a trap. Quickly, man!'

A seething Al-Bitruji repeated the order to a nearby subordinate. He had been barked at like a junior officer, and in front of his own staff no less. He scanned the room for their reaction, but everyone remained diplomatically focussed on their own tasks. Oh, they'd heard it all right. It would be whispered around the command centre until even the lowliest privates would be sniggering at his embarrassment. Well, fuck them and fuck Mousa. He imagined taking Mousa by the collar of his jacket and booting him up the backside, kicking him out into the corridor to the cheers of his own troops. As the clapping subsided, Mousa's snapping fingers cut through his daydream.

'General. Pay attention. There is much to be done.'

Bastard, simmered Al-Bitruji. But he'd get his revenge somehow. After all, he was no fool himself. He'd climbed to the top on others' backs, crushing a few careers on the way. Mousa was a different kettle of fish, of course, being so closely aligned to the Holy One. No matter, he'd concoct a plan to tip the scales in his favour and tarnish Mousa's image in the process. He allowed himself a thin smile as Mousa's grating voice echoed around the basement walls.

Forsythe was reaching for his radio when he heard another noise from the dying machinery. He leaned over the shattered drone as it lay hissing against the tunnel wall. There was still some residual power left and its remaining camera lens whirred loudly as it moved backwards and forwards in the nose cone. Forsythe leaned over the drone, flipped his pistol over and smashed the lens with the pistol grip. It stopped whirring.

His head snapped around as he heard something else. It was a scraping, swishing noise and it was coming up fast behind him. A finger of shadow stretched across the opposite wall, then another. He hopped over the drone and ran back towards the alcove, squeezing himself inside the gap. He quickly changed his pistol magazine and waited in the darkness. Now he heard footfalls, the rustle of clothing, the unmistakeable rattle of equipment. Soldiers.

The shadow fingers stretched across the tunnel wall and then quickly retracted. The footfalls slowed. Whoever it was, they were nearly level with the alcove. Forsythe dropped his chin in an attempt to shield the paleness of his face in the gloom. He looked out from under the rim of his helmet as the first man came into view.

He was a large man, heavily bearded, wearing a sheepskin jerkin and carrying an automatic weapon. Another man joined him, similarly dressed and armed, then another. The sight of these men sent a chill up Forsythe's spine. A lifetime of military service had taught him to recognise elite troops when he saw them. Afghans certainly, sporting ragged beards, their weapons unconventional but deadly, their dress an untidy cultural and military mix.

He could hear the drone being picked over by others who remained out of sight. Forsythe had no idea how many men there were, but he knew he was outgunned. The big man gestured with his hand and, moments later, two soldiers flashed past the alcove and headed towards the platform. They wouldn't know it was there yet; it was still a good distance away around a curve in the tunnel, but they would discover it soon enough. And when they did, Forsythe had no doubt that the ground above their heads would be swarming with Arabian troops.

He had to slow them up, buy the others some time. Which meant one thing: the chances of him making it out of this tunnel alive were very slim. Any second now the enemy troops would suspect that there was someone else down here with them. How else had the drone been so efficiently disabled? And it was only a matter of time before they checked the dark alcoves along the tunnel walls. He had to act now and act decisively.

Forsythe felt a fleeting moment of regret for the way things had turned out. Although he'd spent a lifetime in military service, he'd always assumed that he would see out his days in retirement, tending his modest garden at the Sussex cottage, enjoying the occasional company of family and friends. His wife had died several years before, lost to cancer, but Forsythe had always been an independent, self-sufficient character. Retirement was only eighteen months away. Too bad he wouldn't get to enjoy it. Still, such was a soldier's lot and Forsythe was, if anything, a professional soldier. He'd give these bastards something to think about.

He ran a hand up to the webbing pockets across his chest. In one he found a single fragmentation grenade, in the other a green smoke canister. His hopes rose slightly. If he could create enough confusion and, if his luck held, he might just make it out alive. He moved his head slowly, peering beneath the rim of his helmet. The big man had moved to his left, only part of his shoulder barely visible. There was somebody else to his right, again only half visible. This was his chance. Silently, he holstered his pistol; then, one after the other, he extracted the pins from the grenades.

Haseeb waited impatiently for his two scouts to report back. Behind him, his men had fanned out along both sides of the tunnel walls. It was a pity that the life of the prime minister was to be spared. It would have been a good kill, one to add to the many he'd made during–

His earpiece crackled and Haseeb winced as Mousa's voice barked into his ear.

'Haseeb, we have reviewed the surveillance tapes from the drone. It was disabled from behind. Acknowledge!'

Haseeb spun around, fingers tightening around his rifle. His men squatted along the tunnel walls, awaiting his orders. A few metres away, the shattered drone spat sparks. If it had been disabled from behind, then surely they would have made contact with whoever had–

Two things happened, almost simultaneously. For the first time, Haseeb noticed the nearby alcove in the tunnel wall. He'd seen them before, of course, but dismissed them immediately as tactically inept places to hide, especially for a small group who were running for their lives. The second thing that happened was the sudden appearance of two small objects that sailed out from the recess only a few metres away. The objects bounced across the tunnel floor. There was no time to escape.

As he lobbed the grenades, Forsythe ducked his head and pulled his pistol. Seconds later, the detonation of the grenade almost burst his eardrums and he felt a sharp pain in his left shin as a white-hot fragment of metal buried itself deep into his flesh. The tunnel quickly filled with thick green smoke and he heard screaming and angry shouts.

Keeping low, he crawled forward out of the alcove and turned to his left. A burst of machine-gun fire raked the tunnel wall around his head, soon joined by another. He heard screaming close by and found the source: an Afghan soldier clutching his groin in agony. Forsythe crawled up over his blood-soaked legs and then across his torso. He jammed his pistol in the man's chest and fired twice. The body went limp beneath him and he tore the man's machine pistol from his shoulder strap. He heard voices shouting behind him as thick green smoke swirled around the tunnel.

Forsythe kept moving, crawling away from the smoke towards the distant platform. Soon, the green fog began to thin out and through the haze he could see the lights of the tunnel wall. Now the enemy was behind him. He rose to his knees and checked the weapon. A full magazine; good. Forsythe thought the odds were beginning to stack in his favour.

Apart from the screams and moans of the wounded, he could hear no more firing. The enemy troops were obviously afraid of hitting each other in the confusion and, before the smoke fully cleared, Forsythe decided to create some more havoc. He set the weapon to full auto and raked both sides of the tunnel with two long bursts. He threw the empty weapon to one side and headed towards the platform, rewarded by the sound of fresh screaming.

Ahead of him he saw a pair of boots. They were splayed at an awkward angle and Forsythe realised the man was dead, killed by the grenade by the look of his wounds. He quickly scooped up the man's weapon, turned and fired again across the whole width of the tunnel, keeping his shots low. This time he was answered with a short burst of fire that whizzed over his head and chewed up the concrete ceiling behind him. Forsythe cut across the tracks, trying to keep one step ahead of the enemy. He moved forward, a little more quickly now, eager to escape.

Another movement ahead caught his eye and he dropped to one knee and fired his pistol. The figure cried out and hit the floor hard. He heard a scrape behind him and turned to see another soldier dragging himself along the ground, a slick trail of blood on the floor behind him.

Forsythe surged forward. He had taken three or four steps when he lost his footing. He came down hard, his helmet spinning loose from his head and he cried out in pain as his right arm shattered on the concrete floor. His pistol skidded away from him under the impact. Then he felt a vice-like grip encasing his ankle and he spun around in alarm. His fear increased as the final wisps of green smoke evaporated to reveal the fearsome, bloodied mask of the big Afghan he'd seen earlier. Forsythe pulled back his other foot to kick him in the face but, before he could, the Afghan buried a large knife into his left calf muscle. Forsythe screamed in agony.

Haseeb dragged himself to his knees, the infidel's ankle still locked in his huge fist. He brought the knife down again and again, the thick blade shredding the soft flesh under the infidel's trousers and scraping agonisingly against the bone. The effort was excruciating. Haseeb's body was peppered with grenade fragments and a bullet had lodged under his armpit. Blood coursed down his face from several fragments in his head and his beard was slick and matted with dark blood. It was only pure hatred that kept him moving. He had failed, he knew that. The majority of his SERTRAK team lay dead or wounded, taken out by a single man, the man that lay before him. It was this white-haired infidel that was the cause of his downfall. He crawled forward over the infidel's body.

Forsythe tried to fight the man off as the weight of his body crushed his butchered calf. Never had he known such pain. He saw the knife rise up and he screamed as it plunged into his stomach, then again between his ribs. A hand gripped his webbing and the big man, the leader, muttering through blood-soaked teeth, dragged himself over Forsythe until he straddled his torso. The brigadier felt his strength fading fast. He brought his hand up to his chest, keyed his radio several times, then set it to permanent send. His arm dropped to his side.

'Your friends cannot help you now, infidel,' hissed Haseeb. 'The time of your death has come.'

With each word, blood sprayed across the infidel's face. Haseeb's breathing was laboured now. He thought the bullet might have penetrated a lung because it was getting hard to breathe, but he still had time. He fumbled with the fastenings of the brigadier's body armour and he tore it off. With a huge effort, Haseeb raised the knife in both hands and punched it deep into the infidel's chest. The old man's head came off the ground, his eyes as wide as saucers as his body doubled under the impact of the blow. He let out a blood-curdling scream and Haseeb raised the knife and stabbed him again. This time the brigadier went limp, the knife sunk to its pommel in his bloodied chest.

Exhausted, Haseeb slumped sideways and sprawled on his back, his energy spent. Death would come for him soon. Darkness closed around his peripheral vision and he prayed that Allah would welcome him into paradise. He heard footsteps close by and the next moment two of his men were kneeling by his side. Ah, the scouts. They began to treat Haseeb's wounds, rummaging for field dressings and medicines in their personal kit, but they were wasting their time. Haseeb could no longer feel his legs, a sure sign of massive blood loss. Soon his heart would fail.

As his men busied themselves, the Afghan wondered briefly what they had discovered, then dismissed the thought. It was of little concern to him now. Others would take up the pursuit. Allah had other plans for him.

Haseeb didn't react when the first soldier's face disappeared in a red spray of blood and tissue, but he roared in pain when the other man was similarly despatched and dropped on to Haseeb's shattered body. Moments passed and his breathing became more laboured. A shadow fell across his face and he looked up to see a silhouette looming over him. Another infidel. He smiled. So be it.

Mike Gibson's eyes roamed the tunnel. The two mid-range headshots had been fairly easy, but Gibson was sickened to see the knife that protruded from Forsythe's chest. He stood over the big Afghan and drew his pistol. As the wounded man closed his eyes and began to mutter something unintelligible, Gibson shot him in the mouth.

He looked around at the devastation and was quietly impressed. The Boss had managed to take out a whole squad of troops. A quick scout around revealed that two of the men around him were still alive, but only just. Three blood trails led away from the scene of the action and Gibson decided to let them go. But there was something he could do.

Gathering grenades from the corpses, he booby-trapped several enemy bodies in the immediate vicinity. It was a distasteful task, but the situation was becoming increasingly desperate and he needed to buy as much time as possible. When he'd finished setting the explosives, he leant over Forsythe's body and quickly pulled the knife from his chest, flinging it to one side. He tugged a single dog tag from around the brigadier's neck, slipped it into his pocket and headed back to the platform.

'General, we've lost contact with the SERTRAK team.'

Mousa scraped back his chair and walked swiftly over to the command screen. He could see the glowing icons that represented the individual SERTRAK members in the tunnel near the crashed drone, but they were not moving and all attempts to communicate with them had failed.

'Get another drone up that tunnel fast. And get Major Karroubi on the line. I want a company of paratroopers right behind it!' Mousa walked back to his chair and kicked it hard across the room. He suffered a fleeting bout of panic, realising that his quarry, once tantalisingly close, might now escape. That was unacceptable. Mission failure would be more than a personal blow. It would also dent his credibility with the highest power in all of Arabia. He looked at his watch. The sun would be up soon. Mousa had a dreadful feeling that, with the coming of daylight, the British prime minister would be lost to him, maybe for good. He was racing against the dawn.

He checked the command display again. The tunnel headed north-east towards another so-called royal palace, this one in Kensington Gardens. He barked another order.

'Al-Bitruji! Have two companies of your men proceed to Kensington Palace. Order the engineers to take it apart and find the entrance to the tunnel system. There must be one there. Hurry!'

Al-Bitruji complied, finding it difficult to keep the smile from his face. For the first time since he'd known the man, he thought he detected a hint of panic in Mousa's voice. This mission was everything to the arrogant bastard, and failure might not be taken lightly by the Holy One. Perhaps it would be his downfall. If that were so, then Al-Bitruji would gladly see it happen. There was still a hand to be dealt here, he thought. If he played that hand correctly, maybe he himself would replace Mousa at the right hand of the cleric. This could be the opportunity he had waited for.

Within a few minutes, troop transports and armoured vehicles began to roll out of Buckingham Palace, roaring up Constitution Hill towards the dark expanse of Hyde Park.

Inside the windowless concrete room, Harry and Farrell heard the clang of the steel door at the bottom of the staircase far below them. The sound made Harry jump, rattling his already frayed nerves as he paced backwards and forwards. Farrell went down a couple of flights and returned a moment later.

'It's Mike, sir. Looks like he's on his own.'

Farrell sat down at the single table on which sat a sophisticated military radio set. There were several other monitors built into the wall above the table, each linked to surveillance cameras surrounding the small building in which they now waited. A few moments later Gibson entered the room, breathing hard.

'Anything?' he gasped.

Farrell shook his head. 'Not yet.'

Gibson then briefed Harry on recent events. Harry leaned against the wall, rubbing his tired eyes with balled fists. So much death. God only knew what it was like across the rest of the country. He shivered, despite the stuffiness of the room, and Gibson laid a hand on Harry's shoulder.

'You okay, sir?'

Harry nodded. This was no time to start dwelling on the lives that had been lost on this awful night. He had to keep it together. 'I'm alright, Mike. What now?'

Gibson jerked a thumb over his shoulder. 'No contact with Alternate One yet and the sun will be up in about an hour. If we can't raise 'em by then we'll have to hole up elsewhere during daylight hours. Of course, if we leave here we won't have an encrypted radio set, which means we won't be able to raise Alternate One. In that case, we'll have to head west on our own.'

Harry nodded grimly. 'How would we–'

'Contact! Alternate One, we are receiving you, strength five by five, over!' Farrell turned and gave them the thumbs up, a wide grin on his face. Harry was summoned to the microphone and his voiceprint quickly confirmed. Gibson took the headset next, nodding several times. He asked a few pertinent questions then broke the link. He wrenched the power from the radio and smashed it on the ground, kicking the shattered components around the floor. Harry was horrified.

'For God's sake, Mike! What if–'

Gibson cut him off. 'We've got our orders and we can't leave the kit intact for obvious reasons. We've got to move now. This may be our only chance of getting out of the city before it's too late.'

'What about your other colleagues? Brooks, is it? And the other one?'

'They're trained for this type of work. They'll stay out of the way, head west.'

'But we can't just–'

'We have to,' interrupted Gibson. 'I don't like it any more than you, but that's the situation and your safety is paramount.'

Farrell, scanning the surveillance monitors, interrupted them. 'All clear outside. We're good to go.'

Gibson flicked off the lights in the room. He opened the heavy steel door, inviting a mild breeze in that swirled around the room as their eyes adjusted to the dark undergrowth of Kensington Gardens.

'Let's go,' he whispered. They filed out of the blockhouse, taking up position a few yards into the trees.

'Which way are we headed?' hissed Harry as Gibson scanned the dark, open spaces that sloped down towards Kensington High Street.

Gibson smiled in the darkness. 'We're going shopping. Let's move.'

The party broke cover, Harry scampering after the dark shape ahead of him. Shopping? What the bloody hell did he mean? But Harry decided not to dwell too much on the soldier's cryptic reply. He knew all his questions would be answered soon enough. Instead, he concentrated on keeping Gibson in sight as they headed south across Kensington Gardens.

As they moved through the shadows, the first chirping notes began to echo around the park, the birds in the surrounding trees heralding the fast-approaching dawn.

On the roof of Barkers department store on Kensington High Street, Flight Lieutenant Gavin Lucas sat in silence in the cockpit of his Boeing-Sikorsky Dark Eagle stealth helicopter and waited patiently for his passengers. It had been a long wait, almost three hours now, and they still hadn't arrived, but the trip into Central London had been worth it purely for reconnaissance value, and his multimillion-dollar helicopter was just the bird for the job.

The Dark Eagle was an intelligence-gathering platform like no other. Its on-board flight systems were state of the art and incorporated the latest advances in stealth technology. Its four-bladed rotor, always a detectable heat source on other helicopters, was cooled by a sealed liquid nitrogen system and the rotors spun on a revolutionary bearing arrangement, creating a magnetic field around the blade hub that literally sucked in sound waves. It made the Dark Eagle almost silent.

As a weapons platform, it boasted twin twenty-millimetre electric cannons and two rocket pods, each holding thirty mini rockets. The angular nose, shaped to deflect airborne and ground radar, bristled with thermal, night-vision and low-light optical equipment as well as sideways look-down, telescopic and digital cameras that could track an object on the ground or in the air for 360 degrees. Its air search radar and target-tracking systems were second to none and its own radar signature was equivalent to that of a large bird. The Dark Eagle was American built, of course, but the British Army had six on loan and Lucas was one of the lucky ones who got to fly this impressive machine.

Waiting in the silence of the cockpit, he reflected on the flight to London from Alternate One. As the aircraft glided low and fast across the dark English countryside, its on-board systems had recorded the huge columns of tanks and infantry moving up the M3 and A3 motorways towards London, confirming that England was well and truly in the grip of a massive invasion. As the Dark Eagle gathered data from all points of the compass, it was beamed back to Alternate One by a series of encrypted microwave burst signals that took less than a tenth of a second to transmit. Deep under the Mendip Hills, analysts were already crunching the volumes of data the Dark Eagle was recording on its perilous journey into the capital.

Things had got pretty hairy when they reached London itself. Here, there were many more troops on the ground and someone in the Acton area of West London must have got a brief radar return, firing a surface-to-air missile in their general direction. There had been a few tense moments inside the aircraft, but the missile hadn't achieved lock and had crashed to the ground somewhere to the north-west. Thankfully for the Dark Eagle, the rest of the journey remained uneventful and they landed quietly on the roof of the famous art deco building on Kensington High Street. Lucas had ordered all systems shut down and there they'd remained, an indistinct black mass on a dark rooftop.

His two crew members, one co-pilot and a flight sergeant, had taken up positions away from the aircraft. The co-pilot was on the roof itself, patrolling the perimeter of the building and watching the street below. The flight sergeant had made his way down the darkened fire escape to the staff entrance in Young Street. There he waited, deep in the shadows, until their 'package' arrived. Lucas didn't know who the package was, but he presumed it was a senior member of the cabinet or high-ranking military officer. He hadn't been told, for operational reasons of course, but it was a fair bet they wouldn't risk the Dark Eagle and its crew for the secretary for sport and culture.

They'd waited in virtual silence until, a few moments earlier, the Dark Eagle received an encrypted move order. The package was in the immediate area and en route. About bloody time, breathed Lucas, starting his pre-flight checks. He keyed the transmit switch of his microphone, ordering his co-pilot back to the helicopter and instructing his flight sergeant to hold position at the staff entrance to await the arrival of their passenger. A moment later, the co-pilot climbed into the aircraft and Lucas glanced over his shoulder towards the sky in the east.

Whoever it was had better hurry; they had less than an hour of darkness left.

As Gibson took cover beneath a towering oak, watching the prime minister puffing towards him, he fretted about what lay ahead. The good news was they had transport. On the roof of a nearby department store lay their salvation: a helicopter. But before they broke out the champagne, they had to cross two hundred yards of open parkland, a main arterial road that may or may not have enemy traffic operating on it, then get up on to the roof of the building in question using the staff entrance that was located on a road they couldn't see and didn't have time to recce. Still, it was their best chance of getting out of the city.

Gibson grabbed the sleeve of Harry's jacket as he ducked under the low-hanging branches and pulled him behind the thick trunk. He gestured to Farrell.

'You first. Call us when you're across the street.'

Farrell nodded and took off across the park. They watched him until he was lost in the gloom. Gibson scanned the area around them. The overhead canopy made it hard to see, so he moved out from under the tree's leafy skirt and crouched down on the damp grass, looking to the east. The black horizon was being quickly replaced by varying shades of deep blue and– Oh shit!

He ducked back under the canopy and dragged Harry to his feet. 'Military convoy! Let's go!' As he ran he shouted into his radio. 'Stevie, convoy approaching from the east. How's our route looking?' Farrell's voice hissed in his ear. Gibson shouted over his shoulder as Harry panted behind him. 'We've got to get across the road before they reach the park.' The Arabians must be headed towards Kensington Palace, realised Gibson.

The two men reached the black bars of Palace Gate and ran out into Kensington High Street, dodging between the scores of abandoned cars that littered the road. There didn't seem to be much damage here, although there were one or two bodies lying on the opposite pavement, and it seemed that nearly every shop window had been smashed. Glass crunched underfoot with every step.

Gibson dragged Harry towards the dark mass of the Barkers building. Behind him, he could hear the increasing roar of vehicle engines on the predawn air.

'Where are you, Stevie?' he hissed into his radio. Across the road, red-filtered torchlight blinked out of the dark shadows of a shopfront. Gibson shoved Harry forward. 'Run towards the light. Quickly!'

Gibson pushed him forward and turned back towards the oncoming headlights, whose high beams suddenly washed over the road. He ducked into a shop doorway and watched as the trucks roared closer. Just when he thought that they would bypass the park, the leading armoured vehicle turned sharply to the right and crashed through the iron gates, knocking them both to the ground with an ear-splitting clang.

The vehicle continued on without stopping, accelerating up the wide Broad Walk path to the palace itself. Gibson counted a total of four trucks, three APCs and two Humvee jeeps, all loaded with troops. The rear vehicle, an armoured type with a wicked-looking cannon mounted on its turret, screeched to a halt at the gates and took up position covering the road.

Gibson's heart sank. He was roughly a hundred yards away from the nearest Arabian vehicle, but it was at least another hundred to the corner of the Barkers building and, for some of it, he would be exposed. He looked eastwards along Kensington Gore. Another convoy was on its way. The Arabians were throwing everything at finding them now. Gibson watched the dismounting Arabian troops carefully, waiting for the right moment to make his move.

General Al-Bitruji took the message slip from his communications officer and considered his next move. Whatever it was, it had better be quick. And decisive. Mousa was busy studying the command screen as various units raced into Kensington Gardens. He had no idea that one of Al-Bitruji's loyal communications officers was filtering communications from Major Karroubi, that his precious paratroopers had discovered that the tunnel was a dead end, or that there could be no platform beneath Kensington Palace. Below ground, his crippled lackey was desperately trying to raise Mousa and tell him the news, but Al-Bitruji's man was steadfastly blocking direct transmissions. A message would be passed, the exasperated Karroubi was informed.

Al-Bitruji watched carefully as the minutes ticked by. With each passing second the British prime minister was getting further away. It was clear Mousa was starting to sweat and Al-Bitruji was enjoying every moment. He saw Mousa's hand go up to his ear. Perhaps he had finally heard something on the command net, something that may suggest that there was a communication problem? It wouldn't do to overplay his hand. It was time to act.

Al-Bitruji stepped forward, the message slip in his hand and a blank look on his face. 'I have a communication from your man in the tunnels.'

Mousa snatched the note and quickly scanned the message. 'When did you receive this?' he barked.

'A moment ago.'

Mousa keyed his radio repeatedly but to no effect. He wrenched the device from his tunic and hurled it against the wall, smashing it into pieces. He turned to Al-Bitruji.

'Get me Major Karroubi on the line this instant, or else I will have every man in this room shot.'

Al-Bitruji turned away and repeated the order. He found another radio and gave it to Mousa. The general was quickly patched through to his subordinate.

'Karroubi, where the devil are you?' Mousa was silent as he listened to Karroubi's report. 'Start searching the park,' he ordered. 'They must be close.' Al-Bitruji watched Mousa break the connection and walk away. Maybe he was mistaken, but he thought he heard a slight trace of panic in the general's voice.

Farrell led the way, Harry scuttling behind him. When they arrived at the junction of Young Street, Farrell stopped, peering around the side of the building. With a whisper he ordered Harry to hold his position, then ducked into the side street.

Harry watched him as he disappeared into the darkness beneath the wide canopy of Barkers. He experienced a momentary feeling of panic, his armed escort gone, abandoning him to the dark and dangerous streets of West London. He was scared, of course he was, but his fear was tempered by the thoughts of others out there, the old and the very young, trapped in their homes or caught out on the streets amongst the carnage. Many would be injured, some dying, alone, in the dark. Harry had a chance of escape, whereas the public were at the mercy of the gods. Shame suffocated his fear, but there was nothing he could do until he got to Alternate One. That had to be his priority now.

A movement caught his eye and he saw Farrell race back across the street towards him. He reached Harry and pointed back over his shoulder.

'Other side of the road, fifty yards, a set of glass doors. There's a flight sergeant on the other side. He'll take you up to the roof to the chopper.'

Harry's shoulders sagged in relief. 'Thank God,' he whispered.

'Let's save the prayers until we're away. Mike's got bad guys right on his arse. I'll see if he needs a hand.'

As the soldier turned to leave, Harry gripped his arm. 'Hurry back, both of you. I'm not leaving you behind.' He ran across the street as quickly as he could. One of the glass doors swung inwards as he approached. Behind it waited a man in a flight helmet and black jumpsuit. He also carried an automatic rifle.

'Flight Sergeant Hopkins, sir. Follow me.'

Without waiting, Hopkins turned and made for the stairs with Harry close behind.

With practised rhythm, Flight Lieutenant Lucas brought the Dark Eagle's systems online. Next to him, his co-pilot had strapped in and was going through the same pre-flight checks. They both had hundreds of hours in the Dark Eagle, but they always carried out the checks as if it were their maiden flight. Both men were satisfied to see the status board indicate a solid block of green lights. They were ready.

Lucas reached overhead and depressed another set of switches to engage the main rotor, twisting the power grip on his collective to bring the rotor speed up. A quick scan of his instruments told him that all systems were fully operational and the aircraft was prepared for flight. In fact, he could feel the Dark Eagle just itching to leap into the sky. All he needed now were his passengers. He saw the nearby fire escape door swing open and Hopkins appeared, dragging a sorry-looking figure behind him. He nudged his co-pilot and nodded. The prime minister was alive.

Harry gasped for breath as he staggered out on to the roof. A blast of rotor wash assaulted him, plastering the clothes against his body, and he bent forward against the wind. The strange thing was he could hardly hear the black, angular helicopter that vibrated impatiently in front of him. It was so quiet, just a low, *whupping* noise, like a chopper heard from some distance away. The side door slid back and, with a firm hand from Hopkins, Harry was seated on a bench behind the pilots and securely strapped in. He took the proffered headset and the pilot's voice hissed in his ears.

'Glad to see you made it, Prime Minister. My name is Flight Lieutenant Lucas and this is my co-pilot, Flying Officer Stanton. As soon as your military escort arrives we'll get airborne.'

Harry nodded, still fighting to regain his breath. 'How long have you been here?' he eventually gasped.

'Long enough.'

He saw Lucas glance at his watch, then both pilots shared a look. 'We don't leave without them,' Harry said into his microphone. 'If they stay, I stay.'

Lucas swivelled in his seat. 'Prime Minister, my orders are—'

'Screw your orders. We wait.'

Lucas shook his head. 'Three minutes, sir, that's all I can give you. We can't take the risk, not now you're on board.'

Harry nodded grimly. *Come on, Mike. Where the bloody hell are you?*

Gibson crawled over glass and debris as he inched his way across the road. At least a couple of dozen Arabians were milling around the entrance to the park. A few luminous sticks were cracked and thrown on the ground to mark the entrance, but soon that wouldn't be necessary. In a while it would be light enough to see without artificial aids. If Gibson stood now, he'd probably be spotted. He could continue crawling, using the cars as cover, but it was taking too long. Farrell's urgent voice hissed in his earpiece.

'The chopper can't wait. You've got to move now.'

Gibson considered ordering Farrell to leave him behind. If the chopper waited, then he was effectively compromising the mission and Gibson had never done that in his professional life. He also knew the helicopter was his only real hope of getting out of the city before daybreak, otherwise he might never get out. But the mission was paramount. Evacuate the prime minister to Alternate One.

He was about to reach for his radio when a new voice sounded in his earpiece, a distinctive voice he'd heard a hundred times on the TV.

'Mike, this is Harry. You need to get back here as soon as you can. Our pilots are eager to leave, but I've told them we can't go without you. Do you understand?'

Gibson thought for a moment, then quickly made his decision. He keyed his radio. 'Go now,' he whispered. 'I appreciate what you're saying, but I won't make it. I'll hole up for a few days somewhere, find another way out. But you need to go now. I'm sorry, sir.'

On the roof, Harry nodded to the pilot. With seemingly no effort, the Dark Eagle lifted off the roof and nosed out above the street below. It swivelled under its own rotors until it faced east towards Kensington Gardens. Lucas interrogated his Low-Light Head Up Display built into his helmet visor. Below them, he could see the ghostly images of two trucks, the armoured vehicle and a couple of dozen Arabian soldiers spread out around the entrance to the park. The Dark Eagle's thermal imaging cameras also picked out the ghostly silhouette of Mike Gibson, lying prone behind an abandoned vehicle not fifty yards from the nearest Arabian truck. With a series of voice commands, Lucas alerted his weapons systems to immediate action.

'WepsComp, activate.' The targeting radar built into the nose cone of the Dark Eagle interrogated the ground below. It painted the vehicles and troops below with a single emission sweep, uploaded the information into the weapons system computer and waited for its next command. Lucas glanced at the targeting receptacle that floated over each target.

'Switch target, switch target, target selected. Switch target, target selected.' In less than seven seconds Lucas had targeted the armoured vehicle and both trucks with three forty-millimetre rockets each and a group of Arabian soldiers with a two-second burst of twenty-millimetre cannon. 'Prepare to fire.'

Lucas turned to Harry and gave him a thumbs up. Harry keyed his own radio. 'Gentlemen, we're right above you. Keep your heads down and, when the shooting starts, get up on the roof as quickly as you can.'

On the ground, Farrell ducked back into Young Street and Gibson curled up tight under the abandoned vehicle. They both realised what was coming.

'Fire, fire, fire!'

On the push of a button, nine forty-millimetre rockets hissed from the armaments pods of the Dark Eagle and streaked towards their targets. Almost simultaneously, one hundred and thirty-three explosive twenty-millimetre cannon rounds chewed up the largest congregation of Arabian troops with a loud ripping sound, sending body parts spinning through the air. Before the survivors knew what had happened, the rockets impacted into the vehicles at the park gates and the resulting explosions lit up the early morning gloom. Each vehicle was thrown upwards in separate fireballs, their own fuel tanks erupting and adding to the inferno.

Gibson was up and running as the missiles hit and a blast of hot air washed over him. Seconds later, metal fragments and hot debris rained down around him. As he got to the corner of Young Street, he turned and looked back. A long burst of automatic fire chipped the concrete over his head and smashed windows in the Barkers building behind him. He'd been spotted, and two or three Arabians were already zigzagging through the abandoned vehicles, their silhouettes backlit by the burning vehicles. He turned and raced towards the building. Farrell was waiting, covering him as he sprinted across the side street. As he reached the entrance, Farrell opened fire over his head with a short burst.

'They're right on your arse! Keep going!'

Gibson charged through the open door and both men sprinted across the marble lobby towards the fire escape. Gibson ordered Farrell up the stairs and slammed the door behind him. He grabbed a fire extinguisher from the wall, pulled the pins from two grenades and trapped them between the extinguisher and the door. It was a crude booby trap, but hopefully it would slow their pursuers.

Halfway up the stairs, they heard the twin detonations of the grenades below and a high-pitched scream echoed up the stairwell. A burst of fire from below forced them against the walls as bullets ricocheted off the steel handrail, but they were nearly at the top. They crashed through the door on to the roof.

The Dark Eagle was there, hovering quietly, a crewman waving them furiously aboard. They ran for the side door and clambered over the prime minister, giving the thumbs up to the pilot. Immediately, Lucas increased power, the helicopter rising like an express elevator until it was a hundred feet above street level. He spun the nose around and dipped it, turning the aircraft westwards. Within a few seconds they had accelerated to nearly one hundred and twenty miles an hour as the dark rooftops of West London flashed beneath them.

They'd cut it very fine indeed and everyone on board said a silent prayer of thanks.

The River

The *Kingfisher* slipped quietly along the River Thames, making steady progress westwards under the pale light of the moon. For the crew, the last few hours had been the most traumatic of their lives, but the low throb of the boat's engine combined with the gentle lapping of the dark waters had helped to calm their ragged nerves. While Khan steered the boat, Alex sat perched on the bow, keeping forward watch. At the stern, Kirsty scanned the riverbanks as the *Kingfisher* took them further out of the city. They sat in silence, each lost in their own thoughts, but comforted by the fact that the immediate danger appeared to be behind them, where the sky glowed red and distant thunder rumbled ominously. Every now and then Alex turned to check on Kirsty, and when she caught his glance she smiled.

The river took them past the shadowy expanse of Kew Gardens and they drifted silently under the deserted Twickenham Bridge. Towards Richmond, the river began to narrow and Khan steered the boat midstream, warning Alex and Kirsty to watch the banks for potential trouble. Behind the ornate buildings that lined the riverbank to their left, the sky throbbed with a bright orange glow, a sign that Richmond town centre was ablaze. Burning embers danced lazily in the air and the roar of flames and the crash of collapsing timbers echoed across the rooftops. Khan teased a bit more power from the engine, leaving the depressing scene behind them.

At Glover's Island, the river turned west and then dipped south towards Kingston, where they passed under that bridge without event, chugging past Thames Ditton and moving slowly on towards Chertsey. The only life they saw were bats, flitting silently on the night air, and a family of swans and cygnets, who watched the *Kingfisher* warily as they drifted by.

A short while later, Alex bolted upright then made his way quickly back into the wheelhouse.

'Could be trouble up ahead,' he said.

'Show me.'

Khan throttled back to a couple of knots and left Kirsty at the helm. Out on deck there was little to see, but Khan heard the noise too. Vehicles. Lots of them.

'Do you know where we are?' asked Khan.

'Well, that was Shepperton Lock back there, which means that that must be Chertsey over there.' Alex pointed to the south-west. In the distance, they could see the dark silhouettes of low-rise buildings set against the night sky. 'I'd imagine that's traffic on the M3 motorway, possibly the M25. Either way, there'll be a bridge sooner rather than later.'

'It's the M3,' said Kirsty, leaning out of the wheelhouse window.

Alex raised an eyebrow. 'You're sure?'

'Definitely. Chertsey Lock is up ahead and directly after that is the M3 motorway bridge. I've checked the map.'

While Khan studied the ground ahead with binoculars, Alex joined Kirsty in the wheelhouse.

'You read maps too,' he smiled. 'Smart as well as pretty.' Kirsty didn't reply. 'Sorry. Just kidding.'

'I know.'

'You okay?'

'I like being on the boat, that's all. Feels safe.'

'Once we get to Rob's place it'll be better, trust me.'

Khan returned to the wheelhouse. 'It's getting light. We've got to get off the river as soon as possible.'

Alex pointed through the windscreen. 'There's a spot just ahead that'll give us some cover.'

'Good idea,' Khan said. 'Let me have the wheel.' He spun the helm, turning the *Kingfisher* towards a large stand of willow trees overhanging the water on the southern bank. He cut the engine, steering the vessel silently and expertly under the drooping canopy. Out on deck, Alex used his foot to brace the boat as it bumped against the weed-covered bank, then tied the craft off around an emergency lifebelt stand.

They gathered again in the wheelhouse, Khan scanning the bridge ahead with his binoculars. Through the limp curtain of willow branches he saw movement on the bridge. There were soldiers on the parapet and, behind them, the dark shapes of fast-moving traffic, rubber tyres humming noisily on the air. He watched for at least two minutes then passed the binoculars across.

'That's a lot of vehicles,' noted Alex.

'Sure is,' agreed Khan, 'and all headed for London. Looks like we made the right decision.'

'Agreed. Trouble is, what do we do now?' Alex peered into the darkness. On the shore, the open ground was dotted with oak trees, providing overhead cover for a couple of hundred yards. There were several vehicles out there in the gloom and, as his eyes gradually became accustomed to the shadows on the shore, he realised they were caravans and motorhomes. They looked lifeless and deserted, shrouded in darkness.

'Let's keep going, by road. It's only about thirty miles from here. I know the way.'

Kirsty frowned. 'Really? Aren't we safer on the boat?'

'We can't stay tied up here and we'll never get under that bridge.'

'He's right, Kirsty. The sooner we get moving the better.' Khan turned to Alex. 'It means stealing a car. You okay with that?'

'First time for everything,' Alex smiled.

'Good. Wait here.'

It didn't take long to find a suitable vehicle, a powerful Range Rover parked next to a mobile home where a warm light shone behind the curtains. Khan knocked on the door and, when it opened, he pushed inside. Thirty seconds later he returned with the key. He started the vehicle up and jumped out, beckoning the others with a frantic wave. Alex was impressed until he saw two elderly, frightened faces peering at them from behind the curtains.

'Jesus Christ, Dan. What did you do?'

'They're fine. Get in.'

Alex hesitated. 'We can't do this. Let's find another one.'

'There's no time. Jump in the back. You up for driving, Kirsty?'

'Sure.'

'Good. Alex and I will ride shotgun.'

As they pulled away beneath the trees, Alex offered a sheepish wave to the elderly couple, then Kirsty hit the throttle, accelerating towards the main gate in a cloud of dust and gravel. She kept the lights off, carefully navigating the narrow road that twisted through the trees. They passed the park reception centre and found themselves at the junction of the main road. To their right they could see the smaller Chertsey Bridge. To the left, the road stretched away into the early morning gloom, the emptiness almost eerie.

'Let's keep the lights off for a while and take it real easy,' instructed Khan.

'Which way to the farm?' asked Kirsty, nervous about leaving the boat but grateful to be doing something constructive.

'Go left,' said Alex. 'I'll tell you when to turn.'

The Range Rover spun out on to the road and purred quietly along the darkened street, leaving the *Kingfisher* and the river behind them.

Kensington Gardens,
West London

General Mousa leaned against his Humvee and surveyed the wreckage left in the wake of the Dark Eagle's assault. As he watched, numerous vehicle fires were being noisily extinguished and the blackened and dismembered bodies of the casualties removed in rubber body bags. After a while, all that was left were four burnt out vehicle skeletons and a slick of oil and melted tarmac across the width of Kensington High Street.

Mousa's calm exterior belied his inner turmoil. Cursed infidels, he raged silently. Curse them and the day their whore mothers gave birth to them. How did they slip through? And escape in a helicopter, no less. He would have to communicate with the Holy One soon. Back home it would be after sunrise, and a personal situation report was overdue. He would break the bad news in due course but, before he did so, there was still a straw to be grasped.

Major Karroubi was limping amongst the debris. Mousa beckoned him and he limped over to the Humvee.

'I believe there is a witness to this shambles. Summon him.'

Karroubi barked an order and an Arabian survivor of the rocket attack trotted over. Mousa noticed the soldier was unharmed but terrified. He stepped forward and bowed deeply.

'What did you see? Quickly,' demanded Mousa.

The soldier began to recount his recent near-death experience, telling Mousa of the warm breeze that ruffled his clothing, the black shape silhouetted against the deep blue of the predawn sky. As the missiles were launched and the bullet casings rained down around him, he flung himself to the ground, reluctant to move for fear of being caught in the carnage. When he looked up again, it was just in time to see the helicopter disappear back over the roof of the building across the street. He'd joined in the chase of the English soldiers, following two angry comrades down a side street and into a large department store. The grenades had killed them both. Mousa dismissed the relieved soldier with a wave of his hand.

'They're headed west,' declared Mousa. 'Ground all aircraft west of the city and divert any flights inbound for Heathrow. As of now, the whole of western England is a no-fly zone unless specifically authorised by me. And tell Air Command that I want a Big Eye in the air immediately.'

'At once, General.'

Mousa produced a map and spread it out across the bonnet of the jeep.

'Have a company of airborne troops loaded on to helicopters at Heathrow and ready to move on my order. I want them headed west as soon as the enemy aircraft is located. Tell Al-Bitruji to contact our forces at Southampton docks. I want the next fully equipped mechanised battalion diverted from the coast and have the commander of that unit report to me directly when they have reached this point here.' Mousa stabbed a thick finger on the map.

'But that's Salisbury,' cautioned Karroubi. 'If we send units west, before we've cleared the Hampshire gap, they could be engaged from the rear by British forces escaping the garrisons at Tidworth and Aldershot. Forgive me for saying so, General, but these redeployments run contrary to the invasion plans.'

Mousa quickly folded the map and shoved it into the pocket of his combat trousers. 'And like all battle plans, they tend to change as soon as the first shot is fired.'

'But the Holy One—'

'Let me worry about that,' snapped Mousa. 'Just get the forces to Salisbury and inform me when they're in position.'

They climbed aboard the Humvee and the driver swung the vehicle around, accelerating east towards Knightsbridge. Ahead of them, the sky had taken on a pale hue as the first rays of sun breached the horizon.

Mousa settled back in his seat and considered his impending report to the cleric. His Holiness would not be pleased, but the general hoped he could rectify the situation by capturing the prime minister before the day's end.

Salisbury Plain

The Big Eye surveillance aircraft rotated off the runway at Heathrow and climbed into the dawn sky, headed due west. The flight crew had been in-country for less than two hours when the call came to scramble, but luckily the Big Eye's specialist support team had flown ahead with their equipment and turned the plane around as soon as it landed on English soil.

Captain Ibrahim Al-Sadir pushed the throttles to their stops and gained altitude quickly. Their pre-flight mission briefing had been urgent and to the point: find a helicopter, probably of a stealth variety, headed west. Identify, track and report in. Simple. Except to find a tiny helicopter cloaked with stealth technology and hugging the ground was going to be difficult, even for the formidable electronic capabilities of the Big Eye.

Al-Sadir flexed his fingers inside his flying gloves. He'd expected to fly operations like this, but not quite so soon. The military push to the north and west of England was supposed to start after the major cities had been secured and before the enemy had a chance to muster their remaining forces; H-hour plus seventy-two, according to the crew briefings back in Arabia. Something must have gone wrong. The helicopter they hunted was important, so important that there were other forces out there intent on its capture. Must be something big, thought Al-Sadir. Still, it was not his concern. As he levelled out at seven thousand metres, the young captain pondered the tactical advantages of his situation.

Firstly, domestic electricity supplies were still cut off, which meant electronic background noise would be minimal. The reasonably flat landscape was spread out before him under a cloudless sky as the sun rose behind the aircraft, making visibility almost perfect.

Secondly, all Arabian aircraft to the west of Heathrow had been stood down, decluttering the electronic picture even further and thus aiding the Big Eye in its search. Although it would only take seconds for his on-board computer systems to register friend or foe, that little processing chore had been alleviated by the lack of friendly air activity ahead of him. In fact, his systems registered zero activity on a westerly heading between his aircraft and as far as the Bristol Channel. Perfect. As an experienced pilot, Al-Sadir often had to cope with crowded airspace, but right now he was the only aircraft in the sky and the thought pleased him greatly.

Thirdly, the absence of enemy ground radar gave Al-Sadir additional confidence. According to early reports, the British armed forces had been dealt a massive blow and had been all but neutralised by the invasion forces. Not a single co-ordinated counter-attack had materialised anywhere around the country. Of course, there had been minor skirmishes, but nothing that indicated organised and determined resistance. And the Royal Air Force, once a formidable foe, had been thoroughly neutered by the economic crisis that had plagued Europe for years. What few reports of enemy air activity they'd received indicated they were operating far to the north. It was just his aircraft and a cloudless sky. If there was a helicopter out there, he would find it. He checked the Big Eye's position then keyed the interior comms system.

'Confirm target area. Commence sweep.'

Behind him, in the highly sophisticated main control cabin, the Big Eye's crew of eight technicians finished calibrating their instruments and activated numerous air and ground-search radars, some of the most technologically advanced systems in the world. Outside the aircraft, the air became 'hot' with microwaves as multi-layered search systems swept the airspace before them. The computers and instrumentation aboard were especially designed to filter information from the multiple radar returns and sort them into categories.

Almost immediately they received several contacts. The system identified them as either flocks of birds or similar anomalies, but the computers were programmed to ignore these potential targets and the sweep continued. The returns whittled down on the scopes. Now the remaining targets were classified as military, enemy vehicles and armour on the ground. These returns were plotted and the information sent back to the controllers at Heathrow. They would be dealt with presently.

The target that the Big Eye hunted possessed a specific electronic signature. Speed was also a factor and the computers had been programmed to ignore anything under one hundred and forty kilometres per hour. On its fifth sweep, the air-search system reported a single contact moving at nearly two hundred kilometres per hour, one hundred and seventeen kilometres ahead. The return wasn't strong and the blip kept fading from the display, but it was a positive return and the speed, altitude, direction and lack of transponder signal were enough to confirm to the operator that the target was unfriendly.

'Target acquired. Possible helicopter.'

In the cockpit, Al-Sadir listened to the report and checked his own display, watching the tell-tale blip fade in and out intermittently. It certainly behaved like a stealth aircraft. He banked the Big Eye over a few degrees and increased power, still heading due west. Another radar sweep and the contact firmed up. An enemy helicopter, type unknown and employing stealth technology. And it was where he'd been told to expect it, which made the contact a primary target. Time to call for some help. He radioed the forward air controllers, currently operating out of the main control tower at Heathrow.

'Ground Station Hotel, this is Bravo Echo-Niner. I have probable target acquisition. Request fighter vector.'

'Vector approved, Bravo Echo-Niner. You have command,' Heathrow replied. Al-Sadir then contacted the fighters, two F-22 Raptor Interceptors circling twenty-eight kilometres behind the Big Eye, and fed them the co-ordinates of the target track. The fighters acknowledged and turned west on full afterburner.

'We've got trouble.'

Sixty-eight miles ahead of the Big Eye, above the western edge of Salisbury Plain, Flight Lieutenant Lucas swore into his microphone as the Arabian radar emissions swept over their helicopter once again. They'd been lucky so far. Since leaving London, they'd found themselves in relatively clear country and Lucas had navigated a route away from urban areas and major traffic lanes, taking them in a curving path between the M4 and M3 motorways that saw them skirt Bracknell and Reading. They had detected some feverish radar activity behind them in London as scores of air-search radars began lighting up the sky, but the Dark Eagle was too low, too stealthy and heading further away with each passing second for them to constitute a problem. In fact, it was all going rather well and Lucas had begun to relax a little. Until now.

'They've got us. Positive return that time,' observed Stanton, the co-pilot. It was the fifth emission sweep in sixty seconds. They were being hunted and the radar signature of the hunter meant that it could only be one such aircraft, an Arabian Big Eye.

'What's the score?' hissed Gibson from the rear cabin.

'We've been spotted by an Arabian surveillance aircraft and that means fighters. We don't have long.' Lucas's trained eye took in their immediate environment. The ground beneath them was a patchwork of fields and hedges, with a small village to the north and a cluster of farm buildings to the west. Immediately ahead was a wheat field with a wooden hay barn at its southern end. Lucas banked the aircraft around, circling the large structure, its huge doors flung wide open. Empty. Not perfect but it would do.

'Everybody hang on!'

Lucas pulled back on the control yoke and lifted a foot off one of the rudder pedals, stopping the helicopter in mid-air and putting it into a full one hundred and eighty degree turn. He dropped the craft seventy feet to the ground, twisting the collective back up to increase the power and soften the landing. Lowering the gear, he drove the aircraft right inside the barn and spun her around to face the doors, killing the power to the rotors.

Harry winced as he watched the blades whip up a storm of broken stalks and chaff, the tips thrashing the air only a few feet from the barn walls. He stared at the back of Lucas's head, both hugely impressed and terrified by the manoeuvre. As the rotors dipped and the turbines wound down, they heard the roar of the incoming fighters.

'Signal's disappeared, Captain.'

Inside the cockpit of the Big Eye, Captain Al-Sadir had also noted the loss of contact with the helicopter and scanned his electronic display. Its last known position was a mile or so south of a place called Erlestoke. No matter, the fighters were almost upon them. They would force them down and pinpoint their position, continuing to patrol the area until the helicopter assault teams could get there and capture the infidels. Already Al-Sadir could hear the radio traffic of the helicopter pilots as they clattered off the runway at Heathrow fifty-six kilometres to the east.

Harry winced again as the distant roar increased to an ear-splitting crescendo and two fast-moving shadows suddenly carved across the wheat field in front of them. The barn shook beneath the fighters' thunderous passage and then they were gone, the rumble echoing around the horizon. Harry's ears rang. He looked anxiously at the back of Lucas's green helmet.

'Did they see us?'

'Did you see them?'

Over his headset, the lead Raptor pilot heard the negative response of his wingman. Where the devil had they gone? The Big Eye had vectored them in to the correct co-ordinates and they even had the target on their scopes for a second or two, but now it had gone. Obviously the helicopter had gone to ground, but where? The pilot thought it would be difficult enough to hide a helicopter quickly in all this open countryside, particularly with a couple of supersonic fighters hard on its tail. So where the devil had they gone?

'Wait… wait… shut down now!'

The radar operator obeyed the command and flicked the switch off yet again. He'd done it so often that his thumb was beginning to ache badly.

There were three of them, British soldiers of the Royal Artillery, cooped up inside their MAAT-V air defence vehicle since yesterday. Apart from the odd break to urinate and stretch their legs, they had remained inside the stuffy confines of the armoured vehicle and waited.

Their tracked vehicle was parked in a small but well-camouflaged depression on the eastern edge of the Salisbury Plain training area and, as far as they knew, they were the only unit for miles around. That was fine with the commander. They were tasked to operate independently, such was the nature of their particular function.

Along with other mechanised units, they'd rumbled out from Tidworth garrison two nights ago and scattered across Salisbury Plain for a week-long air defence exercise. Now that exercise had become frighteningly real.

Around six o'clock the previous evening they'd lost contact with their exercise co-ordinating officer, after which they'd been unable to get in touch with anyone, either on the military net or on their personal mobile phones. Something was seriously wrong, but they decided to stay put. Sooner or later someone would get in touch with them.

It was just before sunset when the commander heard the familiar sound of an army Land Rover bouncing along a nearby track. He ran through the trees to intercept it, nearly getting himself run over in the process. The panicked driver had told him that Tidworth garrison had been attacked. Car bombs had been used inside and outside several different barracks and that there were firefights breaking out all over the place. The order to head west had been given and all units and personnel were to make their way towards a marshalling area south of Bristol. The driver scribbled the co-ordinates on a notepad and ripped the sheet off, stuffing it into the commander's palm. The Land Rover sped away in a cloud of dust.

The commander had informed his shocked crew. Only one of them was married and, despite the protests of his comrades, he'd decided to head back on foot to his home on the outskirts of Tidworth and find his family. None of the others could've stopped him.

Now they were three: commander, radar operator and driver. They were to proceed west, which meant the threat was from the east. Four hundred feet away, camouflaged amongst a stand of Scots pines, their air-search radar mast confirmed that threat. The crew had watched with barely concealed anger as enemy aircraft entered British airspace unchallenged. They recorded the mass landings at Heathrow to the east, the high-flying military transports that passed overhead on their way north to God knew where. How could this happen? Where were our lads? As the hours ticked by, it became frighteningly obvious that British forces had been neutralised. Everyone else, according to the panicked jeep driver, was headed west. So be it.

The commander reached another decision. They were well camouflaged and all the air traffic was currently east of their position.

They would stay where they were until first light, recording enemy flight details – course, speed, altitude, probable destinations, aircraft type – dumping the data on to their computers' hard drives. When they headed west, they would go armed with something the top brass could use. The commander was a courageous man; to scuttle away without gathering some intelligence seemed pointless and a little cowardly. So they stayed in place overnight, their instruments quietly recording huge volumes of data. The sun had just risen in the east when they spotted the Big Eye.

As luck would have it, their air-search radar had been flipped to passive when the Big Eye's massive emission sweep washed over them. The commander immediately recognised the radar signature and screamed for all systems to be shut down. As they sweated inside their vehicle, the men listened for the scream of an incoming missile. It never came. After a few minutes the crew began to breathe again. The Big Eye had ignored them, continuing its search elsewhere.

Although they were shut down, there were other ways to maintain their operational effectiveness. The commander ordered the radar operator to switch his search radar on and off intermittently, as quickly as he could. Using this tactic, they could still operate while limiting their electronic exposure, although things would have to be done manually. To that effect, the driver left the vehicle and ran through the scrub to the stand of pines, using the cranking handle at the foot of the mast and manually twisting the radar dish to sweep the eastern horizon.

'There it is again.'

Inside the Big Eye's control cabin, a female operator noted the tiny emission flare on her screen and muttered under her breath. She punched her overhead alert button. Behind her, a senior operator stood up from his own console and watched the radar sweep on the operator's display.

'What is it?'

'Radar signature, type unknown. Very faint but recurring intermittently. Low output, no electronic signature as yet. Designate possible air-search radar. Request sideband sweep.'

'Negative,' snapped her supervisor. 'Priority is airborne traffic to the west. Maintain your watch.'

Fool, the operator cursed silently. It was because she was a woman and women in Arabia were still seen as second-class citizens, even in the military. Her supervisor was one such man who liked women to do his bidding. He had said so on many occasions, particularly when there were other men within earshot. During one incident, the pot-bellied toad had leaned over her console and quietly informed her in a gust of bad breath that he would take great pleasure in bedding her, a mental image that made the operator reel with nausea.

The supervisor was jealous, of course, because the operator was excellent at her job and he was a fat slob who was only on the Big Eye because his wife's cousin was a senior air force colonel in postings and assignments. Well, she would have his job one day. In the meantime, she did as she was ordered and concentrated on filtering the reams of electronic data the Big Eye was gathering as it continued on its westward course.

Twenty-three thousand feet below the Big Eye, the radar operator flipped his power switch every couple of seconds. As the minutes passed, the commander began to see a pattern emerging. As a rule, Big Eyes tended to stay away from danger. They were unsuitable for missile evasion due to their conventional aerodynamics and the sheer cost of the aircraft. The loss of a Big Eye would be a serious blow to any air force. And this one was headed straight for them.

The millisecond radar sweeps had given them course; now, they had both speed and altitude. It was an opportunity too good to miss. He scooped up his radio and a minute later the panting driver dropped into his seat and fired up the turbocharged diesel engine.

'Snap shot! Activate all systems! Prepare to launch!' As the radar operator's fingers ran along the control panel, the commander muttered a silent prayer of thanks that their exercise load out included six Sentry ground-to-air missiles. Four feet above his head, the roof launcher swivelled around and extracted two of those missiles from their magazine tubes. The camouflage net covering the vehicle shimmered as hydraulic arms swept it up and over the MAAT-V, dumping it on to the rear of the roof.

'Designate target Bandit One, tracked and locked. Ready to fire!'

'Fire!' shouted the commander.

'Missiles away!'

Above them, the missiles roared out of their launch tubes, enveloping the tracked vehicle in a cloud of white smoke.

'Shut down all systems! Let's move!' yelled the commander. The driver slammed the vehicle in reverse and roared backwards out of the small depression. He spun the vehicle around and raced toward their next fire position. Their manoeuvrability would make it hard for any enemy aircraft to get a lock-on.

Then again, they'd never taken on a Big Eye before...

'Missile launch!' yelled the female operator. 'Two missiles inbound! They have lock!'

It was the suspicious blip she'd seen only moments before, of that there was no doubt. The sideband sweep she'd recommended would have certainly identified the threat but, as it stood, the Big Eye's automated systems took over and it was now out of the operator's hands. She pulled her safety belt a little tighter.

The Big Eye automatically fired an air-to-ground missile, launched from the weapons bay beneath the cabin, its target the co-ordinates of the missile launch. Chaff pods were fired in self-defence, exploding a million tiny strips of aluminium into the air and creating a huge radar return for the incoming missiles. In the cockpit, Captain Al-Sadir banked the plane south and dived for the ground, launching flares in his wake. He'd never had to evade a missile before. Sure, he'd done it in the simulator, punching a few countermeasure buttons until the threat had disappeared, but that was just an exercise. Nothing had prepared him for the gut-wrenching fear of not one but two anti-aircraft missiles headed for his superheated engines. He pushed the throttles to the stops and began to pray.

The MAAT-V crashed into deep undergrowth and lurched to a halt.

'Status!' shouted the commander.

'Incoming missile, going wide. Standby.' A quarter of a mile away, the Big Eye missile exploded against one of the many rusted hulks on the Salisbury Plain firing range. 'Missile impact. No other inbounds.'

'How are our birds doing?'

The radar operator scanned his instruments. 'Bandit One is diving to the south. Missiles still have lock.'

'You fool!' shouted the female operator, unable to control her anger. 'I warned you about that signal!'

Her superior, strapped tightly into his chair across the aisle, turned away from his subordinate. He was ashen-faced, the sweat pouring from his brow. Like the captain, he was another who had never dreamt of facing the reality of an incoming missile; but now here he was, the G-forces pressing him into his seat as the plane made a steep dive for the ground. His thoughts turned quickly to his own death. He wasn't ready to die, not yet. As the aircraft shuddered around him, he cursed everything – his bad luck, the bitch of an operator, his wife's cousin in postings who said the Big Eye was the safest plane in the air. Stupid bastard.

The Big Eye's airframe groaned as it twisted in the sky, the cabin instruments shaking as it dropped like a stone towards the ground. Panic gripped the supervisor then. He choked back a shameful sob as he urinated involuntarily inside his flight suit, a dark, wet stain spreading down his left leg. Across the aisle, the female operator turned away in disgust and gripped the arms of her flight seat tightly.

'Two more bandits inbound from the west, fifty miles out! F-22s! I have lock on both.'

'Fire!' shouted the commander. The MAAT-V rocked on its tracks as two more missiles blasted out of their launch tubes.

'Move out!'

In the cockpit of the Big Eye, Captain Al-Sadir had only seconds to act. His crew watched with mounting alarm as the incoming missiles bore down on them, ignoring the Big Eye's countermeasures. It was no use. He looked across at his co-pilot and nodded. They both reached under their seats for the ejection handles as the plane thundered towards the ground and the chasing missiles ate up the distance between them.

'Eject!'

Both pilots pulled the yellow and black striped handles simultaneously.

Behind the cockpit, the control cabin automatically sealed itself airtight and two hundred explosive bolts separated it from the Big Eye's main fuselage. Six solid-fuel rockets then fired it upwards and away from the diving airliner. Moments later, the missiles screamed beneath the tumbling fuselage and detonated twelve metres short of the Big Eye's starboard engines, punching a thousand fragments of white-hot metal into the wings and obliterating the Big Eye from the air. The remaining wreckage of Bravo Echo-Niner crashed to the earth, just south of the village of Woodcott in Hampshire.

From the roof of the wingless fuselage, four large parachutes deployed and the cabin snapped upwards as it decelerated. Inside, each operator's face beamed in relief. The Big Eye crews were aware of the escape pods, the astronomical cost of the equipment and the highly trained personnel necessitating the implementation of a system to be used as a last resort. But no one had ever experienced a live test before now.

The senior operator fished a handkerchief from his pocket and mopped his sweating brow. He glanced down at his flight suit, soaked with his own urine. The crew had all seen it, including the bitch. She would make sure that nobody forgot this incident. He could shut her up, of course, but that could lead to more trouble. No, perhaps a transfer might be better. Besides, he'd had enough of flying.

As the ground rushed up to meet them another inflatable deployed, this time underneath the fuselage. They landed in a potato field with a gentle thud as the parachutes fluttered and settled over the aluminium roof.

The Raptor pilots saw the incoming missiles and turned to evade. They had only seconds to react as the F-22s and the British missiles accelerated towards each other with a closing speed of over Mach five. The flight leader heard the threat warning inside his helmet and broke left, heading for the deck.

His wingman wasn't so quick to react. The first missile detonated directly in front of his cockpit, exploding the jet fighter in mid-air. The other missile turned towards its target, now fleeing north at Mach two. The Sentry's solid-fuel rocket was capable of speeds in excess of Mach four; short of a miracle, the fighter ahead had little chance of escape and the pilot knew it. The blip on his scope was gaining horribly fast. He jinked the aircraft up and down, left and right, firing chaff pods and flares as he went, but the deadly missile kept coming. The pilot banked hard to the right and headed east. If he was going to eject, he'd make sure that he'd be picked up by Arabian ground forces. He went to full afterburner, flashing over the asphalt ribbon of the M4 motorway ninety metres below him.

He called in a brief Mayday. As the missile closed to within a mile of the Raptor's engines, the pilot ejected from the doomed fighter. After a short, rocket-assisted flight, his parachute canopy deployed above him while, below him, his aircraft was blown from the sky. The fireball arced down towards the motorway below, narrowly missing the deserted road.

Despite losing his beloved aircraft, the pilot was pretty pleased with himself. He'd survived his first encounter with an experienced SAM crew, his warning systems had proved more than adequate and his reactions were honed to perfection. He hoped his wingman had fared as well as he had.

As he floated down to the green fields below, the pilot gazed around him. The sun was climbing into the morning sky and it bathed the green and yellow fields below in a soft golden light. England really was a pretty place. Once the invasion was complete he could look forward to a short period of leave, when he would take in the sights of this historic land.

Amongst the small stand of Scots pines, the MAAT-V crew quickly broke down their radar mast and loaded it aboard the vehicle, while the commander reflected on their recent engagement. Three kills, two Raptors and a Big Eye. Not bad at all. If it was going to be that easy, they might have a chance of holding the line somewhere, maybe fight back. But they'd need more ammunition for that.

Head west, that was the order. With the skies now clear, the mast was quickly stored away and the MAAT-V was prepped to go. The commander plotted a course across Salisbury Plain, crossing the county border into Somerset somewhere south of Trowbridge. Hopefully they'd locate other stragglers and link up, maybe find out what was going on elsewhere. The driver engaged gear and the MAAT-V lurched away from the copse. They headed west across the plain, keeping to the woodland tracks.

Lucas rolled the Dark Eagle out of the barn and into the field. He eased the aircraft a few feet into the air, while Stanton used the on-board instruments to scan the horizon for enemy aircraft. So far, so good. They climbed higher, increasing the range of their sweep. Still nothing.

'Hang on.' Lucas increased power and dipped the nose, literally brushing the treetops of a small copse to the west. 'We're in the clear for now,' he told his passengers. 'We'll stay low, avoid the towns and villages. We should be home and dry within the hour.'

'Amen to that,' whispered a very relieved Harry.

Central London

Inside the command centre beneath Buckingham Palace, General Mousa's already dark mood turned black. Heathrow had just confirmed the loss of the Big Eye and the two Raptors. The only good news was that the Big Eye's crew had managed to survive unscathed. A helicopter was on its way to pick them up.

'Have them detained at Heathrow and interrogated. I want to know who's responsible for this farce.' Mousa turned on his heel and stormed out of the command centre. It was time to report to the Holy One.

Upstairs in the palace's private quarters, Mousa had one of the king's suite of rooms rigged out with a battlefield command terminal and a secure communications link, while outside his paratroopers guarded the corridor. Mousa powered up the terminal and punched in his personal security code. On the screen, a small video window opened to reveal an ornate, but empty, chair in front of a rough-hewn rock wall. Mousa knew he was looking at the Holy One's private chambers deep under the Jabal Sawda mountains. A few seconds passed and the Holy One entered the screen and sat down. He looks tired, thought Mousa.

'You look tired, my friend,' echoed Khathami.

Mousa ignored the comment and bowed his head. 'Holy One, I apologise for not contacting you sooner, however a situation arose that required my fullest attention. I wanted to rectify that situation before I made my report.' Mousa paused, choosing his words carefully. 'However, events didn't turn out as expected. The infidel prime minister is still at large.'

The cleric stared silently at the camera, his bespectacled eyes unblinking. Mousa swallowed hard and continued.

'The last contact we had was out to the west of England. I have diverted a mechanised battalion from Southampton and sent it north-west in an effort to contain him. There are also rumours of a government facility in the area, and I have ordered the interrogation of every senior civilian and military official we can find to ascertain whether those rumours are true. Nevertheless, I will capture the prime minister in due course, Holy One. Of that, there is no doubt.'

The older man was quiet for some time while Mousa sat straight backed, awaiting his next words. The fate of his career hung in the balance now. No matter how one looked at it he had failed, despite the tactical advantage of surprise and the huge operation to encircle the capital. He sat and waited silently, his eyes lowered in deference. Eventually, the cleric cleared his throat.

'General Mousa, for many years you have been my trusted right arm, the sword in my scabbard. You have never failed me in your duties and your loyalty to me is without question.' Mousa held his breath. 'I believe you have done everything possible to achieve your goal and, for that, you cannot be faulted. If the Englishman has slipped your intricate net, then that is God's will and who are we to question it? I suspect your frustration and disappointment will be a heavy burden for you to bear, but it is a burden that you must rid yourself of quickly, for there is other work to be done.' Mousa exhaled, raising his head. The grand mufti smiled at his favourite general's obvious relief.

'Beecham's escape is a blow to our operation,' continued Khathami. 'However, we must ignore that setback and take into consideration the task before us, the importance of God's work.' He paused briefly, lifting his spectacles off the bridge of his nose and polishing them with a linen handkerchief tucked amongst the folds of his sleeve. Satisfied, he put them back on and continued. 'You will consolidate our hold on the cities, General Mousa. Europe has fallen and Britain will follow, despite Beecham. Report to me again in twenty-four hours. Allah be with you.'

A deeply relieved General Mousa bowed his head.

'And with you also, Holy One.'

Hampshire-Wiltshire Border

Kirsty's fingers played lightly on the steering wheel as the Range Rover cruised along yet another deserted country road. So far, Alex had guided them successfully through the back lanes of Hampshire, the only tense moment being their passage beneath the M3 motorway. Kirsty had steered them through a little-used pedestrian tunnel on the outskirts of Chertsey, where they scraped the paint from the Range Rover's wing mirrors and left the motorway behind them. A few hundred yards beyond the tunnel, Khan ordered Kirsty to pull over while he ran into the woods, not to answer a call of nature as the others soon discovered but to record the military traffic on his mobile phone. Someone, somewhere, might find the images useful.

They drove in relative silence after that, soothed by the smoothness of the ride and the vehicle's plush interior. Alex gave occasional directions and, for the most part, the roads were empty except for the odd pheasant or rabbit loitering on the deserted country lanes.

People were thin on the ground, too. Earlier, as they passed through the village of Bramshill, they saw a small crowd huddled together on the village green. Seeing the startled faces and a few shotguns, Khan thought it best not to stop. Kirsty kept her foot on the accelerator and continued on through the twisting lanes. The villagers watched them until the road took them out of sight. They'd travelled another couple of miles when Kirsty broke the silence.

'The radio,' she said, 'we haven't checked it. Maybe we should.'

Khan leaned forward and punched the button. 'Good idea.' He shot a look at Alex. 'We must be getting slow.'

'Tired, more like,' Alex yawned, stretching his arms. The vehicle filled with a low hiss and Khan began flicking through the pre-sets.

'…a public safety message broadcasting on all frequencies…'

'Stop the car,' Khan ordered. Kirsty stamped on the brakes and came to a halt in the middle of the lane. Khan twisted the volume knob.

'…members of the public are advised to remain in their homes. Martial law is now in effect and all public services, including transport networks, have been temporarily suspended. I repeat, all civilians are to remain in their homes or alternative places of shelter. Stay tuned to this station for further information. This ends this public safety message.'

Kirsty's voice suddenly brightened. 'That's good news, isn't it?' She saw Khan and Alex exchange grim looks and the hope in her voice faded. 'Isn't it?' she repeated weakly. The broadcast looped once more, then a musical track cut in Arabic music.

'Bizarre,' Alex whispered.

Khan snapped the radio off. 'They've thought of everything,' he muttered.

Kirsty gripped the steering wheel, her eyes fixed on the road ahead. 'I can't stay here,' she whispered. 'I have to get back to London. My family, my friends...'

Alex laid a hand on her shoulder. 'Take it easy, Kirsty. London isn't safe, remember? We can't go back, not right now. Let's just get to the farm,' he soothed, 'and we'll work it out from there.'

Kirsty closed her eyes and took a deep breath, exhaling through pursed lips. 'Yes, the farm.' She caught Alex's eye in the rear-view mirror. 'I'm alright, really. Mild panic attack, that's all.' She swivelled in her chair, the cream leather creaking noisily. 'Got to be positive, right?'

'Always,' Khan smiled.

She slipped the vehicle into gear and hit the accelerator, purring smoothly along the lane.

'Want me to drive?' Alex offered.

'No, it's okay. I need the distraction.'

They weaved their way past fields and hedgerows for almost an hour before arriving at a deserted T-junction. Ahead of them was a weather-beaten signpost and, beyond that, a line of distant hills dissected by a black ribbon of road. Alex pointed through the windscreen.

'That's the A34. Cross that and we're in Wiltshire. If we stick to the back roads I reckon it'll be about another hour before we reach Rob's place.'

'Which way?' asked Kirsty.

'Go left. We'll head towards Sydmonton, then cut across country until we get to the A338. It's not far from there.'

'Good,' Khan muttered, shifting in his seat. 'I'm looking forward to getting off these roads.'

Alex glanced behind them. 'They seem pretty quiet.'

'True enough, but you can bet your life they'll start sending aircraft up, if they haven't already. And they won't confine themselves to London, either. Let's keep moving, Kirsty.'

The vehicle spun left and accelerated towards the distant hills. Khan folded his arms, his head against the window, his eyes searching the morning sky.

Alternate One

For the occupants of the Dark Eagle, the remainder of their flight west had been brief and uneventful. As the helicopter hummed across the landscape, the countryside below appeared to be waking up to a normal summer's day – except for the sheer weight of military traffic. Passing north of Frome in Somerset, they saw an enormous bottleneck of vehicles parked along both sides of the town's ring road.

Harry glanced out of the window. There were all manner of vehicles down there: tanks, tracked vehicles, jeeps and trucks of various shapes and sizes. There were also hundreds of British soldiers on foot, milling around in an adjacent field.

'They're being organised by unit type,' said Lucas over the comms net. 'Military vehicles have been arriving since yesterday evening.'

On the ground many, faces tilted upwards, eyes shielded against the sun, watching the helicopter as it flew overhead. To Harry it looked like a chaotic scene and he fought a brief surge of panic. How was he supposed to cope with a situation like this? He hoped that his arrival at Alternate One would offer him a few more options.

They left the traffic jam behind and continued westwards, skirting the town of Midsomer Norton to the south and crossing the A37 between the villages of Emborough and Binegar. Ahead, the Mendip Hills rose up steeply from the flat Somerset plain.

The Mendip Hills were a popular beauty spot, with Cheddar Gorge in the west and Chew Valley Lake to the north attracting tens of thousands of visitors every year. Covering an area of roughly three hundred square miles, the hills comprised steep valleys and gorges to the north and south whilst, to the west, the rolling hills gave way to precipitous escarpments, pushing upwards to form a huge, central plateau that was windswept and sparsely populated.

The plateau itself was punctuated with dense forests, dark valleys, huge rock formations and massive depressions. Large sinkholes bored their way deep into the limestone rock and much of the area was out of bounds in the interests of public safety. It was a beautiful yet desolate area.

The Dark Eagle rose up over the eastern foothills of the Mendips, skirting the town of Wells to the south. Lucas kept the aircraft low. Detection by the locals was always a problem and the Ministry of Defence had gone to great lengths over the years to keep inquisitive civilians away. Usually a few danger signs did the trick, like the ones that dissected the central plateau, but the situation had changed dramatically in the last twenty-four hours and nosy ramblers were the least of their problems now. Although the sun was well above the horizon, Lucas ordered Stanton to keep a close eye on the thermal imaging cameras for any suspicious heat signatures on the ground as the helicopter swept over the plateau and headed north-east towards Mendip Forest.

Harry looked down as the Dark Eagle crested a hilltop and dropped into a deep valley, its steep sides covered in densely packed pine trees. The valley was completely enclosed and ran for a couple of miles or so, with another craggy rock face looming a few hundred yards ahead. Near its summit, jagged limestone teeth jutted into the sky.

At the end of the valley, Lucas banked hard and dropped the helicopter, losing height rapidly. Harry gripped his armrests as the Dark Eagle hovered down below the treetops towards the valley floor. As they approached the ground, Harry realised that the surface comprised of some kind of man-made hard decking, perfectly camouflaged in the mottled green and browns of the surrounding landscape.

The Dark Eagle flared and touched down, rolling forward along the hard deck between the trees. He saw several soldiers and ground crew emerge from the undergrowth as the aircraft rolled to a stop. Gibson and Farrell were first out, helping Harry down from the chopper. He turned and waved to Lucas and his crew, receiving a short salute in return. A hatless soldier in combat uniform stepped forward and extended his hand.

'Good Morning Prime Minister. My name is Major Monroe and I'm the senior security officer here at Alternate One. Follow me, please.'

The major turned on his heel and led the way under the trees. Harry took in the surroundings as they walked quickly up the sloping hard deck. The sun hadn't risen high enough to penetrate the valley and the canopy under the trees was dark and foreboding. High above their heads, Harry could make out thin layers of camouflage netting strung between the treetops. The whole complex must be practically invisible from the air, he realised.

As the hard deck cut deeper into the hillside, the sloping ground on either side rose up to form rough-hewn dirt walls. To his right, a low concrete hangar had been cut into a wide section of the slope and, inside, Harry saw another Dark Eagle being worked on by several technicians. As they passed the hangar, Harry notice more figures in the treeline.

'Security force,' said Gibson, following Harry's eye. 'This must be the main entrance. Look.'

Just up ahead, the hard deck ended at a huge sliding door cut into the rock face that was slowly rolling open as they approached. Harry stopped in his tracks. So this was Alternate One.

The enormous entrance door stood at least thirty feet high, its external fascia expertly camouflaged to blend into the real rock face. It slid quietly open on well-lubricated tracks and Harry was reminded of an old James Bond film he'd once seen. The huge door suddenly changed direction and began to close. Harry stepped quickly over the threshold and found himself inside a large cavern. There were no lights here, but the cavern seemed to stretch away to his right, with yellow-painted parking bays marked on the smooth concrete floor. In the gloom, he could see several vehicles there, all military.

They followed Monroe as he headed towards another doorway. Behind them, the huge entrance door slid closed and Harry felt rather than heard the deep boom that echoed around the cavern. They continued on and found themselves inside a wide tunnel lit by halogen lights, with a single white line in the middle of a road that stretched away into the distance. Ahead of them was an electric buggy; Monroe climbed behind the wheel, inviting the others aboard. The buggy clicked and whined, then accelerated quietly along the tunnel.

'Despite appearances, Alternate One isn't a very big complex,' explained Monroe, his voice echoing off the tunnel walls. 'It's all here under this one hillside.'

'That valley we flew into. It looked like it was closed at both ends. No way in or out,' observed Gibson.

'Well spotted. There's a vehicle tunnel at the southern end that cuts through the hillside. For security reasons we don't use it that often.'

'I never knew the place was so complex,' said Harry.

'Not many people do. We like to keep it that way.'

They continued along the tunnel, the floor sloping downwards and leading them deeper into the hillside, until they reached another large cavern. Here, troops laden with equipment criss-crossed the floor and forklift trucks whirred backwards and forwards, loading supplies on to waiting vehicles. Bellowed orders and revving engines echoed off the cavern walls. The noise was tremendous.

'We're on foot from here,' shouted Monroe. 'I'll escort you to your quarters where you can freshen up, Prime Minister. There's a briefing in the main operations room in thirty minutes.'

'Very well.'

Monroe held up a hand as Gibson and Farrell hopped off the buggy. 'You two will report to the personnel pool. We need every fighting man possible at the moment.'

Harry's eyes narrowed. 'What's this?' Before Monroe could respond, Harry shook his head. 'Out of the question. These men are my security team now. I've lost all the others.'

'Prime Minister, I think we–'

'It's not open for debate, Major Monroe.'

The burly officer cleared his throat. 'Of course.' He turned to the two soldiers. 'I'll arrange accommodation. In the meantime, I'll expect to see you at the briefing.'

They continued across the cavern and Harry noticed the looks from some of the soldiers as they passed. It wasn't optimism he saw in their faces.

'This is the assembly area,' waved Monroe, 'a central distribution point from which supplies and equipment are transferred around the complex. Alternate One can accommodate up to four thousand personnel, although there's nothing like those numbers here at the moment.'

'How many are here?' Harry asked.

'Well, there are always twenty-five permanent staff on duty, twenty-four hours a day all year round. They are backed by a rotational force of another twenty-five. Now, including key government ministers, military personnel and the security force guarding the exterior, there's a total of eight hundred and ninety-one.'

Harry caught Monroe by the arm. 'Nine hundred people? Is that it? Where are all my ministers? Surely some got out?'

Monroe frowned. 'It all happened very quickly, Prime Minister. The initial attacks were far more widespread than we first thought.'

Harry bit his lip. 'Jesus Christ, this is bloody awful.'

'Let's keep moving, please.'

Monroe led them through a corridor until they reached another smaller cavern. Two doors led off it, one on either side. Monroe gestured to the one on the right.

'This is your room, sir. You'll find hot water and toiletries in the bathroom.' He glanced at his watch. 'I'll come and fetch you in twenty minutes.'

Harry stepped inside and found himself inside a simple, yet comfortable room with two single beds, a desk with a computer terminal and a small en-suite bathroom. He turned the shower tap on and was delighted to see a powerful jet of steaming water drum on to the smooth stone floor. He undressed quickly.

By the time Major Monroe returned, Harry had enjoyed a hot shower and shave. For the first time in many hours he felt relaxed and in control. Monroe had some clothes draped across his arm.

'Not quite Savile Row, but they're clean and should fit you.'

Harry changed into a fresh shirt and trousers, feeling vaguely ministerial once again. Outside, he found Gibson and Farrell waiting to escort him and the party moved off. They headed back towards the assembly area, cutting across the cavern towards another tunnel in the far wall. Harry looked up at the high ceiling and wondered how long it had all taken to construct. Monroe caught Harry's look.

'Quite impressive, isn't it? However, our engineers can't take complete credit for the design and construction. Mother Nature and time did most of the hard work. There are a lot of natural caverns cutting through these hills, and large parts of the complex used to be mineshafts dating back to the turn of the twentieth century. In here please, Prime Minister.'

Monroe stepped through a heavy steel door. The operations room was rigged out with a myriad of sophisticated equipment, digital displays and a wall-sized map of Britain. Several soldiers wearing headsets sat in front of a bank of computer terminals at the far end of the room, busily tapping away at their keyboards. Dominating the centre was a large conference table, around which sat a dozen men and women. Chairs scraped back as Harry entered. He waved them back into their seats.

'Please, don't get up.'

Monroe directed Harry to the head of the table, while Gibson and Farrell slipped off to the side and took up positions near the door. As he approached, Harry scanned the faces of the personnel gathered around the table, recognising only two people. The first to approach him was Russell Armstrong. Russell was chief secretary to the Treasury and the right-hand man to Chancellor Stephen Laws. He was a decent chap, Harry recalled, quiet and industrious.

'Prime Minister, so good to see you.' Armstrong pumped Harry's hand a little too eagerly and Harry offered a reassuring smile.

'You too, Russell.'

'Wonderful news that you'd managed to escape in one piece.' Armstrong's face darkened. 'I was so sorry to hear about Anna.'

Unconsciously, Harry bit his lower lip. Anna. Things had moved so fast he hadn't had time to dwell on his emotions. He knew that was a good thing but, momentarily, he fought hard to keep them in check.

'Clare's missing. And the children,' Armstrong announced in a flat voice. Harry could see that the man was close to the edge and he felt ashamed of himself. Yes, his own wife had been killed, but there were probably thousands of casualties out there; men, women and, God help them, children. Russell's girls were quite young, too, and the man had no idea where they were. The very thought must be unbearable and Harry was silently grateful that he and Anna hadn't had any children of their own. He quickly put his own grief to one side. There were others to consider and, as prime minister, he was expected to lead by example. There would be time later to confront his loss.

'I'm sure they're safe, somewhere,' consoled Harry. 'What happened to Stephen?'

'No one knows.'

'Dear God.'

The other friendly face in the room belonged to Peter Noonan, the deputy prime minister. The two men were old friends and they embraced warmly.

'Peter. Glad you made it.'

'Good to see you, Harry.'

'How long have you been here?'

'For some time, now. The meeting at the Press Club overran. I got your message and was on my way over to Downing Street when the first bombs went off. I was taken to Northolt immediately and flown here.'

'What about the rest of the cabinet?'

Noonan's face darkened. 'No word, I'm afraid. The attacks have been devastating and communications have been practically non-existent. We can only pray they're safe.' Noonan paused, laying a hand on Harry's shoulder. 'Harry, about Anna–'

'Thank you, Peter,' he cut in. 'What about your family?'

Noonan lowered his voice. 'I've been very lucky. Jenny's at the house in Gloucester and Toby's in his Bristol dorm. Arrangements have been made to move them north.'

'North?'

'I think we should get this meeting started, Harry. There are a lot of blanks to be filled in.'

Noonan took care of the introductions around the table. Most were members of the armed forces, plus a few mid-level civil servants from London who were fortunate enough to have been evacuated. Harry spent a few moments listening to their tales of escape from the capital and realised how close some of them had come to death. Not for them the services of a stealth helicopter. Most had escaped by car, a terrifying ordeal by some accounts. Many who'd started the journey west hadn't made it, their fate unknown. Harry took a seat along the table and everybody sat down. The deputy PM got proceedings under way.

'Well, Harry, things don't look good. As you're aware, we are now at war with the State of Arabia and God only knows why. It began at six o'clock yesterday evening with a series of co-ordinated terror attacks, focussed primarily in the South East. Casualty predictions are high, both civilian and military. A large portion of domestic utilities have been shut down – gas, electricity, telephone exchanges, even water supplies. Luckily for us, the West Country seems to have escaped the violence, although two car bombs were detonated in Bristol.'

'Jesus,' whispered Harry.

'Now, as far as communications are concerned, all media channels have ceased to operate for the time being. Diplomatically, we've had no word from the Continent, but our communications people here have picked up thousands of garbled messages from the European mainland. Seems they're suffering the same crisis as us.'

'What's the status of our armed forces?'

Noonan nodded to the senior army representative. 'General Bashford will give you the military brief. General?'

Major General Julian Bashford pushed his chair back and stood. He was a tall, thin man with wispy white hair, dressed in combat fatigues. And he looked exhausted, decided Harry. Bashford cleared his throat several times and shuffled the papers at his fingertips, seemingly lost in thought. After a moment, he motioned for the lights in the room to be dimmed and the inbuilt table display glowed brightly in the gloom. It showed several large-scale maps of the UK and the European mainland.

'Prime Minister, we intercepted a radio message at approximately twenty hundred hours yesterday evening from a British Army regiment in the Cologne area. It was a short message, on an open channel. They reported being under heavy attack, that the camp was in chaos, and personnel had scattered into the surrounding streets. A large number of people had also been killed. They also reported seeing at least a dozen Arabian heavy-lift aircraft flying low over their position, inbound towards Cologne airport. We lost communications shortly afterwards.'

Harry twisted his hands on the table. 'My God.'

'There's more, I'm afraid.' Bashford touched the screen and the display changed to a map of the British Isles. 'Many of our main garrisons here in England have been hit, with many vehicles and equipment destroyed. According to survivors, a large number of attacks started inside the bases. Terrorists, posing as civilian contractors and suchlike. Surviving personnel have abandoned many of these bases and scattered far and wide, taking as much of their inventory as possible.'

Noonan cleared his throat. 'Base security was an issue to be addressed in the next defence review.'

'Well, the horse has firmly bolted on that one,' growled Harry. 'Please continue, General.'

'As we re-establish comms, we're ordering all surviving units to make for the Scottish border. There's only been one attack there, a bomb, which detonated in Holyrood.'

'Dear God.'

'The first minister was killed, along with most of his cabinet secretaries and ministers. Lord Advocate Matheson is the highest-ranking official left and is busy forming an emergency administration. They've stated that, in light of the circumstances, all executive authority will be passed to you.'

'I see.'

'Apart from that single attack it appears the rest of Scotland has been unaffected, confirming that it was a decapitation exercise. Instead,

Arabian forces are concentrating their efforts in the south. We have a direct link here with SCOTFOR military HQ outside Edinburgh. Scottish border troops have been deployed and Matheson has issued a general call-up for Territorial and Reservist personnel right across Scotland. They've also closed the border to civilian traffic. Scotland will be sealed up tight.'

'A wise move,' Harry commented.

'As I've mentioned, our southern garrisons have been hit hard, but initial reports are not as bad as we feared. As luck would have it, UK land forces have been running a series of major exercises and a good percentage of our troops were already deployed into the field, mainly across Salisbury Plain. Those units have been ordered to head west. Surviving rear party and HQ staff at Bulford, Tidworth and Aldershot garrisons have been ordered to do the same. The plan was to shorten our defensive line and create a buffer zone across the West Country from which we could organise our defences, using Alternate One as our main base of operations.'

'Was?'

'The situation is fluid, Prime Minister. Let me explain.' Bashford touched the screen, increasing magnification to reveal a detailed view of western England. 'Here we are, deep in the Mendips. The northernmost point of the defensive line is here, at Upper Seagry, a village just north of the M4 motorway. With the intelligence we're getting, the Arabians like to use motorways, which makes sense considering the amount of men and material they're moving.'

'What about their air force?' Harry asked.

'They know we have anti-air capability, and we've already shot down a small number of enemy aircraft. At the same time, they're probably aware we have little or no air forces to counter their threat. They'll be cautious about sending manned air assets against us in the short term and, besides, their ground forces outnumber us massively. We believe that, when the attack comes, it will be a mixture of conventional ground forces supplemented with unmanned reconnaissance vehicles and long-range artillery. To counter that, our defensive line will continue down here to Sherborne in the south and then cut across the A352, the A37 and the A356, just in case they try to bypass our southern flank by hugging the south coast and turning north. Our defences will be arrayed along this line, facing east.'

'I see,' Harry mumbled. Truth was, he was finding it increasingly difficult to relate what the general was saying to events outside. The man was describing the crisis as calmly as if he were giving a lecture at a military college. 'Looks like we'll be spread pretty thin,' he noted. Even a civilian like Harry could see that the area the general was proposing to cover was vast.

'Correct. And because of our lack of resources, we're concentrating our high-mobility armoured units at road junctions, bridges and other major choke points. We're also using the terrain to our advantage by placing fighting vehicles and jeep-mounted anti-armour weapons in other strategic positions, where they can engage the enemy from cover and then escape across country. Some of our Apaches survived the initial attacks too, although they have little ordnance. Still, they can add something to our strategic capability and give the bad guys pause for thought. The order of the day will be to get in, land a solid punch, and get out again. Experienced teams can use this tactic repeatedly, causing advancing enemy units considerable delay.'

'How much time have we got?'

Bashford frowned. 'Not much. We're talking days, rather than weeks.'

Harry studied the map. *Days*. Then what? The countryside laid to waste? Between Alternate One and Bashford's defensive line there were dozens of towns, both small and large, not to mention countless villages and farms. 'You're missing something.' Harry got to his feet, placing his hands on the table. He looked at the faces around him. 'What about the civilians? What provision are we making for them when this attack comes?' Blank faces stared back at him and Harry shook his head. 'What you're proposing here is unacceptable, General. A major battle across the English countryside, with hundreds of thousands of civilians in the firing line? Jesus Christ, it'll be a slaughterhouse.'

Noonan held up his hand. 'Hear the General out, Harry.'

Bashford cleared his throat. 'It's something the people in this room have also considered at great length, Prime Minister. You're absolutely right. The truth is, if we made a stand we'd be neutralised in a few days, resulting in unacceptable civilian casualties. The defence line is in place specifically to buy us time. The real plan is to evacuate.'

Harry raised an eyebrow. 'Evacuate?'

'It's imperative we get you away from here as soon as possible,' urged Noonan. 'The country needs a leader now. Without some form of government and a familiar face at the head of that administration, we stand little chance of negotiating any kind of settlement. And we'll have to negotiate, Harry, sooner or later.'

Harry nodded grimly. The Arabians would want to deal, wouldn't they? But then again, the timing and ferocity of the attacks displayed a frightening lack of concern for the level of casualties in Whitehall and elsewhere. Perhaps the Arabians had no intention of negotiating at all. The thought troubled Harry deeply.

'Where are we being evacuated to, General?'

'Scotland. A little-known facility in the Highlands called McIntyre Castle. It's on the west coast, in Argyll, very secluded, surrounded by mountains and forests. It was last used by the military during the Second World War to train deep-cover SOE agents, but it's always been on the books, so to speak. There'll be a skeleton staff there, plus a small security force. The rest of the operational team will join SCOTFOR HQ outside Edinburgh.'

'How long until the border is secured?' Harry asked.

'In the short term, engineers are constructing razor wire fencing and observation towers, and every cross-border road is being blocked with heavy vehicles or concrete obstacles, backed up with infantry and light-armour support. In addition, anti-aircraft and anti-tank units are being sited at strategic points all along the line. Multiple launch rocket vehicles and conventional artillery are also being drawn up and sited deep into Scotland to give us some long-range firepower. They also have helicopter patrols operating up to three thousand feet, and what fighters we've been able to muster are flying combat air patrols above that. The more troops we relocate north, the more chance we have of preserving Scotland.'

'What about the troops here at Alternate One?' he asked. 'What happens to them?'

'I'm holding a briefing this afternoon for senior officers,' explained Bashford. 'Part of that briefing will include plans for a phased withdrawal. When the time is right, our men and women will withdraw to the coast and board the ships.'

'Ships? We're leaving by sea?'

'Not us, just the bulk of our forces. The navy has four ships that will dock at Teignmouth in Devon when they receive the order. We have two supply ships, a frigate and a small minesweeper at our disposal. Unfortunately, we won't be able to take any of our larger equipment or vehicles, but we can probably squeeze around ten thousand troops in total aboard all the ships. We'll load a majority of them during the hours of darkness, setting sail as we fill the vessels. The ships will then head north into the Irish Sea and rendezvous at Stranraer, on the west coast of Scotland.'

'How many soldiers do we have out there on the defensive line now?' asked Harry.

'Around four thousand. There are approximately another eight or nine thousand troops being held in reserve areas, ready to counter a surprise attack should it materialise.'

'And what about our air force?' A quick glance at the Royal Air Force commodore told its own story. The man sat there with a permanent frown, his eyes cast down towards the display.

'More bad news, I'm afraid,' confirmed Bashford. 'Many of our combat air bases in England were attacked resulting in major aircraft loss and damage. Some planes were able to get airborne and, in some cases, the pilots engaged enemy aircraft, but all in all our squadrons were decimated. Brize Norton itself was attacked by over fifty armed men. At least one transport aircraft was shot down as it tried to escape the fighting. Again, all survivors were ordered north to Scotland.'

'Dear God,' breathed Harry. 'And what about the navy? Please don't tell me we've lost that as well.'

Edward Hughes, First Admiral of the Fleet, cleared his throat. 'The navy has, on reflection, fared rather better than our sister services,' began the admiral. 'We've been unable to contact any of our ships in the Mediterranean, however our presence there consisted of only three small ships as part of our commitment to the Standing Naval Force in the Med. According to the American satellite data we're receiving, Arabian naval forces have sealed the gateway to the Mediterranean at Gibraltar and we've counted several Arabian minelaying ships at work in the area.'

'Our other ships?' asked Harry.

'All intact. We have several ships in dock in Scotland undergoing repairs or replenishments. We have more vessels in the North Sea and Atlantic, plus several patrol craft in the West Indies on exercise.'

'What about the Americans?' enquired Harry. 'Have we had word yet?'

Bashford nodded. 'We've been in constant communication with them via secure links to SCOTFOR. President Mitchell has ordered DEFCON three and closed her borders. During the initial phases of the Arabian operation, the Americans ordered all civilian traffic inbound to the continental United States, excluding US carriers, to divert to US Air Force bases away from metropolitan areas. Unfortunately, two civilian aircraft failed to heed the instructions and were shot down by American air defences. One of those planes was a British Airways flight en route to Washington DC, splashed twenty-five miles offshore. The other one was a Portuguese carrier, en route from São Paulo to Albuquerque in New Mexico. Brought down in the Gulf of Mexico by a US missile boat. They're taking no chances, sir.'

'Jesus,' Harry breathed. Then he bolted upright. 'What about our nukes?'

'All four Vanguard subs have put to sea with a full complement of missiles,' the admiral reassured him. 'Aldermaston has so far remained unscathed, but all weapons programmes are undergoing emergency shutdowns. Fissile materials are being transported north as we speak. The rest of our arsenal is stockpiled in the States.'

'If the Arabians were going to use nukes they'd have used them by now,' Bashford said. 'And they know we won't use them on our own soil.'

'The Israelis wouldn't be quite so squeamish,' Harry pointed out. 'What can we expect there?'

Bashford shook his head. 'It doesn't look good. The Yanks have told us the IDF is considering going to DEFCON one. If Arabia moves against them, which the Americans expect, it'll mean a full-blown nuclear exchange. Baghdad is dismissing any threat to Israel, but the truth is most Middle Eastern countries would secretly revel in their destruction. They'll go down fighting, of that there's no doubt.'

'Dear God in heaven,' Harry breathed. 'Let's just pray cooler heads prevail.'

The general spread his hand over the digital map, now overlaid with various arrows, lines and icons. He began to explain them in detail. 'As I mentioned earlier, we'll concentrate our heavy armour and fighting vehicles near major choke points. If there's going to be a fight, at least we'll be forewarned and the units there will engage the enemy with extreme prejudice. However, our primary objective will be to fool the Arabians into thinking that we possess more strategic assets than we actually have.'

Bashford indicated several icons spread out over a large area, forming a rough half circle near the edge of Salisbury Plain.

'These anti-aircraft detachments are our most easterly units' he continued. 'They'll move every two hours, rotating around the positions you see here. Occasionally, the units will synchronise a sweep pattern at random intervals and blast the air to the east with their search radars. With luck, the Arabians will think that we have a major anti-aircraft capability and hold off any pre-emptive strikes while they figure out a plan. Hopefully, this will buy us a bit more time to make our preparations for departure. Non-essential troops will begin a phased withdrawal towards Teignmouth this afternoon. As night falls, the remainder of our forces will head to the docks. By sunup, all four ships should be fully loaded and deep into the Irish Sea.'

Harry studied the map. It all seemed fairly straightforward. 'Sounds like a decent plan, General. I just want to make it clear that our primary objective must be the preservation of life. And what about here, at Alternate One?'

'A skeleton staff will stay behind and maintain the complex. If it's discovered, they'll use explosives to destroy the command and control sections, then make a run for Scotland.'

'What about stragglers?' enquired Noonan. 'Those who won't make the deadline for the pull-out. What happens to them?'

Bashford shrugged his thin shoulders. 'We have to have a cut-off point. Anyone who hasn't crossed the defensive line and reported in will be on their own. It's a tough call, but the safety and security of the main force must be paramount. However, the rear party here at Alternate One will keep an eye on the roads, send people north if possible.' He studied his watch, a worried frown creasing his forehead. 'Time now is ten o'clock. Last light is approximately nine thirty this evening. Prime Minister, your party must be ready to depart then. Let's pray the Arabians decide to ignore us for the next twenty-four hours.'

Harry studied the screen with its overlay of multi-coloured icons and symbols. It was a decent enough plan and he was suddenly reminded of Dunkirk during the Second World War. Back then, thousands of British and Allied troops had crammed the beaches of northern France to escape the advancing German armies. Although most got away, over five thousand troops were machine-gunned on the beaches or blown up as they boarded the flotilla of small boats that crossed the Channel from England to rescue them. Is that what it would be like here? Harry wondered. Would the Arabians send their forces west before the rest of them had a chance to escape? Bashford had estimated that there were roughly thirteen thousand troops to evacuate. Harry prayed that the plans would run like clockwork, and the Arabians would ignore the desperately inadequate and unprepared forces to the west.

In the prime minister's quarters, the orderly scooped up the filthy black trousers and combat jacket and dumped them into a green refuse sack. His orders were to dispose of the clothes and any other items, then clean the room. In the bathroom, he emptied a waste bin, briefly noting the open pack of disposable razors and the partially squeezed toothpaste by the sink. He gave the room a final once-over then left quickly, picking up another rubbish sack in the corridor outside.

The orderly was eager to finish his duties so he'd be available for the first draft of evacuees. Earlier, Alternate One personnel had paraded in the main cavern where volunteers had been sought to stay behind for the duration of the withdrawal and monitor enemy movements. The orderly had no such intentions. He kept his arms firmly by his side as a large percentage of his stupid colleagues raised theirs. As luck would have it, the orderly had been assigned a place on one of the first transports out of the complex. If that were missed, a later passage would be allocated; *if* transport were still available. For the orderly, missing his slot was unthinkable. He had every intention of leaving this place at the earliest opportunity.

He'd overheard the muted conversations amongst the senior officers, noted the fear in some of the voices. Things didn't look good. The cities were in chaos and enemy soldiers were pouring into the country in ships and planes. Thousands had been killed. Privately, the orderly was terrified.

Clutching his rubbish sacks, he made his way along the warren of passageways to the service shafts, a series of sloping foot tunnels that led to various levels of the complex. He should have headed downwards, towards the lower chambers, where the waste and refuse was catalogued and incinerated, or recycled and packaged for later disposal. But that would have meant adding an extra thirty or forty minutes to his workload and he already had enough on his plate. Instead, he headed upwards.

He moved quickly through the tunnel system, away from the centre of the complex. It was quiet up here, he noted, but still patrolled. He'd have to be careful. After a minute or so he could smell the damp pine of the forest outside. Nearly there.

He negotiated a sharp corner and daylight flooded the tunnel. To his right, a wide opening had been carved out of the rock wall, a discreet observation point that overlooked the valley below. The orderly dropped the rubbish bags at his feet and peered over the rocky lip. In the wide firebreak to his left, he could see the entrance to Alternate One, the huge sliding door locked in place. Beneath the camouflage netting he saw no movement, no guards or patrols, which was to be expected as the whole facility was being rapidly emptied. He glanced to his right, where the densely packed pine forest sloped away into the valley. The tunnels around him, the forest below, were all silent, devoid of life. This was his chance.

He lifted the bags one at a time and dropped them over the edge, watching them as they hit the treetops and disappeared between the branches. He turned away quickly and headed back to the main complex. As he hurried along the tunnels he glanced at his watch. Good, still plenty of time. He would make his transport now, no problem.

Caught amongst the uppermost branches of a particularly tall pine, Harry Beecham's borrowed combat jacket swayed and twisted in the morning breeze. As the morning sun crept above the jagged spires of the hidden valley, the tiny transmitter, still clinging stubbornly to the material of the sleeve, continued to announce its presence to anyone that cared to listen.

LARVE

The umbilical cables were detached from the craft's fuselage and the battery cart wheeled away in preparation for the flight. All on-board systems had been checked by the Arabian ground crew and the remote pilot in the control centre had been given the green light for take-off.

The craft was a UAV, its technical name LARVE, a low altitude reconnaissance vehicle. At four metres long with a wingspan almost double that, the LARVE squatted on runway zero one four at Heathrow Airport like a giant black insect, its fuel-efficient jet engine idling quietly while it awaited its launch command. Half a mile away, parked beneath the airside awning of Terminal Two, sat the command vehicle. This was the LARVE's mobile flight operations control centre and, inside, the pilot and his team gave the LARVE's systems a final check. Everything was online and functioning correctly. The bird was ready for take-off.

On receiving its remote command, the LARVE began rolling along the runway. Inside the mobile control centre, the pilot watched the live output from the digital camera mounted in the nose of the aircraft as the runway rolled beneath it, quickly gathering speed. With a gentle pull on the controlling joystick, it lifted off the tarmac and climbed into the sky, heading due west.

For the pilot, the brief was a fairly general one; enemy forces had escaped to the west and Central Command needed an intelligence-gathering platform in the air and on station to start monitoring enemy traffic. The pilot was aware that a Big Eye and two fighters had already been shot down earlier and correctly assumed that the powers that be didn't want to lose any more aircraft, hence this hastily arranged mission. Once over enemy territory, the LARVE's nose camera would relay real-time images back to Heathrow in an effort to pinpoint enemy troops and equipment detected via the electronic, thermal and magnetic returns the aircraft would record on its travels.

The LARVE was normally a night bird, designed to operate stealthily above any conventional battlefield or behind enemy lines, where it would hide beneath enemy radar, casting out its own electronic net and relaying data back to its pilot as and where it found it. Electronically indiscernible due to its almost wholly plastic body and super cooled engine, the LARVE could be controlled from hundreds of kilometres away by its remote pilots, an aerial surveillance platform that was to all intents and purposes invisible to the enemy forces it was sent against. Invisible at night, that is.

Now, in the bright light of a summer's day, the LARVE climbed to six hundred metres, where its pilot programmed in a search pattern and flipped the craft into autopilot mode. Once activated, the UAV flew itself, making course, height and airspeed changes dictated by its pre-programmed search pattern. As the LARVE headed further west, the pilot back at Heathrow didn't have to wait long for the data to start flowing. The first contacts were Arabian, a huge column of armour, troops and support vehicles moving north-east up the M3 motorway.

As the LARVE crossed Salisbury Plain it began picking up enemy signals, air-search radar sets and electronic returns from other vehicles scattered across the huge training area. Back at Heathrow, the pilot processed the incoming information and uploaded it into the battlefield command system.

The LARVE continued westwards. Above the town of Frome, in Somerset, it ran into a virtual wall of electronic noise, the combined energy of scores of air-search radars forcing the LARVE to set and reset its instruments in an effort to pinpoint the many separate radar sources that probed the air around it. At Heathrow, the pilot's headset warbled an alarm; something on the ground had launched an anti-aircraft missile. Calmly, the pilot watched the incoming blip on his screen. The pilot clicked his tongue in annoyance. He'd warned his superiors that this would happen in daylight but, of course, his objection had been overruled. Still, the pilot had every confidence his craft would evade the missile, but he programmed in a new and more evasive flight pattern anyway, just as a precaution. The LARVE dropped its nose and headed for the deck. The new program called for a low-level high-speed probe, and the sophisticated craft responded immediately. Behind it, the missile continued its futile search into the sky.

The pilot shifted in his seat. The camera continued to broadcast its live feed directly back to the control centre and the pilot watched his large monitor with some interest as the English countryside raced by a mere twenty-five metres below the nose of the aircraft. Green fields gave way to a town here and a village there, and he saw the people of England, their pale faces flashing below as they watched the LARVE skim above the rooftops. As it raced over the village of Bathway, a burst of anti-aircraft fire ripped like lasers across the sky ahead, forcing the craft to bank and drop height, quickly leaving the danger behind. It interrogated its advanced mapping system. In the distance, a major road cut through the countryside. The LARVE was programmed to monitor vehicular traffic and instantly changed course towards it.

At Heathrow, the pilot sat a little straighter as the UAV's on-board sensors suddenly recorded a large enemy convoy ahead, moving south-west. The LARVE mapped the convoy, uploading its speed, direction, vehicle numbers and composition back to the control centre. The pilot's heart raced with excitement. The convoy was huge, consisting of all manner of military vehicles headed south. Small puffs of smoke from the ground indicated that there was some ground fire directed at the LARVE, but its parallel course along the road was partly shielded by trees and its speed made it a difficult target. Satisfied that all available data had been recorded, the LARVE banked sharply and flashed across the heavily congested road, continuing westwards and leaving the convoy behind in seconds.

Ahead, the ground gave way to rising hills and steep limestone bluffs. The LARVE's avoidance radar corrected its height and it climbed over the undulating countryside. At Heathrow, the pilot watched in fascination as the hills gave way to a desolate, high plateau. England really was quite beautiful, he admitted to himself. As the LARVE continued onwards, the pilot noticed a sudden drop in enemy transmissions and reprogrammed another sweep to the south. The craft banked again, climbing above a steep-sided bluff and the rocky fingers at its peak. It flashed above the summit then dropped into a pine-covered valley, skimming across the treetops.

Harry Beecham's discarded combat jacket still clung to the pine tree, swaying as the uppermost branches bent before the stiff morning breeze. Trapped in the folds of its sleeve the transponder, its battery almost dead, continued to broadcast its presence. Above it, something black flashed across the treetops.

What was that?

The pilot's fingers flew across the keyboard, isolating the new signal. A transponder? His sophisticated instrumentation began to decipher the broadcast. Strength two by five and weakening. He hit the manual override and brought the UAV around for another pass over the valley. Definitely a transponder, early model though; more like a solid-signal transmitter, but certainly Arabian in origin. How on earth did it get out here? He entered the data into his computer and, seconds later, the information was displayed on his screen. Mark Three Dedicated Signal Transmitter, a type issued to early infiltration units. The pilot cross-checked it with signals already identified and logged in the battlefield command database since the beginning of combat operations. Well, well, the same coded frequency had already been recorded in London. Where, exactly? His fingers danced across the keyboard. Ah. Whitehall.

'UAV is making another pass, sir. Seems to be flying a racetrack pattern above the valley. Anti-air has it locked on.'

All eyes in the control room turned to General Bashford. *Un-bloody-believable*, he raged inwardly. Twelve more hours and the vast majority of troops this side of Salisbury Plain would be on board the ships or approaching the docks. But the Arabian probe over their heads had sniffed something and had returned for another look. Now it was circling above them, no doubt transmitting whatever data it had back to its base.

Bashford had two choices. The first choice was to order the anti-aircraft crews on the hilltop to destroy it, thereby announcing their presence to whoever was controlling the damned thing; or secondly, leave it alone and pray to God it would fly off somewhere else. But if it happened to fly south it would surely spot the evacuation convoys. If it approached Teignmouth and found the ships, well, that was unthinkable.

'Take it out,' ordered Bashford.

The pilot cursed loudly as the LARVE's nose camera feed suddenly went blank and all electronic contact with the UAV was lost. Quickly, he rewound the footage on his display, advancing it frame by frame a few seconds before loss of signal. There. A flash and a puff of smoke from a nearby hilltop; a missile perhaps, or more likely an electronic weapons system. Either way, his probe was lost to enemy fire. He uploaded that information and the accompanying data into the command system and flagged it as a priority. Someone high up would have to be informed.

General Mousa awoke to the sound of persistent knocking. He'd been sleeping for just over an hour and was momentarily disorientated by his surroundings. The bed that he lay on was huge, the bedspread thick and finely woven, the walls decorated with the paintings of long-dead infidels whose pale, stern faces remained impassive as the knocking continued. Of course, Buckingham Palace. Mousa thought the experience a surreal one. He glanced towards the huge door that led to the corridor outside.

'Come!' he bellowed, swinging his legs off the bed. He hadn't even bothered to get undressed, allowing himself only the luxury of removing his paratrooper's jump boots. He began to lace them up as Major Karroubi entered the room.

'General, we have just received this from a UAV team at Heathrow.' Karroubi handed Mousa a signal slip, which he scanned quickly.

'It's him,' said Mousa. 'It's Beecham. The signal is the same as the one recorded beneath Downing Street. Whoever planted this transmitter was able to attach it to something or someone in his proximity. A map, quickly!'

Karroubi had anticipated his superior's request, rolling one out across a nearby table. Mousa stabbed at it with his finger.

'What is this place, Major?'

'Intelligence suggests a previously undisclosed military bunker system. According to our data it's a local tourist spot, although the grid reference of the transmitter is marked on local maps as a danger area.'

'A ruse to keep prying eyes away.'

'I agree. Beecham must have headed there.'

Mousa was lost in thought for several moments. 'Where is my infantry battalion?'

'Still in position, just south of Salisbury.'

'Get the reconnaissance units moving west. I want to know what kind of resistance to expect. Alert my air force liaison officers and get the field commanders online too. I want a full conference briefing in thirty minutes. This may be our chance to crush any remaining resistance and capture Beecham in the process.'

Karroubi hesitated, a worried frown creasing his face.

'What is it?' Mousa demanded. 'Spit it out, man.'

'The Holy One's orders were clear, General. We are to ignore Beecham–'

'An opportunity has presented itself, Major. We cannot waste time waiting for approval.'

'But–'

'The responsibility is mine alone. Do as I say.'

'At once, General.'

Karroubi limped from the room. Mousa went to the window, looking along the length of The Mall, at the armoured vehicles camouflaged beneath the trees of St James's Park. He had to act and act quickly. Again he considered informing the Holy One, but dismissed it immediately. His mood may be unsettled this early in the day, his mind focussed on more divine contemplations. He was a complex man, the cleric, one who frowned on unnecessary interruptions, particularly if those interruptions questioned his earlier commands. No, contact was unwise. Yet Beecham was out there right now, tantalisingly close, skulking in this secret command bunker and surrounded by the remnants of his forces. It was an opportunity too good to miss, a chance to neutralise remaining opposition in the south of the country and capture Beecham into the bargain. The operation would be swift and decisive, he decided. And when it was over, when Beecham was paraded before the grand mufti, the Holy One would forgive Mousa's earlier failures.

Nothing would be left to chance. Otherwise he was finished.

The Farm

When Khan woke, the afternoon sun was streaming through the bedroom window, its warm bars cutting across the duvet he was curled under. It took a few confused moments to work out where he was, and then the events of the previous day flooded his mind, like an inrushing tide.

He rubbed his eyes and snatched his watch from the bedside table; almost five in the afternoon. He sat up, kicking off the covers. The room was small but cosy – a large bed, tucked under the eaves of a sloping roof, heavy wooden furniture around the walls, a well-appointed en-suite bathroom. The TV was still out, but the radio channels were broadcasting, playing that endlessly looping emergency message.

Khan snapped the TV off and took a shower. As the lukewarm jets drummed his scalp, he wondered if the general population was heeding those warnings. They'd seen people outside, and just a few cars during their journey from London, but that was the suburbs. How would the inner cities react to being confined to their homes? Had they even heard the broadcast? And what would happen when they did? He thought back to the previous night when the battle had erupted on Kew Bridge. No doubt there'd be many more disturbances like that one.

He found clean clothes hanging outside his room; Rob's, no doubt, and the yellow Post-it note stuck to the cellophane confirmed it. He dressed quickly in white shirt and jeans, eager to keep moving, to stay ahead of the invaders. He stood by the window as he rolled up the sleeves, allowing the warm country air to swirl around the room. The farm itself was certainly everything that Alex had promised it would be.

When they'd arrived that morning, the small cluster of buildings had been impossible to see from the road, even from their elevated position in the Range Rover. The lane that ran past the property was narrow, with steep-sided banks of tall grass on either side. As they purred along, Alex had pointed to a wooden post leaning at a drunken angle at the side of the road. The sign read: *Meadow Farm – Bed & Breakfast*. They'd turned on to a gravel track that meandered uphill for a short distance before cutting through a wild flower field. Khan spun around in his seat. From here, the ground was quite elevated and he saw the village of South Lockeridge some distance away. They'd done the right thing by circumnavigating the hamlet. There was no point in announcing their arrival just yet.

The gravel track continued through a small copse and then the farm was in front of them. The Range Rover crunched to a stop, scattering a few protesting geese in the process. They climbed out and Khan's keen eye surveyed his new surroundings. Clearly it wasn't a real working farm, more like a smallholding in a decent plot of land. There were three buildings in all, arranged around a circular courtyard with a small island of grass at its centre, where the scattered geese had regrouped and eyed the newcomers with suspicion.

The main house stood before them, the solar panels arrayed across its roof glinting in the morning sun. There was a converted barn at a right angle to the main house and Khan assumed that was the B&B accommodation. Directly opposite the main house was a large corrugated iron shed, under which was parked a Land Rover and a squat-looking quad bike. There were sacks of grain there too, plus tools and a tidy stack of firewood piled against the rust-streaked walls.

Behind the shed loomed a wind turbine, the large propeller blades spinning lazily in the morning breeze. Off to the side of the main house was a well-populated chicken pen, while the apple orchard beyond stretched towards a distant grey stone boundary wall. The whole place seemed quite remote and very secluded. Khan felt some of the tension leaking from his system.

Rob and Helen came outside to greet them, and Khan noted the physical resemblance between Alex and his clearly older brother. The looks on their faces, especially Rob's wife, quickly turned from surprise to apprehension when they saw the weapons that both men unloaded from the Range Rover. Alex had been quick to placate them. He made the necessary introductions and Rob ushered them all inside.

It was cool and dark in the farmhouse kitchen, the ceiling crossed with low beams, the floor covered with smooth stone slabs. A large oak dining table took up most of the room, backing on to a set of French doors and the garden beyond, where a line of washing rippled before a warm breeze. The smell of coffee and toast lingered on the air and Khan's stomach rumbled noisily.

Rob wanted the weapons placed out of sight and Alex agreed. Khan was more reluctant until Alex pointed towards the French doors. Beyond the patio, in the orchard behind the house, a small boy, legs dangling through a rubber tyre, swung from the branch of a tree, while an older girl pushed him back and forth. Khan handed over the weapon.

'I've got a shotgun myself,' Rob explained, watching Alex hang the rifles behind the cellar door, 'but those things are a bit frightening. I don't want the kids upset.'

'Fair enough,' agreed Khan.

Helen introduced the two children who came running in from outside. Six-year-old Hugo and Daisy, eight, were overjoyed to see their uncle.

Alex scooped them up in his arms and Khan noted Kirsty's approving gaze. The children squealed with delight until Helen shooed them back outside to play. She made a pot of tea and a hearty breakfast of fresh bacon, eggs and home-made bread. Khan declined the bacon, but Alex and Kirsty wolfed down everything that was put in front of them. When they'd finished, the table was cleared and more tea poured.

'So,' Rob began, settling into a chair next to his wife, 'why don't you tell us what's going on?'

For the next hour the three travellers relayed their experiences to an increasingly frightened Rob and Helen. When they'd finished the couple remained silent, their hands clasped tightly together. Helen was the first to react. She let go of her husband's hand and crossed to the French doors, wrapping her arms around her as if she were cold. Outside, the children played amongst the apple trees behind the house. She watched them for a moment and turned to Alex.

'What will happen now?'

Alex shrugged. 'Truth is we don't know, right Dan?'

Khan nodded. 'Look, I won't bullshit either of you. In my opinion, things will get worse. The Arabians are here in force, and they mean to stay. This is an ideological struggle we're talking about here. Muslim armies have invaded Europe dozens of times over the centuries. This is just another attempt, only this time it may well succeed. And if they've got this far, then the rest of Europe must be suffering the same fate too. As far as we can tell, there's been no response from our own armed forces and I doubt very much that anyone else is coming to our rescue. When we left London the power was still out–'

'It's out here too,' Rob confirmed.

'Right. No gas either, and water supplies have been shut off. In my view, that's where the immediate danger lies. If the situation remains the same for much longer things will become desperate. People in the cities will begin to starve and many will scatter into the surrounding countryside. There'll be vandalism, looting, certainly violence. And you can forget about the police.'

'We don't know that,' Alex argued, glancing at his brother. 'In fact, we don't know anything right now.'

Khan could see that he was just trying to soften the blow, to protect his family from the realities of the crisis. He saw Helen's face, a pale face, etched with fear. Beyond the window the children still played, oblivious to the dangers that loomed over the horizon. If the tables were turned, Khan would want to know every detail, every potential danger his family faced, whether real or imagined. And plan for them.

'What about Kew Bridge?' he countered. 'C'mon Alex, you've seen it for yourself. You know what people are capable of in desperate times.' He turned back to Rob. 'Look, I've had some exposure to this kind of thing during my time with the Security Services. I've been involved in a few briefings, taken part in a couple of exercises. I'm talking about highly restricted stuff, national emergencies, major public disorder scenarios, threats to public health. And the one thing the analysts and the planners are sure of is this; civilised society exists only because a vast majority of the general population have neither the need nor the compulsion to break the laws of the land, the same laws that encourage most of us to go to work, pay our bills and treat our fellow citizens with a degree of civility. Now, if those conditions didn't exist, if the legal constraints were removed and people were faced with the prospect of a lawless society, then their behaviour would change accordingly. The lack of food and water is the ultimate motivator and society will revert to the survival of the fittest. Whatever plans the Arabians have for us, I think we'll start to see a general breakdown in law and order as the days go by, replaced by some sort of martial law. Towns and cities will be first. People will try to escape the chaos, head for the countryside. And they'll need food and water. Farms have both. Farms like this one.'

A gentle breeze blew through the open doors, lifting the curtains. The room filled with the sounds of the farm, the children's squeals of laughter, the industrious murmur of chickens, the songbirds that nested in the orchard trees. It was peaceful, idyllic, yet it offered no comfort to any of them. The world had suddenly changed, the air itself tainted with fear.

'I'm sorry,' Khan said, 'but you need to know what you're facing.'

'I appreciate the honesty,' a sober-faced Rob replied, getting to his feet. 'I think you're right, about the potential dangers. The village needs to be told.' He plucked a set of keys from his pocket and headed towards the door. 'I'm going to take a run down there now, speak to someone from the parish council.'

Helen crossed the room, reached for his hand. 'Wait, Rob. It might not be safe.'

'We're okay for now, right Dan? Besides, the rest of the village has a right to know.'

Khan pushed his chair back. 'Don't worry, Helen. I'll go with him.'

'Good idea,' Rob said. 'I might have trouble convincing them.'

Helen reluctantly dropped her hand. 'Don't be long,' she ordered.

Outside, Rob started up the Land Rover and Khan hopped into the passenger seat. He felt naked without the gun, but right now the chance of any contact with Arabian soldiers or screaming mobs seemed pretty remote. And there was more; he needed to keep moving, and if he got Rob and the villagers onside he might be able to scrounge a few supplies off them before making the journey to the coast. If he waited, if the noose tightened and people began to panic, there was every possibility he could become a target himself. So, the sooner he helped out, the better his chances.

Rob crunched the vehicle into gear and sped off, scattering the geese once again.

Khan tucked the shirt into his jeans, checked the rifle hidden beneath the bed, and headed downstairs. It had been a long day but the night ahead would be a long one, too. Thankfully the parish council, or the few members that Rob had managed to muster earlier that morning, had taken the news of the invasion as well as could be expected. Khan wasn't surprised. Isolated communities often felt little or no connection with the wider world and that could work in the village's favour. Khan had told them so, encouraging them to remain that way, for their own safety. The advice had earned him a jerry can of fuel. What he had planned for the meeting tonight should earn him the remainder of the supplies he needed to get to the coast.

Outside the geese had settled down for the day, gathered together on their grass island, grooming their feathers and watching the younger goslings as they pecked at the ground. Khan wandered over to the shed where the Range Rover had been parked. With the aid of a plastic funnel, he emptied the jerry can of fuel into the tank. The vehicle was unlocked, the key still in the ignition, and Khan climbed in, powering up the electronics and paying careful attention to the fuel state.

Even after topping up with the jerry can, the needle still hovered just below the half mark. According to the computer, the estimated fuel range was seventy-nine miles. The satnav mapped the distance to the coast at sixty-six miles. Factoring in unscheduled detours and emergencies, he'd need a lot more fuel. On the floor behind the driver's seat was a road map of Britain and Khan spread it on the bonnet of the vehicle. He was plotting alternative routes south when he heard the crunch of feet on gravel behind him. He turned to see Alex and Kirsty approaching.

'Afternoon, folks,' he smiled, noting their entwined fingers. Well, if they weren't a couple before last night they certainly were now.

'Sleep well?' Alex asked.

'Like a log. You?' He saw the stolen glance, noted the reticent smiles. 'Don't answer that,' he chuckled. Kirsty blushed and Khan quickly changed the subject. 'Well, you were right about this place, Alex. Almost perfect.'

'I walked the boundary earlier. The field at the back of the house runs up to a small wood. From up there the ground drops away and you can see right out to the edge of Salisbury Plain. This place would be pretty hard to find unless you knew where it was.'

'I know. I've been thinking about that.'

Alex was about to say something when Kirsty piped up. 'Still leaving us then?' She tapped the map on the bonnet of the Range Rover.

Khan folded it away and tossed it back inside the Range Rover. 'Does that mean you're staying?'

'That's right,' confirmed Alex. He looked away for a moment, struggling with the words. 'I feel bad letting you go on your own, but my family's here and they're going to need us. And sooner or later we'll have to find Kirsty's folks too.' He gave her a comforting squeeze. 'Sorry, mate.'

'Nothing to apologise for,' Khan assured him. 'I'd made up my mind to head south long before we met. Besides,' he smiled, kicking the empty jerry can at his feet, 'if you're really sorry then you can help me get some more fuel.'

'We can do that,' nodded Kirsty. She squeezed Alex's hand. 'Right, Alex?'

'Sure. Anything you need.'

'Thanks.'

Khan had hoped to persuade Alex to come with him. It would be tough going on his own, not impossible with the right vessel, but hard enough. Yet, since arriving at the farm it was obvious that Alex's place was here, with his family, and now Kirsty was part of that equation too. They needed Alex as much as Khan did. Besides, Khan would have made the same decision if the tables were turned. So, he was on his own again.

'Did Rob fill you in on our little trip to the village?' Alex nodded. 'He told you what the others said, about the riots in Swindon and Reading? About the families that turned up in the middle of the night?'

'They were cousins of one of the villagers. They didn't know where else to go.'

'See, that's the problem, right there,' Khan said, rapping his knuckles on the bonnet of the Range Rover. 'What if word spreads? That South Lockeridge is some sort of safe haven? You could get swamped with refugees in a matter of days. Things could get seriously out of hand.'

'I know,' Alex muttered, squeezing Kirsty's hand. 'Not much we can do about it though.'

Khan caught the gesture, saw Kirsty's worried frown, the hand that gripped Alex's a little tighter. 'Hey, Kirsty.'

'Yes?'

He tapped the side of his head. 'Don't worry, okay? I've got a plan.'

She attempted a smile, but the fear lingered behind her eyes. 'Really?'

'Sure. Everything'll be alright, trust me.' He turned to Alex. 'You know about the meeting tonight? In the village hall?'

'Yeah.'

'Good. There's a lot to go over. I'll fill you in on the way down there.' He leaned inside the Range Rover and took the key from the ignition. It was an unconscious gesture, but the time to leave was fast approaching and he didn't want to run the risk of losing his escape vehicle. He swung the driver's door closed, hit the alarm button – then froze. The sound of helicopters was unmistakable, rolling and fading on the warm summer air. All three of them stood motionless in the shadows of the shed, eyes shielded against the sun.

'A long way off,' Alex presumed, scanning the distant horizon. 'South, I think.' Already the sound was beginning to fade.

'Ours?' asked Khan.

'God knows. Definitely more than one, though.'

The sound faded completely and birdsong once again filled the early-evening air.

'Well, there's no point in worrying about it now,' Khan sighed. He turned to the others, rubbing his hands together. 'I'm starving,' he declared, attempting to lighten the mood. 'I don't suppose there's any more grub on the go, is there?' Alex cocked a thumb over his shoulder, his gaze still wandering the sky.

'Helen's making something now.'

'Good. We need to discuss a few things before the meeting tonight. I've got a couple of ideas that may be of interest.'

Alex raised a quizzical brow. 'What ideas?'

'About this place, the village. To keep you all safe.' He squeezed Kirsty's shoulder and she smiled, a little more relaxed this time. They headed towards the main house, skirting the huddle of geese that watched them from the grass island.

Grovely Wood,
Wiltshire

Mousa tapped the heel of his boot impatiently as the Black Hawk helicopter skimmed low over the fields and treetops of the English countryside. He stared out of the window at the passing ground below, at the four Apache escort helicopters that flew in a loose box formation around his own aircraft. Mousa thought he might well need them. This wasn't London, with thousands of Arabian troops pouring into the capital every hour. There, he was well protected. But out here, they were chasing the tail of the enemy and the information they'd received from the LARVE before it was destroyed made it clear that there were still significant numbers of British troops and equipment scattered around the countryside.

The Black Hawk flared and banked hard, dropping towards a large clearing surrounded by thick forest. Karroubi had chosen well, Mousa admitted, giving his aide seated opposite an approving nod. Grovely Wood was a series of undulating hills that dominated the skyline to the west of the town of Salisbury, the command post near its centre well hidden, the surrounding forest guarded by Mousa's paratroopers. All in all they should be relatively safe. For now.

The helicopter settled in the clearing and Mousa leapt to the ground, followed closely by Karroubi. They strode into the trees, a small detachment of waiting paratroopers falling in around them. A short distance into the wood the ground sloped gently downhill to a wide, flat area beneath the tree canopy, where a large command bunker had been hastily constructed from felled trees. Even now, the massive logs that formed the roof were being covered with earth by scores of shovel-wielding troops. When they reached the bottom of the slope a combat engineer officer, his face streaked with sweat and dirt, saw the approaching party and threw up a salute.

'General, the command bunker is ready and online. We're just finishing the camouflage now.'

'Good. Lead on.'

They stamped down the roughly hewn log steps until they were below ground level, ducking under the low roof and into the command post. It was dark inside, only the bright electronic glow of the large command display screen lighting the gloomy interior. There were a dozen operators with headsets lined around the log walls, busily tapping into their computer terminals while, opposite them, army and aviation group commanders conferred around a large, map-strewn table. The commanders turned as one and snapped upright as Mousa entered.

'Report!' he barked to no one in particular.

A senior army officer stepped forward. 'General. The situation is thus; our forward scouts have moved west to this town here, Trowbridge.' The commander tapped the town's electronic marker on the command display and instantly a new window opened, showing a large-scale digital map of the town and its surrounding area. He pointed to a cluster of glowing green icons to the west of the built-up area. 'These are our reconnaissance units. They've been ordered to hold their position until we can get them more support. Resistance was encountered seven kilometres south-east of the town centre on this road here, the A361.We lost two light-armoured vehicles to anti-tank fire.'

'Where is this convoy going?' growled Mousa. He was referring to the British convoy that the LARVE had detected earlier that morning. Its speed and course had been plotted on the screen with a list of possible destinations. The commander tapped the convoy icon and the black and white footage from the LARVE nose camera began looping in another mini screen.

'General, our concern is that the convoy is heading towards the coast in an effort to move against our southern flank. It may be prudent to shift our axis to the south-west in order to counter the threat.'

'And where is the convoy now?' demanded Mousa.

The army commander circled an area on the display with his finger. 'They could be anywhere in this area here. We haven't been able to establish exactly where, yet.'

'Why not?' Without waiting for a reply, Mousa turned to a senior air force officer. 'Where are my surveillance craft?'

The officer paled before his withering gaze. 'Unfortunately, the ship transporting the LARVE units encountered some rough weather crossing the Bay of Biscay, General Mousa. Seawater entered the cargo hold through an unsealed hatch and corroded the flight instrumentation packages.' The air force officer unconsciously twisted his hands together. Mousa noted the gesture, his eyes boring into the man's sweating face. 'However, I immediately despatched another shipment by transport aircraft to Heathrow,' the officer continued quickly. 'They will be landing in the next two hours.'

Mousa looked at his own watch. Two hours until the new parts arrive, another three or four to mate them with the LARVE units; it would be dark by then and Beecham might have fled his rat hole. He might not get the opportunity to capture the Englishman again.

Right now, Mousa would have given his right arm for real-time satellite imagery, but the retasking of satellites would be brought to the attention of the Holy One and Mousa would be stopped in his tracks. Not only that, but disciplined too, and the punishment for insubordination would be harsh indeed. He looked around the room; if any of the sweating weasels before him discovered he was operating without the consent of the cleric, a call would be made and that would be the end of it. *It's a fine line I have to tread here*, Mousa realised. He had to move fast, achieve his objective, before the game was up.

He balled his fists behind his back. The LARVEs would have given him a big advantage over the infidel forces. With five of those in the air he could have located the British convoy's position in less than an hour, ordering his air assets to advance west to obliterate it. But without the LARVEs he was relatively blind and he dare not commit any more forces in a full-scale attack. Frustrated, he turned away from the air force officer and studied the command display.

'The loss of the LARVEs is unacceptable. You will give the details of the transport ship's crew to Major Karroubi here. In the meantime, tell me about the British anti-aircraft threat.'

In the muffled silence of the bunker, the air force officer retrieved a handkerchief from his pocket and quickly mopped his brow. Mousa turned, noting the beads of sweat glistening on the man's cheeks, the neutral expressions of his comrades as they studied the command display with unnatural attentiveness. Mousa took no satisfaction in the man's distress. More often than not, Mousa's presence had an adverse effect on the performance of his cadre and, right now, he needed these men onside. He decided to soften his tone as he watched the air force officer ball up his handkerchief and shove it into the pocket of his combat trousers.

'General,' the officer continued, 'I have ordered the launch of another Big Eye. It is currently maintaining station well to the east of us. Bearing in mind what happened to the other aircraft, I thought it prudent to keep it out of harm's way.'

'A wise move. And what intelligence is it giving us?'

'We're picking up dozens of air-search radars on various low and high-level frequencies. However, a pattern is beginning to emerge. If I may, General?'

Mousa stepped back and allowed the older man access to the command display. The officer tapped the keyboard and the system began displaying air assets that were already in flight, superimposing them over a map of southern England. To the right of the screen, Mousa noted the position of the Big Eye, its green aircraft-shaped icon moving in slow circles at an altitude of eight thousand metres. To the left of the screen was a multitude of yellow, cone-like radar washes that shimmered from dull to bright to dull again on the display. The officer pointed to them.

'These are the electronic signatures of the enemy search radars, General Mousa. Their points of origin are changing constantly, but the computer has begun to predict the change. For example, this one,' he said, indicating a glowing red icon. 'This is an enemy SAM vehicle and its original position was plotted here. Soon it will shut down its radar and move position, normally just a few kilometres, and once there it will go active again. The same can be said of this unit here.' Another icon close to the first was also highlighted and magnified on the screen. 'When this one moves, the other stays in position and overlaps its search area. Then the roles are reversed. It's a pattern, General; move, search, move, search. And their final positions are always in the same place, give or take a few hundred metres. This pattern is being repeated with nearly all of the enemy anti-aircraft units we have plotted.'

The officer turned to Mousa, swallowed hard and said, 'It is my belief that these units are working in small groups of two or three vehicles, attempting to trick us into thinking that they have a multi-layered air defence capability. I believe they have far fewer assets than we first thought.'

A courageous statement, Mousa allowed, and yet the man was right. He could see the pattern emerging, even as he watched the time-lapse display. But he needed the data firmed up before he committed his air assets to the west.

'Excellent. You have done well, Colonel...?'

'Ahmed,' beamed the officer, stiffening to attention.

'Inform me as soon as you have positive plots on all enemy positions, Colonel Ahmed. The remainder of our forces are ready?'

'We have two squadrons of ground-attack aircraft on the tarmac at Heathrow,' Ahmed declared loudly, bolstered with new-found confidence. 'Your assault troops are already in the air as per your earlier instructions. They will head toward the Mendip Hills as soon as the anti-aircraft threat has been neutralised.' Mousa nodded his satisfaction then addressed the room, keen to extend his uncharacteristic praise amongst the remainder of Ahmed's colleagues.

'Good work, all of you. Ensure everyone understands the importance of this mission and what their objectives are. The success of the operation is vital to our campaign.' He strode away before stopping abruptly, Karroubi nearly cannoning into the back of him. 'That convoy, heading south,' Mousa reminded them. 'Let me know when you locate it. And keep a close eye on our southern flank.'

He marched outside, choosing a particularly stout pine against which to relieve his bladder. The pieces were all in place, and his assault troops would secure the Mendip command centre when the path to the west was clear. There, Mousa would find the infidel, cowering in his hole. Yes, he reassured himself, it was only a matter of time before he had Beecham in custody.

He zipped up his combat trousers and began to pace beneath the trees, his boots stamping an impatient path around the bunker. Time, Mousa pondered. Neither he nor the Englishman had much to spare.

Alternate One

'Wake up, Boss!'

Harry cracked an eyelid then sat up sharply, throwing off the bedcovers. Gibson and Farrell were framed in the doorway of his private quarters, the light flooding in from the corridor behind them. He was confused. Both men were now wearing civilian clothes, T-shirts and cargo pants, but still had their fearsome-looking weapons slung across their chests.

'What is it?' he demanded groggily.

Gibson snapped the light on and marched into the room. He grabbed Harry's trousers and shirt from the wardrobe and thrust them towards him.

'Plan's changed. Time to leave.'

'Now?' Harry rubbed his face, fingering the sleep from his eyes.

'General Bashford's orders. Departure time has been brought forward. Everyone's leaving.'

'Why?' He glanced at his watch. 'I thought we weren't moving until later?'

Gibson ignored the comment. He stepped into the bathroom and turned the shower on. 'No time for chit-chat, Boss. The General's waiting for us.'

Harry did as he was told. Showered and dressed, they navigated the tunnels until they arrived at the operations room. The corridor outside was busy with troops, yet there was none of the squaddie banter that Harry would normally expect to hear. Instead, the soldiers worked in silence, their arms laden with supplies and equipment, urged on by senior NCOs whose hushed voices remained calm and assured.

Harry didn't feel very calm. The tunnel was hot, the air stale and heavy, the abnormal silence of the men around him unnerving. He stayed close behind Gibson, who carved his way through the throng and into the operations room. Harry cuffed a fine sheen of sweat from his forehead, glad to have escaped the claustrophobic corridor.

The first thing he noticed was the conference table, the chairs that ringed it empty, its surface covered with boxes filled with buff-coloured files and computer equipment. The space around the walls was the same, lined with packing crates and more cardboard boxes, while a crocodile of troops filed in and out of the room, grabbing what they could.

Harry felt a hand on his arm and Farrell eased him to one side, out of the way of the busy soldiers. He caught the eye of one man – well, more like a boy, Harry realised, his thin arms straining beneath the weight of a large wooden box stuffed with manuals and rolled up maps. Harry had a mind to help him but, as he moved to do so, the boy gave him a wink, then filed silently out into the corridor with the others. Harry shook his head. Cheeky bastard, he smiled, admiring the kid's impertinence, the absence of fear despite the threat that faced them. Looking around, Harry saw that same expression on all their faces – a steady resolve, a youthful disregard for the dangers ahead. Brave lads, he admitted, all of them. Braver than him, anyway.

General Bashford was at the far end of the room, flanked by Major Monroe and a handful of senior officers in a cluster of camouflage uniforms. They were gathered around a single radio operator, listening to the traffic that squawked and crackled from a wall-mounted speaker. All the other operators were gone, the row of computer screens that lined the wall dark and lifeless. Bashford turned as Harry approached.

'Ah, Prime Minister. Good.'

Harry could see the man was tired, the dark circles beneath his bloodshot eyes, the unshaven cheeks, the dishevelled uniform. The other officers looked the same, exhausted both physically and mentally. A dangerous combination in a crisis, Harry knew. 'What's happened, General?'

'A few hours ago an Arabian UAV was shot out of the sky by one of our air defence teams. Seems it was taking an unhealthy interest in Alternate One. We must assume we've been discovered.' The general picked up a file from the conference table marked *Confidential* and began emptying its contents into a large shredder nearby. It whirred angrily, the plastic sack beneath bulging with paper spaghetti.

'I see,' replied Harry, unsure how to respond.

'It was only a matter of time, anyway. Since then, signals units have been picking up coded Arabian transmissions all afternoon and the volume of messages is increasing. The intelligence suggests an imminent assault.'

Harry paled in the harsh light on the operations room. 'Jesus. How long have we got?'

'Hard to say, but I suspect time is short. I've ordered a wholesale withdrawal and the ships at Teignmouth are to be filled as soon as possible. The Deputy PM and several other senior civilian staff have already departed on my orders. We'll rendezvous again in Scotland, once we're settled. Our own helicopter will leave in thirty minutes.'

'Right,' Harry mumbled, trying to keep up. Like the others he was tired, exhausted actually, despite the couple of hours sleep. He noticed a large urn and a tower of paper cups on a nearby table and headed towards it. Coffee. Perfect. He poured himself a cup, left it black, and heaped in a couple of sugars. He sipped at the dark brew as Bashford emptied the last of his papers into the shredder.

'We need to move fast,' the general warned. 'So far the evacuation has gone smoothly, hardly any civilian traffic on the roads at all. That will change, of course, when the Arabians start advancing towards us. It's imperative we get our forces clear before panic sets in.'

Harry pulled a chair from the conference table and slumped into it. 'Running away,' he grumbled, 'that's the truth of it. Quite frankly, I'm ashamed to call myself prime minister.'

'We have no choice,' Bashford reminded him. 'You know that.'

The general was right, but now evacuation had started, the reality of leaving the civilian population to an uncertain fate left Harry feeling nauseous with guilt. The simple fact was England was lost. She'd been invaded before, many times over many centuries, but it was different now. There would be no secret mustering of an army, no forging of arms by village blacksmiths, their hammers ringing out a message of defiance across feudal England. No, this was the twenty-first century, and history would no doubt reveal that the battle had been fought and won by the Arabians long before a single shot had been fired, that Europe had been conquered by stealth and guile, by agitators, appeasers and fifth columnists. And, like the government itself, the British Army had also been ambushed, its forces scattered and in disarray, leaving a frightened population undefended.

Harry could taste the bitterness of personal defeat in his mouth, his ambitions, his vision for the country's future prosperity, all now consigned to the waste bin of history. After the dust had settled, when everything was said and done, he would only be remembered as the man in charge when it all went wrong. Harry grimaced. If that was the case, then so be it. All he was left with now was the urge to contribute, to do something positive, something that would help save time, or lives. Something. Anything.

He sipped his coffee, feeling the caffeine slowly energising his system, his eye drawn to the huge map of Britain on the wall. He was lost in thought for several minutes, the germ of an idea slowly taking root in his mind. After another minute or so he drained his cup and stood. 'General, how many troops do we have in place to slow the enemy?' *Enemy*. Strangely, the word didn't feel unnatural when he said it.

'Right now, about four thousand, most of them dotted along the predicted routes of advance.'

'And we've no chance of stopping the Arabians?' Bashford shook his head.

'Short of tactical nukes, none.'

'Then let's get them out.'

'Excuse me?'

'Everybody. We don't leave a single soldier behind. You said it yourself General, we'll need all available personnel when we get to Scotland.'

'That may be so,' warned Bashford, 'but the blocking force is vital. Their presence will buy us valuable time and, in the process, save lives.'

'At the expense of their own?'

Bashford held the Prime Minister's gaze. 'Possibly, yes. That's why we asked for volunteers.'

Harry held up his hands. 'General Bashford. I'm not trying to debate with you. You're the senior military commander and I hold your experience and expertise in the highest regard. But legally I have ultimate authority over our armed forces, isn't that the case?'

The other officers in the room ceased their low chatter. Even the speaker on the wall had fallen silent. Bashford folded his arms and nodded slowly. 'That's correct. I can only advise you, Prime Minister. The final decision is still yours.'

'Thank you.' Harry approached the wall map, where a line of coloured markers dissected the western leg of England, the final positions of the men staring down the mouth of the Arabian advance. He studied it for a moment, making sense of the lines and distances involved, believing he had a decent grasp of the tactical situation. Hoping was probably a more accurate word, he chided himself. He stabbed a finger at the map. 'Let's withdraw everybody, General, all four thousand of them. Send the closest troops to Teignmouth right away and the rest of them north to Scotland. They won't make it to the docks in time.'

Bashford joined Harry at the map. He spoke quietly, out of earshot of the other soldiers in the room. 'That's very dangerous, Prime Minister. The moment the Arabians get a sniff of a general withdrawal they'll send everything against us. I don't advise it.'

'I don't want a single drop of blood spilt unnecessarily, not for those bastards.'

'In this situation, bloodshed is unavoidable. What we need to focus on is limiting our casualties.'

'We can still do that though, can't we?' Harry tapped the icons on the map one after the other, the units on the defensive line. 'All these vehicles, tanks and so on, they're as good as written off, correct?'

Bashford nodded. 'We'll lose them, yes. Unfortunate, but necessary.'

'How many men does it take to operate a tank? Or a missile launcher? Obviously I'm no expert, but aren't some of these weapons platforms automated?' The general stared long and hard at Harry. He turned away, studied the map again, his eyes roaming the icons, arrows and coloured lines that constituted the defence of Alternate One and the western leg of England.

Harry moved a step closer, his voice low. 'Do we really have to risk so many men in a futile defence, General Bashford? Is there any way we can appear to be holding the line when in fact we're making good our escape?'

Bashford stroked the white stubble on his chin, deep in thought. 'Excuse me,' he said.

Harry watched him cross the room. Bashford gathered the other military men into a tight circle, the low murmur of their voices drowned out by the noise from the wall speaker. Harry stepped back as they crowded around the map, their language almost unintelligible. But he had them thinking, that much he realised, and for the first time in a while Harry began to feel a little more confident, a little more hopeful that he'd influenced things in a positive way.

After another hurried conference, the military men broke up, some heading for the door, others converging around the radio operator, who began chattering into his headset. Bashford called Harry over to the map.

'Well, you've thrown a bit of a spanner into the works, Prime Minister. But in essence, you may have hit on something.'

Harry nodded gratefully. 'Good. Tell me what you think.'

Bashford picked a china graph pencil and began scoring it across the map. 'Right now the Arabians are reluctant to use their aircraft, no doubt due to our successes against the Big Eye and the Raptors. So, for now, an air assault is unlikely.' The general made more marks with the pencil. 'As you know, we have armour here, Challenger tanks and fighting vehicles, dug in and camouflaged along these probable routes of advance. Hard to detect and excellent firepower, but these particular crews are low on fuel. What we propose is that their tanks are emptied and the fuel redistributed to other crews for their own escape runs. The dry armour will then be left in place, with skeleton crews. Their original orders were to fire and manoeuvre but, obviously, with empty fuel tanks they won't be able to do that. What they can do is engage as many targets as possible, then bug out before the enemy can zero in on them. The crews will then use other transport to make good their escape. As for the infantry units, the order has already gone out – a staggered withdrawal, some to the coast, the rest to the north. In a couple of hours, there'll be less than a thousand men on the line to halt the Arabian advance.'

'That's excellent news. And our air defences will still be operational?'

'As you suggested, the SAM units will be left in place and set to auto mode. It means they'll launch at just about anything, but it'll buy us time.'

'How many units do we have?'

'Twenty-three, each with at least two live missiles. All in all, we can fire over a hundred heat-seeking and infrared homing weapons, plus some turret-mounted electronic cannons designed to engage low-flying enemy aircraft.'

Harry's eyes roamed the expanse of the map. 'Is there anything else we've missed?'

'Probably,' Bashford replied, 'but if you want to get the maximum amount of personnel out as quickly as possible, this is the best way.'

Major Monroe stepped forward. Harry noticed he wore a chest rig like Gibson's, the pockets filled with magazines, the brass of the bullets contained within gleaming beneath the overhead lights.

'The helicopter is ready to depart, sir.'

'Thanks, Gerry. As soon as you've sealed the place, head north, yes?'

'You're staying behind?' Harry asked incredulously.

'Someone has to,' Bashford said. 'Tunnels have to be sealed, equipment neutralised. We don't want to give the Arabs all this on a plate.'

Harry understood, nodding silently. 'Don't hang around,' he ordered Monroe. 'The priority now is to get everyone safely to Scotland. Everyone,' he repeated.

'I understand, Prime Minister.'

Bashford signalled to Gibson and Farrell, waiting patiently across the room. 'Time to go, Harry. Go grab what you need and make your way out to the main entrance. I'll see you there shortly.'

Harry took a deep breath and exhaled slowly. 'I suppose there's nothing more we can do, is there?'

Bashford shook his head. 'We've done as much as we can. It's time to go, while we still can.'

Harry took one last look at the map, at the towns and villages that dotted the countryside around them. 'God help us all,' he muttered. Then he left the room.

On the defensive line, the new orders reached the relieved tank and armoured crews in direct line of the Arabian advance. The northernmost units reversed out of their prepared positions and headed for the Welsh border as quickly as they could. The heavy tank units further south abandoned their vehicles in place. There would be no facilities to load them on the waiting ships and it would take hours to reach the docks and the safety of the sea. The crews emptied their fuel tanks and redistributed it to other vehicles, then disabled their engines and spiked the gun barrels. Some crews even booby-trapped their equipment using grenades and explosive shells.

The remainder, the few who now held the line, quietly sweated inside their vehicles. Hidden along treelines, concealed behind hedgerows and buildings and even parked innocuously in suburban streets, they watched and waited for the Arabian advance units to appear. From their concealed positions they overlooked the main roads, bridges and major junctions that the top brass had predicted the enemy would use to advance west.

For some, it would be their first taste of combat and they relished the challenge. Others were frightened, although they did their very best to disguise it in front of their crew mates. Many more were simply relieved, grateful they were not being committed to an all-out fight. For the most part they were dug in, hull down and well-camouflaged. They would get two, at best three shots at the Arabians, then get the hell out.

Nearby, the jeeps waited, a driver at the wheel, ready to whisk the escaping crew to safety. Those in built-up areas were the most nervous. As time passed, the reckless, the foolhardy and the plain stupid began to drift out on to the streets, drawn by the sight of battle tanks and armoured fighting vehicles. And the anxious soldiers that manned them.

Jim Newman was one such soldier. An infantryman in the 4th Battalion, The Rifles, Newman's unit in Aldershot had been shot up and scattered by a suicide attack inside the camp. He'd headed west on foot with several others, until the tank had roared up the road behind them and offered them a lift. The tank commander wanted to refuel and so he had set a course for Blandford in the south-west, where he knew he could find diesel for his vehicle. It was there that the military police had guided them to a marshalling area further west. Newman had decided to stay and help out the crew. One good turn deserved another after all and, besides, their regular driver had gone missing and they were a man short.

The final order had arrived by messenger a couple of hours ago. Newman was manning the jeep, ready to drive the tank crew to safety after their initial engagement. They'd headed north towards the town of Shaftesbury where the Challenger 2 battle tank took up position inside a large warehouse using the last of its reserve fuel. The warehouse was part of a small industrial estate that overlooked the A30, one of the main routes west from the town of Salisbury.

The tank crew were quite happy with their location, Newman discovered. The industrial estate was on elevated ground, overlooking a shallow valley and the road to be defended. The warehouse walls were made of breeze block and the half-raised metal shutter gave them a wide arc of fire with minimal exposure. The tank was parked deep inside the unlit warehouse and, as the sun began to set in the west, it lit up the ground in front of them perfectly. Anyone advancing up the A30 would have the sun in their eyes, smiled the commander.

But Newman wasn't concerned about the sun, or the Arabians for that matter. At that moment he was two hundred yards away from the warehouse, watching the crowd through the windscreen of his Land Rover. They'd gathered a short while ago near the chain-link fence that separated the industrial estate from a sprawling community housing project, drawn by the sound of the tank's twin diesels. For the most part they stood idle, smoking and chatting in small groups, but their sullen eyes kept wandering back to Newman's jeep.

The soldier cast an eye over the nearby housing. It didn't look very old, but he could see a couple of boarded up properties, the metal grills daubed in graffiti, an abandoned car by the kerbside. Piles of black rubbish sacks had been dumped near the fence, many split open, the contents strewn everywhere. A couple of vicious-looking dogs sniffed amongst the rubbish, tails wagging furiously, jaws snapping and chomping on God knew what. What had no doubt been a clean, tidy housing estate now resembled a Third World slum. You just can't help some people, thought Newman.

As the minutes passed the crowd had swollen, as more residents were drawn to the fence like moths to a flame. There were all sorts, Newman noticed; old people clothed in dressing gowns and slippers, cigarette-wielding mothers surrounded by wailing tots, pale-skinned teenagers in cheap sports clothes and hoods, swigging from cans of lager. He got the impression they weren't a friendly bunch, nor did they look particularly concerned by events beyond the fence.

Newman remained seated in his Land Rover, fifty yards away, his M4 automatic rifle cradled across his lap. Despite the weapon he was nervous. Crowds worried him, especially those intent on violence, and now there looked to be over a hundred people. As he watched, a ripple ran through the crowd. Men, maybe twenty or thirty of them, pushed their way through to the fence. They stared at the Land Rover and Newman could feel their eyes boring into him. His uniform represented authority and Newman figured these men didn't much care for what that meant. Earlier he'd thought about warning them, to get off the streets, to stay in their homes. Now, after watching these new arrivals, their tattooed arms, the bats and sticks they carried in their hands, Newman didn't think it was such a good idea. He was also thinking about reversing the jeep further away, when a shout echoed around the estate. Inside his chest his heart began to pound. Here we go.

'Oi! You! What's happening? What's that tank doing round here, then?'

Newman ignored the man. It was hard to believe that people were still unaware of what was going on. The fence rattled as some of the mob threaded their fingers through the chain link and shook it, testing its strength. Newman wasn't that worried. The fence that separated them was high, topped with barbed wire and pretty strong looking. No doubt the businesses on the industrial estate also had a keen interest in keeping the locals out. A beer can sailed over the fence, hitting the ground near the jeep with a loud smack. The crowd began jeering, the younger kids laughing and pointing. Newman's thumb toyed with the safety catch of his rifle, wishing they could get out of there while they still had the chance.

The last of the anti-aircraft crews behind the defensive line had finally received word and no one questioned their new orders. They'd manoeuvred their SAM vehicles as much as possible, but now their fuel tanks had run dry and they were immobile. Soon their positions would be plotted by the Arabians and the anti-radar missiles would home in on them. Within minutes, most of the crews were already aboard the waiting transports and heading either south-west towards Teignmouth or north-east towards Gloucestershire. The high-tech equipment inside the abandoned SAM vehicles continued to scan the skies to the east aggressively, their missile tubes and gun barrels ready to unleash their deadly projectiles.

For the Arabian technicians, the British anti-aircraft radar signatures were now distinct, their sweeps regular, predictable. Far to the east, their positions were plotted and replotted, checked and double-checked for any evidence of a ruse, a ploy by the infidels to lure in their fighter-bombers and swat them from the sky. They had to be sure. It took another fifteen minutes to confirm the information. When it was, a handset was lifted.

'Get me General Mousa.'

Mousa watched Major Karroubi heading towards him through the trees. He climbed out of the helicopter and met him halfway across the clearing.

'Well?'

'Enemy anti-aircraft units have been located and pinpointed.' Karroubi handed over a slip of paper.

'This is confirmed?'

'Absolutely,' replied Karroubi. 'I confirmed it myself.'

Mousa pushed past his subordinate and ran to the command bunker. His voice boomed around the hard-packed earth walls, startling those inside. 'Engage the enemy SAM units! Order the assault force west and release the fighter-bombers as soon as the SAMs have been neutralised. And get the ground units moving. Now!'

As the stale air hummed with bellowed orders and frantic radio traffic, Mousa's eye was drawn to the battlefield display, where the transmitter icon in the Mendip Hills still glowed faintly. In the reflection of the Perspex, he saw Karroubi limping up behind him. Mousa turned. 'Have my helicopter fuelled and ready to go, Major. We head west as soon as the way is clear.'

In the grounds of Windsor Great Park, twelve multiple launch anti-radar rocket batteries waited for the order. The co-ordinates of the British SAM units had already been plotted and entered into the on-board computers, while sensitive instruments mounted on the roofs of the armoured vehicles continuously tracked wind speed, humidity and air temperature. That data would be factored into the course and trajectory estimates of the missiles' on-board targeting computers.

In the glowing confines of his command vehicle, the battery commander suddenly leapt to his feet as his comms link warbled in his ear. He listened intently for a moment, confirmed the order, then turned to his second in command.

'All units! Execute launch order! Launch, launch, launch!'

South Lockeridge

The village hall was packed, the villagers themselves eerily silent by the time Khan had finished his talk. 'Briefing' was a more accurate word, he decided, as he scanned the worried faces around the stuffy hall. Outside, beyond the tall windows, the sun had begun its descent to the west, casting long shadows across the village green. A group of children played there, their laughter leaking through the windows as they chased each other around the grey stone war memorial.

Khan squinted into the setting sun as it dipped, its fading yellow bars lancing across the room, illuminating a million tiny dust particles drifting lazily on the stale air. Above the stage where Khan stood, a faded Union Jack hung limply from the rafters, framed by a pair of heavy, ruby-coloured stage curtains. Around the walls, hand-made posters proclaimed a recent production of *A Midsummer Night's Dream*, a car boot sale near Swindon, and the Lockeridge Fete and Country Show, scheduled to take place over the August bank holiday. Khan stared at the poster for a moment, guessing that that particular event would not be taking place this year. Maybe for the next few years, he speculated. He hoped he was wrong.

He looked down from the stage at the anxious faces before him and wondered again whether he was doing the right thing. It seemed like a good idea earlier, and Rob had been adamant, but the details of his escape from London had shaken them, had silenced the sceptics around the hall. Now, the pale and frightened faces that stared back at him caused Khan to question his own judgement, but he quickly dismissed those doubts. The villagers had a right to know what was happening in the wider world, in the towns and cities around them. Forewarned is forearmed, Khan had insisted. What he didn't have, though, were answers.

As he took his seat alongside the men and women who made up the parish council, the villagers finally found their voice, and a storm of noise erupted from the floor. Seated next to Khan, Andy Metcalfe, a gruff, no-nonsense scrap dealer in his late fifties, held his hands up for silence. When the hall finally settled down, he spoke in a deep, West Country twang.

'You all know me. I'll say what needs to be said and by the sounds of it we're in serious trouble. Our main concern has to be what's best for the village. We're going to have to pull together, that's the truth of it.' The hall was silent as Metcalfe spoke. It was obvious to Khan that the man had the respect of his community, but there was something else there too – the slight bark to his voice, the challenging jut of his scarred chin, the cautious support of the other council members. How did Rob describe him? A 'character', he'd said, a dealer in farm scrap who'd never served on the council or any other official body. Maybe Rob was jealous, or maybe he was just being diplomatic. Either way, it was in times of crisis that the most unlikely candidates emerged to show leadership, and Metcalfe certainly seemed to fit the bill.

'There are other considerations too,' Metcalfe continued, 'crop harvests, fuel rationing, that sort of stuff. It's my view that the parish council takes the lead on this and they've kindly asked me to join them while this business goes on. We haven't got time to hold elections, am I right?' There were a few polite chuckles around the room, Khan noted, but not many. 'Now, has anyone got any other suggestions for the short term? Make 'em useful or keep 'em to yourselves.'

All eyes swivelled towards Khan as he stood up once more. 'There's one other thing you can do. As I mentioned, many lives were lost last night. The first hours of a conflict are always the most dangerous. No clear battle lines, lots of confusion–' The windows suddenly rattled with the sound of distant thunder. The tremors lasted for several long moments then faded away. Khan traded a worried look with Alex, standing down by the side of the stage.

'Summer storm,' Metcalfe announced, although no one believed it. He looked up at Khan. 'You were saying?'

'Yes. Sorry.' Khan turned to face his audience. 'You need to hide the village.' The suggestion was met with a deafening silence. Even Metcalfe looked baffled.

'Sorry, my old mate, you've lost us there,' the big man snorted, his thick arms folded across his chest. Mild laughter rippled around the hall.

'Like I said, lives have been lost, possibly tens of thousands. Men, women... children too.' The laughter around the hall died away. 'Many would've been killed during the initial attacks, caught in the chaos on the streets, or victims of the sudden lawlessness. I believe you need to isolate yourselves from those dangers, and the longer you avoid contact with the outside world, the better your chances of surviving this critical period of the invasion.'

'So what do we do?' asked Metcalfe.

Khan wheeled a chalkboard to the front of the stage and spun it around. On it was a rough diagram of the village and the surrounding roads. 'You all know the area. There are only two roads that lead into this village, the one from the south and this one here, that runs north-east towards Lockeridge itself. Now, what I suggest will require fast work, some earth-moving machinery and an eye for camouflage. Has anyone got a digger, something with a bucket scoop?' Several hands in the crowd were raised. 'Good,' continued Khan. 'One thing I've noticed around here is that all the country lanes have high-sided banks, correct?' Almost everyone in the hall nodded. 'That's what I thought. My idea is this: take the diggers and block both roads to the village with earth walls. Make them the same height as the existing banks and camouflage them with the same growth and vegetation as the real ones. Even plant a couple of trees, bushes, stuff like that. Then make sure any white lines or junction markers on the road are covered or painted over and, most importantly, remove any road signs that mention this village.'

Khan paused for a moment, but when he realised there were no objections, he carried on. 'I suggest a group of you go farther afield, tell the other villages, remove any road signs you find. The more confusion you create, the better. Of course, the Arabians will have maps and aircraft, but I suspect rural communities are not their priority. The exercise here is to keep out of the way for as long as possible while events run their course. You've heard what a mess London is in, and Swindon too. If people can, they'll try and leave the cities and spread out into the countryside. They'll be scared, hungry, thirsty – and possibly armed. That's why I think sealing off this village is important.'

Khan registered the suddenly frightened faces around the hall. He shrugged and attempted a reassuring smile. 'It probably won't come to that, but it's best to err on the side of caution. Just in case.'

'How do we get in and out if the roads are blocked?' asked Metcalfe.

Khan tapped the chalkboard with a finger. 'Use the bridle path through this wood here, just south of the village. It's wide enough to drive a vehicle through and it'll bring you out on to the main road here, outside the blockade. My advice is to stay put though, unless absolutely necessary.'

The hall remained silent. It was a lot for a community like this to take in, Khan knew, but it might protect them in the long run. And the possibility of marauding gangs had struck a particularly unnerving note. When the Arabians finally discovered the village, Khan doubted whether they'd be too upset about the camouflage tactics. Self-preservation, that would be the agreed cover story. After that, well, the future for the villagers was anyone's guess, but he doubted their way of life would be affected too much. People still needed to eat and farms were the lifeblood of any nation.

Metcalfe lumbered to his feet. 'Sounds like a good idea. We don't want no outsiders coming here, trying to take the food out of our mouths, right? Unless they're family.' A murmur of agreement rippled around the hall. 'Let's vote on it then. All those in favour, raise your hand.'

Almost every hand in the room shot into the air. 'Unanimous,' acknowledged Khan. 'That's it, then. But you must work fast. The Arabians could arrive any day now.' He paused a moment, then nodded. 'Good luck.'

The hall erupted in a cacophony of voices and scraping chairs. Metcalfe's was the loudest of all, as he began barking orders and corralling villagers into work groups. Khan stepped down off the stage where Alex was waiting.

'It's good advice, Dan. When are you leaving?'

'After dark. I need to get back to Rob's place, get organised.' He lowered his voice. 'You hear those rumbles earlier?'

Alex nodded. 'Planes, maybe. Or artillery. Sounded like a long way away.'

'Not far enough,' replied Khan, shaking his head. 'Damn, I should've mentioned lookouts. You'll need them.'

'I'll take care of it,' Alex assured him.

Khan watched the hustle and bustle around him for a moment. A large group of women had converged at the back of the hall while up on the stage Metcalfe had gathered the more able-bodied men around the chalkboard. Through the window the small road that circled the village green was now aglow with brake lights as a dozen vehicles navigated the narrow lanes away from the centre of the village.

Khan's eye caught the parish council members, huddled together at the side of the stage. They were mostly elderly, a mixture of men and women, nervously gathered around the local vicar who was mouthing his own words of comfort. Occasionally, one or two of them would glance in Metcalfe's direction as he held strident court nearby. South Lockeridge had undergone its own power shift, Khan realised.

'You know this guy Metcalfe?'

Alex shrugged. 'Not really. Bit of a loudmouth in the village pub by all accounts. I hear he sails a bit close to the wind, business-wise. Scrap metal and all that.'

'Well, he's certainly risen to the challenge,' Khan observed. 'Just be careful he doesn't dominate the decision-making process. These people will look to you too, you being a police officer.'

'He's alright,' Alex replied. 'We'll sort it out, don't worry.'

Outside, the village green was now deserted, the shadows deepening as night crept towards them. Alex climbed into the Range Rover and Khan fired up the engine, watching the needle climb just above the full mark. The villagers had come through with the fuel, as Rob had promised him. Just as well, he thought; since the briefing, people around here might be a little less inclined to share, especially with a stranger. He slipped the vehicle in gear, hit the lights, then slowly circumnavigated the green.

'Seal this place tight,' Khan warned. 'The Arabians will find you sooner or later. When they do, don't resist. Make sure everybody knows that.'

'Sure,' Alex muttered. 'We'll be alright. I doubt they'll stay long.'

Khan heard the uncertainty in Alex's voice, saw the tense smile that barely creased his face. Khan felt the tension too. They'd enjoyed a brief interlude from the chaos of the invasion, the peace of the countryside seducing them both, but the Arabian war machine waited over the rumbling horizon, moving ever closer. He contemplated pressing Alex again, to try and persuade him to head for the coast, then decided against it. He'd made his choice, the only one he *could* make given the circumstances. So he said nothing, instead easing the Range Rover through the narrow lanes and back towards the farm.

Forty-eight kilometres to the south, General Mousa ducked beneath the thunderous roar of the helicopter rotor blades and strapped himself into his seat. He placed a headset over his ears as the pilot indicated imminent lift-off. Beside him, Major Karroubi did the same and the aircraft leapt into the air, banking to the north as it cleared the treetops of Grovely Wood.

'Over ninety-four per cent of enemy anti-aircraft units confirmed destroyed,' Karroubi yelled above the noise as Mousa watched the ground through the open door. 'Ground forces and helicopter assault teams are on the move.'

Mousa turned away from the fields below, from the back gardens and streets where tiny, pale figures stared up at them in the gathering dusk. It all depended on speed now. All he had to do was punch a corridor through to the Mendips, then get out, quick and clean, before the cleric became aware of the operation. Beecham, paraded before him in chains, would soothe the ire of the Holy One.

'Send in the bombers,' he barked.

Far to the east, eight fighter-bombers of the Arabian Air Force turned into their new heading and went to full afterburner, rocketing low across the English countryside. Their wings were heavy with ordnance as their infrared and thermal-imaging equipment scanned the ground ahead for military targets. In each plane, the two-man crews flipped down their anti-glare visors as they thundered into the setting sun.

The Advance West

It was a gamble, one that could cost them their lives, but it might just work. There were two vehicles, mobile SAM launchers of the Royal Artillery, and both had their systems shut down. They gave off no signature at all, neither electronic emissions nor returns from their armoured hulls. Even their engines were switched off. Everything that could be shut down, was.

The vehicles were parked behind two huge metal grain silos on a farm a few miles north of Andover, the giant containers masking their presence both visually and electronically from anyone watching from the east. They had received the order to evacuate over twenty minutes ago, but the section commander had consulted his crews and decided to wait just a little longer. He felt sure an opportunity would present itself for both vehicles to expend their remaining anti-aircraft missiles. To abandon them just seemed like a terrible waste and they were determined not to leave without a fight. A few minutes earlier, Arabian armour had passed them to the south. They were now officially behind enemy lines, but they would worry about that later. All that mattered now was launching the missiles.

The rumble in the distance grew louder. The lookout on top of one of the silos lowered his binoculars and reached for his radio. Enemy aircraft, coming in from the east, fast movers.

The commander ordered the weapons systems to be powered up. They'd only get one shot at this before they were detected. The distant rumble quickly increased to a roar and then the aircraft were there, passing low to the north in tight formation. There was no time for finesse. Each missile was programmed to auto seek, switching randomly between heat-seeking and infrared, allowing the weapons to choose their own targets. The order was given and the missile tubes swivelled around to face the north-west. Both vehicles rocked on their tracks as the missiles were loaded and launched at two-second intervals. When the last missile had roared from its tube, both crews grabbed their gear and weapons and ran for the relative safety of a nearby wood.

The British commander had done well. Blinded by the low sun and confident in the collapse of the infidel forces, the Arabian pilots were focussed solely on releasing their own ordnance as they scanned the horizon for targets. When their threat receivers screamed in their ears they were momentarily confused, then reacted instinctively as their instruments registered the incoming missiles.

Two fighter-bombers banked left and right simultaneously, veering into each other and obliterating both planes from the sky. In seconds, the missiles had eaten up the distance between the other planes and detonated one after the other, the explosions rippling across the summer sky, filling the air with thousands of deadly metal shards. Another three aircraft exploded, the burning debris spiralling to the fields below.

Now there were just three left. One was badly damaged and limped for home, black smoke trailing from one of its engines. Of the remaining two, one banked hard around and headed for the probable launch site. In the distance, the pilot saw a cloud of white smoke hanging low on the ground and his instrumentation told him that there were two military-spec vehicles parked there. He flipped his weapons control and selected cluster munitions. Less than one minute after the British crews had vacated their vehicles, the whole area erupted in a succession of detonations as the farm buildings, grain silos and everything else in a two-hundred-metre radius was engulfed in a series of fireballs. Leaking fuel from a punctured wing, that fighter too headed back to its temporary base at Heathrow.

The lead plane continued onwards unscathed, its pilot furious at the loss of his flight and desperate to exact revenge. On-board systems reported several possible targets and the fighter-bomber engaged them with extreme prejudice, wiping out six British tanks in a series of low-level sorties.

The pilot checked his instruments. They were still good for fuel and the sun had finally dipped below the horizon. Now he could see. His weapons/navigation officer seated behind him gave him the last-known position of the enemy convoy that had been detected by the LARVE. General Mousa himself had expressed interest in its whereabouts and composition. It would make a nice, fat target, thought the pilot.

He tilted his head and looked below him. He was flying parallel to a main road, which was being utilised by a large Arabian armoured column heading westward. The pilot saw a few arms waving and he dipped his wings in reply. It always made the tankies happier when they had overhead cover. He checked the terrain ahead. There was an industrial estate on a rise a couple of kilometres in front of them and some residential housing behind that. His instrumentation told him there were no immediate threats. The armoured column was safe enough.

The pilot banked the aircraft to the south. The coast wasn't that far away, roughly fifty kilometres. He decided to take a closer look down there.

Jim Newman was starting to get worried, and not because an Arabian fighter-bomber had just screamed overhead; it was the growing mob on the other side of the fence that was making him nervous. The plane had excited them. They'd begun to shake the chain-link violently, the ripple effect causing the metal ties near the ground to come loose from their fastenings. The adults leaned against the fence, pushing the bottom outwards and some of the smaller kids crawled under. They, in turn, held up their side and now the rest of the mob spilled out on to the industrial estate. Some of the kids wandered off to explore the deserted site, but the older ones held their ground, their eyes fixed on Newman and his Land Rover. There was going to be trouble. Fixed to his chest rig, the radio crackled.

'Jimbo, come in.'

Newman keyed the mike. 'Send.'

'We're open for business. Standby, chum.'

That meant the Arabian forces had been sighted and were heading towards them. Newman's heart pounded in his chest. Any moment now the firing would start – and their escape route was blocked.

Newman turned the jeep's engine over and it roared into life. The mob numbered well over a hundred now, strung out across the road. Slowly they began to advance towards him. Newman grabbed his weapon and slid out of the vehicle, leaving the engine running.

'Stay where you are!' he bawled in his most authoritative voice. 'This is a national emergency situation! Go back to your homes!'

Some of the younger kids stopped short at the sight of the gun. The older ones didn't. They kept moving slowly towards Newman. Emboldened by their peers, the younger ones now began to fan out around the jeep. In another minute or so Newman would be surrounded. He didn't want to shoot any civilians, particularly kids, but he might not have a choice here. He'd seen what mobs could do to people caught at the sharp end of their rage. There was no way Jim Newman was going out like that.

He brought his weapon up into his shoulder and looked down the optical sight, taking aim dead centre on the upper torso of a shirtless, muscular man covered in tattoos. He looked to be in his early forties, shaven-headed, wearing heavy gold jewellery around his thick neck. Maybe he was a leader. If Newman dropped him, the crowd might falter. Then again, they may go fucking ballistic. He closed one eye to steady his aim and prayed for the nearby tank to commence firing.

'Target, tank! Twelve hundred yards!'

'Load HEAT round.'

The breech clanged shut.

'Loaded! Ready!'

There was a moment's silence, a segment of time that seemed to stretch beyond all earthly constraints. The air inside the tank was thick with tension.

'God be with us, gentlemen,' said the tank commander quietly. He adjusted the focus of his main battle sight and brought the lead enemy vehicle advancing up the road towards them into sharp relief.

'Fire!'

The deep concussion rang around the industrial estate, startling the crowd. Some of the younger kids screamed and the adults instinctively ducked, crouching on the ground. The tattooed man picked himself up and turned to face Newman.

'What the fuck's going on?' he roared.

Another blast echoed around the estate, quickly followed by two more.

'Get back to your homes!' ordered Newman, his voice shaking with adrenaline, his weapon still levelled at the man's chest.

'What the fuck's happening? Who's shooting?' the tattooed man demanded, his head swivelling towards the sound of the cannon roaring somewhere close by. Worryingly, Newman didn't think the man was scared. His eyes bulged and burned with a manic intensity. He turned back to Newman, the mob bunching behind him. 'I need a gun, gotta defend myself! Gimme that fucking shooter!' he roared, walking quickly towards the Land Rover.

Newman shot the man twice in the chest, the body flopping lifelessly to the ground. The crowd turned and scattered, heading for the safety of the housing estate. Newman kept a careful eye on them but they were dispersing fast, rolling under the chain-link fence. He fired another burst into the air, just to encourage the stragglers. The fear wouldn't last long. He was one man, after all, and the mob had grown large. A member of their community had been killed and that meant that, sooner or later, all hell would break loose.

A nearby warehouse suddenly exploded, sending Newman scrambling for cover behind the jeep. Huge sheets of twisted and blackened aluminium fluttered crazily in the air before crashing to the ground nearby. The Arabians had found their range. Newman piled inside the Land Rover and revved the engine.

'C'mon, c'mon,' he muttered, his hands gripping the steering wheel tightly. Then he saw the crew, racing around the corner of an adjacent warehouse. He slammed the jeep into gear and roared towards them, stamping on the brakes a moment later. The crew piled in, doors slamming. The commander saw the body on the road and the mob that pelted the jeep with stones and bottles from behind the chain-link fence.

'Jesus,' he cringed as the missiles clattered off the roof.

'I don't know what's worse,' Newman said, roaring towards the entrance to the estate. 'That lot or the camel jockeys.' Seconds later they reached the main road. Newman slowed the jeep and checked both ways. To the left the road was clear. Looking right, thick columns of black smoke roiled into the air from the valley below.

'Looks like you got lucky, then,' Newman said.

'Luck had nothing to do with it,' smiled the commander. 'We got three of the bastards.'

It had been a small victory, but a victory nonetheless, and they'd all survived the encounter unscathed. In the gathering darkness, the jeep surged across the junction and headed north-west towards the Welsh border.

The pilot skimmed low over the English countryside, searching the ground, scanning his instruments. Fuel state was pretty fair, enough for another twenty minutes before he had to return to Heathrow. Behind him, his weps/nav officer also scanned his instruments, finding nothing worthy of their attentions. What they needed was something big, something substantial to assuage the anger and frustration that both men felt on losing the flight to a single engagement.

The pilot felt the same mix of emotions, but now, as the adrenaline of the earlier action faded, he felt something else: fear. As flight leader he knew they'd been flying too close together. Despite the warnings, he'd been lulled into a false sense of security by a combination of superior technology, overwhelming numbers and an enemy in disarray. But that enemy still had teeth and the will to use them. They'd turned like rats in a corner and destroyed most of his flight.

Excuses would be wasted on the group commander. This mission was a 'special', an attack that had been hastily prepared using recommended personnel, himself included. And he'd made a rookie mistake. He hoped that other elements of the plan were running well. If the failure of this operation were deemed to have been caused by his error, then his career would be short-lived indeed. The weps/nav's voice hissed inside his helmet.

'Got something.'

'What is it?'

'Air-search radar, forty-nine kilometres south-south-west. Recommend new heading of one eight zero degrees. We could lose some altitude, too.'

'Roger.'

The pilot banked to the left and took the plane due south out to sea, thundering over the coastal town of Seaton and out into Lyme Bay. Behind the pilot, weps/nav began firming up his data on the enemy signal.

'I am now detecting three air-search sets, all low frequency. Designate signals as mobile anti-aircraft batteries, probably in passive mode. Locations are static.'

The pilot maintained his heading. He'd reduced his airspeed in order to lower his fuel consumption, but they couldn't maintain their time on station for much longer. He keyed his microphone.

'Fuel state is low. Do we have a target?'

'Not sure,' came the reply. 'Three mobile SAM units, all in fairly close proximity.' The weps/nav studied the map display in front of him, toggling the view to a more detailed one. The SAM units were a few kilometres apart, their radars looking to the east. He studied the contours of the map. That made sense. They were all on elevated ground that dropped away to–

'Docks! They're protecting something at the docks.'

'What docks?'

'Standby.' The weps/nav keyed in a request for more localised information. Within seconds it was back. Teignmouth dock; five berths, facilities to handle large container ships, warehouses, storage areas, sheltered harbour, good links to the M5 motorway...

'Possible target, Teignmouth docks. SAM units are protecting all easterly approaches. Recommend new heading three four niner degrees.'

The pilot banked the plane around immediately and settled in to their new heading. He had two, one-thousand-pound bombs and one canister of cluster munitions, plus a couple of thousand rounds of twenty millimetre. All he needed now was a target to expend it on.

'What have we got?' he asked.

'Start climbing. Can't see a thing from down here.'

The pilot pulled back on his yoke and increased power. He did it slowly, giving his crewman time to monitor his equipment as their radar coverage increased. It also made them vulnerable to detection, but that was the trade-off.

'Contact! Take us down!'

The pilot pushed forward on the yoke and the plane dived for the surface of the sea. He watched his instrumentation carefully. The sun had set and the gloom was building rapidly. The sea below the aircraft was calm, no whitecaps to give the pilot any points of reference. Flying in these conditions required the utmost concentration and the pilot's eyes flicked constantly between his instrumentation and the sea below. Behind him, the weps/nav firmed up the contact.

'Okay, we've got two ship-borne radar signatures. First contact, military spec, surface type, air-search capability confirmed. Designate target as navy frigate. Second target is stationary, standard sea-set radar signature. Possibly a cargo ship.'

'Did they see us?' enquired the pilot. British frigates were equipped with a variety of anti-aircraft weapons and he didn't want to give the enemy the opportunity to test their effectiveness.

'Negative,' confirmed weps/nav.

The pilot had a decision to make. A frigate was a formidable foe and one he wouldn't normally consider engaging, not without the right ordnance. But the cargo ship was something else. It could be offloading supplies, and those supplies would probably be used to reinforce the infidel troops on the ground. The pilot burned with the desire to avenge his fallen comrades, and engaging the target ahead would go some way to atoning for his own stupid mistake.

'Arm weapons systems and prepare to engage. Recommend simultaneous drop of two LGBs. We're going for the cargo ship.'

'Understood,' the weps/nav replied.

He programmed the laser-guided bombs for low-altitude release as the plane thundered across the surface of the sea. They'd come in hard and fast, right on the deck, popping up at the last minute for bomb release and then bank to the north-west. Weps/nav suggested using the cluster munitions on the westernmost SAM unit on the way out; their course would take them almost directly over it. Perfect, agreed the pilot. He flexed his fingers inside his flight gloves, settled back in his seat and slowly increased power.

The orderly hated ships. In fact, he detested boats of any kind. The water made him ill and the smell of the docks was enough to disrupt his delicate stomach. Add to that the chaos and confusion around him and his nerves were now severely rattled. He just wasn't cut out for this shit. Still, if it helped to get him out of harm's way, he was willing to put up with a few hours of discomfort.

As he squatted on the concrete floor of the warehouse, he reflected briefly on the day's events. If he hadn't dumped the prime minister's clothes like he had, instead of disposing of them properly, he would have definitely missed his allocated transport. He'd probably still be on the motorway now, along with the breakdowns and the other stragglers. There was talk of fighting too, of air attacks and casualties. God knows what would happen if the Arabians caught up with them here, with their backs to the sea.

'You lot! On your feet!'

The orderly swivelled around. The sergeant was shouting at his group! Thank God! Finally they were on the move. He stood up, brushing the dirt from his combat trousers, and looked around the giant warehouse. There must be at least two thousand troops still milling around, waiting their turn to board the container ship tied up outside. The other ships had already left and now there was just this last boat to be filled and then they, too, could leave.

Unfortunately, there were latecomers arriving all the time and their departure had been repeatedly delayed. The orderly was furious about that. *Fuck them!* he'd wanted to scream, *let's just go!* But instead, they were marched into this giant warehouse and told to wait. He'd tried to explain to the burly Royal Marine sergeant that he was a member of the Alternate One permanent staff group, that he was key personnel, but that didn't seem to cut any ice with the man. He was shoved in with a group of strangers and told to wait. Still, at least they were moving.

Outside, the sun had set. Although the sky was a wonderful shade of deepening blues, the shadows on the dockside were long and deep. There were soldiers everywhere, from every unit in the army, and there seemed to be a constant, disjointed chorus of shouts and whistles and the roar of engines. It appeared to be chaotic, but the lines of troops that snaked around the quayside shuffled forward every few moments, waved on by torch-wielding naval types.

The orderly craned his neck as he tramped along the darkened quay. The gigantic cargo ship loomed ominously above him as his group was shepherded towards a wide gangway. As he neared the top of the steep ramp, he turned to look behind him. From here he could see over the roofs of the warehouses towards the dock gates. A crowd had gathered there, a large one, civilians by the looks of them. A couple of tanks were blocking the gates and soldiers had formed a line across the road behind them. It was only a matter of time before panic broke out.

As he stepped over the threshold, the orderly prayed that the ship would get under way soon. The vessel stank of oil and saltwater and the orderly's nose wrinkled in disgust as he entered the darkened ship. He was herded up several tight stairwells, along cramped gangways until he ducked through yet another bulkhead and emerged out on to the open deck. He was facing aft, looking directly at the ship's main superstructure. He could see figures moving about on the dimly lit bridge and, higher up, a thin column of black smoke rose into the darkening sky from the boiler stack. Seagulls wheeled and screeched in the air above them.

He was ordered to keep moving and joined a long line of troops who shuffled forward, cutting across the wide deck. The orderly railed at the thought of freezing his arse off on an open deck overnight, but if that was the price of safety then so be it.

Suddenly, he bumped against the man in front as the column rippled to a halt. The dark line of figures ahead of him snaked around a huge, open hatch that looked down into the bowels of the ship. Fear gripped the orderly as the column moved forward again and he found himself alongside the hatch. Carefully, he peered over the edge. There were men down there, hundreds of them, like a scene from Dante's *Inferno*. He could see their pale faces looking upwards, the mass of tightly packed bodies ebbing and swaying under the influx of a never-ending line of figures climbing down two bulkhead ladders to join the throng below. The orderly instinctively backed away, but a rough hand grabbed him by the shoulder.

'Back in line. Keep moving.'

The orderly turned to see a ship's crewman, a green luminous wand in his hand, his body silhouetted by the fading sky behind him.

'I can't. I mean, it's–'

'Don't worry,' smiled the crewman, only his crooked teeth visible beneath the wide brim of his cap. 'It's only temporary. We underestimated the numbers, see? The other ships have already sailed and everybody has to get on this one.'

'But I–'

The crewman grabbed his elbow, moving him forward along the line. 'That's it son, one foot in front of the other. As soon as we've rounded Land's End you'll be able to come up on deck, stretch your legs, get a bit of fresh air. Captain might even let you stay up here.' He jabbed a finger down into the hold. 'In the meantime, you're down there with the others. Only take us a few hours to round the point. The frigate will look after us.' He cocked a thumb over his shoulder.

The orderly looked past the crewman and out to sea. He saw the dark silhouette of a warship, maybe a mile away, the sea churning to white foam in its wake. There was something else out there too, a dot on the horizon that was growing larger even as he watched it.

'What's that?' asked the orderly.

'What's what, mate?'

'That.'

The crewman turned, following the orderly's pointed finger.

'Arm LGBs!' barked the pilot.

Behind him, weps/nav flipped the switch to arm the fuses for the laser-guided bombs. Nothing. He tried it again, several times. A red light blinked on his display.

'Arming failed! Arming failed!'

The pilot smiled, recognising the subtle touch of God's hand. A price had to be paid for his failure, and Allah, knower of all things, had decided it must be here, now. Nothing mattered any more, not the humiliating debrief, nor the wrath of the group commander. Only paradise awaited. *Insha'Allah.*

The frigate was coming up fast on their left wing, the fighter-bomber a mere ten metres above the waves. He dropped the nose a touch and pushed the throttles to the stops. Weps/nav shuddered in fear as he realised what the pilot was about to do. They were travelling too fast and too low for him to eject. A flash of tracer from the frigate lanced behind the fighter-bomber as it headed directly for the grey hull of the huge container ship. The pilot depressed his cannon trigger as the starboard beam loomed large in front of him. Behind him, weps/nav closed his eyes and hung his head in a final prayer.

The ripping sound made the orderly yelp in fear. Others spun around as the thunder echoed across the bay. Some saw the speeding object and screamed for cover before heavy-calibre rounds began impacting across the crowded deck. The crowd surged and the orderly screamed as he lost his balance. He tipped sideways, then backwards, plunging with several others into the gaping deck hatch and tumbling sixty feet towards the squirming mass below.

He hit the crowd, arms and legs flailing, crushing those beneath him. His eyes remained open, registering the forest of legs around him, sensing the irreparable damage to his body. Someone writhed beneath him in the darkness, moaning in pain, cursing. The crowd around him surged, the heavy boots crushing his broken chest, his shattered legs and cleaved skull. He gasped in pain, praying for release from the hell into which he'd descended.

A moment later, the fighter-bomber ripped through the side of the ship, the twin one-thousand-pound bombs detonating almost immediately. The resulting explosion lifted the vessel from the sea before blasting it to pieces across Teignmouth docks, hurling steel, concrete and bodies over a half-mile radius.

Western Scotland

The Dark Eagle came in low and quiet over the treetops, barely visible against the night sky, flaring gently between glowing markers in the secluded grounds of McIntyre Castle. After the rotors had wound down, General Bashford stepped out of the aircraft and motioned the others to follow him.

Harry hopped out on to the grass, stretched his aching limbs and took a deep breath. For the first time since the invasion had started he was beginning to feel a little more composed. The air was cool this far north and he stood there for a moment, enjoying the peace and tranquillity of his new surroundings. Nobody rushed him here and there, nobody bawled commands or brandished guns in his face; the threat of imminent violence appeared to have receded.

Although night had fallen, the sky was clear and visibility was good. Above him, the heavens were dusted with stars and a soft breeze whispered through the surrounding pine forest, carrying with it the gentle lap of water against the distant shoreline of the Sound of Kerrera. It really was quite beautiful, sighed Harry. A pity he'd arrived under such godawful circumstances.

With Gibson and Fuller trailing behind, Harry followed Bashford towards the turreted building that loomed ahead. As they drew closer he noticed a figure waiting in the shadows, torch in hand, beckoning them. When the man spoke it was with a strong Scottish accent.

'Good evening gentlemen, and welcome to McIntyre Castle. My name is Bill Kerr, the duty keeper here. Everything's been prepared, so please follow me.' They climbed a wide set of stone steps and crunched across a gravel courtyard, surrounded on three sides by the building before them. Harry saw it was a traditional Scottish baronial castle, shrouded in darkness, its distinctive high towers spearing the night sky. Not a single light shone from any window.

Kerr twisted a large iron ring and pushed one of the heavy arched doors open, its considerable weight swinging silently on well-oiled hinges. He pulled back a heavy inner curtain to reveal a large entrance hall that shimmered in a flickering light. He ushered them in, drawing the blackout curtain back across the threshold.

'This is a fully staffed facility, Prime Minister, so if you have any questions or requests, please ask. We'll try to make your stay as comfortable as possible.'

Kerr appeared older than Harry first thought. In the dark, he'd noticed the wide shoulders and the strong, confident stride, but in the light of the hallway it was clear that Kerr was in his mid to late sixties, with receding sandy-grey hair and weathered features indicative of a life spent outdoors. He was dressed in civilian clothes, but Harry suspected that for most of his life he'd worn a uniform of some sorts.

He looked around him, at his home for the foreseeable future. The large entrance hall was deserted, lit by a single oil lamp that cast a flickering glow across the grey stone walls, the smooth granite slabs underfoot, the high-vaulted ceiling above. Where the shadows were deepest Harry caught a movement, then registered the armed soldier who lurked there, watching them. Kerr moved past him towards a wide staircase that wound its way up to the floors above.

'If you follow me, sir, I'll show you to your rooms so you can freshen up.'

A whole suite of rooms had been allocated to Harry, with Gibson and Farrell bunked immediately next door, the landing outside patrolled by more armed guards. It was the safest Harry had felt in quite a while. He took a hot shower and changed into the fresh clothes that had been laid out on his bed. As he dressed he felt a quiet vibration in the air. He went to the window overlooking the grounds and saw another Dark Eagle settling on the wide lawn.

A short time later, Kerr escorted Harry to a well-appointed drawing room in one of the castle's towers, where the windows were covered by heavy green curtains and a fire crackled in the stone hearth. The walls were decorated with heraldic shields and oil paintings of local wildlife, sympathetically portrayed against traditional Highland backdrops. In front of the fire were arranged three large sofas, a thick oak coffee table between them.

General Bashford waited, as did Deputy PM Noonan and Admiral Hughes. They stood as Harry entered, but he waved them back into their seats. Two stewards appeared with trays of tea and coffee then silently retreated, closing the door behind them. Harry poured himself a cup of tea and slumped on to one of the sofas.

'How are your quarters?' Bashford enquired.

'Fine,' Harry replied, sipping his tea.

'We're completely off the map here,' the general explained. 'Not a military base for fifty miles, so we shouldn't draw any attention. All approach roads are under constant surveillance and the whole area is patrolled by a very discreet security force. The cover story we've put out is that you've relocated to a Cold War command facility near Aberdeen. Planning and operations will continue to be run out of SCOTFOR, where the rest of my team are now based.'

Harry leaned forward and spooned sugar into his cup. 'What's the latest, with the evacuation?'

The question hung on the air. Harry glanced up, the crackling fire illuminating the troubled faces of the men around him. Noonan dropped his eyes to the floor and Harry felt the hairs prickle on the back of his neck.

'Something's happened. What is it? General Bashford?'

The soldier took a deep breath and levelled his gaze at Harry. 'I'm afraid one of the container ships was hit at Teignmouth. Details are sketchy at the moment, but it would appear that it was struck by a low-flying plane. We think it was a suicide mission. The loss of life has been, well, considerable.'

Harry set his cup and saucer down, spilling the contents across the table.

'How bad?'

'Two thousand at least.'

The blood drained from Harry's face. *'What?'*

'I'm afraid so. The escort ship spent some time recovering survivors but, with the threat of another attack and the light gone, they've had to put out to sea.'

Harry's eyes bored into the general's. 'Are you telling me people have been abandoned?'

Bashford nodded. 'As I said, the threat–'

'No!' stormed Harry, banging his fist on the table, rattling the cups and spilling more tea. 'We have to do something. We just can't leave people in the water to die.' Admiral Hughes leaned forward, frustration and anger evident in his face.

'And run the risk of losing another ship, Prime Minister? That escort frigate is overloaded, too. We can't afford any more loss of life.'

'But we–'

'They had no choice. They had to pull out,' the admiral stressed, 'and you can be sure that the decision wasn't taken lightly.'

Harry slumped back into his chair. Hughes was right, of course. The naval man was clearly feeling the loss more than most, yet the sheer horror of the event had affected them all, especially Harry. He felt hot, the air around him suddenly thicker, making it difficult to breathe. He ran a finger around the collar of his shirt and swallowed hard.

'I'm sorry, Admiral. This constant loss of life, I...'

'Don't apologise. This is war,' Hughes reminded him, 'and the sooner we all get our heads around that reality, the better.' He picked up his own cup, taking a moment to sip the hot beverage, easing the tension around the table. 'Now, surviving personnel at Teignmouth will head north, as per the plan. With a little luck and decent transport they'll start arriving at the border in the next twelve to twenty-four hours. We should have a clearer picture of what happened then.' Harry nodded silently. They were getting hit from all sides and the casualty list must be… well, he didn't want to dwell on that. However, the mere thought of it made his stomach churn. He realised that the time to negotiate may come sooner rather than later, if only to end the chaos. If the Arabians were willing to negotiate, that is. The thought of dealing with those bastards made him feel equally sick, but if it prevented any more loss of life then Harry would do it without question. It was the steady ticking of the antique clock above the fireplace that brought his focus back around the table.

'Any word from the Arabians?' he asked.

Noonan shook his head. 'Not directly. Their ambassador in Washington was summoned to the White House. Apparently, Baghdad is citing some sort of provocation. They have intelligence they say, some sort of European plot to destabilise North Africa and the Middle East. Like the Arab Spring back in twenty-eleven. They're saying the invasion is a pre-emptive defensive action.'

'Defensive? Killing God knows how many people?' Harry snarled. He turned to the general. 'Can't we hit back at the bastards? There must be something we can do.'

'There is,' Bashford nodded, 'but right now we need to consolidate our forces, build up the intelligence picture, our strategic options. We're in uncharted waters here, Prime Minister. There's no model or war game scenario for this.'

'One big missile, that's all we need,' Harry fumed, twisting his hands together. 'Punch a bloody hole right in the middle of Baghdad.'

'And kill Arabian civilians?' tempered Noonan. 'No Harry, we'd open the door to retaliatory attacks, reprisals against our own citizens. Let's not forget international condemnation, too. It's important we maintain the moral high ground.'

'For God's sake, wake up,' Harry snapped. 'Didn't you hear, Peter? We're at war. To hell with the UN, we have to do something.' The anger was giving way to something else now, an unfamiliar emotion that made his heart race and a sheen of perspiration form across his brow. He struggled to think rationally as a sudden wave of panic flooded his thoughts. He took a deep breath, willing himself to relax.

He watched Bashford cross the room and retrieve a bottle and glasses from a drinks cabinet. Harry took the offered malt whisky and belted the contents back in one. He held his glass out for a refill and the general obliged.

'As painful as it is,' Bashford began, 'our best course of action now is to consolidate our position. We have had some successes, but we can't deliver a decisive blow without a strategic plan. For now, we think we may have some breathing space and I suggest we use that time to rest and recuperate. The Scottish border is not directly threatened, and the nearest Arabian forces have stopped just north of Leeds. We have two ASTOR aircraft – that's Airborne Stand-Off Radar – operating sixty miles behind the Scottish front line, monitoring enemy air and ground movements to the south. If the Arabians start to move in our direction, we'll know about it. In the meantime, we need to gather our strength.'

Harry rubbed his face, grateful for the alcohol that had momentarily stemmed the rising panic. The exhaustion wasn't just physical, it was emotional too, he realised. And it wasn't just military expertise that would be required in the coming days. Diplomacy was key, and if there were talks to be held, with Baghdad, with Washington, he had to be on top of his game. Bashford was right. What he needed – what they all needed – was rest.

'Look, there's nothing much we can do here tonight,' Bashford concluded. 'SCOTFOR is monitoring the situation, so I suggest we all retire for the evening, try and get a good night's sleep. We have some intelligence people coming in from Edinburgh in the morning for a briefing session and you'll be able to speak to the Lord Advocate via telephone. Things will look a little clearer then.' The general got to his feet and picked up a wall phone. Moments later there was a soft knock on the door and Bill Kerr entered the room.

'Ah, Bill. Can you escort the Prime Minister back to his room and ensure that he is not to be disturbed? Breakfast at seven for everyone else, if you please.'

Harry got to his feet, feeling too tired, too fragile to argue. His thoughts returned to Teignmouth, to the cold, dark waters of the English Channel, where he heard the cries for help, saw in his mind the oil-covered faces bobbing in the sea, condemned to die by fate and circumstance. Harry paused by the door, slowly turning to face Bashford. When he spoke he felt his voice tremble.

'Somewhere down the line, those bastards are going to pay for what they've done. In blood. Do you understand, General?'

Without waiting for a reply, Harry left the room.

Alternate One

Mousa felt the rumbling beneath his feet, despite being told that the main cavern was deep below him under thick rock.

The attack on the infidel command post was going well, and Mousa had landed in the Mendip Hills a mere five minutes after the area had been secured by his airborne troops. He paced around the helicopter on the ridge above while, far below, two SERTRAK units were fighting their way through the tunnels and caverns of the underground facility. There was also contact nearby, in the town of Wells, where British soldiers were engaging his forces in house-to-house fighting. Mousa smiled in the darkness. Not only did he enjoy a fight, but the ferocity displayed by the defenders meant that his quarry was close. It was only a matter of time now.

A short distance away, Karroubi conferred with Mousa's signaller. The general strode over and joined them.

'Well?'

'The SERTRAK commander reports that the enemy forces have been neutralised, General. There are several prisoners, military and civilian.'

'Lead the way!'

A short while later, Mousa found himself in the main cavern of Alternate One. The huge chamber was littered with debris and bodies, and the air was thick with the smell of spent cartridges. In the centre of the cavern a small group of prisoners squatted miserably on the floor, their uniforms bloodied and filthy, surrounded by a large number of SERTRAK personnel. Mousa searched the terrified faces of the civilians amongst them, but Beecham wasn't there. He noticed a British officer amongst the huddle and had him hauled to his feet. The officer was bleeding from a head wound, and held a field dressing against his temple to stem the flow of blood.

'Name?'

'Monroe. Major Monroe.'

'Where is the criminal Beecham?'

Monroe stood a little straighter. 'Under the provisions of the Geneva Convention I am only–'

Mousa slapped the major so hard the sound echoed around the rocky walls. Only the smirking Afghans holding him prevented Monroe from falling to the ground.

'Last chance,' warned Mousa. 'Where is Beecham?'

Monroe spat blood on to the floor, the field dressing dangling from his head. He straightened up, and Mousa recognised the spark of defiance in his eye.

'Under the provisions of the Geneva Convention I am only–'

Mousa pulled his pistol, jammed it into Monroe's chest and shot him. The sound was deafening in the cavern and Monroe flopped, wide-eyed, to the floor. Mousa stepped over the still-breathing body and approached the prisoners. Before he could say a word one of the civilians, a bald man in his fifties, scrambled to his feet.

'He's gone to Scotland,' he blurted. 'Left by helicopter some time ago. That's all any of us know.'

Mousa stared at the man for several seconds, trying to control the rage that was beginning to boil inside him. 'Where?' he said slowly. 'Where in Scotland?'

'No one knows,' the man stammered. 'The orders were clear. All troops and equipment are to head for the border.'

The pistol shook in Mousa's hand. How he wanted to shoot the man in the face, unload the magazine into his fat head until it was empty. But that would be foolish. There was more to discover here, of that he was sure. He turned to the SERTRAK team leader. 'Interrogate them all, one by one, until you discover where the infidel has fled. Use any means necessary.'

Back on the ridgeline, Mousa paced around his helicopter in the darkness. A cool night breeze gusted across the ridge top, tempering his anger. He'd failed. There weren't many times in his career when he would freely admit to it, but this was one of those times. Not only that, but he'd disobeyed the Holy One, his insubordinate actions not only costing lives but also the loss of some very expensive military hardware. Mousa had never seen the Holy One angry before, but he had a feeling that that might change in the near future.

On the plus side, his forces had discovered a previously unknown military complex that could give his intelligence people some high-grade material, and there was also a spectacular attack on an enemy ship on the coast, so the news wasn't all bad. But would it be enough to save his skin?

'Let's get back to London,' he informed the loitering Karroubi. Moments later, the air filled with the whine of powerful turbine engines. The general climbed aboard the helicopter and strapped in, Karroubi jumping in beside him. The pilot immediately pulled up on his collective and the helicopter rose into the air, the escorting gunships falling into position on either side. Mousa watched from the window as the helicopter banked over and headed east.

Scotland. That would be where the real battle would take place. The British forces would reorganise, strengthen their positions, but they would be squeezed tight, with nowhere to run but north, where the sea would trap them. They would fight like cornered rats.

As the helicopter skimmed east towards the capital, Mousa prayed he would survive the wrath of the Holy One, allowing him the opportunity to take part in the inevitable campaign to the north. For a moment he forgot his mounting troubles. He smiled in the darkness, relishing the thought of the bitter fight to come.

The Road South

Khan finished packing the last of his things into a small rucksack. It wasn't much – a few clothes, some food and water, a couple of items kindly donated by the villagers. He hefted the rucksack over his shoulder, snapped off the light to his room and went downstairs.

Outside, the night was clear and bright, made brighter by the earlier flashes in the western sky, a sign that the war machine had finally outpaced them. All they could do now was avoid the danger as best they could. For Khan, he was sticking his head back into the lion's mouth, but that was preferable to hiding here in the village, hoping and praying that the outside world would pass them by. It wouldn't, of that he was certain.

He climbed inside the Range Rover, stowing his gear on the back seat and programming the satnav for the forthcoming journey. He heard a chorus of protests from the geese, then the crunch of gravel. He looked through the windscreen to see the others approaching. He switched off the ignition and climbed out to greet them.

'We've come to see you off,' Kirsty told him.

'Thanks. Nice job with the blackout curtains,' he told Helen, pointing at the darkened farmhouse.

'You think?' She glanced over her shoulder. When she spoke again her voice shook with emotion. 'The kids think it's all a game. I wonder how long we can keep that up?'

'I want to thank you,' Khan said quickly, stepping forward. He held out his hand, saw the tears on Helen's face glinting in the moonlight as she took his hand in hers. Her grip was warm and firm. Then she snatched it away, turned on her heel and headed back the farmhouse. Rob watched her go.

'She's not coping too well,' he admitted. 'She'll come around, though. She's tougher than she looks.' He shook Khan's hand warmly. 'Thanks for everything. You can always come back here, if things don't work out. Whatever happens, I wish you all the best.'

'Thanks, Rob. You too.'

Kirsty stepped forward and kissed him on the cheek. 'Thanks, Danesh. Without you, we'd still be stuck on that riverbank.'

'Nonsense,' protested Khan.

'She's right,' Alex said, snaking an arm around Kirsty's shoulders. 'We owe you. Thanks, mate.'

'Let's just call it a team effort, eh?' smiled Khan. Then the smile faded. 'Just remember, you'll be discovered eventually. Plan for that, and when it comes, don't resist. Okay?'

'Oh, wait,' Kirsty exclaimed. She produced a mobile phone from her jeans' pocket and gave it to Rob. 'Take our picture, please Rob. You know, two or three, just to be sure.'

He did as he was told and Kirsty flicked through the results, smiling as she did so. Then Khan realised she was upset too. 'For posterity,' she explained, trying to fight the tears and failing. 'When you get to America you can email us and I'll send you a copy.'

Then she turned and headed for the house. 'Jesus Christ, I'll be next,' Alex joked. He slapped Khan on the back and headed towards the Range Rover. 'C'mon, I'll ride with you to the roadblock.'

The short drive was made on sidelights. On arrival they were surprised to see that the earth bank was almost complete. It was being hastily camouflaged by a couple of dozen people, the only sound the low murmur of their voices, the stamp of their feet and the slap of shovels on the hard-packed earth. Metcalfe loomed out of the darkness to greet them.

'Well? What do you think?'

'Very impressive,' Khan said. They all clambered to the top of the barrier. Here they were a good eight feet above the road, the barrier merging subtly with the banks on either side.

Khan noticed that some enterprising soul had painted over the junction markings on the road. Once the vegetation took hold it would be hard to spot another road behind it. It wasn't fool proof, but it would do for now.

They climbed back down and assembled around the driver's door of the Range Rover. Metcalfe handed Khan a slip of paper.

'I sent some lads out to chop down as many signs as they could, so these are your directions. If you don't balls them up they'll get you into Hampshire. You'll have to use a couple of major roads, mind. No choice.'

Khan took the slip and studied it carefully. He leaned inside the cab and entered the details into the Range Rover's on-board satnav system. Satisfied that the route reflected the one given to him by Metcalfe, Khan tore up the paper, stamping the fragments into the ground.

'Thanks for all your help, Andy.'

'See you, mate.' Metcalfe slapped him on the shoulder and walked away.

Urgent whispers carried on the night breeze warned everyone to stop talking. They stood motionless as the sound of distant helicopters clattered around the northern horizon. After a minute or so, the sound faded and the work continued.

Khan watched Metcalfe a short distance away, his bulky shoulders silhouetted against the night sky, his gruff voice still issuing orders.

'Just keep an eye on Andy,' he said to Alex. 'It's probably just a rush of blood to the head, but he seems to be enjoying the role of leader right now. Make sure you don't get side-lined.'

'Okay.'

They shook hands, then embraced; for a moment Khan hesitated. It would be so easy to stay, to get lost in the English countryside. Compared to stealing a boat and sailing solo across the Atlantic, remaining on the farm seemed like the sensible option. But he put a lot of faith in instinct, and this time his gut feeling told him that staying wasn't a healthy option.

He started the Range Rover and turned into the adjacent field, while Alex walked ahead with a torch. When they reached the bridle path at the bottom of the woods, Khan swung the vehicle through a gap in the hedgerow and out on to the road. He powered down the passenger window.

'Take care of yourself,' he said.

'You too,' Alex replied, his face bathed in the red wash of the Range Rover's brake lights. Khan hit the accelerator and drove slowly down the lane, away from South Lockeridge. He glanced at the rear-view mirror but Alex was gone, swallowed by the darkness.

The initial thirty miles were uneventful. Khan eased the powerful Range Rover slowly along the country roads, paying close attention to the computerised female voice of the satnav system. He drove on sidelights in an attempt to draw as little attention as possible, but he didn't expect that to last. Sooner or later he would be stopped and challenged.

He was kitted out in the clothes that Rob had given him and the identity card he carried declared him to be the same man that had worshipped at the mosque in Morden. The ID card was real, as was the National Insurance number displayed upon it. His Security Services warrant card had been carefully hidden under the thick carpet in the rear passenger compartment. The automatic rifle he'd left behind, exchanged for Alex's ten-millimetre Glock, hidden in the air filter compartment under the bonnet.

It was past midnight by the time Khan turned on to the A338 and headed south towards Tidworth. He flicked on his headlights. The wide road was empty in both directions, which Khan didn't really expect but welcomed all the same. The last thing he needed was to get caught up in a sea of cars all trying to escape the chaos.

The miles slipped slowly by. The only other sign of life were the bugs that flickered in and out of his headlights and a lone fox caught in the middle of the road just north of Tidworth. To the south-east the sky glowed red around the horizon. There were large fires somewhere out there. Khan knew that Tidworth military garrison was in the general area and he assumed the fires were the aftermath of a terrorist attack. He increased speed, eager to clear the area.

At the junction with the A303, Khan negotiated an empty roundabout, then headed south on a quiet back road that would take him as far as Romsey in Hampshire. From there it was roughly ten miles to Southampton, but he intended to skirt the city and loop around the eastern side towards the village of Hamble. It was there that he'd learned to sail and he knew the area was littered with marinas, sea schools and boatyards, all potential sites for finding the—

He slammed his foot on the brake as the Range Rover slewed across the narrow country lane. The nearside wing clipped a hedgerow, forcing Khan to swing back the other way. His chest snapped against the seat belt and he rocked back in his seat as the Range Rover came to rest six feet from the steel track of an Arabian battle tank that squatted menacingly across the road.

Within seconds his door was wrenched open and Khan was dragged out of the vehicle. He stumbled and sat down heavily on his backside. Two soldiers pulled him roughly to his feet. The tank lit up a searchlight mounted on its turret, washing the scene in harsh white light. Khan looked up, shielding his eyes with a hand. The tank was parked broadside across the narrow lane, forming a giant roadblock. Its massive gun barrel was pointed out over an adjacent field, but a fifty-calibre heavy machine gun was aimed directly at the Range Rover.

There were three or four other soldiers on the tank and one of them jumped down to the ground. He strode slowly up to Khan, studying him as one would study an insect caught in a spider's web. Khan saw the officer's shoulder boards and lowered his eyes in submission, a gesture not without meaning in the Middle East.

'Who are you? Where are you going?' barked the man in heavily accented English. The other soldiers remained silent, watching the exchange carefully. He felt the grip on his arms tighten. Khan had the impression that this was the first contact with a British person that this crew had experienced.

'I have ID. In my pocket,' Khan replied.

The officer nodded and the soldier to Khan's left quickly emptied his pockets, dumping the contents on the bonnet of the Range Rover. The officer held up each item carefully, examining them in the glare of the tank's searchlight. He noticed the name on the ID card.

'Fawad? You are Pakistani?' he asked, switching to Urdu.

'By blood. I am a British citizen,' replied Khan in the same tongue.

'You are Muslim, no?'

Khan nodded, holding his breath. The officer studied the fake ID card a moment longer, then began picking through the other items, finally unfolding a drug prescription. He peered inside Khan's vehicle. Seeing a brown paper bag on the passenger seat, he retrieved it and spilled the contents on the bonnet. He picked up one of the pill bottles and read the label carefully.

'What are you doing on this road?'

Khan pointed to the prescription, to the drugs supplied by the village pharmacist in a fictitious name.

'For my nephew, to treat the child's epilepsy. He's only six years old.'

'You're a doctor?'

'Medical student,' Khan lied, 'at the hospital in Swindon. I haven't heard from my brother in Southampton. I'm worried about the boy.'

The officer eyed Khan for several moments, then waved his hand. The soldiers suddenly released him from their grip. He jerked a thumb at the Range Rover.

'Expensive vehicle.'

'A friend's,' Khan explained.

The officer turned back to the tank and made a signal. The turret searchlight was extinguished and its powerful twin diesels roared into life in a cloud of exhaust smoke. The tank jerked into gear and surged forward into the adjacent field, clearing the road. Behind it were parked two Humvee jeeps.

'Things are about to change here, my friend, but good Muslims have nothing to fear.' The officer reached into his pocket. 'Take this.'

Khan took a laminated card from the officer's outstretched hand. He studied it for a moment and then looked quizzically at the officer. 'What is it?' he asked.

'A temporary movement pass. You may travel freely for the next twenty-four hours. You must carry it with you at all times and present it when ordered. Your business is urgent, I can see that. When you have tended to it, remain indoors and listen for information broadcasts on your radio. Do you understand?'

Khan turned the card over between his fingers. 'Thank you. May Allah bless you for your kindness.'

'On your way,' the officer ordered.

Khan jumped into the Range Rover and started the engine, edging the vehicle past the Humvees. In his rear-view mirror he saw the tank reverse back across the road. Once again the roadblock was lost in the darkness. He powered down the window and let the cool night air wash over him. Close one, he thought to himself. But the cover story held up and, as a benefit, he'd been issued some sort of movement order. He reprogrammed the satnav to find a quicker route.

When he reached the M27 coastal motorway some time later, his movement order was checked again by another Arabian patrol. He was asked a couple of questions and waved down the ramp and on to the motorway. He was ordered to keep to the left-hand lane and out of the way of military traffic.

Travelling along the unlit motorway, the view was unsettling. The other side of the road was choked with Arabian military traffic, all streaming out from Southampton docks. Khan saw troop transports, towed artillery, tanks and jeeps all rumbling past in the darkness. As he neared the interchange for the road to London, Khan saw that that road, too, was solid with military traffic. He kept going east.

The enormity of the operation was staggering, the repercussions yet to be felt. The world had changed overnight. Everything Khan knew was gone now, and something dark had taken its place. He'd made the right decision, of that there was no doubt. But he wasn't clear yet.

Thirty minutes later, Khan eased the Range Rover gently under a large stand of trees near Andrew's Marina in Hamble. He parked on the eastern edge of the village, the nearby buildings silent and shrouded in darkness. The approach to the village had been quite tricky, the dark roads narrowing as he headed towards the spit of land that Hamble nestled on.

Khan turned off his headlights, unwilling to broadcast his arrival as he negotiated the tight country lanes. In one particularly heart-stopping moment, a car had careered past in the opposite direction, its headlights burning through the darkness. Khan had got a brief glimpse of the driver; young, male, the other occupants shouting and screaming as it barely missed the side of the Range Rover. Joyriders, Khan assumed, making the most of the blackout. He hoped that that would be his only human encounter here.

He stepped out of the vehicle, closing the door with a soft click. He popped open the bonnet and retrieved the pistol, which he checked and shoved into his waistband. It was time to go shopping.

Back at the farm, he'd made a list of items he'd need for the long trip across the ocean. He'd secreted that list under the carpet of the Range Rover and now he studied it again by the light of a small torch. The list wasn't long. If he was lucky, the boat he chose would have most of the items aboard. But first he had to find the right boat.

He walked beneath the trees until they gave way to an eight-foot high chain-link fence. Ahead, he could see the dark waters of the estuary that led out into the Solent, the moonlight dancing off its surface. He peered through the fence into the marina for several minutes. He didn't spot any movement, but he could hear the soft slap of water on fibreglass hulls, the unmistakable sound of yachts tied alongside jetties. A soft breeze moaned through the mastheads and, somewhere across the estuary, a dog barked.

Khan lifted himself over the fence and dropped noiselessly to the grass on the other side. Ahead of him was a vast network of moorings that looked to be pretty full. He walked slowly across to the nearest jetty and began his search. If he was going to find a boat it would be here.

Khan took his time, walking slowly up and down the network of jetties and inspecting the myriad of different boats. Everything seemed to be moored here, from small dinghies and skiffs to luxury motor cruisers and–

The boat that grabbed his attention suddenly loomed out of the darkness in front of him. He stopped, turning slowly as he scanned the area around him. Still nothing. Good. He turned back and walked towards the yacht, running a hand admiringly along her stainless steel rail. She was beautiful.

The *Sunflower* was an Oyster 68, a sleek, superbly appointed ocean-going yacht that had a solid reputation for strength and reliability. It was the type of boat he'd learned to sail on, although that was the much smaller model. The *Sunflower* was not that much different in terms of sailing, although she was probably designed to be handled by more than one person. But so far it was the only boat that Khan had seen that he felt immediately comfortable with. It wouldn't hurt to take a look. He checked the area once again and slipped quietly aboard.

On deck, the first thing he noticed was that all the ropes were where they should be, the right amount and length, all expertly tied off. The boat was secured fore and aft and the fly bridge situated amidships was sealed tightly with a waterproof cover. Except for one corner. Khan lifted up the flap and peered underneath. The cabin below was in complete darkness. He reached for his torch and flicked it on, waving it around the cabin area. Satisfied, he crouched under the flap and stepped down the short staircase below.

The blow caught him full in the face and he staggered backwards in the darkness, cracking his skull on something hard. He bit his tongue sharply and cried out in pain, ending up on his backside in the gloom, the pistol skittering across the cabin floor. The taste of blood was thick in his mouth and his lip was split. He scrabbled around for his weapon, then froze when he heard the distinct *click-clack* of a round being chambered. A light shone in his face and a male voice, full of menace, spoke quietly in the darkness.

'What the hell do you think you're doing on this boat?'

Khan almost smiled. Just his luck to pick a boat that was occupied. Still, the man was hiding too, so maybe they had something in common. Instinct told him to tell the truth.

'Well, I was planning to steal it. Looks like I'll have to try elsewhere. Now, if you'll excuse me…' He made an effort to get up, but the pistol was suddenly thrust in his face, the barrel an inch from his nose. He eased himself back down and leaned against the cabin wall.

'Don't be so bloody smart. And don't think I don't know how to use this.' The man rattled the gun in the darkness. 'Now, who are you and what the hell is going on?'

Khan was beginning to lose patience. In a few hours the sky would start to lighten in the east. His plan was to be on the water before dawn and to have cleared the Solent by the time the sun had fully risen. It wasn't a journey he wanted to attempt in daylight, mindful of Arabian shipping. He reached into his pocket for a handkerchief and dabbed at his mouth. With his other hand he felt the growing lump on the back of his head. Luckily the skin was unbroken. Khan squinted, looking up into the light, his own pistol pointed at his chest. He was wasting time here.

'Look, I'm sorry, okay? I'm taking a long voyage and I need a deep-water vessel that's up to the trip. This boat fitted the bill.'

'Where are you headed?' asked the voice behind the torch.

Khan squinted into the light. 'The States.' He was desperate to get going. He jerked a thumb over his shoulder. 'Don't you realise what's going on out there? Where have you been for the last thirty-odd hours? The country's under attack, did you know that?' Khan pushed himself to his knees and this time the voice didn't object. 'Look, I'm sorry about your boat, but if I don't leave, then my life will be in danger. So either shoot me or let me go.'

The torch clicked off, replaced by the warm glow of cabin lights. The man that stood before him appeared to be in his mid-forties, with short-cropped grey hair and sporting a couple of days' worth of stubble. He wore a pair of khaki trousers and a blue, open-necked shirt. The gun was still in his hand, but the barrel was now pointed at the deck. He held out his other hand, which Khan took, and helped him to his feet.

'Thanks,' said Khan.

'Sorry about your jaw. Couple of the boats here have been stolen since yesterday.' The man opened an overhead cupboard, producing a large medical kit. 'Here.'

Khan fished inside and dabbed his lip with a cotton ball and some antiseptic, wincing painfully. He looked around the cabin. It was magnificent, almost brand new he guessed, with teak decking and wall panelling, and a luxury raised seating area that looked out through forward-facing windows. There was a well-appointed kitchen and all the other fineries that one might expect from a state-of-the-art boat. Khan was impressed.

'She's beautiful.'

'She is. What's your name?'

'Danesh. Danesh Khan.'

'Patrick Clarke. So, what's going on out there? All I get on the radio is some bloody government message, some sort of national emergency or something. I heard there'd been rioting in Southampton. A lot of people here have packed up and gone.'

'There is no government,' Khan told him. 'London is a war zone and you can forget Europe too.' Khan spent the next few minutes explaining who he was and recounting the events of the last thirty-six hours.

'Jesus,' was all Clarke could whisper when he'd finished. He flopped down at the chart table, the Glock still in his hand. 'That explains the helicopters, the flashes on the horizon. No wonder it's deserted around here.'

'It's going to get worse. Right now, the Arabian military is pouring equipment into the country. They're using the docks at Southampton, probably others along the coast. The clock's ticking, Patrick. Pretty soon they'll have everything locked down and we'll be under martial law. That's why I'm leaving. I think the only friends we have left are the Yanks, so I'm heading for the States.'

Clarke stared at the table, deep in thought. Then he looked up. 'You've done that route before?'

'No. Been as far as the Azores though, several times. I was planning to pick up the trade winds from there.'

'Tricky this time of year,' Clarke warned. 'Almost hurricane season. Better to head further south, Cape Verde, then head westwards. What about your family?'

Khan shrugged. 'I'm single. Parents are dead. You?'

'Wife and sons are in Martha's Vineyard. I've got a place out there. They left a week ago.'

'Lucky.'

'Right. I'm supposed to join them next week, but then all this kicked off. I was here in Hamble when it started. Came down to do a bit of work on the boat.'

Khan held out his hand. 'Think I could have my weapon back?'

Clarke stared at him for a moment. 'What?' He looked at the gun in his hand. 'Oh. Yes, of course.'

Khan took the gun and made it safe, tucking it back into his jeans. 'Where did you learn to shoot?'

'The States. I keep a gun on the property there.'

'Very wise. How long do you intend to hide out down here?'

Clarke shook his head. 'I'm not hiding.'

Khan frowned. 'What d'you mean?'

'I've been watching the chandlery,' Clarke explained, 'but I fell asleep.

Then you woke me up.'

'The chandlery? What for?'

'Supplies. Place has been closed since I got here. Obviously the owners have other priorities, but I need to get in there. I've got a very long shopping list.' Clarke smiled. 'You're not the only one with dishonest intentions around here.'

Khan raised an optimistic eyebrow. 'What do you need supplies for?

'You say you want to head for the States?' Khan nodded. 'Good, because that's where my family is. I've done the crossing before and the *Sunflower* is certainly up for the job, but I could really use a mate. Help me skipper her home, Danesh. You'd be doing us both a favour.'

Khan let out a long breath. He'd been lucky so far, but this bordered on something else, a more divine hand at work. For the last few years he'd used his religion like a tool, a key to a door behind which lurked a shadowy world of terror cells, plots and conspiracies. He'd lost touch with the true meaning of faith, its purpose and strength. And its signs.

'You're on,' he said, taking Clarke's outstretched hand. 'I'll push the trolley, but let's make it quick. The noose is already tightening.'

They put to sea almost two hours later. Under engine power, the *Sunflower* cruised quietly through the still waters of the River Hamble and out into the Solent, turning south towards Cowes on the Isle of Wight. Khan and Clarke stood behind the twin steering wheels as the boat made steady progress towards the open waters of the English Channel. Clarke suggested that they wait until they were out of the Channel before unfurling the huge white sails that would be seen for miles.

The boat was indeed everything Khan thought it would be. Everything was automated, including the sail rigging and the boat's navigation systems, and the automatic pilot was online and functioning. The sophisticated radar told them that there were two large freighters steaming up from the south towards East Solent, but the *Sunflower* would pass well ahead of them. It turned out Clarke was a serious sailor, a hobby that had blossomed into a passion over the years, financially aided by the public floatation of his communications company. He recommended hugging the coastline until they were well clear of the major shipping lanes, before heading out into the Atlantic. Khan agreed.

As they reached Calshot Spit, Khan turned and looked back towards the eastern docks a few miles behind them. The horizon was dotted with powerful arc lights that blazed along the miles of dockside. The Arabians weren't bothering with camouflage or light-discipline drills, unconcerned by a British counter-attack. That in itself spoke volumes. The *Sunflower* continued onwards, rounding the point and heading south-west towards Hurst Spit. Beyond that, the open waters of the English Channel beckoned.

The helicopter came in unexpectedly from the north as the *Sunflower* glided past the Beaulieu Estuary at four knots. In a few seconds, the distant throbbing turned into a thunderous hammer beat as an Arabian gunship headed straight for the sailing boat from the darkness of the New Forest. Khan shoved Clarke below and ordered him to stay put.

Suddenly, the *Sunflower* was bathed in a powerful searchlight. Khan's hands went immediately to the boat's controls, quickly setting their course and flicking on the autopilot. The helicopter, a huge, black shape silhouetted against the night sky, spun over the boat and hovered fifty feet off the port bow like a giant, deadly dragonfly. Khan could see the pilots, their faces lit by the green wash of the cockpit instrumentation. His eyes tracked slowly back to the open compartment behind the cockpit, where a crewman sat behind a wicked-looking mini gun. Waving stupidly and sporting a wide grin, Khan reached for the rope behind him. Earlier, while Clarke prepared the boat for sail, Khan had slipped back on shore. There was one other item he wanted, something he thought may come in useful.

As the rotor wash of the gunship battered the *Sunflower*, Khan's hand yanked the rope and the large, green and white Arabian flag unfurled on the flagpole and snapped outwards, fluttering behind the *Sunflower* in the offshore breeze. Khan continued to wave and grin stupidly, all the time praying that the helicopter would leave them alone.

'What do you think?' asked the captain of the gunship.

'Nice boat,' replied the co-pilot. Their earpieces hissed as the door gunner behind them keyed his microphone.

'Want me to put a few rounds into the water, get him to heave to?'

The captain considered that while he interrogated his on-board camera system. Khan's beaming face was displayed in tight close-up, his hand shielding his eyes from the searchlight, while his hair and clothing were whipped by the downwash of the helicopter.

'He looks like one of ours. Besides, we're low on fuel and we haven't got the time. Funny hour to be out sailing though.'

'Agreed,' said the co-pilot. 'Pick him up later?'

The captain traced his finger along an electronic map display. 'Maybe.'

'Shall we alert a patrol boat?'

Khan's beaming smile and continuously waving arm filled the screen inside the gunship. 'Negative. Look at that stupid grin. He's probably an officer, helping himself to some local booty. If that's the case, then good luck to him. I'm looking to get something out of this myself.'

'Oh? Like what?' asked the co-pilot.

'I hear apartments will be made available to officers who were in the first wave. Accommodation in the more fashionable districts of London.'

'Really? Who told you that?'

'Just a rumour I heard. In the meantime, let's get this bird back to base. I could use a coffee.'

'Roger that.'

Khan lowered his arm as the searchlight blinked out and the helicopter banked away, lost in the darkness. A million coloured spots danced before his eyes as they grew accustomed to the gloom once again. At his feet, the cabin door moved a crack and he heard Clarke's voice.

'Have they gone?'

'Looks like it. Stay put a while longer, just in case.'

Khan's heart pounded in his chest. Another gut-wrenching moment, one of a series that seemed to have lasted for days. In reality it was less than two. I'll be grey-haired by the time we reach the States, he thought.

The *Sunflower* continued onwards without further incident, cutting quietly through the dark Channel. Clarke was back skippering the boat when Khan appeared from below with two cups of freshly brewed coffee. To the east the sky was just beginning to lighten.

'Thanks,' said Clarke, sipping the steaming brew carefully. 'So far, so good, eh?'

'We're not out of the woods yet.'

'True. But I've got a good feeling, same feeling I had about this boat the first time I stepped aboard her.' He put his brew down and smiled. 'This is going to sound a bit weird, but three days ago I was in London, working, when I got a sudden urge to come down here, to the *Sunflower*. That night I packed a bag and drove down to the coast. Didn't think much of it at the time.' Clarke gently tapped the gleaming fibreglass of the instrument housing. 'You may laugh, but the more I think about it the more I believe she was calling me. She called you too, you know, brought us together. That's why I've got a good feeling about this trip.'

Ordinarily Khan wasn't superstitious. He was more used to living and working on the darker fringes of society, where sound intelligence and careful planning altered the gameplay, not luck or chance. But Clarke had a point, had felt compelled to travel to Hamble on a feeling. And it had saved him.

Khan's thoughts turned again to the possibility of a more powerful force at work, the same force that had protected him thus far, had guided him to the *Sunflower* where another man waited in the darkness, a man who'd also been called. Clarke was almost right; it wasn't the *Sunflower* that had brought them together. It was God. And He would see them safely across the ocean.

Khan took a deep breath of salty air and smiled in spite of himself. 'I think you're right, Patrick. I think we're going to make it.'

'Look.' Clarke pointed to a dark headland off the starboard bow that jutted out into the sea. 'That's Hurst Spit. After that we're in the Channel.'

'Open water,' realised Khan.

'Correct. Once we're past the spit we'll set the pilot and go below, take a look at the charts.'

'Aye aye, captain,' smiled Khan, throwing up a mock salute. Their laughter echoed across the dark waters of the Solent.

Baghdad

It could have been much worse, Mousa reflected, stamping on the accelerator and powering the Mercedes saloon past a slow-moving livestock truck. He could've been demoted, flogged – even executed – but deep down he knew it wouldn't have come to that.

He glanced out of the window as he swept past the rumbling vehicle, at the rows of sheep that stared back at him from between the wooden slats, marking his passage with tired bleats and cold, dead eyes. Mousa smiled. They reminded him of the elders, the twelve jurists and clerics of the Guardian Council who'd presided over his recent military tribunal at the Palace of Justice in central Baghdad. The cleric, clearly intending to distance himself from the proceedings, had observed them discreetly, sometimes seated near the back of the hall, occasionally settling into the witness gallery above the marbled floor.

Mousa had dreaded meeting him, for once at a loss as to how to explain his actions, his blatant insubordination. But after arriving in Baghdad, the Holy One hadn't summoned him at all. For the first time in his life Mousa had felt exposed, naked. That first morning, standing alone in the defendant's box (he'd refused legal counsel), Mousa had briefly caught the Holy One's eye. When he did, he'd registered the disappointment behind the round spectacles and felt utterly shameful. He cared not for the judgements of the old men ranged before him on their ornate stage, only for the approval, and absolution, of the Holy One whom he'd so publicly disobeyed.

Mousa turned the wheel and cut across the highway, hitting the off-ramp at al-Qahira, squinting as the rising sun caught the burnished domes of the grand mosque that dominated the near horizon, casting its golden rays across the city. He fished in the glovebox for a pair of sunglasses and slipped them on, heading north on the empty Ali-Talib highway that would take him beyond the city limits. He crossed the Army Canal, leaving the gleaming towers of the business district behind him, and cruised by the smarter suburbs of Ash Sha'b and Hayy Sumar, their palm-lined avenues giving way to open fields beyond.

Mousa still marvelled at Baghdad's transformation, its once-teeming slums bulldozed, the residents banished to other districts, the new suburbs a lush network of low-rise homes and green parks. Now only the affluent and the influential travelled the city's wide highways and occupied its gleaming marble and glass buildings, the capital of Arabia twinkling like a diamond in the sand by day, and like a bright constellation of stars at night.

Until recently, Mousa thought of himself as one of those influential personalities, his rank, reputation and proximity to the Holy One ensuring no door remained unopened, no order questioned. Now it was different. Word had spread of his tribunal, of the witnesses that had flown in from the European front to give evidence against him, including the preening Al-Bitruji, who'd marched into the courtroom with a confident stride and a grave look across his fat face. Mousa knew it was an act, knew the man was revelling in Mousa's downfall.

Mousa had glowered at him as he gave evidence, causing Al-Bitruji to stumble and stammer through the weasel words of his prepared statement, the one that told of lost aircraft, tanks and men. He could've killed him on the spot, knowing that Al-Bitruji had leaked news of Mousa's failure and insubordination to his contacts in Baghdad, that he lacked a soldier's guts to do anything decisive himself, preferring instead to gossip like an old woman in the marketplace. Others had stepped forward too, from the command bunker in Grovely Wood, from Air Command at Heathrow, all allied to Al-Bitruji and eager to drive another nail into Mousa's coffin. And that, Mousa was now convinced, had been their undoing.

As day three of his hearing had opened, the remainder of Al-Bitruji's snakes had slithered into the witness stand and hissed their betrayal. Forced to endure their whining condemnations, Mousa had burned with rage as he glared at the traitors across the marble chamber.

It was then he'd noticed the Holy One again, flanked by two bodyguards as he watched from the shadows of the pillars that circled the hall, his lined face suddenly pained. No, it was more than that, Mousa had decided; there he stood, the Holy One's trusted confidant, having to suffer the betrayals of those less loyal, less devoted, and certainly less capable than himself. Mousa had felt it then, a shift in the wind that blew against him, a turning of the tide indicated by the subtle nod of the Holy One as he caught Mousa's glance. To be summoned here, to face the shame of a public hearing, was punishment enough for a man like Mousa. The Holy One must have known that, had seen the indignity etched on Mousa's face, but the rituals had to be observed, the game played out to its conclusion.

The Guardian Council had made him wait for its judgement, three more days in fact, but the final outcome was one Mousa had begun to suspect. He'd stood straight and tall, resplendent in his best dress uniform, his back ramrod straight, his eyes staring off into the middle distance as the elders passed down their judgement: banishment from the European theatre, a temporary attachment to an obscure military academy in Damascus, and a purse to be paid to the families of the dead soldiers and airmen, all one hundred and seventy-four of them.

The council had been lenient, their spokesman informed him. Mousa was relieved to have avoided the disgrace of demotion, yet it was on his lips to demand it, to be sent back to the European front as a mere private; combat was a far more attractive proposition than wasting his days giving lectures to officer cadets. Instead, he kept his mouth shut. He'd been saved by the Holy One, of that he was sure. Only time, and the course of action he'd now chosen to take, would tell whether he was right or not.

So now, the road ahead was practically empty, only the odd farm truck or military vehicle sharing the six-lane highway with his Mercedes saloon. He powered the window down, letting the warm breeze ruffle his hair. It needed cutting, as did the dark stubble on his face that reached down to the thick black curls that sprang from the open neck of his navy linen shirt. But he would get around to it, when the movement order to Damascus finally materialised. In the meantime, he would relax, keep a low profile. And visit old friends.

He was dressed casually, in jeans and trainers, a white *galabiyya* gown on the seat behind him should the need arise to change into more modest attire. He didn't expect to today, however. At the side of the road a movement caught his eye, and in the shadows of a nearby palm grove he spotted a cluster of military vehicles, one of the many air defence teams that marked the outer boundary of the city. The wind snatched at the smoke of cooking fires and ruffled the camouflage nets, the sun dappling across the tips of the surface-to-air missiles beneath. So far Baghdad hadn't been threatened, and nor did Mousa expect it to be. As long as the Israelis stayed out of the fight.

Another two hours had passed before Mousa turned off the highway, heading north-east across the flood plains of southern Salah ad Din, the fields on either side of the road thick with summer crops, the water treatment systems whipping spray across armies of swaying corn stalks. Ahead, the Tigris river beckoned, marked by the thick forests of palms that lined its banks.

He turned off the asphalt, on to the dirt track that twisted its way deep into the palms. The track ended at a large clearing, the steel gate of the compound opened by a young boy who swung it closed again and slammed the bolt home as Mousa drove through. He watched the boy scamper inside the villa as he climbed out of the dust-covered Mercedes and stretched his limbs. The sun was higher now, climbing towards its zenith, but the rising heat was tempered by the surrounding forest, by the breezes that came off the nearby Tigris.

'You're getting old, General.'

Mousa spun around, surprised to see the man behind him, his approach silent, the two fingers jammed into his spine like steel rods. For a man in his seventies it was impressive.

'Bullshit. Those creaking bones of yours make far too much noise. I was just being polite.' Then they embraced and shook hands warmly, each man planting a small kiss on the other's cheeks.

'It's good to see you, Zaid.'

'Salaam alaikum, my friend. It's an honour to have you here,' smiled the old man. 'Come.' He beckoned Mousa to follow him. Zaid had aged some, but remained fit, the barrel chest that swelled against the white vest still formidable, the posture erect, the stride confident. And he still wore the trademark combat trousers he'd always worn, the green and black tiger stripes of the old Iraqi marines. No boots though, Mousa noticed, just the leather sandals that slapped against his feet as they circumnavigated the villa. How had he managed to sneak up on him wearing those?

The place hadn't changed much since Mousa was last here. The cars and pickups still nestled in the shade of the palms, all foreign imports of course, as was the impressive cluster of high-tech satellite dishes that beamed their unfettered TV and radio signals directly into Zaid's home. The grounds were well kept, the lawns trimmed, the vivid flowerbeds carefully attended to, and Mousa had to smile. Zaid had done very well for himself, had worked hard to maintain his privacy. Beyond the walls of the compound he was a man of mystery, the old soldier that lived quietly out by the Tigris with his extended family, with connections to powerful people in Baghdad. People like Mousa.

He followed Zaid around the grounds of the whitewashed villa to an impressive shaded veranda where lunch was being prepared. Mousa caught the smell of barbequed lamb as a group of women in colourful saris and sequinned headscarves fussed over a huge table laid out with covered plates of bread, rice and salads. Beyond the veranda, a grass bank sloped down towards the clear waters of the Tigris. A group of children played football nearby, while a couple of older boys sat on the edge of a small wooden jetty, fishing rods dipping towards the slow-moving waters.

'Allah has truly blessed you,' Mousa observed.

'In every way,' Zaid agreed. He led Mousa to a table in the shade of a tall palm. A few metres away, the river lapped against the bank. A pot of coffee was delivered by a middle-aged woman, her attractive face framed by a white veil. No doubt one of Zaid's eight daughters, Mousa guessed. Then they were alone.

'Speaking of blessings, I hear you got lucky with the council,' Zaid observed.

Mousa raised an eyebrow. 'Word travels fast.'

'I still have contacts.'

'In any case, the council had little to do with the decision.'

'You always were his favourite,' Zaid remarked with a wry grin.

'You know what that's like.'

'Different rulers, different times,' the older man observed. 'Saddam was a little more intense. Even bodyguards like me were not immune to his rages.'

Mousa took a careful sip of the bitter coffee. 'Still, the Cleric is a different man entirely. He dislikes the base nature of politics, the compromises, the infighting. And yet, look at us now, how he's brought us together, under one flag, one nation.'

'I never thought I'd see it in my lifetime,' Zaid admitted. 'The caliphate restored, an empire stretching all the way to the English Channel and beyond. Makes an old man's heart sing.'

A dhow drifted into view around the bend in the river, its sail filled, its small deck laden with cargo. The children ran to the end of the jetty, waving frantically. The distant pilot waved back and the children squealed with delight. Zaid chuckled and lit a cigarette with a Zippo lighter, the emblem of the United States Marine Corps emblazoned on its brass flanks. He caught Mousa's inquiring eye.

'Fallujah,' he explained, sucking the strong Turkish tobacco deep into his lungs. 'So, Faris, what brings you here, to this quiet little backwater? You know I'm retired, yes?'

Mousa saw the glint in the old man's clear blue eyes and chuckled. Zaid would never retire, not until he took his last breath. He'd first met Zaid Hadi when he'd joined the military academy all those years ago, the tough combat instructor who'd fought the Americans across Iraq, the British in Helmand, the Jews in Gaza. When the caliphate had risen once more and Mousa had moved into special forces, he'd called on Zaid's skill and experience many times, fighting side by side on countless operations in Nigeria, Kurdistan and across the Middle East. Zaid was a legend, a man whose speed and agility had long deserted him, yet even today his formidable reputation remained unequalled.

Mousa glanced over his shoulder, at the women who were preparing the food, at the children playing and fishing nearby.

'They are deaf and blind to your presence, Faris. You may speak freely,' invited Zaid.

Mousa settled back into his chair. He kept his voice low, his eyes watching the surrounding trees, the river, the shadows of the opposite bank. 'So, these contacts of yours, did they tell you of my punishment?'

Zaid nodded. 'Banished from Europe. For men like us, a life without the taste of combat is a life barely worth living. Am I right?'

'As always,' Mousa admitted, 'but it gets worse. I have spoken with my subordinate in England, a Major Karroubi. You know of him?' Zaid shook his head. 'He informs me that the British continue to strengthen their defences along the Scottish border. Our own forces are moving steadily north, taking control of more towns and cities. There has been some fighting, but not much. Most of the infidel soldiers have escaped across the border. They are digging in, preparing for a fight. This could be the last campaign for the foreseeable future. Perhaps the last significant one of my career.'

'What about the Chinese?' Zaid remarked, crushing the butt of his cigarette on the sole of his sandal.

Mousa shook his head. 'The Cleric is wary of their power. Besides, Europe must be conquered first before he'll consider such a campaign. Peace and stability must exist across the empire before we turn our guns to the East. His words, not mine.'

Zaid nodded. 'So, the clock is ticking.'

'Correct.'

'You want back in.'

'Of course. The battle for Scotland will be significant,' Mousa breathed, 'and the infidels will fight like cornered rats. The thought of watching it all on TV in some Damascus officers' mess is... well, I'd rather put a bullet through my brain.'

'Enough of the drama,' Zaid laughed. He leaned forward on the table, his fingers toying with the brass lighter. 'I get it. And frankly I'd feel exactly the same. So, what is it I can do for you?'

'I need a team,' Mousa explained, 'all professionals, discreet. And loyal.'

'To you?'

'To you,' stressed Mousa. 'You once said you knew London. You had people there.'

'Since the early days,' admitted Zaid. 'They are old now, like me, but the flame of jihad has always burned brightly in England. The right people will be found. What's the job?'

So Mousa explained. When he was finished, Zaid leaned back in his chair and lit another cigarette. 'It can be done. The repercussions, however, will be another matter. Are you sure about this, Faris?'

'Let me worry about the fallout. In the meantime we plan, nail down the details. The good news is it isn't a complex op. It's merely about timing and execution. And deniability. Karroubi will provide the necessary local intelligence. The rest will be up to you.'

'Okay.'

'And from now on, no direct contact. We'll use the Baghdad Business News forum to update each other. You still have the usernames and ciphers, yes?' Zaid nodded. 'Good. We'll keep our distance, until it's over and the dust has settled. And today's visit–'

'–never happened. I know the drill,' smiled Zaid. He took another pull of his cigarette and let the smoke drift slowly from his nostrils. 'What a gift to be young again, eh? I would go to London myself to squeeze the trigger.'

'I know.'

'This kind of op reminds me of North Africa, during the Arab Spring.'

'I was a teenager,' Mousa reminded him. 'I watched it on the TV.'

'The uprisings, the assassinations, ops on the fly, no satellites or intel briefs, just six guys around a kitchen table, map spread out, AKs and grenades at the ready. Those were good times.'

'The birth of the caliphate,' stated Mousa.

'Right. And the West just lapped us up, all those infidel governments cheering us on, wailing about democracy, only to see their puppets eventually replaced by true Islamic governments.' Zaid shook his bald head. 'Fools. Blind and stupid.'

'Their naivety has always been pitiful,' Mousa agreed, finishing off his coffee. The children were called to the house and they raced across the lawn, their laughter filling the air. Mousa watched them as they scampered around the dining table and took their places, tiny legs dangling from chairs, wide eyes staring at the feast before them. He glanced at Zaid. 'Like I said, you're truly blessed.'

'Grandchildren,' Zaid sighed. 'Wonderful to have, but so many? What were my girls thinking!'

Mousa smiled. Zaid's family was everything to him. It was one of the reasons the man had fought so hard on the battlefield, had killed with a ruthlessness Mousa had rarely seen, believing at one time that Zaid's character was flawed, that perhaps his mind had been scarred by the experience of war. But he'd been wrong. As Mousa had discovered as the men had grown close, Zaid had killed so that he may live and return home, to the wife he loved, to his children.

Mousa looked around again, at the sprawling villa, the sculptured grounds, the idyllic setting. This is what Zaid had fought and killed for, a chance to see out his days in peace and comfort, to care for his family, watch them grow. Mousa was troubled by a sudden pang of envy, the choices he'd made, the Spartan existence he led, the loneliness that sometimes woke him during the night. He quickly banished the thoughts, mindful of the reasons that brought him here today, the days and weeks, perhaps months ahead that would pass agonisingly slowly as he cooled his heels in a Damascus military camp. This was no time for sentimentality.

'You'll stay for lunch,' Zaid said, rising to his feet.

'Of course.'

They strolled towards the veranda, where the women were shuttling in and out of the villa, their arms laden with platters of barbecued lamb. The children cooed and gasped excitedly.

'There is another matter,' Mousa ventured quietly as they crossed the lawn.

Zaid came to a stop. 'Oh?'

'The death tax, the payment to the families of the dead,' Mousa explained quietly, turning his back to the veranda. 'All one hundred and seventy-four of them.'

'Yes, the other terms of your punishment,' Zaid chuckled. 'I was wondering when you'd get round to that. What with travel and funeral costs, compensation to the families, it'll all come to a pretty penny, even on a major general's salary. Still, since you've been away I guess you haven't spent that much.'

Mousa could see amusement dancing behind the man's eyes, the lines that deepened as the smile widened. He tried and failed to control his own smile.

'Don't play with me, Sergeant Hadi. Saddam's gold – I take it you haven't spent it all?'

'It would take several lifetimes to spend what is buried under our feet,' Zaid laughed, tapping the grass with his sandal. 'Take what you need, Faris. But first we eat.'

Mousa nodded his thanks, the financial burden lifted from his shoulders at least. The rest was out of his hands, but the dice had now been thrown and Mousa had always been lucky. He smiled and slapped his old staff sergeant on the back.

'Lead on, my friend. You know, for the first time in a week I'm actually hungry.'

McIntyre Castle

Harry trudged along the narrow woodland path, wet ferns brushing against his legs. A bird screeched high overhead, its forlorn cry echoing around the forest. Harry craned his neck, trying to catch sight of it, but the thick canopy above and the gloom of the dawn gave him little chance, and soon the screeching faded into the distance. He kept walking, head down, his hands thrust deep into the pockets of his raincoat.

He'd woken before dawn and breakfasted alone, eager to escape the confines of the castle, deciding to take a long walk through the grounds. Clothed in wet-weather gear, Harry had left the castle just as the first of the sun's rays painted the eastern horizon. Halfway across the gravel drive he'd heard the crunch of footsteps behind him. Gibson and Farrell had appeared, dressed in civilian clothes, and Harry had waved them away bad-temperedly. However, despite his protests, he knew they were still out there somewhere, amongst the trees, shadowing his movements. Their unseen presence only added to the mounting stress he'd begun to feel as the days turned to weeks. He knew the breakdown was coming, could feel it building with each passing day, the outbursts of temper, the lapses in concentration, the worried glances of those around him.

He wanted to run, to escape the eyes and whispers, to confront the demons that plagued him and scream until his lungs burst. But he didn't. He kept it in, lied to the doctor, flushed the pills down the toilet and drank too much at night. Walking, that was good – the fresh air, the exercise. So he'd taken to following the paths each morning, stamping around the surrounding forests, hoping for the weight to lift from his shoulders, for the black clouds to clear from his mind. The weeks had passed and he'd remained shackled by the chains of his emotions. Until this morning.

The tears had started not long after Harry had risen. He'd cuffed them away, stifled the involuntary sob that escaped his lips as he shaved. At breakfast he'd pushed the food around his plate, frightened by his fragile emotional state. Now, deep in the forest, the tears came again, coursing down his cheeks, the panic building in his chest. He began to speed up, walking faster along the path, trying to outpace the building pressure. He broke into a jog, his breath coming in ragged gasps, his vision blurred by tears.

He stumbled, then fell, lying prone on the woodland path. He rolled over on to his back, unable to move, paralysed by fear, guilt. And sorrow. He gave into it then, made no attempt to stem the tears, the mournful wails that broke the silence of the morning, echoing through the trees.

He beat his fists on the ground until his hands hurt. He curled into a ball, clutching his knees tightly, rocking himself on the forest floor, crying until he was spent.

Eventually, the convulsions stopped and Harry lay motionless, listening to the breeze that whispered through the shifting treetops above him. Time passed, how long Harry didn't know, but the grey clouds overhead eventually brought a fine rain drifting through the trees. He sat up. The demons had finally been confronted, the weight that had crushed him lifted. How long for he couldn't know, but the panic had abated. Slowly he dragged himself to his feet and brushed away the woodland debris that clung to his clothes. He felt spent, but better, if that was the appropriate word. He believed it was.

'Anna's dead,' he told the trees around him. 'She's not coming back.' It felt right to say it aloud, to face the reality of life without her. The road ahead would be tough, the future uncertain, and the pain... well, like all things, that would pass in time. He felt his strength returning, the black fog drifting away towards the far reaches of his consciousness.

There was work to do, a crisis to focus on. The weight of expectation lay heavy on his shoulders. He was prime minister after all, and he had a duty to a country that was still in turmoil. That had to be his motivation now. Like so many others, he'd suffered devastating loss, but there were other considerations too, the details that would help him put his own loss into perspective.

Anna was an adult, and had died instantly. She hadn't suffered, was probably unaware of the danger to her life, even up to the moment of her death. But what about the others, the children dying in front of their parents, the old and the infirm cowering in fear behind their front doors, the system that cared for them suddenly snatched away? He was joined to these people now, connected by the horrors of war, a war being fought and lost on English soil, the population reduced to a frightened herd. They needed him, as much as he needed them.

He resumed his walk, conscious of the time that had passed. With each step, Harry began to feel a little better. He knew the pain would be back, but maybe not for a while and maybe not as intense. For now he felt he could function again.

The path led Harry out of the forest and along the shoreline. Around him, steep hillsides swept majestically upwards towards the grey skies above, their sharp flanks dotted with swathes of purple heather. Harry walked down to the shoreline and stood for a moment, the cold, slate-coloured waters of the Sound of Kerrera lapping at his feet. A mile away, across the sound, the island of Kerrera was still shrouded in an early-morning mist. He pulled the map from his pocket, deciding to loop back around McIntyre through the forest to the north. The peace and solitude of the morning were comforting, and Harry had no desire to rush back to the business of war just yet. Another hour's exercise would do him some good.

He pushed on, through the northern forest and up through the rocks of a prominent escarpment that overlooked the sound. Above the treeline, limbs aching, Harry sat down on a smooth rock to catch his breath. From up here the view was magnificent. He could see the turrets of the castle in the distance and, out on the sound, a small motor boat left a wide wake on the glass-like surface. It really was a–

'Nice view, eh Boss?'

Harry spun around, startled to see Mike Gibson several feet above him, perched on a higher rock. He was dressed in waterproof trousers and a green fleece jacket, an automatic rifle cradled across his lap.

'Jesus Christ, Mike, you nearly gave me a heart attack. What are you doing up here?'

Gibson jerked a thumb at the escarpment behind him. 'There's an anti-aircraft battery up there near the summit. We saw you heading this way, so I thought I'd get here first, just in case you stumbled into them. Everyone's a bit jumpy at the moment.'

'Of course,' said Harry soberly.

Gibson climbed down. There was an awkward silence for a moment or two and Harry could see doubt etched on the soldier's face, the unspoken question forming on his lips. He didn't want people worrying about his emotional state any more. There were so many other issues at stake and, besides, Harry had no room for self-pity.

'The business in the woods, Mike. I don't want you to be concerned.' Gibson started to protest but Harry held up a hand. 'It's been building for weeks, everyone knows that. I've been a bloody mess since we got here – the pressure, my own personal loss. Since all this started I've had no time to confront my grief. I think this morning, down there in the woods, my grief confronted me. Do you have family, Mike?'

Gibson shrugged. 'Got a sister. She lives in France, but we haven't spoken in years. Dad died before I was born and my mum went a few years later. There's no one else.'

'I'm sorry,' Harry murmured sympathetically, 'yet in some ways we're luckier than others. At least we're free of the burden of uncertainty.' He paused, then said, 'I take it Farrell saw my little episode too?' Gibson nodded. 'No one needs to know about this, Mike. I'm alright, really. Besides, there's work to be done and I need the distraction. I'd appreciate it if we could keep this between ourselves.'

Gibson looked at him long and hard, clearly making his own appraisal. Then he nodded. 'Sure, Boss. It's nobody's business but yours, anyway.'

Harry's eyes narrowed. 'Not true. My mental health is everyone's business, including yours. People's lives will depend on any future decisions I take. You could end my career with what you've seen today, and I wouldn't blame you if you felt that that was the right thing to do. But I feel I've got something back this morning. I feel ready again. You need to believe that, Mike.'

'No pressure then,' quipped Gibson, then the smile slipped from his face. 'Look, we all deal with things differently. I had problems when I was a kid, after mum died. Usual stuff – booze, scrapping. I could've gone bad, but the army saved me, gave me direction. I got a second chance. I understand what you're going through, Boss. I won't say anything.'

Harry closed his eyes for a moment, then held out his hand. 'Thanks, Mike.'

Gibson grasped it and the two men shook. 'No probs.'

Harry got to his feet, his eyes searching out the distant castle below. 'They're worried about me down there, and rightly so. I know there's been talk of replacing me.' He turned to the soldier beside him. 'I've been gone a long time, Mike. Questions will be asked.'

Gibson tapped the radio fixed to his chest rig. 'Already told them you're inspecting the hilltop defences. That you might be a while.'

Harry smiled. 'Thanks, Mike. I mean it.'

'We should get going,' Gibson replied, staring at the clouds overhead. 'Looks like more rain.'

Harry headed off, stepping carefully down between the rocks towards the treeline below. 'By the way, where is Farrell?' he asked over his shoulder.

'Waiting for us lower down. Said you were a fit old boy, that he couldn't keep up with you.'

Harry recognised the gesture for what it was and silently thanked him for it. He smiled to himself, feeling the strength returning as they headed down into the trees.

Consolidation

Dearest Brother,

I hope you and the family are well. At last we have been given a few days leave, so I thought I would write and tell you of some of the things I have seen during my time here in England. No doubt you've seen much of it on the news back home but I know you'd want to see it from a soldier's eye.

I should start by saying that the months of training, the secrecy and the enforced absences were all worth it; the drop over London was one of the most exciting things I have ever done. The jump itself lasted only a few seconds because we came in so low, but to drift down over one of the most famous cities in the world, to see it blacked out from horizon to horizon, was a surreal experience. My platoon was the first into Downing Street, into the heart of the enemy, and the destruction was unbelievable; praise to the martyrs for their sacrifice. We exchanged fire with some British troops later that night but suffered no losses, as their numbers were few and they had little ammunition. We took many prisoners in the first twenty-four hours.

You know of General Mousa, of course. Soon after we arrived in London he ordered us west, in helicopters this time, to attack a strong point in a place called the Mendip Hills. There was much fighting in the area and we lost several of our company. You remember my friend Rashid, from Mosul? He was killed by a British mortar round during the fighting and his loss was a real blow to us all. Such a funny guy, always joking. We've missed him a lot since then. To make things worse we later discovered that the operation was an unauthorised one and the general has been relieved of his command, which was regrettable because we'd all grown to respect him. He was a tough man, but fair.

Since that operation the fighting has more or less stopped. We've been told the British have fled to the north and have dug in all along the Scottish border. They're preparing for a fight, which is good. Maybe we'll get to jump again, into Scotland, behind their lines. As for our own forces, we've pushed as far north as Newcastle and Carlisle, which is about twenty kilometres from the border. (Funny names, I know. Look them up on a map.) For now we're keeping our distance, which is a mistake in my opinion. In the meantime, we've been ordered to hold and secure our positions. No one knows why, but the only thing we do know is that we've turned from soldiers into policemen.

The daytime curfew in London has been lifted and people are now venturing out on to the streets. Many of our Brothers and Sisters have turned out to greet us and there has been much celebration across the city. Arabian flags are flying from buildings and rooftops and it is a wonderful sight. I hear this is going on around other parts of the country and across Europe too. Have you seen much of it? The only thing being transmitted on the TV stations here are information messages, and all Internet and telecoms links are still shut down so we're in the dark most of the time.

As for the infidels, they are sullen and angry. You can see it in their faces, when they queue at the standpipes for water, or when they pass us on the street. Their eyes are downcast, but I do not believe they have accepted defeat yet. There have been one or two violent incidents and several rebels were publicly hanged in Hyde Park just last week, although I think these punishments may only strengthen their resolve. I'll be glad when we go operational again, get us off these dirty streets.

The good news is many British Brothers have joined our ranks as auxiliaries, manning roadblocks and policing their own communities, which has taken the burden off us a little. Many more have been helping to put out the fires around the city, some of which have been burning for weeks. A huge building near St. Paul's collapsed a few days ago, killing over a hundred people, and we've seen a couple of plane crash sites too, the biggest one in Trafalgar Square, an airbus. The square was obliterated and Nelson's Column was lying across the street in pieces. Someone had already taken off the head, a souvenir no doubt. But don't worry, little brother, I've kept a couple of things for you too.

Bodies are a real problem. When we find a Muslim victim they're handed over to the burial teams for interring according to custom. All the rest are loaded into trucks and dumped in pits outside the city. I've also heard there's an incinerator working around the clock somewhere in East London which wouldn't surprise me, considering the amount of corpses we've seen.

We were posted for a week to Wembley Stadium where a reception centre had been set up. It really is a magnificent sight and it reminded me of all the matches we watched together at home. Couldn't see the pitch though, as the grass had been covered with crates of supplies and other equipment. We used loudspeakers and leaflets in the area and the local population turned out in their thousands, queuing right around the outside of the stadium. In exchange for personal registration and an Arabian ID card they were given access to food stamps and medical care. Many of them were a real mess, while others had brought their dead with them, wrapped in sheets and plastic rubbish bags. Things must've been desperate in the early days. Still, no more desperate than those in Baghdad or Kabul, when the Crusaders invaded, am I right little brother? In any case, I had little sympathy for them.

Gas and electricity supplies are still scarce, but the water's back online and repairs are being carried out by forced labour gangs, infidel prisoners and suchlike. From what I've heard they're the lucky ones, but I'll get to that in a minute.

The only other action we've seen was the riot in Brixton, a slum district in South London. Apparently the invasion triggered a huge uprising there and the main street was burned to the ground. By the time the first Arabian forces got there hundreds had been killed, and gangs were still shooting each other across the whole area. We were bussed in from Central London a few days later. By that time the gangs had been pushed back into a row of tower blocks and surrounded with armour. We spent a couple of days getting civilians out of there and picking off the Kuffar with sniper fire, but they continued to fight, mostly with each other. We couldn't believe it. Rashid would've laughed at their stupidity. Anyway, the local commanders were keen to crush the uprising. They said it could sow the seeds of rebellion around the country and had to be stopped quickly. At that point we all thought we'd be tied up for days in house to house fighting, but the local command wanted to end the stalemate quickly so they came up with another solution.

On day three, just before dawn, everyone was ordered to withdraw from their positions. Me and a couple of other guys were manning an observation post in an apartment block opposite the estate when we got word, so we bugged out very quietly and pulled back to a point five hundred metres from our original position. Then we were told to take cover. A few minutes later, an air force transport flew over and dropped something. I must admit, when I first saw it floating down under a big white parachute I thought they were dropping supplies or something. Then I realised, and we scrambled behind a tank that had reversed behind a row of garages. Have you ever seen a MOAB bomb go off? Search for it on ArabNet and take a look. It's a thirty-thousand-pound airburst bomb.

The detonation was so loud, the ground shook so hard, that I thought the end had come. Even the tank rattled like a toy. It seemed to last for ages, and when the noise finally died down all you could hear were dogs barking and car alarms going off (well, the ones that weren't burned out anyway). Then we were ordered back to our positions. Every window in our observation post had been blown out. In fact, every window I could see. And the tower blocks? Gone, my brother. Vanished, vaporised, call it what you will. Just gone. When the dust *settled, all that was left were huge mountains of rubble, every building flattened like pitta bread.*

Some survived the detonation, though. They looked like ghosts because they were covered head to toe in white dust and they staggered all over the place. It was funny to watch them. Only a few made it out and that night the bulldozers came in. It took another two days but, by the time we got the order to withdraw, the roads had been cleared and the rubble piled high. The smell was getting very bad though, so it was a relief to leave. Since then there's been no trouble.

I guess that's because so many men and much equipment has arrived since June. Civilian transport is banned and the streets are busy with trucks and jeeps, with APCs and tanks at some of the more sensitive locations. Every plane and helicopter in the skies is one of ours, every ship at anchor offloading Arabian supplies. If there was any doubt that England is now ours, that doubt has been laid to rest. The rest of Europe, we are told, has already fallen.

Remember the 'lucky ones' I mentioned earlier? I got talking to a guy recently, a military cop, just arrived in London. He'd been here in England from the beginning and had seen quite a lot of action, mostly around the city of Birmingham to the north. Shortly after the British fled, his unit was tasked with administering to the prisoners, not POWs but the ones in England's gaols. It was a tough and gruesome job by his account.

Some prisons had been abandoned by the staff and many prisoners had died of thirst and malnutrition. Other prisons were destroyed, the rioters making off and leaving a trail of corpses in their wake. Those that remained were processed and formed into work groups to clear roads around the cities or remove bodies. As I said before, those were the lucky ones.

Of the thousands of prisoners taken into Arabian custody, many had committed appalling crimes: murder, rape, child abuse, drug trafficking. A decision was taken at the highest level, the cop told me. These men – and some women – were separated from the common criminals and bound in chains, along with the criminally insane from secure hospitals. The cop was there when they were transported to the east coast, thousands of them, and loaded on to a giant freighter that put to sea after dark. Thirty kilometres off the coast, the engines were cut and the crew, plus the cop and his escort team, climbed down on to a waiting navy boat. Ten minutes later and two kilometres away a button was pressed and an explosion ripped out the hull of the freighter.

He watched it go down. He said it sounded awful, the screech of metal as the vessel nosed beneath the sea, but not as bad as the screams of those still aboard. He said he could hear them as their cries echoed across the water. He said the sound would haunt him forever.

Anyway, it's good to know that we've rid ourselves of such animals. As for the other prisoners, the soldiers and policemen we've captured, they're also being ferried to ports on the south coast. They're headed back east to be processed, so I suppose you will see them before I do. Their fate will be a lot kinder, I'm sure.

So now we wait, little brother. The hope is we will head north soon, and prepare for the assault on Scotland that must surely come. Right now the curfew sirens are sounding across the city, so I must finish up and prepare for tonight's patrol. I will write to you again, when time allows and I have more news. I hope this letter finds you well. Give my love to mother and father, tell them not to worry and tell them, Insha'Allah, I will see them again.

Your loving brother, Rahman

Atlantic Ocean

The *Sunflower* sliced noiselessly through calm blue waters as it headed towards the eastern seaboard of the United States at a steady six knots. She was still over forty nautical miles off the North Carolina coast, but her recently issued orders were to maintain a specific course and speed and the *Sunflower* was adhering rigidly to those instructions.

For Khan and Clarke, it was their fifty-third day at sea. Although the *Sunflower* had performed beautifully, they'd encountered a depression eighty miles east of Cape Verde and that, combined with the weight of their overcompensated supplies and spares, prevented them from going faster than four knots in frustratingly calm seas. The autopilot and rigging system problems caused further delays, forcing the journey across the Atlantic to take much longer than expected.

Despite the temptation on seeing the lush coastline of Barbados, the *Sunflower* had bypassed the Caribbean and steered north under blue skies and fair winds, both men unsure of the political situation that could easily have changed across the islands in light of the crisis in Europe. The US was their destination and they were stopping for no one, avoiding the shipping lanes and steering clear of any distant vessels. It was time-consuming but safer, and safety had to be their main priority.

Three days earlier, with Bermuda far off their starboard bow, Clarke had finally reached his family on the satellite phone, and the two men had celebrated that night with an extra ration of tinned chicken curry and a bottle of Merlot. Khan cooked the curry but stuck to orange juice and they enjoyed a pleasant evening, Clarke's relief and excitement infecting them both. Later, Clarke had offered the phone to Khan, but he'd politely declined. There was no one to call.

The plane had appeared the day before, a rapidly approaching dot on the northern horizon that had morphed into a low-flying US Navy surveillance aircraft. As it circled above them, Khan had answered the urgent radio enquiry with the necessary information: boat name, registration, port of origin, crew details. The interrogation lasted over ten minutes until the navy radioman sounded satisfied. Their last instructions were to change course and maintain their new heading unless instructed otherwise.

After the aircraft had disappeared over the horizon, Khan and Clarke had checked the charts and plotted their probable destination – Virginia. They had originally planned to make landfall further north but, when the US Navy issued orders, it seemed prudent to follow them.

Khan emerged from the galley below with two steaming mugs of coffee. Clarke was up on deck behind the wheel, his eye monitoring the boat's systems. He took the proffered mug in both hands. The dawn air held a chill that both men felt and they protected themselves against the elements with fleece-lined waterproof jackets, courtesy of the marina in Hamble.

'Is it still there?' enquired Khan.

Clarke pointed to the console. The radar echo had appeared during the night and had shadowed the *Sunflower* ever since, sailing somewhere off their starboard bow. It was now moving towards an intercept point ahead, the courses slowly converging. There was a ship out there, a large one, and it was heading their way.

Khan gazed out at the early-morning mist that shrouded the *Sunflower*. It had appeared at dawn and descended over them like a grey cloak, restricting their visibility to a couple of hundred yards. The blip on the screen was big, and it was drawing steadily closer. A collision would be disastrous. As Khan slopped the dregs of his coffee over the side, the radio crackled on the control panel. Clarke twisted the volume knob.

'*Sunflower, Sunflower,* this is US Navy ship *Denver* requesting you heave to immediately.'

'Heaving to now,' replied Clarke. He glanced nervously at Khan. 'Here we go, then.'

The *Sunflower's* sails were lowered, while her twin engines gave them steerage control only. After a couple of minutes, the sailing boat was drifting with the current and riding the rhythmic swell of the Atlantic. The mist that enveloped them created an eerie backdrop to the tension of the moment, and the only sound they heard was the slap of water under the hull.

It started as a quiet hiss that grew in volume until a sharp, battle-grey bow with huge white lettering on its hull knifed through the mist and drifted smoothly past them. Khan and Clarke held on tight as the wake of the battlecruiser pitched the *Sunflower* from side to side. Along its rails, marines in full battle gear studied them with interest. Then the stern was past them and, once again, the ship was swallowed up by the mist. Silence descended on the *Sunflower*, broken only by the firm, southern twang of the voice behind them.

'Hands on your heads, please, gentlemen.'

Khan and Clarke nearly jumped out of their skins. Spinning around, they found themselves confronted by four US Marines in black tactical gear spread across the deck, their weapons held low but ready. Khan saw the small assault boat just off the port stern, its pilot holding the vessel steady as it bobbed up and down on the swell. Crafty bastards, admitted Khan. They had obviously used the battleship to disguise the smaller boat's approach. Both men put their hands on their heads. They were quickly and expertly frisked and their identification documents confiscated. Then the marines' attentions focussed on the *Sunflower*, which underwent a lengthy and thorough search. Khan and Clarke sat on the deck and watched. The marines hadn't bound their hands, simply requesting that the two Brits sit down and keep out of the way, which they did. After an hour the boarding party officer approached them.

'Gentlemen, thank you for your co-operation. Your ID checks out and the boat is clean, so you can continue on your journey. You are requested to head for the US naval base at Williamsburg, where you'll be debriefed. I believe you have the GPS co-ordinates and the *Denver* will escort you part of the way in.'

'Debrief?' Clarke looked worried.

'Standard procedure now,' the marine informed them. 'All our borders are closed. World's gone to shit, in case you hadn't noticed.'

'We noticed all right,' smiled Khan. 'Why d'you think we're here?'

'Smart move,' the marine replied. 'Well, that it. The *Sunflower* is cleared to proceed.' With that, the officer waved the assault boat alongside and the marines climbed aboard. As it pushed off, the officer shouted to them. 'You may want to get a shake on. We got some weather coming down from the north that could get ugly. Suggest you make all possible speed, gentlemen. You'll be contacted again when you reach the outer buoy at Williamsburg.'

Khan and Clarke gave them a wave and got to work hoisting the sails. As they prepared the *Sunflower* for departure, the marine officer cupped his hands around his mouth.

'Oh, and by the way, welcome to the United States.'

The assault boat accelerated away and disappeared into the mist. For a moment, Khan and Clarke watched in silence as the white foam of the wake dissipated across the glassy surface of the ocean. Then they turned to each other and embraced, smiling broadly. They'd made it.

For Khan, it was the end of a nightmare. He didn't know what the future held for him, but at least he had one. He glanced over his shoulder, through the mist, towards the distant horizon they'd left behind, and his thoughts turned to Alex and Kirsty. He hoped they had one too.

September

Harry stepped down from the helicopter, grumbling as he worked the stiffness from his tired limbs. It had been a long week and he was glad to get back to McIntyre Castle. In spite of everything, he was beginning to regard the place as home. The accommodations were comfortable and the privacy and solitude had given Harry time to successfully traverse his personal minefield of emotions.

He felt a lot better now, much more so than when he first arrived over three months ago. Harry shook his head. Hard to believe it had been that long, but the many hours he'd spent walking the forest paths and along the shores of the sound had regenerated him both physically and mentally, and the despair he'd felt in the early days was a now distant recollection. He'd come to terms with Anna's death and, occasionally, he found himself smiling at a memory of her in happier times.

In the darkness, Harry and his SAS escort trudged towards the castle, their footsteps now finding the familiar route with ease. Later, after a shower and a light supper, Harry retired to his private drawing room where a fire crackled in the hearth. He settled himself down into an overstuffed armchair and sipped at a cup of tea. His eyes were drawn to the dancing flames that flickered beneath the granite fireplace and his thoughts turned to the events of the previous week.

The tour of the front line had taken six days, visiting the troops and inspecting the layered defences that stretched from coast to coast. General Bashford had warned against the tour, declaring it too dangerous, but Harry had insisted. Despite his love for McIntyre Castle and the daily video link briefings with Lord Advocate Matheson and the military personnel at SCOTFOR, Harry had begun to feel rather like a fifth wheel. He'd even suggested a regular trip to Edinburgh to attend at least some of the briefings in person, but again Bashford had argued against it, explaining that the SCOTFOR base was a potential target for Arabian missiles, despite its underground location.

Harry had relented, resigning himself to dealing purely with the politics of the crisis. But the truth was, there was little to deal with. Negotiations of any kind still hadn't materialised. Baghdad knew that a British government-in-exile was functioning north of the border yet the Arabians had made no effort to end hostilities. It was a very bad sign.

Determined to make himself useful, Harry had decided on the front line tour, even overruling Bashford and visiting SCOTFOR in Edinburgh, on spending four productive days with Matheson's fledgling administration and conducting face-to-face briefings with the military commanders. After his final night, spent in a comfortable safe house outside the city, Harry boarded the Dark Eagle and headed east towards the coast and the border with England.

They touched down outside the busy fishing port of Eyemouth, where Royal Navy frigates and submarines patrolled the coastal waters. The surrounding cliffs and bluffs were dotted with surface-to-surface missiles and anti-aircraft batteries, giving the land-based forces some protection against any potential threat from the sea. But would it be enough, Harry had asked the local commanders. In the long run, probably not, was the answer he feared.

Across the sea, to the north-east, Norway was still functioning, but only just. Civil unrest, sparked by the huge numbers of immigrants that had flocked to the liberal state over the decades, had thrown the country into turmoil. To add to their problems, Russian forces were massing along the Finnish border. It was only a matter of time before Scandinavia fell. When the Russians reached the North Sea coast, then the British Isles would be directly threatened on two fronts. Militarily it would be an impossible situation. Despite repeated attempts through a variety of diplomatic channels across the world, neither the Arabians nor the Russians were talking. War in Scotland was inevitable.

Still, Harry was encouraged by the scale and complexity of the border defences. The undulating countryside had been extensively criss-crossed with deep trench and bunker systems that ran almost the whole length of the border, and every observation point, every listening post and every command centre was linked by a telephone system running on copper wire. It was primitive, Harry was informed, but virtually impossible to eavesdrop on and, therefore, an extremely effective way of communicating between the various sectors in clear speech. Even dispatch riders had been employed, able to travel over rough terrain on powerful motorbikes.

From a deep trench just outside Saughtree, Harry had surveyed the gorse-covered no-man's land to the south through powerful binoculars and had been instantly reminded of grainy First World War footage he'd often seen on television. Of course, it wasn't as pitted and shelled as the landscape back then, but Harry wondered how long that would last when hostilities finally commenced.

A mile ahead of him, the highway had been dug up and blockaded with a pile of huge, reinforced concrete posts, each over twenty feet long and several yards in diameter. On either side of these massive obstructions, the roadside verges had been deeply excavated and the trenches flooded with water to drive enemy troops and armour on to soft, open ground, ground that had been liberally sown with anti-tank mines.

He'd visited the machine-gun nests and anti-tank batteries, had peered out through the camouflaged fire slits of the logged trench walls, and had even spent a night in one of the accommodation bunkers, a gesture that endeared him to the soldiers but unnerved Harry as he struggled to sleep inside the poorly lit, claustrophobic chamber. He was assured that the timber ceilings could withstand an artillery attack, but Harry wasn't so sure.

Eventually he reached the west coast near the town of Eastriggs, overlooking the grey waters of the Solway Firth. There, as darkness fell, he spoke informally to the troops, listening to their various contact reports, nodding in sympathy as many recounted the loss of friends, family and loved ones. Others grinned in the failing light, relishing any opportunity to even the score a little and Harry felt humbled by their courage.

After a dinner of hot rations in a draughty tent, he delivered an impromptu speech, using the back of a truck as a temporary platform. Harry had assured the tired, dirt-streaked faces gathered beneath the trees that he'd do all he could for them, that diplomatic efforts were still ongoing, that a truce could still be negotiated that would see families and friends reunited once again.

Clambering down from the truck, with handshakes and words of encouragement paving his route to the Dark Eagle, Harry had felt ashamed. He'd lied, of course. To tell them the cold truth would have broken their already fragile spirits. For now, they had hope. Their tired smiles and optimistic banter had told him that much and to extinguish that hope would have been criminal. Harry could have told them that the Russians were about to invade Scandinavia, that churches and synagogues had been boarded up, that there were rumours of deportations, that most of England had returned to a begrudging normality, but he didn't. Far to the south, beyond the horizon, street lights once again painted the sky with their orange glow. People had returned to work, the TV stations were broadcasting their censored schedules, the pubs remained closed, alcohol banned, and there was still a curfew in place. But life went on.

In stark contrast, the border was a black region, a dark stage set for war. All along the border British troops were dug in, ready to face the enemy whatever the outcome. And there could be only one outcome. Yes, Harry had lied to them, but only to spare them from the hopelessness that he'd begun to feel himself. Leaving the front line behind, Harry watched the dark ground pass below the helicopter and wondered, yet again, how many had died, and how many more would die until the fighting stopped. No, he decided, this wouldn't end with more British deaths, lost in a futile attempt to stop the Arabian war machine. There had to be another way out, for all of them, and he had to find it quickly.

There was a soft knock on the door and Bill Kerr entered the drawing room, a thankful interruption to counter Harry's darkening mood.

'Anything else this evening, Prime Minister?' the Scot enquired.

'Nothing, thank you Bill. Early call tomorrow, please.'

Kerr nodded and retired from the room. The fire in the grate had diminished somewhat and Harry debated whether to place another log on top. He decided not to, instead watching the blackened wood burn to a deep red. It was time to ask for some serious help. He wasn't sure if he'd get it, but it was his duty to ask. They'd been called on before, many years ago, when another enemy had stood on England's doorstep. As friends they had answered that call and, together, they'd been victorious.

This time, however, there would be no D-Day, nor even a VE day, when celebrating crowds would flock to Trafalgar Square to sing, dance and rejoice in the outbreak of peace. No, this time all they could do was attempt to escape the coming maelstrom that threatened to engulf them all and lay waste to a land that Harry had grown to love.

North-East England

Major General Mousa shielded his face as the Kiowa scout helicopter behind him leapt back up into the air and twisted away over the rooftops. Bodyguards in tow, he straightened up and headed through the rain towards a nearby stairwell, the last gusts of the rotor blades whipping around his uniform. He made his way down to the fire escape stairs of Corbridge's central police station, currently being used as the temporary headquarters of the Northern Army Group. And General Mousa, taking those stairs two at a time, was its newly appointed commander.

He dismissed his bodyguards and strode along the busy corridor to his office, ignoring the hurried salutes of his staff. Colonel Karroubi, recently promoted on Mousa's personal recommendation, got to his feet in the outer office as Mousa entered. He beckoned Karroubi to follow him into his inner sanctum and slammed the door. Mousa flopped into a high-backed swivel chair and swung his boots up on the desk, waving Karroubi to a seat. The wood panelled walls were decorated with dozens of maps and high-definition photographs.

'How was the field inspection?' his subordinate asked.

Mousa scooped up a remote control from the desk and powered up the command system screen mounted on the wall to his right. He called up the military dispositions of the Northern Army Group and the display filled with electronic information.

'Unsatisfactory. Those three brigade commanders you reported? I've had them arrested for gross negligence, amongst other crimes. The military court in Baghdad will hear their pathetic excuses in due course, but in the meantime it leaves our assault capability undermined. We need replacements flown in from Arabia and brought up to speed as soon as possible. Here are the names.' Mousa fished inside the breast pocket of his combat jacket and produced a slip of paper.

'They're all Iraqis, Ashira men, so they can be trusted. And the LDDs?'

'En route. They passed through Gibraltar yesterday.'

The layered defence destroyers were enormous armoured bulldozers, powered by massive turbocharged diesel engines and fitted with giant bulldozer blades which were used to literally scoop out and bury enemy defences. Armed with mini missile launchers and electronic guns, the LDDs could deliver a withering storm of fire as they approached dug in positions while, inside their cavernous holds, a platoon of infantry would be ready to storm enemy positions once they had been breached. In addition, wide caterpillar tracks and Kevlar-plated bodies allowed them to surmount almost any terrain and sustain considerable damage, making them a formidable weapon indeed.

After studying camera footage from penal troops and LARVE surveillance birds, Mousa had ordered two LDDs to be shipped from their base in North Africa. The infidel defences along the Scottish border were multi-layered and complex, he knew. There were concrete roadblocks, anti-tank pits and vehicle traps, and other obstacles too numerous to mention. In border towns, approach roads had been excavated and buildings demolished to form enormous rubble mountains. In sprawling forests, the roads and tracks had been blocked by felled trees and anti-tank teams watched and waited along every possible approach.

Elsewhere, thousands of artillery and mortar crews changed position on a daily basis, adding further complications to the attack plans. And that was just the ground forces. While British air assets had been depleted, the sky above the border hummed with air-search radars, an indication that the infidels still possessed significant surface-to-air capability. Mousa had to be careful, particularly with his own air assets. He couldn't afford another debacle.

With such formidable defences facing him, Mousa had decided that the LDDs would be invaluable. Deployed skilfully, they would clear a path clean through the British lines, scooping up concrete and dirt, weapons and bodies, and allowing the tanks and troops behind to breach the defences and attack the enemy from the rear. Once that happened it would be over very quickly.

But the LDDs were still en route, lashed down inside a transport ship that was at this very moment steaming up the western coast of Portugal towards the port of Sunderland, a mere fifty kilometres from where Mousa now sat. He did the calculation in his head. Seven more days at sea, a day to offload, three days to move them along a specially cleared route to their new bases, another three days for their crews to prepare them for battle – the huge blades were removed for shipping – and another two days to advance them towards their jump off point. Three weeks then, maybe a month. A long time. Still, since his exile to Damascus Mousa had learned to become a patient man; besides, the delay would give the replacement officers more time to familiarise themselves with their new commands.

'What about our sea defences?' Mousa enquired. 'I needn't remind you of the importance of security in our northern ports.'

'Of course,' Karroubi acknowledged. 'Since the sinking of the two transport ships in Sunderland, we've erected anti-mine nets and doubled our sea patrols. However, the British still own the waters further north. Their submarines pose a significant threat, coupled with the prolific use of sea mines.'

'They can keep their cold waters,' Mousa sneered. 'Besides, the Russians will deal with them soon enough. As long as our ports and the shipping lanes to the south are secure, the infidels can do what they like. It will be of little consequence in the long run.'

Karroubi shifted in his chair. 'May I ask, General, how was the funeral?'

'Tiresome,' Mousa sighed. 'The multitude of wailing relatives, the screaming brats, the obituaries; I had a headache for most of the day, I can tell you. Still, Al-Bitruji would've enjoyed the send-off, in particular the media coverage. Did you see it?'

'On Al Jazeera,' confirmed Karroubi, a smile playing at the corners of his mouth. 'We can only pray that paradise has welcomed him like a true soldier. It seems he underestimated the anger and determination of the British rebels.'

Now it was Mousa's turn to smile. The attack on Al-Bitruji's three-vehicle convoy as it headed to the Regent's Park mosque for Friday prayers was particularly devastating. While negotiating the narrow streets to the east of Park Lane a team of masked attackers had unleashed a hail of anti-tank rockets and automatic weapons fire that destroyed all three vehicles and left Al-Bitruji plus three of his most senior officers and thirteen other personnel dead, not to mention eight bystanders. One terrorist even fired four rounds into Al-Bitruji's corpse to be sure.

The attack had left a leadership vacuum, one that was quickly filled by Mousa's appointment to Northern Army Group commander by the Holy One. He was back, without supreme authority it was true, but with the approval of the cleric and with an army at his disposal, their one aim being to crush the remaining British forces in Scotland and bring the whole nation to heel. It couldn't have worked out much better, he admitted. And when the campaign was over, when the dust had settled and enough time had passed, he would again travel to the villa on the banks of the Tigris and thank his old friend.

But, for now, there was work to do. For the next hour he filled Karroubi in on his recent trip to Arabia, where he'd consulted with the Holy One and the other European commanders at the cleric's marbled summer palace on the shores of the Red Sea. Huge maps of Northern England and the Scottish Borders had been pored over for weeks, as were thousands of photographs and aerial footage. Plans were formulated, rejected, reworked and tested.

All the while, Mousa had sensed the mood in the palace, one of a conquering army on the verge of an historic victory, just a single battle left to win before ultimate conquest could be achieved. He'd seen his own eagerness reflected on the faces of the other commanders too, each contemplating their own special place in Arabian history, the desire for a last push on a scale not seen since the days of Saladin, an Islamic army sweeping across Europe, crushing everything in its path.

But the Holy One had urged caution, perhaps sensing the determination amongst his officers in the room. They were close to victory in Europe, he'd said, but they would wait, until the Russians had taken Norway and faced Scotland unopposed across the sea, until Europe was fully pacified. Then, as the world watched, the final battle would begin. They had the luxury of time on their side, the cleric had explained. Besides, there'd been enough civilian deaths, even if they were infidels.

At the time, Mousa had sat at the long, ornate table in the palace conference hall and considered trying to change the Holy One's mind. By disengaging, it would allow the infidels time to strengthen their own defences on the ground, which would ultimately result in a longer, more drawn-out campaign. He quickly decided against it, choosing instead to nod in agreement like the other commanders around the table. He wouldn't make the same mistake twice.

Yet, it was agreed that things had gone remarkably well. Of course, other countries across the globe had been outraged at the military campaign and, at the United Nations in New York, several delegates had protested long and loud at the scale of the invasion. Predictably, the US had objected the loudest, but America on her own did not present the problem she might have done at the end of the last century. Instead, the US had pursued a somewhat isolationist policy since its expulsion from the Gulf region, concentrating instead on domestic issues rather than taking its assumed role on the world stage as a leading superpower.

The other big players were Russia and China, the former now firmly in the Arabian pocket and the latter, emboldened by Arabia's conquests, now eyeing Taiwan hungrily. The other countries that made up the United Nations were either now living under the Arabian yoke or were too insignificant to consider. Their protestations had faded and the more forward-thinking delegates among the international community were already attempting to open channels of dialogue in the hope of rebuilding pre-war diplomatic and commercial ties, particularly with the now reshaped European continent.

As Mousa concluded his debrief, he glanced at the little island of Britain on the map behind Karroubi's head. This once-powerful empire had folded as easily as the rest of Europe and, in a way, Mousa was disappointed. As a soldier, he'd anticipated fast-moving tank battles across patchwork green fields and savage street fighting to rival even Stalingrad, but none of these events had fully materialised.

Mousa had expected more from the British. Maybe the coming conflict to the north would provide an opportunity to test their resolve? Or maybe the passing generations had lost their stomach for a fight? If that was the case, it was easy to see why. Before the invasion, life in the West had been very comfortable for most. The sudden loss of utilities and the inability to be able to purchase food at overstocked shops had terrified a population that had become a demanding consumer society. The West had grown soft and fat, become slaves to greed and the consumption of everything that could be consumed. Western society was a heartless, godless organism that would pollute and destroy its citizens and the very ground they walked on. The invasion had changed all that.

Now, only Scotland stood in the way of total domination. How tough a battle that would prove to be, only time would tell.

'How long?' Karroubi asked after Mousa had finished his brief. 'The Holy One must know that delay only strengthens the infidel's hand.'

'He does,' Mousa shrugged. 'But when he finally issues the order we must be ready. A month, two at most.' He swung his chair around and stood, ambling over to the window behind his desk. He looked down into the small courtyard below. There were one or two jeeps there and several soldiers hurried to and from the building, bent against the driving rain. He stared across the wet rooftops towards the town centre, contemplating another eight weeks in this damp, dreary town.

The weather in Scotland was even worse, by all accounts. North of the border, it seemed to rain constantly. He made a mental note to address the tactical implications of the weather at the next briefing. Mousa sighed, already missing the hot sun of Arabia on his back, but this is what he'd worked for, had killed for, so the weather be damned. He turned away from the dull landscape outside the window.

'There's not much more can be achieved here now,' he said to Karroubi. 'I will travel to London tonight and return for the briefing next week. In the meantime, you'll remain here and oversee the preparations. Think you can suffer the rain for a few weeks longer, Colonel?'

Karroubi's shoulders slumped dramatically. 'How do these people stand it? If it's not raining, then the sky is just a solid grey ceiling. The men are getting depressed. We may have to issue Prozac, as well as ammunition.'

Mousa laughed. 'An impractical combination, I think. Still, I'll inform the Holy One of your suggestion.' As he started to leave the room he glanced at the command display one more time, the smile slipping from his face. 'Ensure our forces are ready when the time comes, Colonel. This will be our last key offensive in Europe and the Holy One expects it to be a decisive one. We must not fail him. I must not fail. Do you understand?'

'Of course,' nodded Karroubi.

There was a light tap at the door and an orderly stood to attention in the outer office. 'Your helicopter is on final approach, General.' Mousa grunted an acknowledgment and Karroubi flashed up a salute as he swept past.

'Have a safe journey, General.'

'Carry on,' ordered Mousa. 'And try not to get too wet,' he smiled, marching from the room.

Camp David, Maryland

President Scott Mitchell peered through a frost-crusted window of the presidential lodge and watched the departing SUV as it wound its way out of the high-security compound. Further down the hill, a Black Hawk helicopter waited, its rotors chopping the cold air, the whine of its jet turbines echoing across the densely wooded slopes. The SUV's brake lights bloomed crimson in the darkness and then it was lost, sinking behind a thick stand of black birch that marched across the ridgeline.

Mitchell's recent guest, the British ambassador to the United States, was in the back of that SUV, returning to the embassy on Massachusetts Avenue in Washington, his request for assistance, any assistance, yet to be answered. He took a breath and turned away from the window, gratefully sinking into the deep cushions of the Jackson sofa.

White House Chief of Staff Zack Radanovich and Eliot Engle, the president's national security advisor, sat on the opposite sofa, waiting patiently as Mitchell dug into his trouser pocket and extracted a pill from a small plastic box. He popped it on to his tongue, then washed it down with the dregs of a cold pot of coffee perched on the low coffee table between them.

'Blood pressure's up again,' he grimaced, setting the mug with the presidential seal down. 'Jesus, what a mess.'

'We have options here,' Radanovich pointed out. 'Saying no is one of them.' He wore charcoal-grey trousers and a blue shirt and tie, the collar loose, sleeves rolled to the elbows. 'The fact is, the old Europe has gone, and the UK with it. If we side with them, with Beecham, we undermine our position regarding Israel. That has to be our primary focus now.'

'This isn't a legislative government we're talking about here, Mr President,' the similarly dressed Engle added. 'This is an administration staffed by a handful of government and military personnel running a country the size of South Carolina. They're under siege, their position is completely untenable, and Khathami isn't negotiating. In one respect, Zack is right; we have to give the Israeli situation our fullest attention, because that one has the potential for global disaster.' Engle paused. 'On the other hand, we can't just ignore the situation in Scotland either. We have to do something.'

'What are we giving them now?'

'Satellite data, mostly. Some low-grade human intel from our assets in Baghdad. As much as we can without tipping our hand.'

'Jesus, what a mess,' Mitchell repeated, shaking his bald dome. He exhaled long and loud, stretching his legs out before him. 'Brings to mind something I heard once, something my old law professor at Yale said.'

'What was that, sir?' enquired Engle in his soft Tennessee drawl.

'He said, "Tell your grandchildren if they want to do business in Europe when they graduate, they'd better learn to speak Arabic." Clever guy, old Harpenden. Saw the writing on the wall way back when.'

'Maybe we should've hired him,' Engle quipped. 'Question is, can we afford to escalate things with Baghdad right now? Diplomatically, they've reached out to us, kept the channels open, left our embassies intact, repatriated US citizens from Europe–'

'Not all of them,' Mitchell growled. 'Some are never coming home.'

'That's true,' said Radanovich, 'and somewhere down the line they'll pay. But we have to look at the bigger picture here, Mr President. Arabia has just inherited France's nukes, on top of the old Iranian weapons they already have, and the way Europe folded has given the Arabian military machine a huge confidence boost. Right now they think they're invincible. How long will it be before they turn their attentions towards Israel? Any assistance we offer Beecham could give Khathami the excuse to make his move.'

'He wouldn't dare,' Mitchell countered, but his words lacked conviction. Arabian territory now stretched from the North Sea to the foothills of the Himalayas. If the worst happened, if old hatreds prevailed and Arabia launched against America's only ally in the Middle East, then any retaliatory nuclear strike against Baghdad or Islamabad wouldn't make any difference. The destruction of Israel would simply be total. He pondered the scenario for a moment, the tension in the room far below ground, the assembled military personnel, the loud snapping of plastic, the confirmation of the launch codes. The final order. Mitchell's blood ran cold, and it was Engle's voice that brought his attention back into the lodge.

'You heard what the ambassador said, Mr President. Beecham has offered us his support in that regard. They're prepared to use their nuke subs under our command should things deteriorate. That's gutsy talk for a guy who's lost his country and is now staring down the barrel of a gun.' He glanced at Radanovich.

'The real question is, do we desert our friends when they need us most? If we do, what does that say about us?'

'Damn it,' breathed Mitchell. 'We can't help one without compromising the other. What's the latest out of Jerusalem?'

'Sec State's brief is right there,' Radanovich replied, sliding a buff-coloured folder marked 'RESTRICTED' across the table. 'Right now,

Baghdad is maintaining cordial relationships with Israel. All diplomatic channels are open and the Knesset has been assured that Arabia harbours absolutely no hostile intentions towards its neighbour. They're insisting it's a European problem. Meanwhile, the IDF is on full alert and Israeli citizens are digging bunkers and stocking up on tinned foods. It's a goddam mess.'

Radanovich got to his feet, crossing the handwoven rug to the hostess trolley. He poured three coffees into white enamel mugs emblazoned with the logo of the United States Marine Corps, avoided the sugar and cream, then placed the mugs on the coffee table. The president took his, watching his chief of staff sip the steaming liquid through pursed lips, noting the worry lines around the red-rimmed eyes, the runner's frame that appeared to have shrunk even further over the last few weeks. Mitchell recognised the signs, the fear and stress that gnawed away at all of them.

'You okay, Zack?'

Radanovich nodded, running a tired hand through his thick curly hair.

'Israel will be next, Mr President. We all know it. Fifteen hundred years of anti-Semitism doesn't disappear overnight. Synagogues have been razed to the ground all over Europe. The Arabians are saying it's localised, mob rule, whatever. But it's clear what's really happening.' He set his mug down, his voice low, his hollow cheeks flushed with anger. 'That's how it started in Germany. It's happening again, I can feel it. It's a goddam nightmare.'

'We hear you, Zack,' Mitchell soothed, feeling the pain of the young New Yorker opposite him. Yet the reports coming out of Europe were ominous. Synagogues had indeed been destroyed and, worse, there were rumours of disappearances and deportations. How much of it was organised was impossible to say – all transport and communications links between Europe and North America had been suspended – but Mitchell was publicly concerned and privately fearful.

Israel, naturally, had protested the loudest against the reports of religious violence, but those protests had fallen mainly on disbelieving ears, its delegation storming from the UN negotiations to the jeers of the Arabian members. She had no friends left, save the US, and was surrounded by her historical enemy, an enemy that had embarked on a conquest of Europe under the pretence of securing the safety and well-being of the ninety-two million Muslims who resided there. No wonder Zack, whose own family had survived the Holocaust nearly a hundred years ago, was scared. They all were.

'Israel is expecting an attack,' Radanovich warned. 'They've been under constant assault since 1948, but now they're facing impossible odds. If the pogroms in Europe start all over again, if they so much as smell Arabia cranking up their missile programme, or making a move towards their borders, they'll get the first punch in. That means we'll be sucked into an intercontinental shooting war. Then it's game over.'

'Let's pray that doesn't happen,' replied Mitchell.

'Prayers might not be enough.'

'Then keep a lid on the rumours,' the president countered. 'Do what you have to do. Call the media guys in, brief them, get them onside. We can't let this thing gain momentum Zack, or God knows where it will lead us. Besides, we have five million Muslims living right here in the US. That gives us a fair amount of leverage with Baghdad.'

'With respect, Mr President, you really think they give a shit?'

'Don't get me started,' Mitchell snorted, anger briefly replacing his unease. 'They invaded Europe without giving a rat's ass what we think, and now they've got Russia playing offence for them too. As for China, well, they're not so much sabre-rattling as waving a switchblade in Taiwan's face. And all because of Khathami. Any influence we ever had in the Middle East evaporated overnight when that guy stepped up. Arab Spring my ass,' the president scoffed. 'The truth is, they think we're a busted flush. Our disengagement from Europe and the Middle East has opened up this goddam Pandora's box and now we'll be lucky if we get the lid halfway closed.'

His bones protested painfully as he pushed himself off the couch and crossed to the stone fireplace, where a fire crackled brightly in the hearth. He selected a poker from a brass stand and teased the flaming logs, dislodging one and sending a shower of tiny embers billowing up the chimney.

Mitchell stared into the flames where the fire burned brightest, the flame almost white. He was approaching the end of his first term and the economy was at last recovering. His approval rating was holding steady and the media had finally called off the dogs, focussing instead on the corner that America had turned. Mitchell couldn't take credit for the economic recovery; he was simply lucky enough to be in the right time at the right place. Wasn't that the difference between success and failure in life? Good timing?

He was fortunate to have been elected just as the breakthrough was made, when Arabia's oil embargo suddenly no longer mattered, when he'd flown in the dead of night to the facility deep in the Nevada desert to witness the energy miracle, made possible by the tireless work of generations of faceless men and women after the crash of forty-seven.

Now, the lights were back on in California, the very tip of the energy revolution he'd been told to expect, the first of many still-classified programmes to be rolled out across the country that would change lives and reshape history. But, once again, war had raised its ugly head in Europe, threatening that future for all. What the hell was the matter with the human race? Why did it have to be so goddam destructive?

The heat of the fire wrapped Mitchell in its comforting embrace and warmed his aching bones. At sixty-seven, he wasn't getting any younger. He'd won the party nomination by a slim margin, the presidency by even less, his campaign focussing on reigniting a patriotic flame, on extolling the conservative values of hard work and self-sufficiency, in the belief that America, above all others, was God's own country. No one had been more honoured, more proud to serve, than Scott Mitchell on inauguration day. Yet, since then he hadn't given the American people much opportunity to warm their hands around that flame of patriotism he'd talked so much about. America's stock was low and it pained him.

His eyes wandered up to the oil painting that hung over the fireplace, a Leutze reproduction of General George Washington crossing the Delaware River. Mitchell understood the painting was more symbolic than an accurate historical representation, but he found it inspiring nonetheless, the moment when Washington led his troops in boats across the icy river to surprise and defeat the British at Trenton. The physical hardship back then was unimaginable, the sacrifices too numerous to mention. For Mitchell, the picture said more about the American spirit than any Independence Day speech or schmaltzy movie.

'Mr President?' prompted Engle from the sofa.

Mitchell stared at the tiny boats a moment longer, crammed with revolutionary musket men, the frigid waters breaking over the wooden bows. The solution lay there, right in front of him.

'What were the figures the ambassador gave us?'

Engle reached for a printout on the table. 'The numbers aren't concrete, but they're predicting initial casualties of over fifty thousand. Ten times that figure will become refugees in the first forty-eight hours, all heading north to avoid the conflict. The Arabians will squeeze them until their backs are against the sea and there's nowhere left to run.'

'Nowhere,' Mitchell echoed softly. He studied the painting a moment longer, then turned and faced the men on the sofa. 'For as long as I can remember, Britain has been a close friend and ally of the United States. It's been a complex relationship, that much is true, but what isn't in doubt is the history we share. The blood that ran through the folks at Jamestown runs through us both today, blood that's been spilt on battlefields for centuries, as friends as well as enemies. It's my belief we're bound by that blood. The United States is tied to Britain in fundamental ways that transcend politics. It's a relationship we cannot ignore.'

'You're going to help them,' Engle said quietly.

Mitchell nodded. 'As best we can. Now, this is what I had in mind...'
He spoke for several minutes and, by the time he'd finished, both the chief

of staff and the national security advisor were stunned into silence.

'Jesus Christ. That's a big task, Mr President,' Radanovich finally whispered.

'But doable, right Eliot?'

'I believe so,' Engle agreed after a moment.

'There's a lot to consider,' Radanovich frowned, but this time Mitchell noticed the anxiety had been replaced by a steely focus. 'Security and diplomatic issues, statements of intent...'

'Let's not forget the rules of engagement,' Engle reminded them. 'International waters are dangerous places. Anything could happen to spark an incident.'

'Work it out with Sec Def and the NSC. Zack, you speak to State and Justice,' Mitchell ordered. 'I'll speak to the Israeli ambassador and the attorney general myself. And keep Connie up to speed. When the news breaks, the UN and Baghdad will demand answers. I want to make sure she's equipped to bat any arguments from the Legal Counsel's office out of the park. Our case has to be absolutely airtight, got it? And make sure she reminds the Security Council that we've lost many of our own citizens during this conflict. Remind them that we won't tolerate the taking of another American life, collateral damage or otherwise. I want that point rammed down the secretary general's throat. See to it, please.'

As Radanovich scooped up his jacket and left the cabin, the president turned to Engle. 'The military aspect will be delicate, to say the least. Time is running out, Eliot, so we'll have to move fast.'

'We're already at DEFCON three, Mr President. Mobilisation shouldn't be an issue.'

'Good. I'm going to recommend raising the alert level to DEFCON two as a precaution, just to give our detractors something to think about. In the meantime, I'll need to speak to the NMCC and, in particular, COMLANTFLT at his earliest convenience. We'll need time with Langley and Fort Meade, too.'

'Yes, Mr President.'

'The commercial shipping aspect is crucial. I want a conference call set up with the owners of all major lines by the morning. We can't do this without them, Eliot, so be nice.'

Engle left the lodge and Mitchell was alone, turning to bask in the warm glow of the fire. He looked at the painting once more, at General Washington standing in the bow of the lead boat, wrapped in a thick cloak, his jaw set resolutely, carving across the dark waters towards an enemy that was both numerically stronger and technically superior. And still they followed him, thought Mitchell.

That was the true nature of the American spirit right there; the willingness to risk one's life for freedom, for liberties earned by the blood of millions, the countless sacrifices remembered by so many, yet truly understood by so few. Now the people of England were labouring under the yoke of a new oppression, while those in Scotland waited fearfully, their future uncertain, their freedom, their very lives, at stake. It was time, Mitchell decided, to remind the world exactly what America truly stood for.

He crossed the room and picked up the phone on the table. 'Patch me through to the ambassador's Black Hawk.'

November

The US Air Force C-5B Galaxy rumbled along the runway, then clawed its enormous airframe into a leaden sky, its four turbofan engines powering its massive grey body up through low cloud and out of sight. It was the eighth transport departure in less than four hours, the senior RAF air traffic controller had informed Harry, and there were still fourteen more flights to go until operations were curtailed for the day. After that, a four-hour window would enable essential maintenance to take place. Once that was completed, evacuation flights would recommence with all possible speed.

Standing in the control tower at Glasgow Airport, Harry took the proffered binoculars and focussed on a distant C-17 Globemaster as it taxied for take-off. After a few teething problems, the evacuation was starting to run smoothly and they were now averaging around twenty-five flights per day, moving roughly twelve thousand people every twenty-four hours. And that was just here at Glasgow. Thanks to the Americans and their fleet of huge transport aircraft, they were also managing to evacuate the same kind of numbers further down the road in Edinburgh. That was about twenty-five thousand civilians a day and the operation had started seventeen days ago without pause. In eastern Scotland, there were several daily outbound flights from Dundee and Aberdeen airports using civilian airliners, plus military transports from the RAF bases at Kinloss and Lossiemouth, transporting roughly fifteen thousand evacuees a day.

And then there were the ships, of course. The sea routes to the west were a lot slower but they carried more people, particularly in the six vast vehicle-transporter ships that the Americans had supplied for the duration of the evacuation. The numbers were impressive. In total, the number crunchers were reporting nearly nine hundred thousand people out already. The logistics of the operation were astounding and Harry was amazed that things were running as smoothly as they appeared to be. Like any good operation, it was all about preparation and planning and, in the previous weeks, Harry had witnessed levels of co-operation between government, military and civil administrations that he doubted would ever be repeated in his lifetime.

Still, it would be a close-run thing. Since the middle of September, over one hundred Arabian surveillance craft had been shot down by British anti-air defences. On the ground, the border fortifications had been probed by what intelligence officers later discovered were Arabian penal troops, kitted out with remote cameras and sent forward unarmed and under cover of darkness to find potential weaknesses along the British lines. Many had drowned in the deep anti-tank pits or been killed or wounded by the sniper teams that watched the border at night. Those they did capture were often elated at surviving the ordeal and were eager to co-operate. But the signs were obvious. The threat from the south was growing and time was running out. Thank God the Americans had thrown them a lifeline, thought Harry.

The plan, the seed of which had taken root in a log cabin three and a half thousand miles away, was an audacious one: evacuate every soul possible, an impossible task without the might of the US and the assistance of the Canadians. Their old allies had stepped up to the plate, constructing vast resettlement centres in various northern US states and across the border in Canada. At the same time, the British front line had been reinforced with American UAVs and munitions, while military transport planes would fly evacuees to US bases in Iceland. From there, a steady convoy of ships and aircraft would take them to the North American mainland, an operation as impressive as the airlift.

Once the plans had been finalised, the public were informed. It was a no-frills address aired on the country's single remaining broadcaster, BBC Scotland, and a grim-faced Harry had delivered the very worst news: England was gone and Scotland would be next. All attempts at diplomacy had failed, the UN cowed before the power of Arabia and its new allies. Arabian troops were massing south of the border and war was inevitable. Whatever the outcome, the future for the civilian population looked bleak.

But there was another alternative. The US and Canadian governments had graciously opened their doors and were willing to accept those who wished to flee the coming conflict, to offer them the chance of a new life. The public were urged to register for evacuation, to listen for details of their evacuation day and departure points. Normal media broadcasts would be cancelled, replaced by information messages announcing evacuation procedures and giving advice on clothing and documentation that each individual should take on their journey.

Demonstrations followed Harry's speech, anger at the Arabians, anger at the administration in Scotland over money, the collapse of the stock market, lost pensions, plummeting house prices, worthless cars, fuel rationing. In the end, none of it mattered. There were only two choices: stay and face an uncertain future, or go, taking whatever one could carry.

The first to leave were those who lived near docks and airports, evacuated early in order to clear the approaches for the huge numbers of refugees expected to descend on local towns and cities. Women and any children under sixteen were also prioritised, along with pensioners, the disabled and hospital patients well enough to travel. With the vulnerable safely away, the main evacuation began in earnest. Those who had cars took them, abandoning them near their designated ports and airports. Each evacuee was allowed only two items of luggage, although many people tried to bring more. At departure points across the country, car parks and loading areas were full of containers, each one overflowing with clothing, luggage and thousands of other confiscated items. It was a question of space and weight, the civilians were told. There could be no exceptions.

Airport terminals were particularly eerie places. Normally bustling with lively activity and awash with light and colour, war-footing regulations had transformed the terminals into gloomy, unlit halls flanked by shuttered and darkened shops. Military personnel waving torches ushered the evacuees quickly along jet ways or out on to windswept tarmacs, where the huge mouths of waiting US transport planes swallowed them like plankton before embarking on their flights to Iceland.

For many others, the journey westwards would be less comfortable. Directed to ports all around the rugged coast of Scotland to await evacuation by a variety of ocean-going vessels, from giant American container ships to rust-stained ferries and cruise ships, their journey across the stormy North Atlantic to the United States would be a long and uncomfortable one. On the way, some ships would dock in Belfast or Larne, depositing those who wished to rejoin their families in an as yet unscathed Ireland. How long this would last was unclear, but many who watched and waited by those Irish docksides, where their own descendants once waited to embark on a similar journey, were taking no chances. The ships would be back.

Yet, despite Harry's pleas, despite the inevitability of war and the uncertainty of occupation, there were many in Scotland who simply refused to leave. There were a multitude of reasons why just under half the population failed to register for evacuation. In many cases loved ones were still missing, husbands, wives, brothers, sisters, fiancées and friends, trapped in England or elsewhere when the invasion had begun. For most, there had been no contact, no word from those who were missing and who may still be desperately trying to reach home. To abandon them was unthinkable. Someone would be waiting when they finally made it back to Scotland.

Others simply had no intention of deserting the country of their birth, the homes they'd grown up in, the streets and parks they'd played in as children, the property that they'd worked hard to purchase and maintained with loving pride. If anything bad was going to happen then at least they would be on familiar territory, surrounded by friends and family. They would take their chances when the Arabians came. After all, what was the alternative? To start all over again in a foreign country, common language notwithstanding?

Some argued that it would be years before so many people could be housed properly, before the economies of America and Canada could absorb the sudden, massive influx of immigrants who would all have to be fed and sheltered and then assimilated into society. And what was a resettlement camp anyway? What happened when the winter storms blew south and the snow piled high? In Canada, the temperature dropped through the floor. How were the very old and the very young supposed to survive that? So, despite Harry's calls for reason, despite the warnings and the dangers, many stayed. But no matter what course of action people decided on, the future was uncertain for everyone.

Harry lifted his binoculars and tracked another transport aircraft as it rotated off the runway and thundered upwards into the grey skies. He watched it bank across the city, climbing to the west until it was lost in the clouds. So far the operation had been a success. The numbers were looking good, but there was still another million evacuees to get out, give or take the odd thousand. After that it would just be Harry, his staff, the senior military commanders and the British forces that were mostly concentrated along the border.

Inspired by the bravery of those that had decided to remain behind, Harry briefly contemplated staying himself, but General Bashford and just about everybody else had overruled him, including President Mitchell in Washington. They were right, of course. Not that Harry was scared; since his acceptance of Anna's passing, since the true scale of events at home and across Europe had become known, death no longer held the fear it once did, but his responsibilities now lay with the evacuees. Harry's final destination was to be a newly established camp on the windswept plains of Montana, where he would spend the winter with his people, working alongside the US and Canadian administrations, making plans for all their futures. And it was up to Harry to lead them into that future.

After all, fate had already decided he would survive the bomb at Downing Street, the Arabian troops who hunted him deep below the streets of London, the flight to Alternate One. He had a purpose now, a responsibility to those who were facing a life filled with uncertainty, and it gave him strength. His duty was to oversee the ongoing evacuation and get as many out as quickly and efficiently as possible. That was his focus now.

He raised the binoculars to his eyes as he watched an ageing American Airlines 747-400 start its take-off run, urging it along the runway and up into the sky as it thundered past the tower. But they'd better be quick. Time was running out.

Wiltshire

The village of South Lockeridge had escaped detection for just over four months when the first Arabian troops appeared at the northern and southern barricades. Behind the bulldozers, armoured vehicles and trucks full of soldiers waited to advance towards the village. The deception was over, but for Alex and the others it wasn't unexpected. A week before, Arabian helicopter gunships had flown over the village several times, proof that they'd finally been discovered.

A village meeting was quickly convened and their original strategy reiterated. No resistance. A delegation was formed to greet the Arabian troops on the village green. Alex stayed out of it, while Andy Metcalfe decided he would act as spokesman, the remainder of the delegation consisting of his small clique and some of the older folk. Metcalfe reckoned any Arabian anger would be diffused by the sight of the old 'uns as he cajoled and bullied the pensioners to stand around the war memorial. As Alex waited with the other villagers across the green, he noticed Metcalfe and his boys burying themselves in the middle of the seniors.

He was reminded of the other gathering he attended a few weeks ago.

Wearing a borrowed suit, Alex had waited nervously at the altar of the village church as Kirsty glided slowly up the aisle towards him, radiant in Helen's flowing white wedding dress. The celebrations had lasted well into the night and Kirsty drove back to the farm with an extremely drunk, but very proud, new husband slurring his love for her.

Alex hadn't intended to drink quite so much, but Kirsty's refusal to touch alcohol at the reception and the village doctor's visit the week before confirmed what Alex had begun to suspect. Their emotions had ranged from fear to joy and everything in between. What kind of world would their child grow up in? Was there a future for any of them? They'd decided that they would be positive about the baby and what life would bring. They would face it together, as a family.

Still, the apprehension was almost palpable as the noise of the Arabian armour rumbled along the lanes towards them. A couple of villagers bolted away but most held their ground, the men and women watching nervously, the younger children giggling with excitement. The lead Arabian vehicle roared into view, its wicked-looking machine gun sweeping left and right. Several troop trucks followed, rolling around the village green and disgorging troops.

Initially there was a lot of shouting and Alex saw Metcalfe almost pleading with a couple of Arabian officers before being led away, but surprisingly the new arrivals didn't seem overly concerned with the attempts to conceal the village. Similar tactics had been used in other parts of the country, as they'd explained over loudhailers, but registration was necessary and there would be no exceptions.

The villagers gathered together for processing in the village hall, men, women and children, forming long queues that snaked towards the hastily arranged trestle tables beneath the stage, where the Arabian clerks waited behind a bank of computer screens. Alex and Kirsty queued patiently, chatting quietly with the other villagers and shuffling forward every few minutes. Alex was surprised by the mood in the hall. It wasn't jovial, of course, but neither was it apprehensive. In fact, he sensed an undercurrent of relief in the room, a resigned acceptance of the circumstances and the probability that the Arabians would fill in their forms and leave, allowing life to return to some sort of normality. At least they wouldn't have to hide any longer, thought Alex. With the onset of winter, trying to conceal the lights at night had been tough enough.

'Next!'

Alex put a gentle hand in Kirsty's back and guided her towards the stern-faced Arabian behind the trestle table.

'Your name?'

'Kirsty Taylor. Recently married,' she smiled, glancing at Alex. He could see the relief in her eyes too, the hope that things might return to normal, that their son or daughter might be born in a clean, efficient hospital rather than a cramped farmhouse bedroom with only a midwife to oversee the daunting ordeal of childbirth. Kirsty handed over her driving licence to the Arabian clerk. Fingers hammered the computer keyboard.

'Address?'

Kirsty gave the farmhouse address. Then followed the standard questions: age, date and place of birth, children's ages. Kirsty beamed at the last one. She blinked as the camera flashed, then held out her hand for the shiny ID card spat from a small printer. Alex smiled at her, then stepped up to the silver gaffer tape line stuck to the wooden floor.

'Name?'

'Taylor. Alex Taylor.' He produced a Visa credit card.

The Arabian studied it, turning it over in his fingers. 'This is all you have?' Alex shrugged. The man was a typical-looking bureaucrat: skinny, round glasses, soft hands, receding hairline. And full of his own self-importance. The clerk continued with his questions and Kirsty, standing directly behind Alex, squeezed his hand when he enquired about children. Alex squeezed back.

'Occupation?'

Alex frowned. The litany had been the same as they neared the line of tables, the questions never deviating from a seemingly prepared script. Until now. 'Excuse me?'

The Arabian's eyes remained fixed on his keyboard, his fingers poised above the keys. 'Occupation?' he repeated, an edge to his voice.

The murmur in the hall faded to silence. Heads swivelled towards Alex, glowering guards that lined the walls clutched automatic weapons.

'I... I don't understand,' he stammered. He looked around the hall. Other faces caught his eye, villagers who'd laughed and sang and slapped him on the back only a few weeks before. Now they were strangers, their eyes turned away. At the far end of the room, Andy Metcalfe was locked in deep conversation with a gaggle of Arabian officers.

'Occupation?' the voice barked.

'Alex!' Kirsty hissed.

Alex saw Metcalfe watching him, saw the officers watching him too. 'Farmer,' he said loudly.

'Liar!' The Arabian pushed his chair back. There was shouting behind him, the sound of boots and curses. Suddenly Alex's hand was snatched from Kirsty's, his arms wrenched up behind his back.

'What the hell are you doing?' he cried. The Arabian guards held him tight and dragged him towards the table. Kirsty was pushed back into the crowd of suddenly frightened villagers, now hemmed in by armed guards. The mood in the hall crackled with tension, the guards' hands tightening around their weapons. The Arabian behind the desk pulled his arm back and slapped Alex hard across the face.

'Liar!' he repeated. 'You are a police officer. You have weapons, equipment. Speak!' He slapped his face again, the sound echoing around the hall. Alex staggered under the blow, blood pouring from a cut lip. He struggled but his arms were bent behind him, secured by the guards' strong hands.

'I'm a farmer,' he protested.

The Arabian shook his head, worryingly calm again. 'It is unwise to lie. We have been informed of your true profession.' He looked past Alex, to the villagers now pressed up against the back of the hall. 'To lie is a crime,' he bellowed. 'Your help in rooting out such crimes and bringing them to the attention of the authorities will be rewarded. You have nothing to fear from us.'

He sat down again, using a handkerchief to wipe his knuckles. He pulled his chair in, flexed his fingers.

'Take him away,' he said, without looking up.

'What? No!' Alex dug his heels in as the guards swivelled around and frogmarched him across the hall. Kirsty screamed. She tried to rush the cordon but was held back.

'Him and his mate had guns,' he heard Metcalfe announce in his gruff voice. 'Up at the B & B.'

The doors were wrenched open and Alex blinked in the bright winter sunlight, feet dragging behind him. Nearby was an open flatbed truck, the driver casually smoking a cigarette in the cab, the tailgate hanging down. Beyond that, a small group of villagers had gathered on the green. They watched Alex with guilty eyes as he was dragged towards the truck and bundled aboard. It was clear to him now that a deal had been done, that Metcalfe had sacrificed Alex so any collective punishment would be spared. He could see it in their faces, the shame, the relief, as his hands were flexi-cuffed behind him and he was forced to sit down on the hard wooden bench.

Fear gripped him then, his mouth suddenly dry, his heart pounding in his chest. Then he noticed the two other men on board, cuffed in a similar fashion, their faces bruised and bleeding, shivering in the November chill. Alex recognised them, the brothers who'd escaped from Swindon and sought refuge with a relative here in the village. Now they were all just Metcalfe's bargaining chips. The guards jumped down from the truck as Kirsty burst from the hall, running across the grass towards him. They closed ranks and she struggled against their arms.

'Alex!' she cried, tears streaking her face. 'Alex!'

'Find out where they're taking me!' Alex shouted. 'Then get back to the farm, tell Rob. Tell him Metcalfe's sold us out. He'll know what to do.'

Suddenly the truck's engine rumbled into life. Commands were shouted, whistles blown, the tailgate raised and slammed home with a loud clang. The soldiers dispersed, some climbing on to another truck as it hissed to a stop outside the hall. Kirsty broke free and ran to the tailgate. Alex shuffled along the bench and leaned over. She reached up and held his face in her hands.

'Alex, please,' she whimpered.

He looked down at his wife and smiled, the fear suddenly gone. 'Listen love, you've got to be brave. Take a deep breath then go and speak to one of the officers, find out where they're taking us. It'll probably be Swindon or Reading, one of the big towns. We'll just be interviewed, that's all. Trust me.'

The truck revved several times then crunched into gear. A soldier stepped forward and pulled Kirsty back.

'Don't leave me,' she sobbed.

'Just tell Rob!' he yelled above the revving engine. 'I'll be back later, I promise!' His voice was lost as the truck lurched forward. Kirsty ran after them, quickly falling behind as the vehicle accelerated around the village green. Then she stopped, sinking to her knees on the road, her hands clasped to her face. For the briefest of moments the roar of the truck faded to nothing. Their eyes locked and all they saw was each other, the fear, the love, the reality of what was happening to them. And in that instant they both knew.

'I love you,' he mouthed, then the truck rounded a corner and Kirsty was gone.

December

With the evacuation almost complete, many urban areas across Scotland were transformed into desolate, windswept ghost towns. Normally hectic city centres were devoid of life. No pedestrians bustled along the pavements, no music drifted from pub doorways, no conversation hummed from restaurants and coffee shops; every business was boarded up and shuttered. Darkened buildings stood sentinel along lifeless streets, where traffic signals blinked robotically at empty road junctions.

In the surrounding suburbs things were much the same. Along endless rows of terraced housing, abandoned and ransacked homes lay open to the elements, the winter winds whipping curtains in and out of open windows. Litter scraped and tumbled along deserted streets, and here and there an unsecured door or window banged loudly in the icy gusts.

A lone fox, emboldened by the scarceness of human activity, sniffed the air warily outside an open front door, then disappeared inside, re-emerging several minutes later with the remnants of a rubbish bag hanging from its jaws. There was no one there to chase him away, no shouts of alarm or objects hurled in its direction. Everywhere had been abandoned. The fox rummaged amongst the rubbish for a few moments, then loped off.

Halfway along the street, light flickered in the window of another empty house and the sound of music carried on the wind. This home had been vacated recently, and in a hurry. There had been no time to secure the windows or lock the front door, or even to turn off the television that hung on the living room wall.

Suddenly the music stopped and the screen went dark. A banner appeared. *Important Announcement – Please Wait*. The words remained frozen on the screen for several seconds, then a sudden flash of coloured bars and the picture changed. Harry Beecham, wearing an open-necked shirt and pullover, sat in a wing-backed chair, a backdrop of grey stone behind his head. He looked off camera briefly, nodded, then stared directly into the lens. He cleared his throat, and when he spoke his tone was measured, his gaze strong and resolute.

'Citizens of Britain. This may be the last time that I address you as your prime minister here within these islands. There was much I had planned for our nation, so many shared goals that I believed could be accomplished, but it was not to be. My hopes and dreams, along with everybody else's, were shattered on the eleventh of June. Since then, our country has suffered great loss and hardship, a state of affairs we could barely have imagined six months ago. Yet, when all hope seemed lost, salvation came to us from across the ocean, offering many of us the chance of a new life, a safe life, on the other side of the Atlantic. Many of us have taken that opportunity and we have become pilgrims once more, seeking a fresh start in the New World. It will be tough and it will be challenging, but we have the advantage of being British. There isn't another nation on this planet that possesses such an indomitable spirit as us. History has proved that, and in the coming years we will rely heavily on that spirit to see us through the hard times.'

On the screen, Harry paused and looked down. He seemed to struggle momentarily with some inner emotion, and then continued. 'Even as I speak, there are many of you that have chosen to stay. Your reasons are numerous, not least for some a simple love of their country and the will to defend it against the advancing enemy. All along the border tonight our troops are dug in, ready to defend this land against the invaders. Like you, I am deeply humbled by their courage. And the civilians amongst you, you too have shown bravery not seen since the last century, when this nation of ours was threatened by another enemy, in another time and place. We could not be cowed then and nor will we–'

The picture flickered several times, Harry's image scrolling across the screen before settling once more. 'The opportunity to evacuate has now passed,' he said gravely. 'Even as I speak, the last transport plane has left Scottish airspace and is headed for safety. All that remains now is to wait. As of midnight tonight, electrical power, gas and water supplies will be shut off for the duration of the coming conflict. I hope you've all taken the necessary precautions and gathered the requisite supplies. Head north if you can.'

Harry paused for a moment. When he began again his voice was heavy, his brow deeply furrowed. 'Darkness will descend upon us tonight and it is uncertain when light will shine again over our green and pleasant land. I ask all of you to offer up your prayers for each other, for our troops on the front line and for those who have crossed the ocean to begin a new life. It is our friends and families that honour us most. Let us pray that we will always remember them and that they will never forget us. Goodnight and God be with us all.'

General Mousa scooped up the remote control and turned the TV set off. His face wore a smile of grim satisfaction. 'I told you that bastard was still here. A nice speech though, for what little good it will do them. Everything is ready?'

Colonel Karroubi, wearing body armour and full battledress, nodded curtly. 'Everything, General.'

'The LDDs?'

'Fuelled, armed, and with their infantry complements ready to board.'

'Excellent.' Mousa glanced at his watch. Eleven hundred hours; seven hours to go. He stepped outside the armoured personnel carrier, closely followed by Karroubi. The command vehicle was dug into a wooded hillside near the village of Nether Denton, twenty-two kilometres south of the Scottish border. Nearby, his communications vehicles were similarly dug in and camouflaged, and a company of infantry patrolled the woods around them.

Mousa walked a few metres away and looked down the hill towards the east, where the rolling landscape was blanketed in darkness. Out there, three hundred thousand Arabian troops waited, ready to advance north. This was it, the final stage of the European campaign, and Mousa offered up a silent prayer of gratitude. It was monumental what had been achieved and the general had been here to see it all. He turned to Karroubi.

'Wake me at one. The attack will commence at four as planned.'

'Yes, General Mousa.'

For the British troops on the border, the night was a restless one. They knew that the Arabian assault was imminent. Reports were coming in of firefights breaking out all along the border as Arabian Special Forces tried to penetrate the trench system. So far, they'd been unsuccessful.

The attack had to come by land and both the Arabians and the British knew it. With each flight into the country, the Americans had delivered dozens of portable air-defence systems, a lightweight unit the size of a telephone booth that held a magazine of four surface-to-air missiles controlled by a simple yet powerful fire-and-forget air-search radar system. The PADS were deployed at regular intervals along the border and their radar envelopes washed the sky to the south. In addition to the PADS, the overhead shield was augmented by standard ground-to-air defence systems, creating a formidable anti-air screen over southern Scotland. Until these systems were disabled, the Arabians would have to fight their way across the border without air support.

On the high ground of Northumberland's Cheviot Hills, British soldiers peered out over trench tops and squinted through their camouflaged gun slits into the darkness before them. According to intelligence reports, this was where the main axis of the Arabian attack would strike. Every few minutes a flare would pop high over the sloping ground below, bathing the shallow valleys below in ghostly white light. A rolling sea of razor wire shimmered under the harsh glow of the flares until the light faded, once again plunging the landscape into blackness.

In the sky above, Arabian UAV surveillance craft buzzed low across the British defences, mapping targets. It would start soon, of that there was no doubt. Every soldier on the border that night could feel the tension rising as the minutes ticked by. At midnight, two-thirds of the troops were ordered into hardened shelters that would shield them from the worst of the artillery barrage that was sure to signal the start of the Arabian offensive. Those that remained on the line were mainly Royal Engineers and they had work to do.

Behind the front line, in towns, villages and forests along the border, every tank and armoured fighting vehicle the British could muster waited nervously in their pre-battle positions, engines shut down and heavily camouflaged. Ten miles behind the armour, artillery units were redeployed in a deadly game of hide-and-seek, constantly changing their firing positions in an attempt to fool the Arabian rocket batteries that were no doubt attempting to target them.

Further north, the remnants of the Royal Air Force were ready for the coming attack. Scattered across several military and civilian airfields, scores of planes lined up along runways ready for the signal to commence operations, their wing mounts and gun pods filled with imported US munitions. Already in the air, combat air patrols flew racetrack patterns, topping off their fuel tanks from several USAF KC-135 tankers that flew in support. In all, the British had managed to assemble a total of eighty-seven aircraft, forty-eight of which were fighter-bombers. The remaining aircraft were a mixture of air-to-air fighters and electronic warfare platforms, and all waited nervously for the order to fly south into battle.

Inside British military headquarters, now relocated from Edinburgh to an underground command post just outside Fort William in the Highlands, General Bashford and his remaining staff watched and waited for the impending attack. Every man and woman in the command post, and those along the border, had volunteered to stay and fight. Their numbers were woefully inadequate, but they had a few tricks up their sleeve that they hoped would give the Arabians pause for thought.

The plan was to save as many lives as possible. The war was already lost, and the forces that were about to be hurled at them would guarantee that the forthcoming battle would be lost too. Their only hope was to ensure that as many people survived the coming conflict as possible. The plans were in place and, in the command post, operations staff talked in hushed tones as they pored over maps and computer consoles. Everyone watched the clock as the minutes ticked slowly by. It wouldn't be long now. The attack would come before first light.

In the darkness, Harry Beecham trudged across the courtyard of McIntyre Castle, an overnight bag in his hand. There was no moon, only the reflected light of a recent dusting of snow, and a cold wind sighed through the surrounding forest. He stopped short of the small party that waited for him, veering off towards a single figure dressed in full combat gear who stood quietly to one side. Harry set his bag down and thrust his hands inside his coat pockets, the man before him barely recognisable, his body festooned with equipment and weaponry, his face streaked with dark camouflage cream.

'Where's Farrell?'

Gibson jerked a thumb over his shoulder. 'Already on the transport, Boss. He doesn't like goodbyes.'

'I see. Well, this is it then,' Harry sighed. He studied his shoes for several moments, unsure of his words. 'You know Mike, for the first time in my career I'm actually speechless. Saying thanks just doesn't seem enough. I owe you my life, everything.'

Gibson shrugged and smiled. 'Don't mention it.'

They shook hands, Harry closing both of his over Gibson's. 'It doesn't have to be this way,' he said. 'I could order you to accompany me north, get you both out of this godawful mess.'

Gibson shook his head in the darkness, his breath fogging on the cold air. 'Tempting, but we'd have to decline. The lads would never forgive us.'

Harry nodded. It was worth a try, but he knew that every man was needed on the border, particularly the men of the special forces. To be allowed to sit it out, to avoid the fight while others faced the full brunt of the enemy attack, was anathema to men like Mike Gibson. Harry understood.

'Then take good care of yourselves,' he urged, 'and try not to do anything too brave or too stupid. You know the radio frequencies, yes?' Gibson nodded. 'We'll be monitoring those frequencies from Iceland. If you can, make contact. Transport arrangements will follow. Get as many out as you can, Mike.'

'I'll do my best, Boss.'

'I know,' Harry smiled. 'Good luck, then. And Godspeed.' He patted Gibson's arm, then quickly turned away. Ahead of him shadowy figures waited patiently, feet stamping on the snowy ground. On the far lawn the Dark Eagle idled, its ultra quiet rotors spinning noiselessly as it prepared for imminent departure.

The group closed in around Harry as he approached. Two of them were soldiers, a newly appointed close-protection team to take the place of Gibson and Farrell. The other two were Deputy Prime Minister Noonan and a military liaison officer whom Harry had only just met. Bill Kerr stood to one side as the liaison officer reached for Harry's holdall.

'We really must push on, Prime Minister. The attack could start at any time now and we're quite exposed here.'

Harry nodded grimly. The troops that had provided perimeter defence around McIntyre had been transported south four hours ago to fill gaps in the defence line. There now remained only a single company of soldiers providing security and they, too, would be leaving on waiting trucks, just as soon as Harry was airborne. The liaison officer was right. McIntyre felt suddenly naked, exposed by its dwindling security force. Still, that was okay with Harry. There were thousands of ordinary people across the country whose safety was also compromised. Why should he be any different?

He turned to look for Gibson but he'd disappeared into the night, towards the troop trucks that rumbled on the road beyond the trees. All that remained were his footprints in the snow, snaking towards the distant forest. His eyes travelled across the familiar silhouette of McIntyre Castle, a place that had become home for the last few months and a place that he would probably never see again. Harry fought back a wave of emotion. Time passes, things change, even more so in wartime. It was an inevitable fact of life.

'I'll look after her, don't worry,' Kerr assured him, as if reading his thoughts. 'She'll be here for another five hundred years, I'd imagine.'

Harry turned and forced a smile for the old Scot. 'There's still time for you to join us, Bill. Plenty of room on the chopper.'

Kerr shook his head. 'I'm not one for travelling, Prime Minister. Besides, it'll be much too cold for them heathen bastards up here. I've a wee feeling that, if they dare come this far, they won't stay for long.'

Harry gripped the old man's hand. 'I hope to God you're right, Bill.'

'I generally am,' smiled Kerr.

They parted as they'd met, in the black of night, by the windswept shores of the Sound of Kerrera.

Battle Zone
3.59 A.M.

On the British front line, the men of the Royal Engineers finally finished their preparations. Scrambling from the trenches, they ran to the hardened shelters just as the horizon to the south lit up the predawn sky. Within seconds, tens of thousands of artillery rounds began impacting on the border in a barrage not seen since the Second World War.

The first rounds fell purposely short, chewing up the fields of razor wire and tank traps, as Arabian forward artillery observers hidden near the British lines radioed back new targets to the heavy gun and rocket crews. High explosive rounds rained down on the defences themselves, while airburst shells detonated above the front line, sending millions of white-hot fragments down into empty trenches. Starburst shells lit up the sky, and long-range rockets sought out tanks and armoured vehicles hidden behind the front line. For forty-five minutes the earth shook and the sky glowed red as the storm erupted along the length of the Scottish border. Then, as suddenly as it had started, the shelling stopped.

Inside the command post at Fort William, General Bashford and his staff watched their display screens intently. The images they were watching were being broadcast from UAVs circling high above the front line, the border transformed into a landscape of huge, muddy craters wrapped in a drifting curtain of smoke. Slowly, as the fog began to clear, more distinct objects began to take shape. Some trench systems were still intact in places, along with their supporting fire point and gun emplacements. Above the Cheviot Hills, where the main Arabian thrust was anticipated, the UAVs were piloted further south as their on-board cameras swept the darkness beyond the pitted battle lines. And that's when they saw them.

All along the border, whistle blasts brought troops sprinting from the shelters to their defensive positions. They poured into the trenches to discover that a great many had been chewed up by the massive artillery barrage, and their well-constructed and expertly camouflaged fire points had been reduced to mud-filled craters and splintered timbers. Entrenching tools were produced and the battered defences shored up as quickly as possible. With the hasty repairs completed, all eyes turned to the south.

Thousands of flares were fired into the sky. The razor wire fields were gone, scattered in twisted clumps across the scarred landscape, or completely obliterated by the artillery storm. On the approach roads, the concrete tank obstacles had been mostly reduced to rubble or simply pulverised by the massive force of the barrage.

As thousands of phosphorous parachute flares drifted towards the ground, the defenders looked beyond the nightmarish scene to the south. The glow of the flares cast long, dark shadows, reflecting off the curtain of smoke that had begun to dissipate on the predawn breeze. The British troops were dug in as best they could. Every soldier was equipped with more ammunition than they could possibly carry, plus several light anti-tank weapons each and, as the minutes ticked by, the tension mounted to almost unbearable levels. As the troops waited nervously for the Arabians to appear, an eerie silence descended along the border.

The soldiers defending Keegan Fell heard it first, the clank of steel and grind of caterpillar tracks that echoed menacingly over the hills. A hundred pairs of binoculars were trained south and a thousand pairs of eyes strained to catch the first glimpse of the enemy. A whistling sound that grew into a screaming crescendo signalled another barrage that had every British soldier hugging the bottom of his trench. It lasted for two long minutes and, when the shell-shocked troops finally peered cautiously over their defences, they discovered that they couldn't see more than fifty yards. The thick smokescreen swirled and eddied before them, but the noise behind it grew louder. Tanks, lots of them, advancing up the broken tarmac of the A68 and through the forests of the Northumberland National Park. All along the trenches, heads swivelled and eyes strained to pierce the clouds of smoke, flickering beneath the harsh light of the flares. Hearts hammered, weapons were cocked and bayonets fixed with trembling fingers. It was going to be hand-to-hand combat when the Arabians broke through, of that there was no doubt.

Now another sound penetrated the fog, a deep rumble that grew into a metallic roar, advancing up the slope towards the dug in soldiers on Keegan Fell. The ground began to shake beneath them. A heavy machine gun opened up to the west, but stopped after repeated shouts of cease fire echoed across the ridge top. All that could be heard now was the eerie clank of tracks and the whine of gas turbine engines that increased in volume with every passing second.

Suddenly the wind picked up, gusting from the north. Like a curtain drawn back, the smokescreen across the battlefield was blown away in a matter of seconds. As the fog swirled and dissipated, the troops on Keegan Fell saw the monstrous layered defence destroyer less than one hundred yards away, its huge caterpillar tracks whipping up sprays of dirt as it bore down on the nearest trench. Packed tightly behind it, hundreds of Arabian troops stumbled through the mud, ready to fan out once their giant protector had breached the trenches. Further behind, scores of tanks and thousands of troops advanced in a great wave towards the fell across the pitted terrain.

Within seconds, British troops launched a fusillade of anti-tank rounds at the LDD, whose wedge-shaped blade seemed to deflect the swarm of missiles as they bounced and skimmed crazily into the sky. Others aimed their missiles at the massed ranks of Arabian soldiers immediately behind, who struggled up the slick, muddy slope in an effort to keep up with the LDD. The detonations sent bodies spinning through the air like rag dolls. More British troops, suddenly aware of the imminent danger to their defences, opened fire with heavy weapons and small arms, cutting down hundreds of Arabians in a withering crossfire. More flares lit up the sky as the defenders further along the fell saw the strength of the enemy before them. The call went out.

Ten miles behind the front line massed British artillery opened fire on pre-programmed co-ordinates. Along the fell, the defenders roared with delight as a curtain of steel erupted across the battlefield, sending huge columns of black earth into the sky. But the rounds had fallen short and someone else had also anticipated the artillery attack.

Inside two Big Eye surveillance aircraft orbiting seventy-five kilometres behind the battle zone, Arabian operators noted the heat blooms of the British guns and the arc and fall of the initial bombardment. In a matter of seconds, the data had been downloaded to several Arabian artillery batteries positioned twenty kilometres behind the front line. They immediately launched a deadly salvo of over four thousand high explosive missiles, averaging over two per target.

Nearly sixty per cent of British artillery was destroyed in that first barrage and those units that did survive thanked their lucky stars, shut down their systems and quickly moved position. The best they could hope for was to get off maybe two or three rounds before they had to change position again. It wasn't going to be enough.

On the front line, British joy turned to despair when the artillery rounds stopped falling amongst the Arabian tanks. Illuminated by a constant shower of flares, the ground below the fell was now an undulating mass of Arabian troops and vehicles as wave after wave crossed the muddy, cratered earth below. Scores of tanks nosed their way out of the treeline further to the south and opened fire, adding to the crescendo of noise and screams that threatened to deafen everyone on the battlefield.

With a thunderous roar, the LDD reached the nearest trench line, the log walls collapsing beneath its massive tracks as the giant vehicle shuddered to a halt near the crest of the fell. British troops scattered left and right along the forward trench line, running through the mud to new positions. The LDD gunners inside their reinforced hull directed their weapons and hosed the trenches in either direction with machine-gun fire. Grenade tubes fired round after round of high explosives along the defence line and the detonations banged and cracked along the muddy channels.

But the driver of the LDD was having difficulty moving his massive machine. This wasn't like the exercises on the hard-baked terrain of the North African desert. Here, the slope rose steeply and the ground was a quagmire. As he tried to coax the LDD up toward the flat ground beyond the peak the giant machine stubbornly refused, slipping sideways, then backwards. The caterpillar tracks were thick with cloying mud and, in his ear, the driver could hear his superior yelling at him to continue over the crest of the fell. But getting there was proving to be the devil's work. The shouting in his earpiece got louder as an anti-tank round detonated against the side of the hull.

The driver reversed a few metres, crushing several Arabian soldiers sheltering behind its massive bulk, then applied full power. The LDD lurched forward again, clearing a wide gap in the British defences that the following Arabian troops began to pour into. The driver accelerated the LDD further up the slope and finally crested the summit of the fell, crashing down on the other side with a deep, seismic concussion. Immediately, the rear ramp went down and the Arabian infantry inside the LDD split left and right along the rear trench lines to engage the British.

Above the ear-splitting wall of noise that greeted them, they heard the unmistakable blast of whistles.

The whistle blasts pierced the roar of battle and shrilled all along the British defences. Sector after sector acknowledged the signal and retreated north as planned. In many areas, the defenders fell back under heavy fire as the Arabians pursued them relentlessly, spilling into trenches and bunkers behind them like an unstoppable tide. Less than half of the British troops in these sectors managed to escape. The rest were either dead, wounded or simply cut off by the fast-moving Arabian forces.

Perversely, in other sectors along the border, not a single shot was fired as the defending troops listened to the sound of distant battles rumbling across the night sky. When the whistle blasts echoed over the hills and through the forests the defenders withdrew, moving quickly and quietly to the waiting transports.

In the black shadows of Ker Hope Forest, near the Cumbrian border, Mike Gibson dived for cover yet again as more debris rained down around his trench. For the last twenty minutes Gibson and his fellow defenders had managed to keep the Arabian troops at bay with sustained heavy weapons fire, mortars and anti-tank rounds, but now the enemy had drawn close all around them and the heavy weapons were out of ammunition.

The trench line ran along the southern edge of the forest, where Gibson and Farrell had finally joined a mixed unit of British Paras and Special Forces one hour before the attack began. After the initial Arabian barrage, Gibson and his men had managed to stem the ground assault for some time, but Arabian infantry soon flanked their trenches and there was now intense fighting to the rear. Pinned down in his trench, Gibson heard the whistle of the withdrawal signal, but some of the lads were still fighting close by and he wouldn't leave them. He was surrounded now, cut off from his escape route.

He leaned against the rear wall of the trench, raised himself up and peered carefully in all directions. Through the trees behind him he could see muzzle flashes and heard the sharp detonation of grenades. The Arabians were clearing the trenches one by one, and all around him he could hear shouting and screaming in a foreign tongue.

He looked down at Farrell's body. A round had taken him straight through the temple and he lay sprawled at the bottom of the trench, his legs twisted beneath him. Gibson had no illusions about his own fate and he certainly wasn't going to surrender. He called out, trying to make contact with someone, but this time his calls went unanswered, the radio strapped to his body armour lifeless. The sound of the British guns fell silent and Gibson realised he was the last man standing.

Suddenly a dark shape ran towards him from the trench to his right, silhouetted by a burning tank nearby. He opened fire with his rifle and the figure hit the ground hard with a low grunt. He swivelled around as he heard the sharp crack of snapping branches behind him. Two more figures rushed through the pine trees, screaming in an unintelligible tongue. Gibson dropped them both with another short burst.

The punch in his back winded him, sending him crashing into the trench wall. He spun around to see another Arabian charging out of the smoke ten feet in front of him. Gibson fired a single round and missed. His rifle was empty and he threw it at the advancing shape, then drew his pistol. He fired two quick rounds and the Arabian fell headlong, landing a few feet from the trench. Gibson thought about taking his weapon, but the man had fallen on top of it and suddenly it seemed like too much effort to recover it.

He must be winded, because his chest hurt and he was having trouble breathing. He reached around under his left armpit and felt the warm stickiness beneath his body armour. His head swam and his knees began to buckle. He slid down the trench wall and slumped heavily on the dirt floor, his breathing laboured and a sudden tightness constricting his chest. Farrell stared across the trench at him with lifeless eyes and Gibson looked away, towards the sound of movement close by.

Using his remaining strength, Gibson pulled the pin from a grenade and lobbed it over the lip of the trench. He was rewarded with a scream of agony as the weapon exploded and forest debris rained down on top of him. There were more footfalls above him, harsh voices whispering in the darkness. He tried to bring his pistol up but his arm wouldn't respond.

Mike Gibson knew the end was close and he was surprised to discover he was frightened. What lay ahead he couldn't possibly know, but he was about to find out and the thought chilled him. His paratrooper grandfather had died in similar circumstances, killed while attacking a trench during the Falklands War. Now Gibson was about to die defending one and the irony of the moment wasn't lost on him.

The sound of battle suddenly faded as a childhood memory jolted him; he was home again, a child, squatting on a patterned carpet as his chubby fingers fumbled with a pile of coloured building blocks. He saw an electric fire, felt the warmth of its single bar on his bare legs. Above the fireplace was a photograph, a man in uniform with a maroon beret, staring proudly out into the living room. In the background a radio played, and he saw his mother standing in the kitchen, humming softly as she chopped vegetables. Then she turned and smiled, and suddenly Gibson wasn't afraid any more.

He opened his eyes as a silhouette loomed above him, then another. He tried to raise his pistol, hoping that someone, somewhere would remember Mike Gibson. His life ended in a blinding flash.

When the order came, forty-eight RAF fighter-bombers thundered south on afterburner, hugging the earth at a dangerously low level. They were split into eight groups of six aircraft, each formation headed for the sectors where Arabian forces had broken through the defence line in significant numbers. It would be a deadly game they were about to play. The PADS were still operating on automatic mode and the fighter-bombers had to ensure that they didn't fly above four hundred feet or else they would fall prey to their own missiles. The pilots pushed on, rumbling across the predawn landscape. Towns, roads and forests flashed below them, barely visible in the darkness.

And then, quite suddenly, they were over the front line.

At Keegan Fell, the Arabians were still clearing the trenches. The main road that dissected the border was being hastily repaired by Arabian combat engineers, as more than fifty tanks queued along the broken tarmac to head north. The terrain around the road had proved too waterlogged and pitted for the fifty-tonne monsters, so they waited on the hardstanding for the engineers to finish their work.

Around the tanks, thousands of troops were headed up the face of the fell and dropping down into the trenches. Already, the infantry were reforming, preparing to head further north. Recce units had pushed forward and checked the roads, reporting that they were clear and serviceable. At the top of the fell, mud-caked Arabian troops shuffled up the ramp of the LDD and filed inside, ready to head deeper into enemy territory. The sudden, ear-splitting scream of the lead British jet had everyone in the open running for cover.

One by one the pilots released their munitions. Cluster bombs, smart weapons, bunker busters, dumb iron bombs – everything that could be dropped was dumped on to the enemy forces below. The fighter-bombers flashed above the front line, spilling their deadly cargoes in their wake before turning north on full afterburner. Keegan Fell erupted in a huge sheet of flame as bombs carpeted the summit.

The lead pilots thundered over the tank column below, marking the target with strobes for the following aircraft. The tanks, forming a line over two miles long, tried desperately to get clear of the road. Most made it, but at least twenty tanks were destroyed by low-flying bombers and cluster munitions. The survivors up on the fell managed to fire a few handheld SAMs, but they were too late. They watched with mounting rage as the bright blue exhausts of the British planes shrank to tiny dots and disappeared over the northern horizon.

The trench system was devastated and hundreds had been killed or wounded in the attack. Rescue teams fought hard to dig out the casualties from the mud and smoking craters that dotted the rugged contours of the fell.

On the flat ground behind the ridgeline, the Arabian infantry corporal muttered a silent prayer of thanks as he looked out over the hellish scene below. Yes, they had been victorious, but the infidels had made them pay for every foot of ground. He cursed the British pilots, the Yankees who helped them, his own comrades who'd been too slow or too stupid to shoot them down. Still, at least he had the luxury of being able to curse. Lucky for him he'd been sent over the ridge with his section to check for enemy activity. The cowards were on the run, he was told. Pursue them, and kill as many as possible.

He turned to wave his crouching section onwards when he stopped in his tracks. The bomb crater near the treeline wasn't a large one, probably the result of a mortar round, but the wires that protruded from it headed off into the trees. He looked back towards the fell. The wires were also headed in the direction of the British trenches. Strange. The Arabian ordered his section to fan out into the trees, while he splashed into the water-filled crater and ran the mud-caked lines through his fingers. Were they telephone wires? He plied and twisted the thick black sheathing; too strong for telephone wire. What was it then? He tugged it hard. The wire was buried deep but it finally sprang free from the mud, disappearing into another crater nearby. The corporal followed it and discovered another tangle of wires, all headed in different directions, twisting all over the fell.

His eyes suddenly widened.

'Now.'

Four miles to the north, inside a tracked command vehicle, the combat engineer pushed a green button on his control panel. The three soldiers inside the vehicle watched through their vision slits as the night sky to the south lit up with the pulsing intensity of a nuclear detonation. Seconds later, the shock wave passed over them, rattling the windows of nearby houses and dislodging tiles from roofs. Beneath their feet the ground shook for several seconds.

The Royal Engineer captain breathed a sigh of relief. Thank God the wires had survived. It had been a time-consuming and laboriously long operation, burying over two hundred tonnes of explosives at a dozen predicted choke points along the length of the border, linking it all up to the electronic triggering systems, then testing and retesting the links. Some of it would work, had worked, but other links would have been broken by the storm of artillery and rockets. Thankfully, the Keegan Fell site had worked perfectly.

When the Arabian forces had attacked, when there was no hope of holding them, the prearranged signal had gone out. As the sound of massed whistles shrilled along the border, the defenders had fled their positions and headed north. Even now, jeeps and trucks were passing their position, roaring through the village in blacked-out convoys. It wasn't a great plan, but hopefully it had saved a lot of lives and would slow up the Arabian advance in the process. To the south the sky still glowed, now a deep red. It was time to move.

The camouflage nets were rolled up and lashed down, then the command vehicle roared into life. It lurched out from its hiding place in the car park of a village pub and rumbled along the narrow country lanes, chasing a speeding troop truck, its rear filled with smiling, muddy soldiers. Ten miles to the north was the town of Jedburgh. There they would dump the tracked vehicle and find a truck themselves, something that would transport them into the Highlands that much quicker.

Behind them, Keegan Fell had disappeared off the map. On open ground below the fell, the advancing Arabians slowly picked themselves up out of the freezing mud. They'd spent the last twenty minutes trudging across the battlefield in long columns, laden down with equipment and heading towards the ridge in front of them. They had missed the earlier battle and, as they filed around the deep craters, slipping and stumbling on the chewed up earth, they saw the piles of dead bodies and screaming wounded and were grateful that they had been selected for the second wave. Then had come the blinding flash and the world had erupted in front of their very eyes. A wall of mud had covered the leading troops and it was several minutes before anyone moved.

When they did, they saw that two massive chunks of earth had been scooped out of the ridgetop and the trees up there were gone. It resembled the aftermath of two huge landslides. The LDD that had squatted on top of the fell was now on its back at the foot of the slope, half buried in mud. Hundreds of troops had been instantly wiped out and hundreds more buried under the giant wave of earth, mud and trees that rained down over the whole area.

At other strategically crucial points along the border, similar detonations shook the earth and stopped the Arabians in their tracks. From inside his command vehicle, General Mousa ordered his forces to hold their positions until engineers could be brought up in strength to clear the whole line. The combined air attack and explosive traps had cost the Arabians dear and brought the advance to a grinding halt. Intelligence from the Big Eyes reported the presence of hundreds of PADS still operating far behind the front line. Until these were taken out the Arabian troops would remain in position and hold at the border.

For now, the battle was over.

Departure

The US Navy Sea Dragon helicopter circled the wide valley once before making its final approach, flaring and landing a few yards away from the strobe marker that pulsed near the centre of the snow-encrusted field. Overhead in the dawn sky, a flight of four fighter jets rumbled unseen around the horizon. Just inside the treeline of the surrounding forest, Harry stood under the damp canopy of pine branches and watched the helicopter settle a short distance away. So, this was it.

His gaze wandered beyond the aircraft, to the dark sky behind the eastern peaks of the valley. On the other side of the country, Russian naval forces were already probing the Scottish coastline, filling the void left by the Royal Navy after their escape towards Iceland. Surprisingly, to the south, the bulk of the Arabian forces had remained in their pre-battle positions, just short of the border. No one knew why, only that they were grateful for the opportunity to evacuate more troops out of the country.

Harry glanced to his right. A short distance away, General Bashford stood quietly beside his senior staff officers, locked in whispered conversation. Most of the British military forces had escaped across the sea, packed into US Navy logistics ships and transport aircraft. The airports were now abandoned, the runways silent.

The cause was lost, as Bashford had known from the start it would be, but in the final reckoning the general had found it hard to accept. It really was time to leave, Harry had privately urged him. They'd had a good run, he reminded the soldier; they had given the enemy several bloody noses and saved countless lives, but the stark realities of their situation had to be faced. The game was finally up.

But not for everyone. Lord Advocate Matheson and his small administration had decided to stay behind, along with several senior officers and over four thousand soldiers, most of them from the Scottish regiments. Matheson was taking his people further north, where the rugged beauty of the Highlands offered many places from which to launch a guerrilla war against the invaders. The Scots promised to make the enemy pay in blood for every inch of Scottish soil.

Harry had felt a chill run down his spine as Matheson's senior military commander, a colonel in the newly re-formed Black Watch, declared his murderous intent to the room at Fort William. Despite himself, Harry pitied those who found themselves on the receiving end of that cold fury. They'd left the command bunker shortly afterwards, driving in a small convoy to the coastal valley, where they now waited.

Harry shivered in the cold air as he watched four heavily armed US Marines leap from the helicopter and jog through the snow towards the trees. The lead marine was a tough-looking man in his mid-forties, with black paratrooper's wings sewn above his breast pocket. He had a no-nonsense air about him and, as he approached Harry, he threw up a quick salute.

'Prime Minister, my name is Captain Van Buren. I'll be your escort out of here. The *Arizona* is waiting offshore, so I would advise we move quickly. Are you ready to leave, sir?'

Harry took a deep breath and nodded. 'Thank you, Captain. Yes, I think we are.' He turned around and shook hands with the officer of the patrol that had guided them through the forest to the pickup point. These were some of the men who would be staying behind and Harry had the utmost admiration for their bravery. 'Good luck,' he said.

'You too, sir,' replied the officer. Without waiting, the soldier turned away and faded back into the trees with his patrol. Harry, Bashford and the others watched them go, then head out into the valley.

Leading the way, Van Buren strode towards the helicopter, its rotors lashing the field in a violent downdraught. Harry followed, bent against the blizzard of snow and ice. When everybody was safely aboard, the helicopter quickly lifted off the ground, dipping its nose and banking towards the western end of the valley. Gradually, the massive aircraft gained altitude and cleared the ridgeline, then headed in a north-easterly direction, a route that would take them out over the Atlantic towards the waiting aircraft carrier.

Harry looked down at the passing treetops below and all the emotions of the last few months came rushing up to meet him. He cuffed a damp eye with his sleeve; so many lives lost, so much destruction. It was difficult to comprehend that just a short time ago Harry's major concern was the economy and how to fix it. He had a wife then, and a home.

In a modern world it was so easy to take things for granted, to go about one's daily business, to make plans for a future that no one truly believed was uncertain. People always assumed that bad things happened to others, not themselves. But bad things had happened, terrible things, and nearly everyone in the country had been affected. No, Harry corrected himself, this wasn't just a British problem; the whole of Europe had been affected and the crisis had yet to play out globally. Only God knew where that would lead. He was still dumbfounded as to how such an audacious plan had ever succeeded, but succeeded it had and Harry would be left to ponder over the reasons, the failures, in the years ahead. For his own reputation he didn't much care. What's done is done, he realised, but for those left behind, they were already paying the price, living under the yoke of Arabian rule.

The Sea Dragon thundered low across the coastline, where rolling green waves pounded themselves to white spray on the jagged rocks below. They skimmed above the water, climbing as they headed out to the safety of the sea. Harry rested his forehead on the Perspex window and watched the white-capped waters roll beneath them. The sun had risen behind the aircraft, its light smothered by heavy grey cloud cover. Ahead the sky was still dark, the ship that would transport them across the ocean as refugees still hidden by the stubborn cloak of night. Harry closed his eyes and offered up a silent prayer, for the wife he could not bury, for the countless others who'd died, and for the living who were still caught up in this nightmare. He prayed that they would find some kind of peace in the years to come and, in that uncertain future, Britain would be a free nation once again.

He opened his eyes. As the coastline receded to a dark line on the horizon, Harry Beecham whispered farewell to the land of his birth, knowing he would never set foot on her soil, or breathe her air again.

Somewhere in the Arabian Desert

Alex brushed aside the tent flap and straightened up, stretching his limbs and scratching at the lice beneath his thick beard. He wiped his hands on the black smock that draped his bony frame, then made his way slowly between the endless rows of white canvas marquees that stretched in all directions across the flat, sun-baked desert. Tent City was expanding all the time, to accommodate the growing numbers of prisoners that were still arriving from Europe, and Alex cursed his ever-lengthening journey, the mounting workload, the relentless sun. The surrounding terrain was featureless in every direction, except for a thin ridge of hills to the east. Beyond those hills was the Site, a place that people only spoke about in quiet whispers. Alex had yet to see it, and prayed he never would.

The Site was supposedly the largest single construction project ever undertaken. Out there, across the arid desert, a whole city was being built, a city that consisted of huge mosques with soaring minarets, of marbled palaces, residential complexes and luxurious hotels, all surrounding some kind of giant monolith that held enormous religious significance for the Arabians. Mecca II, some called it. Not in earshot of the Arabians, though.

The remote location of such a project was a familiar topic of discussion around the cooking fires in the evenings. Some said that an artefact had been found beneath the desert floor, an artefact so important to the Islamic faith that the Site had been decreed a holy place above all others. Others said that an ancient mosque had been uncovered by shifting desert sands, a mosque where Muhammad himself was rumoured to have dispensed his divine wisdoms.

Alex didn't know what to believe, but the nuclear exchange between Israel and Arabia, the one that destroyed Jerusalem, Mecca and Baghdad, was the most likely reason for construction on such a scale. It also explained the intense lights that had pulsed on the northern horizon, the shock waves that had rolled across the desert floor and rippled through the massed ranks of canvas tents. It was only after those terrifying nights, now over eighteen months ago Alex calculated, that construction had begun. Almost overnight the bleak desert prison had been transformed into a work camp, and seen the arrival of so many important Arabian political and military figures.

The Site was to be built by the hand of man alone and without the help of labour-saving machinery, the prisoners were told. A never-ending supply of slave labour was required to carve stone and marble from distant quarries, to transport it to the Site and carefully construct the buildings that were springing up beyond the hills. It explained the endless stream of prisoners transported in from Europe and from the irradiated wastelands of Israel.

The parallels drawn with ancient Egypt were unmistakable. All that was missing was the crack of whips, and Alex didn't rule that out either. He'd heard about conditions at the Site and thanked God he didn't work there. The hours were impossibly long, the workload brutal, and many of the occupants interred beneath the sands of the workers' cemetery had died because of heat exhaustion, many more by industrial accident. It was not quite as bad in Tent City, but the heat was a killer. Find every shadow, he'd been warned on arrival, every wedge of shade no matter how small. It will save your life.

Alex was surprised he still clung to that old life, but not as desperately these days. He'd arrived in a batch of over two hundred prisoners on a windowless cargo plane, one that had flown them from a holding camp in Morocco to this remote, unknown area of desert. Prior to that, he'd spent several months in a clean-up crew in Madrid, a city that had been effectively reduced to rubble after heavy fighting during the invasion.

Talking had been forbidden during shifts, but there was always an opportunity for a clandestine conversation with a shackled neighbour. Alex discovered that most of his fellow prisoners were police officers from a variety of European countries. Each man had similar stories to tell about their experiences, but most of them agreed that the sheer scale and audacity of the Arabian operation had caught them unawares. Others were more cynical, grumbling that the invasion had been an event waiting to happen. It hardly mattered now.

Alex spoke of his final days in England, how he and several thousand other prisoners had been paraded along a packed Mall in London. They had shuffled past the jeering crowds, past the Arabian cavalry in their ceremonial dress, flanked by the combat troops who marched in tight formation around them until they eventually rippled to a halt in front of Buckingham Palace itself. There, outside the former home of the British royal family, they had listened in silence as the Grand Mufti Khathami himself spoke passionately to the crowds, and the throng gathered before the palace had cheered and waved in ecstatic response. The ceremony over, the prisoners were marched away and transported to the docks in Portsmouth.

There was a sense of finality about that night, Alex remembered. As he'd boarded the cargo ship, a feeling of despair overcame him and he wondered how long it would be before he saw the dark coastline of England again. As the months passed, that hope had faded to a point where his previous life felt like a dream. It all seemed so long ago now, the heat of the desert evaporating his memories, stifling his emotions. Which was probably for the best.

The hot sun was beginning to dip towards the horizon as Alex trudged between the long rows of tents, grateful for the slight drop in temperature. The black linen smock and pants they all wore were designed to soak up the heat, to make life uncomfortable, to make it easier for the Arabian patrols to locate the bodies of escapees against the white sands of the desert. With no guard towers or fences, plenty of prisoners had tried, heading out into the desert under cover of darkness, but their bodies had always been recovered and returned for burial. Every escapee was accounted for, a reminder to those who might contemplate fleeing that only death awaited them out beyond the sun-baked horizon. The simple truth was that escape was futile and Alex discovered that most of the prisoners had come to accept their fate. As he had too.

He skirted around the ropes of the last tent and the empty desert opened up before him. A mile away was the burial ground and Alex could see the multitude of small white grave markers shimmering in the distance. It was a predominately Christian cemetery, tolerated by the camp administrators and divided by nationality for practical purposes. There was a Jewish graveyard too, ten times the size and located far beyond the hills to the east. All Jews went to work at the Site, without exception. No one gave much for their survival and no one dared ask.

As he shielded his eyes against the setting sun, Alex could see several others making their way to and from the gravesite, their silhouettes quivering in the heat haze. He took a long swig from a water bottle and set off across the desert floor.

By the time he reached the cemetery, the shadows were beginning to lengthen. He moved slowly through the centre, past the neat rows of German, Italian, French, Dutch and Spanish graves and towards the far edge of the burial ground, where the new arrivals waited, wrapped in white sheets and bound by ropes. His fellow gravediggers waited too, shovels in hand, playfully teasing Alex for his tardiness.

They got to work, scratching at the hard desert floor until the sweat dripped from their beards and the dirt piled high beside them. It took an hour to complete the pit and lay the bodies to rest. The Dutchman, Boeker, recited some lines from the Bible, the freshly painted head board was hammered home with a shovel, and that was that. After the others had left, Alex reached inside the pocket of his loose trousers and produced a handful of small pebbles. Kneeling down, he placed them on the ground around the grave, forming a loose border, something that would give this final resting place a little more permanence and dignity. Besides, he was in no rush to get back.

He stood up, dusting the sand off his knees. The graveyard had grown fast in the last year, and wooden grave markers stretched for hundreds of yards in all directions. Here and there, men walked between the rows of white-painted head boards in silent contemplation or chatted quietly in small groups. People spoke of a sense of peace here, a place where man could find solace and comfort in the quiet of the desert and the stillness of the cemetery. Alex had never been particularly religious, but he often thanked God that he'd been selected as a gravedigger. It kept him away from the Site and, for that, he remained grateful.

But lately, as the last vestiges of hope faded, he'd become resigned to his fate. Only one thing kept him going, stopped him from following the sun out beyond the horizon.

Shielding his eyes, he watched the huge red orb as it dipped to the west. Somewhere out there his son was growing up in a world without him. Yes, a son, Alex smiled to himself. Something told him the child was a boy. In many ways Alex considered himself lucky, that he didn't have a memory of a baby that had features and a personality all of its own. Occasionally, he would try and form a mental image of what the child might look like, or sound like, how he slept, ate and played. Or how he smiled. It was natural curiosity, of course, but when the images became too painful he banished them from his mind. Alex didn't harbour any illusions that he would ever see the kid, but he hoped he would grow up safe and happy, and that Kirsty would make sure that his father wouldn't be forgotten. Because, short of a miracle, this was where his life would end, buried out here in an empty desert with only a wooden head board to mark his final resting place.

Alex watched the setting sun for a few more minutes then headed off. He made his way slowly through the lines of graves and set off across the white sands of the desert, back to the sprawling camp that shimmered in the distant haze.

Epilogue

Inside the walls of his opulent home in Warwick Square, the emir led the two brothers down a narrow staircase into a large basement area. They were perfect candidates, the emir decided. They had carried out a difficult task already, finding their way back into the city after dark, but the remainder of the mission was still fraught with danger. What they required now was intelligence as well as courage, qualities he'd been assured both men possessed. But they also needed faith. To put one's life willingly into the hands of others, especially when those others were strangers with strong ties to Arabia, took a giant leap of faith. Yet, faith in the success of their mission and its aftermath was all the boys had. Without it they were nothing, doomed to a servile existence within the city walls and a life of squalor outside them.

The boys followed the emir through the brightly lit basement to a large steel locker that was fixed to a whitewashed wall. The emir opened it, revealing polishes and cleaning rags, bottles of detergent and several pairs of overalls. He squatted down with some difficulty, fumbling around inside the locker until he heard a soft click. Satisfied, he lifted a false panel to reveal an empty space below the floor, retrieving a clear plastic pouch that contained a roll of black cloth.

'Come,' he puffed. They sat down at a long wooden bench in the middle of the basement. The emir opened the pouch and laid the transparent dark cloth on the bench. He pointed to the red-haired boy, the one with steel in his eyes.

'Put this on beneath your clothes.'

The boy quickly removed his black smock and pulled the wafer-thin vest over his head. He swung his arms about and stretched, testing the flexibility of the strange material. He eyed the emir quizzically.

'It is comfortable, is it not?' noted the emir. 'Yet the material is strong and possesses a certain quality. It is the latest technology from the Americas.'

The boys' eyes met at the mention of the word. The Americas, where lives were lived long and fruitfully, where light and power were never rationed, where poverty and sickness were non-existent, where there were mountains and lakes and the freedom to roam them. It was paradise.

But to get to paradise one must first sacrifice, the emir often reminded young fighters like these. There was a price to pay for everything, and the price for a place on a ship to the New World was a mission of great importance. Like this one. The attack would remind the rulers that there was still some fight left in this nation, that its people hadn't forgotten a history that successive regimes had stifled and buried. When the blow was struck the word would spread, even to the camps in the north, and maybe as far as the Borderlands, from where the first fighters had originated.

History told that the invading Arabian armies had stopped short of the cold, snow-capped hills that heralded the gateway to the Borderlands, had tired of the struggle against the guerrilla fighters who lived in the impenetrable forests and beneath the deserted cities. Even now, over two hundred years since the Great Invasion, the guerrillas continued to probe the Wall, the massive fortification that stretched from coast to coast, constructed to keep Arabia's enemies penned inside what was once called Scotland. Border troops manned its high walls and gazed out across the stormy frontier, shivering in the cold winds and thick snows that swept down from the north.

The emir spent the next hour explaining how best to use the vest and where to place it for maximum effect, outlining the plan on a simple chalkboard. They went over the instructions several times; the boys were not stupid, but speed was of the essence and they rehearsed the practical side of the operation with specially constructed props.

He watched them carefully as their hands displayed a speed and dexterity that was impressive beyond their years. Despite their mundane lives and menial employment, they had maintained a decent level of physical fitness and mental sharpness. That in itself was an achievement for mere Workers, realised the emir. The drudgery of their existence, the poor diet and squalid living conditions tended to crush a man's spirit long before he reached his middle years. But these young men were different, their courage to be applauded. Secretly, of course.

The emir checked the time; it was almost sunrise. Soon the first Worker trains would enter the city, the buses would fill, the subways transporting them to their places of employment. The boys had to report to the Chambers of Justice by seven o'clock. It was time to leave.

On the emir's instructions, the brothers snapped new security bracelets around their wrists. He ushered them upstairs and out through the kitchens to a large garage, where they came face to face with the emir's official vehicle, a silver Bentley limousine. It was a splendid vehicle, petrol driven of course, a symbol of the emir's rank and standing within Arabian society. The emir nodded to his manservant Ali, who quickly removed the rear seat. Underneath was a hollow compartment.

'Do not worry,' the emir assured them. 'The ride is short and the space below is adequate. Here are the tools you will need.'

He handed over a small nylon bag, indicating they should climb into the recess. Ali locked the thick leather seat back into position and the emir settled his heavy frame on top of it. At six thirty a.m. precisely, the car glided out into Warwick Square and turned east towards the river. There was no traffic to speak of and the emir noticed only one or two pedestrians on the streets. So much the better, for today was all about timing. Now that the sun had risen, the night patrols would soon be stood down, the shift changes meaning fewer uniforms on the streets. And he had timed it well. As the car continued on its journey, the emir didn't see a single policeman.

When they reached the road that swept past the lush, well-tended gardens of the Chambers of Justice, the emir looked beyond the neat rows of palms that ringed the building and up towards the dome that glowed a warm bronze in the morning sun. So many laws passed under that high arch, so much oppression heaped upon the people that inhabited the derelict Workers' camps around the country. The military battles may have been won long ago but, for the Workers who inhabited this island, the struggle continued.

The emir thought about the site on which the chambers stood, the significance to British history that the whole area held. It was the site that once housed the first parliament building and an abbey that had crowned British kings and queens for a thousand years. Both buildings were gone now, replaced by a symbol of Arabian occupation that gave so much freedom to the few, while denying it to so many others.

The emir seethed at the injustice of it all, his plump fists balling in his lap. He himself had hidden his own past well, rising to his present position of moderate power and influence amongst the Arabians. He held a seat on the city's policy committee and governed his own protectorate down in the Southern Territories, far beyond the wastelands, where the rich enjoyed the sea air in their coastal palaces. Yes, the emir had achieved much through his wide network of powerful connections and his faithful obedience to the system. But it only served to mask his true motives, to free the Workers from the poverty in which they existed, to end the persecutions they endured, condemned for the faith that some still practised in crude places of worship across the camps and in the wastelands beyond.

There were others like him too, decent Arabians who secretly served another God, determined to change the laws of an empire that stretched from the Borderlands to the foothills of Kazakhstan far to the east, where the battles with the Chinese still raged. It was an empire vast in size and the emir often felt like a single ant nipping at the thick hide of a giant elephant, tiny, inconsequential. But, if enough ants could be persuaded to attack that great beast, well, maybe things could change.

The Bentley hummed past the Chambers of Justice and continued north before gliding to the kerb by a large, well-kept park adjacent to the riverbank. His eyes drifted across the road, to the twenty-metre high statue that dissected the highway, up towards the chiselled marble features of General Faris Mousa, one of the first Arabian soldiers to land on these shores during the Great Invasion. Mousa had been a much-admired soldier, earning his place in Arabian history as one of the architects of the fall of Europe. He'd died, along with thousands of others, when Chinese Special Forces had detonated a tactical nuclear weapon in New Delhi, just before the Nepalese offensive.

Beyond Mousa's gleaming edifice stood another memorial to the Great Invasion. The small street had been preserved for historic purposes and already a small crowd of tourists, fresh in from the Gulf no doubt, had formed a queue outside the bomb-damaged and pockmarked buildings. It was a strange site, incongruous amongst the ornamental gardens that now surrounded it, but the remnants of Downing Street still drew the crowds.

Further to the east, the Gold Mosque squatted magnificently where Buckingham Palace had once stood, its towering minarets reaching up into the dawn sky. Soon the call to prayer would begin, and he intended to be in his usual place inside that magnificent building as the first notes echoed across London.

The emir slid across his seat and powered down the window, glancing at the pavement. The front tyre was directly in line with the faint chalk mark on the kerbstone. He nodded to a watching Ali in the rear-view mirror and the Bentley's engine was shut off. That was the signal.

As Ali feigned concern over the off side front tyre, the boys twisted beneath the rear seat and slid open the lower floor of their hiding place. Beneath them was the surface of the road and a wide drainage inspection cover. From the nylon bag, one of the boys produced a special tool and twisted it into a central slot on the face of the cover, lifting the metal grid out of its recess. He placed it carefully to one side and pulled himself down into the drain, twisting his body around and descending the iron ladder cemented into the drain wall. The other boy did the same, tapping three times on the exhaust pipe before sliding the inspection cover back in place above his head.

He joined his brother down on the lower level, finding himself in a wide, dry intersection of rainwater drains. The rainy season was still some months off, so they were safe from the annual deluges that London endured. Above them, the Bentley's engine purred into life and the car pulled away from the kerb. So far, so good. Now it was in God's hands.

One of the boys produced a compass and a small, hand-drawn map from the bag. Taking a bearing, they headed south along the tunnel, darting through the shafts of sunlight that beamed down from the drains above. They continued for another hundred metres and stopped. There.

At their feet was another inspection hatch, thick with filth and rusted around its edges. Using the same tool, one of the boys knelt down and, with a stifled grunt, heaved the cover off. The other man clicked on his pen torch and shone it down the black shaft at their feet. Handholds cut into the old brick walls served as ladder rungs and the bottom of the shaft looked to be about five metres below them. Quickly, both boys climbed into the shaft, replacing the cover above them. At the bottom they found themselves in a well of darkness. With the help of the torch, they discovered a long, narrow tunnel that disappeared into inky blackness in either direction, exactly as they had been told to expect. Down here, the tunnel was smaller and the air was musty and damp, a thin layer of moisture coating the curved brick walls. This was part of the old city that was built many years ago, long before the invasion, and the smell of the river was strong down here. Another compass bearing was taken and the boys headed south.

As they moved they felt a deep rumbling beneath their feet that reverberated around the walls. They were getting closer. Presently they found themselves in a darkened cavern, the brick ceiling arching high over their heads. There seemed to be lots of old equipment here, much of which they didn't recognise. There were piles of steel rails and indistinguishable metal objects, old crates filled with rags and brushes and wheeled trolleys full of portable warning signs. To their right, rail tracks snaked away into the darkness alongside a concrete walkway. It appeared to be some kind of workshop, except that this equipment hadn't been used for years.

With no further use for the contents, the boys dumped the nylon bag, moving silently along the concrete walkway until they reached another tunnel. The torch beam glinted off the tracks to their left and the rumbling they'd heard earlier grew louder and more frequent. Ahead they could see a dull wash of light against the far wall and switched off the torch. The tunnel curved to the right and now they slowed their progress. The distant rumble grew in volume until it seemed to shake the very ground beneath their feet. Using the noise as cover, they scurried towards the tunnel junction.

The Underground train roared past them, the light of its carriages banishing the darkness. The boys waited until the train's brakes squealed in protest and the last carriage flashed by. The torch was discarded and they turned quickly into the tunnel, following the rapidly slowing train. With a loud blast of compressed air it shuddered to a stop, and ahead they saw the platform of Justice Station. They passed the rear carriage of the train and walked quickly up a small ramp that led to the passenger concourse.

As the doors hissed open, a crowd of Workers spilled out on to the platform and the two boys moved rapidly up behind them, melting into the throng. There were no guards down here and the camera system was old and poorly maintained. The boys merged effortlessly with the crowd and discreetly slapped at their clothing in order to remove the dust, shuffling towards the wide staircases that led to the upper levels.

A few minutes later, the boys were checked through the basement security point beneath the Chambers of Justice and collected their work cart. Stopping briefly at the basement toilets, the red-haired boy disappeared inside, emerging a few moments later with the thin undervest rolled up in his hand. He hid it amongst a pile of polishing cloths in one of the cart's many storage bins and they continued about their chores.

Their workday was much the same as any other until they reached the Inner Chamber. As usual, they started at the dome, while the guard below leaned against the wall and inspected his fingernails. They dusted, polished and cleaned and then the boys went about their separate chores, one heading up the terraced seating while the red-haired boy walked towards the raised lectern in the centre of the chamber.

A shout of alarm followed by a curse brought the guard quickly off the wall. Liquid polish ran freely down the stairs, spreading across the marble tiers. The guard panicked, taking the steps two at a time, joining the boy on the highest terrace as he slapped at the spreading puddle, tossing ornate cushions out of its way. Down at the lectern, the red-haired boy clicked the small wiring cupboard shut and stood up, making a careful show of polishing the glass autocue. The Arabian hissed and beckoned him angrily, and between them they managed to clear up the mess in a few minutes. The grumbling guard ordered the boys to finish their task and then they were dismissed.

They continued along the corridors, pushing their cart before them. A few more hours, that was all. They would finish up their day and take the train from the Victoria Terminus, once more dropping to the tracks and finding their way back to the house in Warwick Square, where they would begin the first leg of their journey to the New World. Their hearts beat fast in anticipation.

In the small wiring recess beneath the lectern, the slender black vest had been crammed inside, the miniature magnetic clamp attached to the correct cable, the wire threaded into the cloth. A quick inspection wouldn't reveal anything untoward, but a continuous electrical pulse triggered by the human voice would result in a small positive charge being generated and fed into the black cloth.

The material was American in design, an extremely advanced piece of technology. When enough pressure was applied to it, the subsequent chemical reaction turned the thin material into a solid, pliable mass. That mass was now placed carefully out of sight and wired into the lectern's microphone system. What was only moments earlier an innocent-looking undervest was now a solid block of extremely powerful explosive, a device that was prepared, charged and armed. All it required now was the microphone to be powered up and the subtle reverberations of the human larynx to detonate it.

The chamber lay empty today, but tomorrow morning an assembly of the high council would take place; the first speaker on the agenda was the prosecutor general with his monthly briefing. The man had a reputation as a brutal overlord, someone who enjoyed the suffering and degradation he inflicted on the Workers.

And, according to the emir, the man had a unique baritone voice too.

The emir glanced in the Bentley's rear-view mirror, watching the boys' faces as they studied the passing landscape. The black hills were behind them now and the emir relaxed a little more, his fingers resting lightly on the steering wheel. There were no mobile patrols this far south, only quiet security posts where the guards enjoyed an easy existence far from the cities. The chances of discovery now were remote indeed.

The emir had dismissed his manservant and left Warwick Square earlier that evening. With the boys once again hidden inside the rear compartment, the emir headed south across the river on the elevated highway. A short time later he reached the Wimbledon checkpoint, where an Arabian escort jeep shadowed the Bentley along the motorway that dissected the wastelands, passing crumbling factories, office blocks and suburbs that lay half submerged beneath a sea of vegetation, a civilisation lost amongst the wild countryside.

Beyond the southern checkpoint, after the escort had peeled away, the emir pulled into an empty lay-by and let the boys out. They stretched their cramped limbs by the roadside, marvelling at the fresh country air, the soft night breezes that teased the crops in nearby fields. The wastelands were behind them now, the emir explained. These were the Southern Territories, where the soil was rich and farms and vineyards abounded. For the first time in their short but difficult lives, the boys were in unknown territory.

They drove on, the tarmac smooth, the ride comforting. The boys had their windows down, watching an unfamiliar world pass them by. They marvelled at the beauty of the terrain, pointed with wonder at the luxury estates and the ornate and well-lit grounds that surrounded them. Soon the houses fell behind them and all they could see were endless, undulating fields and dark woodlands.

Presently the Bentley purred to a halt and the lights were

extinguished. The boys climbed out of the car and the emir joined them. They were on a small country lane, on top of a rise, the road falling away in both directions. Not a single light shone in any direction and black woods bordered the surrounding fields on all sides. Above them, a million stars littered the heavens and the breeze, blowing from the south, brought the tang of salt to their nostrils. It was a beautiful evening.

'There are no patrols this far south,' the emir reassured them. He pointed across the adjacent field to a thick copse that crowned a nearby hill. 'There is your destination. Go now, quickly. The ship will not wait.'

The boys hesitated, bowed as one, then vaulted the wooden fence. The emir watched them go until their tiny figures were lost in the darkness, then returned to his vehicle. He kept the lights turned off for a mile or so then turned south, towards his coastal residence.

As the kilometres passed he thought about the boys and what they were about to experience. Nothing could prepare them for it, no words would suffice.

The emir had made the trip once, as a boy, and would probably make it again when the noose tightened and he could operate no more. He remembered his own journey to a woodland clearing, his fear of the dark countryside, the men who waited for him, their uniforms that bore the stars and stripes, the advanced aircraft that barely made a sound, that climbed effortlessly into the heavens and landed him safely in the New World a short time later. How lucky he'd been. How lucky the boys were. But they would return, when the years had passed and their training was complete, to fight again.

As he had returned.

The emir reached his coastal residence some time later, a well-appointed two-storey villa that sat on a prominent bluff overlooking a wide bay. He retired upstairs to his private study, throwing open the French doors and inviting a gentle sea breeze into the dimly lit room. He took a seat on the terrace, watching the wind ruffling the tall grasses, listening to the hiss and sigh of the tide beyond the sand dunes.

The meeting in the Inner Chamber would begin at ten the following day and the bomb would detonate shortly afterwards, killing the prosecutor general and many of the high council. Naturally, the boys would be the main suspects, and the police would soon discover that they lived together in the Workers' enclave in Vauxhall, that they had no blood relatives nor friends with whom they socialised, that their employment at the Chambers of Justice had been secured by a man who'd died over a year ago, the victim of a hit-and-run accident that bore no witnesses. The emir himself had carried out the repairs to the paintwork of the Bentley.

But there would certainly be reprisals. It would be the first attack within the city limits for over twenty years, a deadly assault aimed at the very heart of Arabian power. The prison cells would soon be full, no stone left unturned as the investigation followed every twist and turn.

It was possible the emir's behaviour might eventually be questioned, the unusual stop near Mousa's statue, or the boys' shadowy figures seen entering his dwelling the previous evening. Deniable of course, yet maybe his loyal manservant Ali would betray him. Maybe they no longer shared the same loyalty to the cause; maybe Ali sought allegiance with a new master. So many possibilities. Still, he would know soon enough. If the net began to close he would hear of it and make good his escape. But he hoped it wouldn't come to that. He was, after all, a fighter.

The emir recalled his own long-buried past, how he'd killed as a boy, escaping to the New World then returning with an education, with money, documents and training. How he'd mastered his orphan cover story, his fluency of Arabic, honed his business acumen to become a valuable friend and patron to his enemies.

Yet, despite his new life, despite the respect and privilege he'd earned over the years, it was the legacy of his family's resistance that provided his true motivation; his father killed in the New Forest battles when the emir was a baby, his mother tortured to death in the cells of the Khali Detention Centre before his second birthday. He himself had been spirited away before the authorities could snatch him, taken in by distant relatives and reared as one of their own. Nothing survived the bulldozing of their family home, nothing but the items he kept hidden in his study.

The emir walked back inside, closing the French doors behind him. He went to a bookshelf and reached for one of the heavier gold-leafed volumes on the higher shelves. Crossing to a deep sofa he sat down, placing the volume carefully on his legs and gently turning its thick cover. The book was a study of Arabian culture through the ages, but he skipped past the historic distortions and blatant propaganda until he reached the back sleeve. Carefully, he peeled away the outer layer of the cover and retrieved the small plastic envelope secreted within.

The emir extracted the photograph and the faded, handwritten note it held. The note explained much, yet left so many questions unanswered. He laid his mother's fragile missive to one side and held up the photograph, a digital image of the only family members he'd ever seen. The emir reached for a magnifying glass and studied the photo intently, as he always did. He was approaching his sixtieth year and had scrutinised the snapshot hundreds of times, yet it always held a unique fascination for him. It represented his past, a tangible link to events that had shaped his personal history and the history of his country.

It was a group portrait, taken on a summer's evening in front of an old-fashioned farmhouse, sometime during the Great Invasion. The woman was very pretty, with dark hair and olive skin, the camera lens picking out her soft brown eyes and wide smile. Her husband was a little more reserved, a handsome man, tall with short dark hair. There was another man in the photo too, an Arabian by the name of Khan, but the emir could only speculate on the relationship between them. Everybody smiled at the camera but he thought the cheerfulness a little too strained, the eyes reflecting some inner sadness. But perhaps he was wrong.

He studied the young couple again. Alex and Kirsty Taylor, the names of his distant, long-dead ancestors. The emir smiled; Taylor was a proud English name, too. He was fortunate to have been bestowed such heritage.

He carefully returned the items to their hiding place and put the book back on the shelf. He sat down and poured himself a cup of sweet tea and leaned back into the sofa's deep cushions. Tomorrow would indeed be an eventful day. Many would die, as others had died over the years, but if the operation brought justice for his people one day closer then it would be worth it.

The emir wasn't a terrorist, or a fundamentalist, or any of those other words used to label a just cause with the stain of criminality. Throughout history there had been many examples of wars against oppression, wars that pitted ordinary men against the ruthless power of the state. Almost every country on the planet had, at one time or another, been witness to similar struggles, struggles that had spilt the blood of many a loyal citizen, yet ultimately led to the downfall of such regimes. The emir's cause was no different.

He was a patriot, a freedom fighter, a man who simply loved what his country had once represented, a place where liberty and justice were once valued over all other things. A place where they would be treasured again. And he would do anything to achieve it.

Now where was the crime in that?

The End

Also by DC Alden

The Angola Deception

Roy Sullivan, an immigration officer working at the UK's busiest airport, is in deep trouble. Haunted by the disappearance of younger brother Jimmy in Iraq, Roy's relentless search for the truth has reached curious and dangerous ears. Sammy French, a violent south London criminal and former childhood associate, is in need of a favour, one that a suddenly compromised Roy has no choice but to grant. Forced to take part in a perilous criminal conspiracy, Roy must exploit his position at Heathrow and risk his own liberty before he can be free of Sammy's debt and live his life again.

Yet as the walls close in around him a mysterious stranger enters Roy's crumbling world, a former Navy Seal who knows the truth about the Nine Eleven attacks, a man haunted by demons and hunted by powerful forces determined to silence him, a man who holds the key to the mystery of Jimmy Sullivan's disappearance while guarding a covert facility deep in the Iraqi desert.

For an increasingly frightened Roy, this troubled and dangerous stranger will come to represent a chance to escape, not only from the uncertainty of his brother's fate and the clutches of a vicious gangland criminal, but also from the coming storm, one that threatens to decimate humanity and usher in a ruthless and terrifying New World Order.

The Horse at the Gates

Whitehall is in ruins, Britain's most significant mosque destroyed, the country adrift on a tide of political turmoil. As war rumbles on in the east, millions of refugees head west, desperately seeking the safety of Europe's borders. The conspiracy to change the course of European history has begun.

At the heart of that conspiracy are three men, each divided from the other by birth-right and status, all of them integral to the success of an operation that has been meticulously planned and ruthlessly executed.

Yet before the gates of Europe can be thrown open, before the maps of the continent can finally be redrawn, two of them must be removed from the field of play.

Permanently.

For more information,
please visit the official website at
www.dcaldenbooks.com

Printed in Great Britain
by Amazon.co.uk, Ltd.,
Marston Gate.